NEW

倍斯特出版事業有限公司
Best Publishing Ltd.

全新制 新多益 金色證書 閱讀

一次滿足所有師生需求
集三種動物特長
一舉奪「金」

莊琬君、韋爾◎著

U0066422

應考＋備考　　　獵豹

像獵豹一樣反應快，能即刻
秒殺試題。

教學解說　　　貓頭鷹

學貓頭鷹的特長，能查覺問題、
找到問題癥結。

解題＋靈活運用　　浣熊

跟浣熊一樣思考靈活，能應對
考題變化。

AUTHOR

在 2018 年改制的新多益在閱讀測驗的 Part 6 及 Part 7 更加靈活，新題型甚至類似新托福 iBT，須要考生運用更多推理能力，也必須考慮空格前後文的連貫性來解題，無法單純以單字字義或單一文法觀念來解題。例如在 Part 6，多了四個選項都是完整句的題型，而在 Part 7，除了保留舊制多益的單篇及雙篇題組，更多了三篇題組。Part 7 中，新題型出現在單篇題組，格式模仿托福 iBT，須將一個完整句插入文章中恰當的位置。台灣考生在面對以上新題型的挑戰時，很可能遭遇的瓶頸是無法以狂做模擬試題的題海戰術因應。針對新題型的思考模式應該要調整成探討深層句意，思考句與句及篇章與篇章之間的關聯性，也就是 look at the big picture 的模式。

相信此書三種層次的特殊解析方式，能幫助讀者快速衝破瓶頸，更能磨鍊分析能力。

莊琬君 敬上

AUTHOR

　　游泳健將費爾普斯的教練 Bowman 曾要他在黑暗中的密西根湖游泳，因為認為他需要對任何意外的事做好準備 (needed to be ready for any surprise)。其實不只是游泳，小至準備比賽、考試大到工作上許多上司交辦的事項，我們都需要做好萬全的準備。傳統的題海策略和準備模式（即寫題目模擬試題對完答案就報名考試）就等同還使自己置身在室內大型泳池游泳一樣，儘管每天有教練指導，進步的成效有限且無法有極大的突破。考生需要的是更靈活的準備方式，像費爾普斯那樣將自己置身在黑暗中的密西根湖那樣，做最充分的準備，只有這樣才能在不管題目如何變化或生活中遇到甚麼挑戰，都能臨危不亂。

　　在新制改制下，訊息量的增多、投機跟技巧性試題減少、需運用考生整合和推測能力的題目的新增，都使得舊有的學習模式無法應付新制題型。這本新多益閱讀規劃了三個動物的學習方式，能激盪考生的思考力，浣熊學習方式的設計也很靈活，同篇文章除了本來

設計的題目外，還多了加碼題，讀者可以寫完例如 part 7 雙篇文章的 5 題題目且對完答案後，測試自己再回過頭寫加碼題兩題，檢視自己在面對同樣的文章換了其他方式詢問是否也能答對，因為許多考生其實面對的困惑是明明寫了很多題目且都對完答案了，但是始終不知道自己是哪方面有問題。其實解除困惑點的關鍵在於「確實理解」，其實寫完同篇題目且對完答案，或自己都答對，都不代表自己完全理解意思了，只是再寫該篇時題目正好都問到你會的。確實理解才能讓你達到你想要的成績。確實理解代表的是同篇文章換個出題方式你也都能答對，這也是這本書與仿間書的不同之處，書中的學習方式都朝著靈活學習、提升思考力和以更萬全的狀態下應試，而非填鴨式的學習或狂寫題目。（例如：A 考生寫了模擬試題用答對的題數換算對應的成績 850，其實更該著重的不太是是否達到某個分數段，而是是否確實理解文章中每句的意思。）

　　這次很感謝合著作者莊琬君，很慶幸可以跟她一起合寫這本書，其實從求學時期就一直希望自己可以跟很優秀的人一起做個專案、完成某個計劃、學習別人優點讓自己更好，我覺得合寫這本書是 2017 年一件令我感到很開心的事之一。自第一本書《文法狀元的獨家私藏筆記》出版後不知不覺時間過得很快，也很感謝幾個國外友人對我寫那本書的肯定。然後要感謝的是倍斯特出版社給予本人出書機會。最後祝考生都能獲取理想成績，一舉拿下金色證書。

韋爾 敬上

使用說明

INSTRUCTIONS

★ 新題型均有 **NEW** 圖示更便利學習。

★ 圖檔即為段落填空題新增的完整句子的題型。

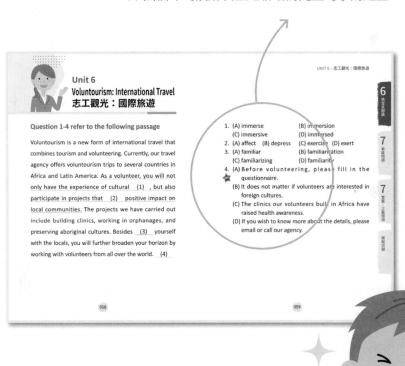

★Part 6 段落填空題（Test Completion）由原先的 12 題調整成 16 題。131-146 題為句子填空題。另外新增了完整句子的選項，更能檢測考生對整個段落的理解程度，減低了靠文法或單字等較片面的理解就能答對題目的比例，考生要更注意時間上的掌握跟多練習這類題型。

新多益模擬試題解析

PART 6

Directions: Read the texts that follow. A word, phrase, or sentence is missing in parts of each text. Four answer choices are given below the text. Select the best answer to complete the text. Then mark the letter (A), (B), (C), or (D) on your answer sheet.

Questions 131-134 refer to the following advertisement.

To Whom It May Concern,

I'm honored to announce that the Craft & Hobby Fair will ___(131)___ in the World Trade Center on July 2nd.

The fair gathers designers, craftsmen, retailers, distributors, buyers and suppliers. Attendees will not only familiarize themselves with traditional American crafts, but also interact with the ___(132)___ craftsmen from around the globe.

I'm also pleased to inform you of a new sector, the upcycling sector, which is highly informative on ___(133)___ lifestyle. The fair has received accolades for the diverse products in the paper and textile sectors. Besides, the jewelry sector has seen unabated boom according to our statistics of visitors and orders.

___(134)___ If you have any questions, please contact us via e-mail or phone.

400

Sincerely,
Jeff Benson
the Craft & Hobby Fair Organizer

131. (A) command
(B) commence
(C) commend
(D) comment

132. (A) promised
(B) prominence
(C) prominent
(D) compromising

133. (A) sustainable
(B) sustain
(C) sustainability
(D) sustaining

134. (A) Attached is the information of the schedule, exhibition booths, and transportation.
(B) We have invited craftsmen from Asia.
(C) It takes only 10 minutes to walk from the MRT station to the World Trade Center.
(D) The number of transactions is the highest in the

6 填空式短語

7 單篇閱讀

7 雙篇閱讀、三篇閱讀

模擬試題

401

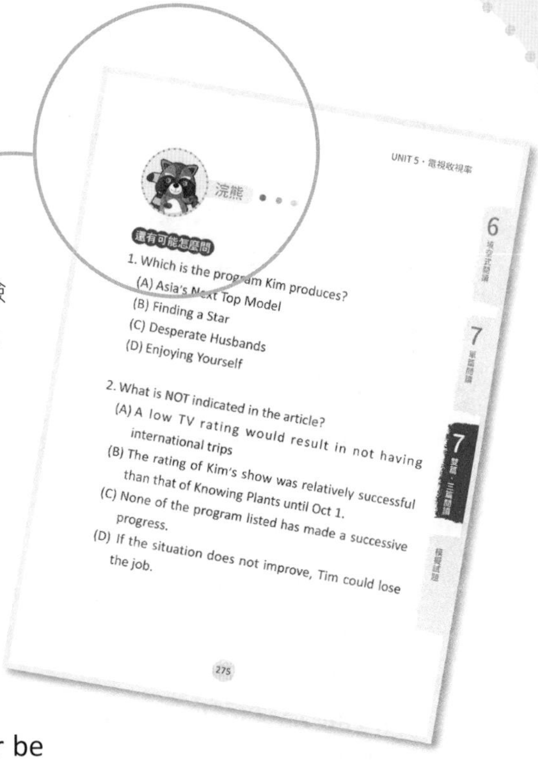
UNIT 5・電視收視率
浣熊
還有可能怎麼問
1. Which is the program Kim produces?
(A) Asia's Next Top Model
(B) Finding a Star
(C) Desperate Husbands
(D) Enjoying Yourself
2. What is NOT indicated in the article?
(A) A low TV rating would result in not having international trips
(B) The rating of Kim's show was relatively successful than that of Knowing Plants until Oct 1.
(C) None of the program listed has made a successive progress.
(D) If the situation does not improve, Tim could lose the job.
275

★每篇文章均附加碼題設計，能更充分檢測出考生的應考實力，並協助考生更全面掌握每篇章的閱讀訊息。

★例如萬聖節派對這篇是多篇閱讀題，有 5 題試題，但寫完此篇也達對這 5 題，僅代表剛好都掌握這 5 題的閱讀訊息，其實你還需要寫加碼題替自己做更完備的準備才應考。

1.What kind of party might this company hold?
2.What does Neal mean by “Better be safe than bold”?
3.What does Neal mean by “It's going to stay with me”?
4.What can be inferred about Lucy?
5.What does Katie imply by “You beat me on this one”?

★加碼題，當題目又換成加碼題的題目你也確定自己能答對嗎？
1.Which is most likely to be the costume Neal dresses up at the party?
2.What is NOT indicated in the article?

★考生可以更充分利用書中浣熊學習設計，強化自己應考的實力。

★此設計也適合老師教學，對於程度更好的學習者，可以請學生也試試浣熊試題，教學滿意度滿分。
（通常老師僅能滿足 70%的考生，讓頂尖的考生也有些事情做吧！浣熊試題還有計算題不妨一試 ^^）

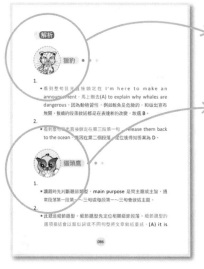

★ 獵豹的學習法，能更快速的答題，在閱讀訊息增多的新制測驗中，答題速度顯得更為重要。

★ 貓頭鷹的學習法，能進一步了解原因跟理解閱讀訊息，更多時候題目牽涉的不僅僅是單字和文法的掌握，還包含掌握同義字轉換等的能力和組織跨篇章訊息的整合能力，你確實需要貓頭鷹的幫忙 trust me。

★ 例如：同義字轉換/重述的能力

‧細節題型的選項描述會以類似詞或不同句型將文章敘述重述。

‧(A) it is difficult for the staff to maintain the operation. 意思近似 They do cause problems for our staff to maintain the overall stability of our operation。

‧(B) The glass wall is too fragile 重述 the glass wall can't seem to endure their pouncing。

‧(C) Adult whales and young whales cannot get along 重述 Adult whales are too aggressive. It's pressuring young whales…。

★Part 5 句子填空題（Incomplete Sentence）由原先的 40 題調整成 30 題。101-130 題為句子填空題。此舉也表示能靠技巧性得分的文法和單字題降低了比例。

READING TEST
In the Reading test, you will read a variety of texts and answer several different types of reading comprehension questions. The entire Reading test will last 75 minutes. There are three parts, and directions are given for each part. You are encouraged to answer as many questions as possible within the time allowed.

You must mark your answer on the separate answer sheet. Do not write answers in your test book.

PART 5
Directions: A word or phrase is missing in each of the sentences below. Four answer choices are given below each sentence. Select the best answer to complete the sentence. Then mark the letter (A), (B), (C), or (D) on your answer sheet.

Part 5

101. People working in an underground tunnel for a long period of time are exposed to harmful chemical substances, which can ultimately lead to ------- illness.
(A) regular
(B) unharmful
(C) chronic
(D) sustained

102. Health experts are constantly reminding people of not taking foods that contain cholesterol, but totally forgetting the fact that cholesterol does have a -------

390

★ Part 7 單篇閱讀題（Single Passages）由原先的28題調整成29題。且篇數由9篇閱讀文章增加到10篇閱讀文章，考生需要更注意時間分配並於平常多閱讀文章。

★ Part 7 多篇閱讀題（Multiple Passages）由原先的20題雙篇式的閱讀文章調整成25題包含雙篇和三篇式的閱讀文章。另外還增加了文字簡訊、即時通訊軟體和聊天室對話的內容等搭配文章的出題模式，以更逼真生活情境的方式呈現，其實更有利於較靈活思考和口語表達佳的考生，考生可以多練習這方面的題目，其實還蠻有趣的！比較不像是在寫呆版的閱讀考試內容，可以抱著像是跟同事跟朋友聊天的模式去理解就會很容易掌握新題型。

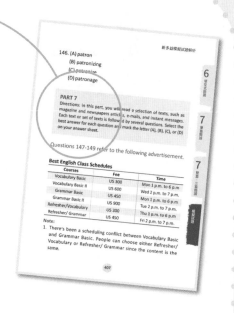

★ Part 7閱讀新題型，三篇式的閱讀文章包含臉書公告文、佈告欄公告訊息和信件。

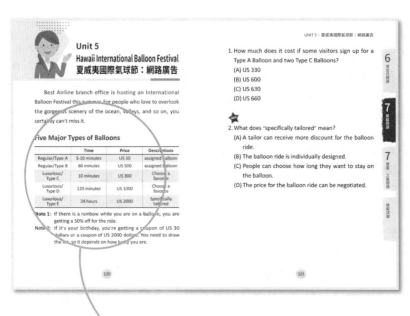

★ Part 7單篇閱讀，快點來挑戰新制新題型吧！

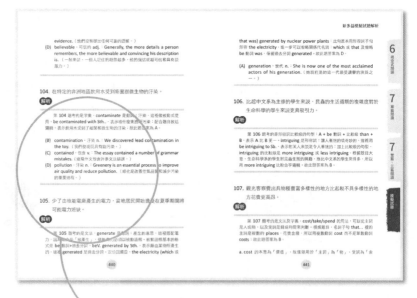

★詳盡的解析，徹底了解各選項的字彙跟相關用法。

★選項中英對照設計，閱讀起來更方便。

目次

CONTENTS

填空式閱讀　新多益 Part 6

1. 聖誕節採購 / 018
2. 信件：餐飲部門 E-mail 公告 / 026
3. 倍斯特寵物美容坊和旅館徵才 / 036
4. 抱怨信：購買泰迪熊後的不滿 / 046
5. 退休員工告別派對 / 054
6. 志工觀光：國際旅遊 / 062
7. 泰國北部清邁的大象庇護所 / 070
8. 市政府公告：健身中心公告 / 078

單篇閱讀 新多益 Part 7

1. 倍斯特水族館：新聞發佈文 / 086

2. 倍斯特旅館：結束營業公告 / 094

3. 倍斯特動物園：招聘 / 104

4. Skywriting（空中文字）：演講稿 / 114

5. 夏威夷國際氣球節：網路廣告 / 124

6. 倍斯特酒席承辦：網路廣告 / 134

7. 倍斯特禮堂：海報 / 144

8. 倍斯特醫療中心：廣告 / 154

9. ABC渡假村和SPA：招募：招募 / 164

10. 常綠安養社區：公告 / 174

11. 倍斯特安卓電視盒保固書：使用說明書 / 184

12. 倍斯特加勒比海郵輪：廣告 / 194

雙篇、三篇閱讀 新多益 Part 7

1. **兼職男友與兼職女友** / 204
   - Line 對話：與分公司經理的對談
   - 信件：主要服務項目表

2. **臉書聊天室談論小孩舞台劇表演** / 218
   - 臉書對話：母親們談論小孩舞台劇表演
   - 信件 1：冰品價格和口味表單
   - 信件 2：其他資訊

3. **書籍推薦：森林秘境 The Forest Unseen** / 236
   - 臉書公告：生物學院院長臉書公告文
   - 公佈欄：生物學系公佈欄
   - 信件：在校生致生物學院院長信件

4. **生日禮物挑選** / 252
   - Line 對話：生日禮物討論

・信件：芭比娃娃目錄表格

・Line 對話：生日禮物後續

5. 電視收視率　　　　　　　　　　　　　　　 / 266

・電視收視率表格

・員工們於臉書聊天室討論

・會議室對談 0

6. 萬聖節派對　　　　　　　　　　　　　　　 / 280

・Line 對話 1：萬聖節裝扮討論

・公司公告欄：人事部公告新的萬聖節服飾

・Line 對話 2：萬聖節後續

7. 報考空服員　　　　　　　　　　　　　　　 / 294

・信件 1：ABC 航空公司第三回合面試通知

・Line 對話：與友人的討論

・信件 2：向師長尋求意見

8. 訂購書籍 / 308
・信件 1：訂單
・信件 2：客戶信件回覆
・信件 3：公司信件回覆

9. 內部升遷名單 / 322
・會議
・Line 對話：員工間對話
・公告欄：公司內部公告欄

10. 運送動物 / 336
・信件 1：犀牛運送狀況
・信件 2：動物保護中心來信

11. 倍斯特商業會議中心 / 350
- 信件 1：會議中心活動表單
- 信件 2：更正後活動表單

12. 倍斯特運動場 / 364
- 信件 1：販售食物價格表
- 信件 2：主管回信

13. 韓國自助行 / 378
- Line 對話 1：關於最後登機呼叫
- Line 對話 2：登機後對話
- 公告欄：航空公司公告欄

模擬試題 / 392
- 試題
- 答案表

Unit 1
Christmas Shopping
聖誕節採購

Question 1-4 refer to the following passage

Get ready for the Christmas shopping spree and   (1)   yourself in the Christmas spirit. Located in downtown Sydney, Best Shopping Mall is not only the   (2)   shopping destination for local Aussies, but also a must-visit for   (3)   from around the globe. Be sure to take a photo with the Santa Claus in our courtyard, and   (4)   the holiday cuisines in our food plaza.

1. (A) hug   (B) immerse   (C) dedicate (D) play
2. (A) prime   (B) basic   (C) trivial   (D) festive
3. (A) tour   (B) tourism   (C) tourists   (D) tour guides
4. (A) save   (B) savior   (C) saving   (D) savor

中譯

　　準備好聖誕節大採購，＿＿(1)＿＿在聖誕精神裡。倍斯特購物中心位於雪梨市中心，不只對當地澳洲人是＿＿(2)＿＿購物目的地，也是來自世界各地的＿＿(3)＿＿必須造訪的景點。務必和我們中庭的聖誕老人拍照，並＿＿(4)＿＿美食廣場的節慶美食。

1. (A) 擁抱　　　(B) 沉浸　　　(C) 貢獻　　　(D) 玩耍
2. (A) 最佳的　　(B) 基本的　　(C) 瑣碎的　　(D) 節慶的
3. (A) 觀光　　　(B) 觀光業　　(C) 觀光客　　(D) 導遊
4. (A) 存　　　　(B) 拯救者　　(C) 節約的　　(D) 品嚐

答案：1.B　2.A　3.C　4.D

獵豹 ● ● ●

1.

- 看到整句目光直接鎖定在 yourself in，並掃描選項，因為選項全是動詞，馬上判斷此題主要考字義，不是考詞性變化。

- 首先刪除(D) play，因為無 play yourself 這個搭配詞，接著刪除(C) dedicate 貢獻，與空格後的聖誕精神字義上搭配不通順。dedicate 雖然能搭配反身代名詞，但介系詞是搭配 to。
比較(A) hug 和(B) immerse，因為要搭配 yourself in，考慮 in 有在裡面的意思，(B) immerse 是「沉浸」之意，字義搭配 in 比較合理，所以刪除(A) hug，得出正確選項(B) immerse。

2.

- 看到整句目光直接鎖定在 shopping destination，正確選項應該是形容詞，因為形容詞修飾後面的名詞。

- 選項都是形容詞，因此主要考字義。搭配上下文語意最通順的是(A) prime，主要的或最佳的。

3.

- 看到整句目光直接鎖定在 from around the globe。

- 此題可從文意解題，空格後的文意是來自世界各地，因此(C) tourists 才合理。

4.
- 看到整句目光直接鎖定在 cuisines... food，從這兩個字義判斷空格應該選品嚐的動詞。

- 此題主要考文意。

6 填空式閱讀

7 單篇閱讀

7 雙篇、三篇閱讀

模擬試題

貓頭鷹 ● ● ●

1.

- 此題正確選項的字義必須和空格上下文的大意通順地搭配。也必須考慮空格之後的介系詞，因動詞片語的特色即是動詞搭特定的介系詞。正確答案的字義及文法必須能搭配空格後的反身代名詞 youself 及介系詞 in。

- (C) dedicate 能搭配反身代名詞，但介系詞是搭配 to。dedicate 有致力於、貢獻之意，與下文的聖誕精神語意不連接。搭配反身代名詞的片語是 dedicate oneself to N.。

2.

- 此題主要的解題線索是空格後的名詞 shopping destination，購物目的地，也就是購物地點，因為所有選項都是形容詞，所以主要考點是哪個形容詞的字義修飾購物目的地最恰當。

- 從字義判斷先排除(C) trivial，瑣碎的，而(D) festive，節慶的，雖然好像跟第一句的聖誕節有關係，但 festive 通常形容抽象的氣氛，不適合形容購物中心或地點，因此也刪除。而考慮此篇是購物中心的廣告文，(B) basic，基本的，也不適當，因為廣告文傾向使用意義正向的形容詞。(A) prime 意為「最佳的」，最適合使用在廣告文形容產品或地點。

3.

- 除了空格後的 from around the globe，空格前的 a must-visit for... 也是線索。複合字 must-visit 指一定要拜訪的景點。綜合以上線索，能聯想正確選項是觀光客，才能形成意義通順的片語：「來自世界各地的觀光客一定要拜訪的景點」。

- 所有選項都是 tour 衍生的單字或片語，所以此題主要考 tour 的詞性變化，tour 是名詞也是動詞，兩個詞性都有「導覽」之意。(B) tourism 及 (C) tourists 都是 tour 加上不同字尾衍生的名詞，(D) tour guide 指導遊或嚮導。

4.

- 空格前的對等連接詞 and 暗示正確選項必須與 to take 形成平行結構，即 to take... and (to) V。因此正確選項是原型動詞，對等連接詞連接兩個不定詞（不定詞的格式是「to +原型動詞」）時，第二個不定詞裡的 to 會省略。

- 先排除(B) savior，拯救者，因為字尾-or 是表達身份或職業的名詞字尾，由於此題正確選項要選動詞，可刪除(B)。savior 只是剛好拼法與品嚐的動詞 savor 類似，是類似拼字的陷阱選項。

浣熊 • • • •

改寫

1. All of the employees at Best Shopping Mall <u>dedicate</u> ourselves to making sure that all of our consumers have a fantastic shopping experience. 此時要選 (C)。

2. Local people enjoy the <u>festive</u> atmosphere during the holiday season at Best Shopping Mall. Besides, the mall has become a must-visit for foreign tourists. 此時要選 (D)。

中譯

1. 所有倍斯特購物中心的員工致力於確保我們所有的消費者能有很棒的購物經驗。

2. 在節日時分，當地人在倍斯特購物中心享受節慶氣氛。此外，此購物中心已經變成外國觀光客必須造訪的景點。

解析

1.

- 主詞 All the employees 是第一個解題線索，按照基本肯定句句型結構：主詞+主要動詞，推測底線是主要動詞的位置，先看

懂底線之後的大意，再從下文大意倒著推測哪個動詞的字義搭配下文是最通順的。下文大意是「……我們自己以確定所有我們的消費者能有很棒的購物經驗」，因此字義有「致力於」的動詞最適合。

● 要特別注意「致力於」或「貢獻」的動詞片語有固定的搭配詞：dedicate oneself to N.，如此句是搭配身代名詞 ourselves，介系詞 to，動名詞 making。也就是說 ourselves 也是重要解題線索。也要注意 to 在此片語是介系詞，介系詞之後只能接名詞或動名詞，所以之後的動詞 make 一定要加 ing 改成動名詞。另一同義的動詞片語是 be dedicated to N.。

2.

● 空格之後是名詞 atmosphere 氣氛，因此要找能合理形容氣氛的字義。由此篇章第一句，即知道主題與聖誕節有關，這篇是購物中心為了聖誕節推出的廣告文。下文也有 holiday season，節日季節，暗示正確選項應該跟節慶有關，才能呼應下文。綜合主題和節日季節一詞，推測出(D) festive，節慶的，是最合理的選項。

● 此外，可先把最不合理的形容詞刪除，先刪除(B) basic，基本的，和(C) trivial，瑣碎的。接著刪除(A) prime，最佳的，要注意中文雖然會說最佳的氣氛，但在英文 prime 鮮少形容 atmosphere。也要特別注意 prime 是多重意義的形容詞，除了強調品質上、時間上、或重要性佔第一的，也有壯年的、信用最高的、（電視節目）黃金時段的等意義。

Unit 2
E-mail Announcement
信件：餐飲部門 E-mail 公告

Question 1-4 refer to the following passage

E-mail Announcement

From: Director of the Dining Department

To: All employees of Best Biotechnology

Subject: Major Changes in the Cafeteria and Coffee Shop

Dear All,

 (1) our CEO's mission statement to take further steps towards a green enterprise, the Dining Department will (2) several main changes.

Please note that these changes will (3) from October, 1st.

1. Plastic bags will no longer be provided for take-out, but can be purchased for 50 cents each.

2. 60 cents will be deducted for every coffee take-out if you bring your own mug or beverage bottle.

3. Disposable utensils will not be provided for eat-in. They will be replaced by stainless steel utensils. <u>All utensils are strictly high-temperature   (4) </u>.

We appreciate your cooperation.

Frank Lin

Director, Dining Department

1. (A) Responding   (B) In response to
   (C) Responsive to   (D) Responds to
2. (A) commence   (B) compliment
   (C) complement   (D) commend
3. (A) affect   (B) effect
   (C) take effect   (D) have affection
4. (A) sterilization   (B) sterilized
   (C) sterilize   (D) sterilizing

中譯

E-mail 公告

From： 餐飲部主任

To： 所有倍斯特生物科技的員工

Subject： 自助餐廳和咖啡店的主要改變

親愛的各位，

　　(1)　 我們總裁提出的更進一步朝向環保企業的企業宗旨，餐飲部將　(2)　 幾項重要改變。

請注意這些改變將從十月一日　(3)　。

1. 外帶不再提供塑膠袋，但可以 50 分美元購買一個塑膠袋。

2. 如果你帶自己的馬克杯或飲料瓶外帶咖啡，每杯折抵 60 分美元。

3. 內用不再提供拋棄式餐具。它們會被不銹鋼餐具取代。所有餐具都經過嚴格的高溫　(4)　。

我們感謝您的合作。

法蘭克・林

餐飲部主任

1. (A) 正呼應　(B) 為了呼應　(C) 對…有反應的　(D) 呼應
2. (A) 開始　　(B) 稱讚　　　(C) 補充　　　　(D) 讚揚
3. (A) 影響　　(B) 效應　　　(C) 生效　　　　(D) 有感情
4. (A) 殺菌過程 (B) 被殺菌　　(C) 殺菌　　　　(D) 正在殺菌

答案：1.B　2.A　3.C　4.B

解析

獵豹 ● ● ●

1.

- 看到整句目光直接鎖定在名詞 mission statement，並掃描整句結構。完整句是 the Dining Department will __(2)__ several main changes，因此能判斷句首的片語是修飾完整句的副詞片語。因副詞片語的格式是「介系詞+名詞」，所以選 (B) In response to。

2.

- 看到整句目光直接鎖定在 several changes。此題考能搭配受詞 changes 的動詞字義。

3.

- 看到整句目光直接鎖定在 these changes 及 from October, 1st。空格前是助動詞 will，因此正確答案是原型動詞。考慮與下文 from October, 1st 的連貫，正確答案應表達從十月一日「生效」，「生效」的動詞片語是 take effect。

4.

- 看到整句目光直接鎖定在 All utensils are。考慮整句大意，應該以被動語態表達，所以要選過去分詞(B) sterilized。

貓頭鷹 ● ● ●

1.

- 此題選項包括動詞 respond 衍生的詞性變化及不同詞性搭配介係詞 to 的片語，首先考慮 respond 的搭配詞，respond 是不及物動詞，須接介係詞 to，而且空格後面是名詞 mission statement，沒有介係詞 to，因此刪除(A) Responding。

- 接著刪除(D) Responds to，因為空格在句首，不可能以動詞字尾加 s 當作句首第一個字，原型動詞字尾加 s 只會搭配主詞是第三人稱單數，簡單現在式的動詞時態。要特別注意(B) In response to 及(C) Responsive to 這兩個容易混淆的片語。(B) In response to 意為「為了呼應，作為呼應」，意思搭配空格後的受詞 our CEO's mission statement，我們總裁（提出）的企業宗旨，是合理連貫的，所以正確選項是(B)。而(C) Responsive to 這個片語前面須搭配 be 動詞：beV. responsive to，responsive 是形容詞，beV. responsive to N.意為「對…反應積極的、易受感動的、有反應的」。

2.

- 每個選項都是原型動詞，能搭配空格前的助動詞 will，因此主要考點是哪個動詞的字義搭配上下文最合理通順。此空格所在的子句的主詞是「餐飲部門」，空格後是受詞「幾項改變」，從主詞、受詞的意思聯想動詞的意思應該是「開始」。

- 只有(A) commence 有「開始」之意。其餘選項的意思搭配受詞「幾項改變」意義都不通順。(B) compliment，讚美，(C) complement，補充，(D) commend，讚揚或推薦。注意「開始」的動詞有幾個類似字：begin、start、incept、commence。

3.

- 雖然(A) affect，(B) effect 都是原型動詞，(D) have affection 有原型動詞 have，但字義都無法和下文搭配。affect，影響，是及物動詞，要馬上接受詞，搭配 from October, 1st 是錯誤的，所以 (A) affect 是錯誤選項。effect 有名詞及動詞兩個詞性。當名詞使用時，意思是「影響」。當動詞使用時，意思是「實現」，是及物動詞，即之後馬上要接名詞當作 effect 的受詞。因此若空格套入(B) effect，之後接副詞片語 from October, 1st.，文法上的搭配是錯誤的。

- 同時考慮主題及空格上下文大意，推測出字義搭配最合理的選項。主題是向所有員工宣佈自助餐廳和咖啡店的主要改變，通順的句意應是「請注意這些改變將從十月一日生效」，故選(C) take effect，「生效」的動詞片語。

4.

- 由主詞 utensils，餐具，可推測主要動詞是用被動語態表達「餐具被…」，被動語態的格式為 be 動詞+過去分詞。此句有 be 動詞 are，能進一步推測正確選項是過去分詞。

- 選項都是原型動詞 sterilize，殺菌，的詞性變化。符合過去分

詞的只有(B) sterilized。過去分 sterilized 前面搭配 high-temperature，形成 high-temperature sterilized，「高溫殺菌」的意思。(A) sterilization 由字尾 tion 判斷是名詞，(C) sterilize 是原型動詞，(D) sterilizing 可能是動名詞或現在分詞。

浣熊 ● ● ●

改寫

1. We believe the changes will not <u>affect</u> most of the employees. 此時要選 (A)。

2. The Dining Department will ensure that the process of <u>sterilization</u> is strictly carried out. 此時要選 (A)。

中譯

1. 我們相信這些改變不會影響大部份員工。

2. 餐飲部門將確保消毒過程是嚴格地執行。

解析

1.

- 空格前是助動詞 will，因此正確選項應該是原型動詞。(A) affect 是「影響」的原型動詞，套入空格，句意合理，文法也正確。此句的主要動詞是 believe，believe 之後以名詞子句當受詞。名詞子句的結構是：主詞 the changes+否定助動詞 will not+動詞 affect+受詞 most of the employees。因此刪除(C) take effect，「生效」的動詞片語，因為 take effect 之後不會接受詞。

- 刪除(B) effect，effect 當名詞使用時，意思是「影響」。要注意 effect 雖然也是動詞，但當動詞使用時，字義是「實現」，也無法和空格後的受詞「大部分員工」，搭配成合理通順的句意。effect 是及物動詞，effect something 意思類似 achieve something 或 cause something to happen，例如 effect changes，造成改變，effect a purpose，達成目的。(D) have affection 是「有感情」之意，與篇章主題和此句句意完全無關。

2.

- 此句的主詞是 The Dining Department，主要動詞 ensures，類似 makes sure of，「確定」之意。ensures 的受詞是 that 導引的名詞子句，名詞子句的主詞是 the process，而 of sterilization 修飾 process，表達「殺菌的過程」。

- 另外，空格前是介系詞 of，介系詞的文法重點是之後一定要搭配名詞或動名詞，因此先刪除(B) sterilized 及(C) sterilize。(B) sterilized 可能是動詞過去式或過去分詞。(C) sterilize 是原型動詞。接著比較(A) sterilization 及(D) sterilizing。sterilization 是表「滅菌，消毒」的普通名詞，sterilizing 可能是動名詞或現在分詞。

- 因為在英文的修辭原則裡，普通名詞通常被視為優先於動名詞，所以(A) sterilization 會比(D) sterilizing 更適合當正確選項。

Unit 3
Best Pet Grooming Parlor & Hotel
倍斯特寵物美容坊和旅館徵才

Question 1-4 refer to the following passage

Best Pet Grooming Parlor & Hotel is seeking an animal caretaker.

OVERVIEW: Responsible for the proper care of our furkid clients and providing assistance to the grooming services

Description of Duties:

*   Clean the cages, individual rooms and play areas.

*   Provide food and water to furkids   (1)   SOPs or   (2) __.

*   Decontaminate all areas of the facility.

*   (3)   waste from the parlor & hotel under guidelines.

*   Perform daily animal health   (4)   checks and report any abnormal conditions to supervisory staff.

*   Help organize and sanitize grooming equipment & tools.

1. (A) followed   (B) follower
   (C) follows   (D) following
2. (A) protection   (B) brochures
   (C) pamphlets   (D) protocols
3. (A) Dispose of   (B) Throw
   (C) Discard of   (D) Dispose
4. (A) surveys   (B) momentary
   (C) surveillance   (D) temporary

倍斯特寵物美容坊及旅館正找尋一位動物照護員。

概述：負責對我們的毛小孩客戶提供適當照顧及對美容服務提供協助。

職務描述：

* 清理籠子，個別房和玩耍區。

* __(1)__SOP 或 __(2)__ 提供食物和水給毛小孩。

* 消毒整棟建築。

* 按照規定 __(3)__ 美容坊和旅館的垃圾。

* 進行日常動物健康的 __(4)__ 檢查並向上級報告任何的異常狀況。

* 協助整理並消毒美容器材及工具。

1. (A) 追隨/ 被追隨　　　　(B) 追隨者

　　(C) 追隨　　　　　　　　(D) 按照

2. (A) 保護　　　(B) 小冊子　　(C) 小冊子　　　(D) 規則

3. (A) 拋棄　　　(B) 丟　　　　(C) 拋棄　　　　(D) 拋棄

4. (A) 調查，民意調查　　　　(B) 短暫的

　　(C) 檢查、監測、監視　　　(D) 暫時的

答案：1.D　2.D　3.A　4.C

獵豹 ● ● ●

1.

- 看到整句目光直接鎖定在 SOPs，推測正確選項應該有「按照」的字義。

- 首先刪去名詞(B) follower，追隨者，字義搭配 SOP 不合理。又由句首 provide 知道此句是祈使句，正確選項可能是原型動詞 follow，以表達另一個祈使句，刪去(A) followed，因為 followed 可能是動詞過去式或過去分詞，也刪去(C) follows。注意空格前缺少連接詞 and，所以此句應該是把 and follow 的 and 省略，follow 改成現在分詞 following 的分詞構句。故得出正確選項(D) following。

2.

- 看到整句目光直接鎖定在 or....。

- or 是對等連接詞，連接名詞 SOPs 和另一名詞。因選項都是名詞，只須考慮字義。有規則之意的只有(D) protocols。

3.

- 看到整句目光直接鎖定在 waste。由空格之後的大意：按照規定…美容坊和旅館的垃圾，推測正確選項是「拋棄」之意。

- 「拋棄」的動詞有幾個類似詞：throw away，dispose of，discard，因此正確選項是(A) Dispose of。

4.

- 看到整句目光直接鎖定在 health... checks。

- 字義必須與健康檢查連貫，因此選(C) surveillance，surveillance 也有檢查之意。

1.

- Follow 是多重意義字，應考慮後面的受詞再推測 follow 的意思。

- 此句屬於職務描述，而且其它職務描述的句子都是原型動詞開頭的祈使句，因此推測正確選項是表達「按照」的原型動詞，但因為無原型動詞選項，所以要考慮其它可能性。既然空格前沒有對等連接詞 and 連接 Provide...... 及 follow...... 兩個子句，可推測此句是將 and 省略，follow 改成現在分詞 following 的分詞構句。原本的句型是 Provide...... and follow......，分詞構句會將對等連接詞 and 省略。也要考慮「按照」是主動語態，主動語態是以現在分詞 Ving 表達，而不是用過去分詞。

2.

- 因為所有選項都是名詞，能判斷此題主要考字義，不是考詞性。建議考生先掃描選項，當選項詞性都相同時，再依上下文文意判斷字義搭配最通順的選項。

- 考慮此句是描述動物照護員的職責，且為了符合空格前的大意：「按照 SOP 或⋯提供食物和水給毛小孩」，將(A) protection，保護，先刪去。(B) brochures 和(C) pamphlets

是類似字，都是「小冊子」之意，因此也刪除。最適合搭配上文大意的是(D) protocols，規則或規範。

3.

- 此題所有選項都有原型動詞，主要測試考生在記憶動詞片語時，是否細心注意到動詞之後要搭配不同的介系詞或副詞。dispose 是不及物動詞，固定搭配的介系詞是 of，因此正確選項是(A) Dispose of。

- (B) Throw 不能選，因為後面搭配 waste，垃圾或廢棄物時，throw 後面要搭配副詞 away。而(C) Discard of 是錯誤的，因為 discard 是及物動詞，及物動詞的意思是動詞後面要馬上接名詞，當作動詞的受詞，動詞之後不能直接接介係詞，所以 discard of 裡的 of 是多餘的，discard 之後應該馬上接受詞。(D) Dispose 的錯誤則是缺少介係詞 of。

4.

- 除了考慮空格前後文意連貫，正確選項也一定與主題有關，因主題是動物照護員的職責描述，因此選擇與「照護」關係最密切的選項。

- 首先刪去(B) momentary，「片刻的」及(D) temporary，「暫時的」，因為意思與空格前後的 health... checks，健康檢查無關。而(A) surveys 是「調查，民意調查」，survey 比較偏向大幅度的調查，(C) surveillance 是「檢查，監測，監護」之意。將(A)和(C)比較，(C) surveillance 比較適合搭配健康檢查，也呼應此句描述動物照護員的職責的大意。

浣熊 ● ● ●

改寫

1. The animal caretaker should <u>follow</u> our SOPs and protocols. 此時要選 (C)。

2. Occasionally, the animal caretaker needs to conduct <u>surveys</u> on the feedbacks from furkid owners. 此時要選 (A)。

中譯

1. 動物照護員應該遵循我們的 SOP 和規則。

2. 動物照護員偶爾需要執行關於毛小孩飼主的回應的調查。

解析

1.

- 空格前是助動詞 should，所以空格應該填入原型動詞 follow。follow 的受詞是 our SOPs and protocols，從受詞的字義能推測 follow 是「遵循，遵守」之意。類似動詞有 obey，stick to，abide by，comply with，act in accordance with。也須注意 follow 是多重意義字，意思主要依賴其後的受詞字義去推測。

- 例如「追隨，跟隨」：Disease follows intemperance，疾病跟隨著放縱的生活而來。The child followed his mother home，小孩跟著媽媽回家。也有「理解」之意，例如 to follow an argument，理解一場爭辯，此時 follow 的類似字是 understand。或「接替」之意，例如 Who will follow the president after he retires? 總裁退休後，誰將接掌他的職位？此時的類似字是 succeed。

2.

- 因為空格前是 conduct，執行，空格應填入名詞，當作執行的受詞。先刪去(B) momentary，因為 momentary 是形容詞，意為「片刻的，稍縱即逝的」。也刪去(D) temporary，「暫時的」，也是形容詞。

- (A) surveys，(C) surveillance 都是名詞，這時就要考慮主題及空格上下文大意，比較哪個字義套入空格能讓整句句意最通順。survey 有「意見調查」之意，呼應下文的毛小孩飼主的回應。surveillance 是「監視，檢查」。所以(A) surveys 比(C) surveillance 更適合當正確選項。

Unit 4
A Complaint Letter
抱怨信：購買泰迪熊後的不滿

Question 1-4 refer to the following passage

To whom it may concern:

I'm writing this letter to express my disappointment in a recent purchase of your Teddy Bear (1) .

I have been a (2) collector of your Teddy Bear series for more than 20 years. When I learned about the release the centennial Teddy Bear, I placed my order via mail immediately.

  (3) , as soon as I received the package, I was dismayed to find out that there are not only scratch marks on the display case, but some fur has fallen off from the teddy bear.

Obviously, your quality control has not been (4) . I'm returning the defective collectible along with this letter, and expect a full refund.

Sincerely,

Jessica Wang

1. (A) collecting   (B) collectable
   (C) collective   (D) collector
2. (A) transient   (B) keen
   (C) kin   (D) temporary
3. (A) Thus   (B) Hence
   (C) Moreover   (D) However
4. (A) at close range   (B) up to speed
   (C) up to par   (D) within reach

敬啟者：

我寫這封信以表達對最近購買你們的泰迪熊 __(1)__ 的失望。

二十多年來，我一直是你們泰迪熊系列的 __(2)__ 收藏者。當我得知百年版泰迪熊上市，我馬上下了郵購訂單。

__(3)__ ，我一收到包裹，我很不高興地發現不只展示盒上有刮痕，泰迪熊有些毛也掉了。

明顯地，你們的品管 __(4)__ 。我正要把這瑕疵品隨這封信寄回，並期待完整退款。

誠摯地，

潔西卡・王

6 填空式閱讀

7 單篇閱讀

7 雙篇、三篇閱讀

模擬試題

1. (A) 正收藏　　(B) 收藏品　　(C) 集體的　　(D) 收藏者
2. (A) 片刻的　　(B) 熱衷的　　(C) 家族　　　(D) 暫時的
3. (A) 因此　　　(B) 因此　　　(C) 此外　　　(D) 然而
4. (A) 在近距離　(B) 速度夠快的　(C) 達到標準的 (D) 垂手可得的

答案：1.B　2.B　3.D　4.C

獵豹 • • •

1.

- 看到整句目光直接鎖定在 Teddy Bear 及空格的位置位於句尾。因為句尾的位置不可能是 Teddy Bear 接形容詞，所以選名詞，收藏品的名詞是(B) collectable。

2.

- 看到整句目光直接鎖定在 collector。因選項都是形容詞，只須考慮字義。字義能合理修飾 collector 的只有(B) keen，熱衷的。

3.

- 看到整句目光直接鎖定在 I was dismayed...及空格的位置位於句首。因為 dismayed 是非常不悅的意思，與上一段落的大意形成反差，所以正確的轉折詞選(D) However，然而。

4.

- 看到整句目光直接鎖定在 Your quality control has not been...。因上文是否定句，推測是批評品管達不到標準，所以選(C) up to par。

貓頭鷹 ● ● ●

1.

- 此題主要考動詞 collect 的詞性變化。大部份有-able 字尾的單字是形容詞，少數同時也是名詞。也能考慮字義解題，例如首先刪去(C) collective 集體的和(D) collector 收藏者。(B) collectable 是雙重詞性，形容詞是「可收藏的」，名詞是「收藏品」，搭配空格前的泰迪熊是最通順的。另外，檢查此題的上文: purchase of your Teddy Bear，由 purchase，購買，可 知 道 空 格 應 該 套 入 商 品 之 類 的 名 詞，因 此 刪 去 (A) collecting，collecting 可能是「收集」的現在分詞或動名詞，但無收藏品之意。

2.

- 此題考字義，考生須注意拼法及發音類似，但詞性及意義不同的字，如(B) keen 和(C) kin。

3.

- 轉折詞的詞性是副詞，副詞在句首後面要逗號，因此逗號也是詞性的線索。

4.

- 此題主要線索是主詞 quality control，品質管理，正確選項在意義上要能合理修飾品管。由品管一詞聯想合理的修飾詞有「達到標準的」意思。因此先刪除(A) at close range，在近距離或逼近的，和(D) within reach，垂手可得的。名詞 par 有「usual standard，平常的標準」之意，所以(C) up to par 是正確選項。

浣熊 • • •

 改寫

1. I have been <u>collecting</u> all of the editions of your Teddy Bear collectables for more than 20 years. 此時要選 (A)。

2. The wait for the release of the new Teddy Bear collectable was too long. As a loyal customer, I had hoped that the manufacturing process of your Teddy bears could have been <u>up to speed</u>. 此時要選 (B)。

中譯

1. 我蒐集所有你們的泰迪熊收藏品版本已經超過 20 年了。

2. 等待新的泰迪熊收藏品上市的時間太久了。身為忠實顧客,我原本希望你們的泰迪熊製造過程能達到該有的速度。

解析

1.

- 此題主要線索是空格前的 have been,由 have been 聯想動詞時態是現在完成進行式: have been Ving,have been 搭配現在分詞 collecting。

- 另一線索是句尾的 for more than 20 years，因為現在完成進行式主要的功能是描述從以前直到現在，長時間持續進行，幾乎沒有中斷的動作，呼應「超過 20 年」。

2.

- 第一句 The wait... too long 的句意是主要線索，既然消費者認為等待過程或時期太久，很有可能是他原本希望廠商能更快推出新產品。第二句主要動詞 had hoped 的受詞是由 that 導引的名詞子句，名詞子句裡的主詞 the manufacturing process，製造過程，也是解題線索，即正確選項必須在意義上合理修飾製造過程。

- 從慣用語的意義判斷，可先刪除(A) at close range，在近距離或逼近的，也刪除(D) within reach，垂手可得的，因為都無法修飾製作過程。再比較(B) up to speed，速度夠快的，及(C) up to par，達到標準的。考慮第一句的目的是抱怨等待太久，最合理修飾製造過程的慣用語是跟速度有關，換言之，消費者原本希望製造過程速度能快，因此(B) up to speed 比(C) up to par 更適合。

- 另外，可注意 up to speed 有兩個意義。除了「達到該有的速度或效率」，也有「瞭解最新情況或得知最新進展」之意，例如 bring someone up to speed，讓某人知道最新進展。

Unit 5
Farewell Party
退休員工告別派對

Question 1-4 refer to the following passage

Dear faculty members,

__(1)__ the university, I would like to invite you to the farewell party for Mary Townsend, which will be held at 7 p.m., Oct. 5th, at the Oriental Culture Center, located at Sandburg Hall __(2)__ campus. As you might have heard, Ms. Townsend, the director of the center, is going to retire next month. __(3)__, and her contribution to the center has been __(4)__. It is Ms. Townsend that pioneered the research of oriental calligraphy in our university, and thanks to her leadership, the center has grown into one of the leading establishments focusing on oriental calligraphy.

Please join me at the party to show our appreciation for Ms. Townsend, and I look forward to seeing you.

Cordially,

Sam Johnson

University Dean

1. (A) Behalf of   (B) Behaving
   (C) On behalf of   (D) On behalf for
2. (A) in   (B) on   (C) at   (D) within
3. (A) Refreshments and drinks will be served
   (B) She has served the university for 35 years
   (C) The center holds many exhibitions every year
   (D) Please contact the center for more information
4. (A) valuable   (B) worthy
   (C) worthwhile   (D) invaluable

親愛的教職員，

僅 ___(1)___ 本大學，我想邀請你們來瑪莉·湯森的告別派對。派對將在十月五日晚間七點，於東方文化中心舉辦，東方文化中心 ___(2)___ 校園的桑柏大樓。你可能聽說了，此中心的主任湯森女士下個月要退休了。 ___(3)___ ，她對中心的貢獻是 ___(4)___ 。在我們大學，湯森女士引領東方書法研究，由於她的領導，此中心已經成長為專精東方書法的領導機構。

請在派對和我一起表達對湯森女士的感謝，我期待看到你們。

誠摯地，

山姆·強森

大學校長

1. **(A)** 代表　　　**(B)** 正做出行為　**(C)** 代表　　　　**(D)** 代表

2. **(A)** 在　　　　　**(B)** 在上面　　　**(C)** 在　　　　　**(D)** 在裡面

3. **(A)** 有提供點心和飲料

　　(B) 她在大學服務 35 年了

　　(C) 中心每年舉辦許多展覽

　　(D) 請聯絡中心以獲得更多資訊

4. **(A)** 有價值的　　　　　　　　**(B)** 值得的

　　(C) 值得的　　　　　　　　　**(D)** 極為重要的、無價的

答案：1.C　2.B　3.B　4.D

 獵豹 • • •

1.

- 看到整句目光直接鎖定在 ...the university, I would like to invite...。從「大學…想要邀請…」推測空格字義是「代表」，所以選(C) On behalf of。

2.

- 看到整句目光直接鎖定在 campus。campus，校園，固定搭配介係詞 on。

3.

- 看到整句目光直接鎖定在 is going to retire next month... and her contribution...。由(B) ...has served... for 35 years 這兩個線索得知此選項的描述與退休之間的關係最密切。

4.

- 看到整句目光直接鎖定在 her contribution... has been...。正確選項是形容詞，形容 contribution。因 contribution 意思是貢獻，最適合修飾貢獻的是(D) invaluable，極重要的。

貓頭鷹 ● ● ●

6 填空式閱讀

7 單篇閱讀

7 雙篇、三篇閱讀

模擬試題

1.

- 此題須同時考慮文意及配合詞性觀念。句首的片語是修飾完整句的副詞片語。副詞片語的格式是「介系詞+名詞」，所以先刪去(A) Behalf of 和(B) Behaving。On behalf of... 僅代表...，是常放句首的慣用語。(D) On behalf for 其中的介係詞 for 是錯誤的。

2.

- 此題測試考生對慣用語的熟悉度。某些慣用語要注意無法只依賴中文翻譯判斷選項的狀況。例如「在校園」的慣用語並不是 in campus，而是 on campus。

3.

- 空格之前的句子描述湯森女士下個月即將退休。空格後提到她對中心的貢獻，因此正確選項應該呼應上下文，必須與她的工作內容及退休一事有關連性。

4.

- 此題因為所有選項都是形容詞，所以主要考點是字義的合理搭配，正確選項必須能合理地形容主詞 her contribution，她的貢獻。考生要注意容易混淆的單字，如 valuable 及 invaluable。valuable 通常形容可被定價的具體物品或商品，所以不能形容抽象意義的 contribution。invaluable 的類似字是 priceless，有極重要的、極珍貴的、無價的意義，比起其它選項，最適合形容抽象意義的 contribution。

浣熊 ● ● ●

改寫

1. She has served the university for 35 years, and during her term of service, she has introduced many <u>valuable</u> artworks to the center. 此時要選(A)。

2. During her term of office in the center, she has organized numerous exhibitions on oriental art, and all visitors to those exhibitions found it <u>worthwhile</u> to spend their time appreciating the artworks. 此時要選(C)。

中譯

1. 她在大學服務已經 35 年了，在她任職期間，她為中心引進了許多有價值的藝術品。

2. 在她於此中心任職期間，她組織了許多東方藝術展覽，而且所有的參觀者都覺得花時間欣賞這些藝術品是值得的。

解析

1.

- 空格後是名詞 artworks，藝術品，因此必須選形容詞修飾藝術品。特別注意(A) valuable 及(B) worthy 不是類似字。(A) valuable 意為 worth a lot of money，值錢的，具備高金錢價值的或貴重的，類似字是 expensive，costly，換言之，如果要修飾的名詞是可被定成高價格的物品，應該以 valuable 修飾，不是以 worthy 修飾。

- 按照此意，以 valuable 修飾藝術品是合理的。另一意思是重要的，有用的，通常形容 advice，information 或 support。(B) worthy 是多重意義形容詞，意思有（1）值得欽佩的或尊敬的，例如 make a donation to a worthy cause，捐款給值得欽佩的事業。（2）值得注意的，例如 be worthy of consideration，值得注意或考慮。（3）受之無愧的，例如 a man worthy of confidence，值得信任的人。（4）匹配……的，符合……特徵的，例如 a party worthy of a millionaire，符合百萬富翁特色的派對。

2.

- 此題主要線索是空格之後的 to spend their time，因為(C) worthwhile 是形容「某個活動值得花費時間、金錢或勞力的」，與其它選項比較，worthwhile 最適合搭配下文的「花時間欣賞這些藝術品」這項活動。

Unit 6
Voluntourism: International Travel
志工觀光：國際旅遊

Question 1-4 refer to the following passage

Voluntourism is a new form of international travel that combines tourism and volunteering. Currently, our travel agency offers voluntourism trips to several countries in Africa and Latin America. As a volunteer, you will not only have the experience of cultural __(1)__ , but also participate in projects that __(2)__ positive impact on local communities. The projects we have carried out include building clinics, working in orphanages, and preserving aboriginal cultures. Besides __(3)__ yourself with the locals, you will further broaden your horizon by working with volunteers from all over the world. __(4)__

1. (A) immerse   (B) immersion
   (C) immersive   (D) immersed
2. (A) affect   (B) depress   (C) exercise   (D) exert
3. (A) familiar   (B) familiarization
   (C) familiarizing   (D) familiarity
4. (A) Before volunteering, please fill in the questionnaire.
   (B) It does not matter if volunteers are interested in foreign cultures.
   (C) The clinics our volunteers built in Africa have raised health awareness.
   (D) If you wish to know more about the details, please email or call our agency.

中譯

　　志工觀光是一種新型態的國際旅遊，結合觀光業和志工活動。目前，我們旅行社提供在非洲及拉丁美洲數個國家的志工觀光旅行。身為志工，你不但能擁有文化 ___(1)___ 的經驗，也能參與對當地社區 ___(2)___ 正面影響的計畫。我們已經進行的計畫包括蓋診所、在孤兒院工作及保存原住民文化。除了讓你和當地人 ___(3)___ ，你也能藉由和來自世界各地的志工工作拓展視野。 ___(4)___

1. **(A)** 沉浸   **(B)** 沉浸   **(C)** 浸入的   **(D)** 被沉浸

2. **(A)** 影響   **(B)** 使憂鬱   **(C)** 運動   **(D)** 施展

3. **(A)** 熟悉的   **(B)** 熟悉的過程   **(C)** 熟悉   **(D)** 熟悉

4. **(A)** 當志工前，請填這份問卷。

    (B) 志工對外國文化有沒有興趣不重要。

    (C) 我們志工在非洲蓋的診所提升了健康意識。

    (D) 如果你想知道更多細節，請 email 或打電話給我們旅行社。

答案：1.B   2.D   3.C   4.D

解析

獵豹 ● ● ●

1.

- 看到整句目光直接鎖定在 cultural。因為 cultural 是形容詞，後面要修飾名詞，所以選(B) immersion。

2.

- 看到整句目光直接鎖定在 impact on...。因選項都是動詞，所以從字義判斷能搭配受詞 impact，影響或效應的動詞，選項中唯一有「發揮」之意的是(D) exert。

3.

- 看到整句目光直接鎖定在 Besides... yourself with。選擇能搭配反身代名詞 yourself 的動詞 familiarize，又因為介係詞 besides，正確選項必須將動詞改成動名詞 familiarizing。

4.

- 看到整句目光直接鎖定在此空格的位置。考慮文章類型是旅行社介紹某種特殊行程的內容，通常在此文類最後會提供旅行社聯絡方式、如何洽詢等。所以選(D) If you wish to know more about the details, please email or call our agency。

貓頭鷹 ● ● ●

1.

- immerse 是原型動詞，其它選項都是從原型動詞衍生出的不同詞性單字，所以此題主要考詞性的搭配，可以從字尾判斷詞性，如 -sion 是普遍的名詞字尾。

- cultural immersion 有融入文化的過程、文化沉浸及文化滲透之意。

2.

- exert 有施展、發揮(力量)之意。常搭配的受詞有 influence、impact、effect、pressure、power 等。

- 正確選項 exert 是形容詞子句裡的動詞，形容詞子句由關係代名詞 that 導引，關係代名詞 that 同時代替先行詞 projects，同時也是形容詞子句的主詞，所以其後馬上接動詞 exert。exert positive impact，發揮正面效應，是意思合理的片語。

3.

- 此題考 familiar 的詞性變化，考生也須累積動詞片語，使某人熟悉…的動詞片語是 familiarize oneself with N.。注意 familiarize 一定要接反身代名詞。

- 介係詞之後要接名詞或動名詞。

4.

- 完整句選項的題型也能從此題目所在的位置推測答案。考生也
  須注意不同的文類有不同的結構，按照句子的意義安排在不同
  的位置。

浣熊

改寫

1. Volunteers will have the invaluable opportunity to immerse themselves in the local culture and mingle with the locals. 此時要選(A)。

2. The projects volunteers carry out affect the local communities in a positive way. 此時要選(A)。

中譯

1. 志工將有珍貴的機會可以融入當地文化，並與當地人打交道。

2. 志工們執行的計劃以正向的方式影響當地社區。

解析

1.

- 此句的 have the opportunity to 是第一線索，因為 have the opportunity to 之後馬上要接原型動詞，「to+原型動詞」形成不定詞，不定詞的功能是暗示未來有機會或可能進行的動作。只有(A) immerse 是原型動詞，故答案是(A)。

- immerse 有「沉浸，融入於......」之意，之後的介系詞常搭配字義搭配 in，介系詞也是另一解題線索。(C) immersive，形容詞，浸入的，身歷其境的。(D) immersed，可能是動詞時態過去式或過去分詞，(C)，(D)都無法搭配 have the opportunity to。

2.

- 從空格下文的大意可以倒著推測該套入的動詞，下文大意是「以正向的方式......當地社區」。由於選項詞性都是動詞，因此主要以字義判斷哪個動詞接受詞 the local communities，且被副詞片語 in a positive way 修飾是最適合的。由正向方式聯想，動詞字義應該是影響，最恰當，所以選(A) affect。

- 事實上，(B) depress 使憂鬱，(C) exercise 運動，(D) exert 施展，馬上接「當地社區」這個受詞，大意都不通順，這三個選項可刪除。

Unit 7
The Elephant Sanctuary
泰國北部清邁的大象庇護所

Question 1-4 refer to the following passage

The Elephant Sanctuary located in Chiang Mai, Northern Thailand, has played an __(1)__ part of __(2)__ elephants that are kept in captivity or injured in the wilderness. Since the inception in 1980, the sanctuary has developed from a local center to an internationally __(3)__ organization. Visitors from around the world come here to learn about the herds or volunteer to help with rescue projects. __(4)__ Other than making donations and volunteering, please stop buying ivory products; If the demands for these products lower, deaths of elephants incurred by poaching will lessen.

1. (A) indispensable   (B) avoidable
    (C) profitable   (D) measurable
2. (A) rescue   (B) rescuing
    (C) rescuers   (D) rescuing from
3. (A) fame   (B) famous for
    (C) renowned   (D) anonymity
4. (A) Elephants are intelligent animals.
    (B) The sanctuary cooperates with several international travel agencies.
    (C) The sanctuary also takes care of stray dogs and cats.
    (D) There are several ways you can help preserve these majestic animals.

位於泰國北部清邁的大象庇護所在 ___(2)___ 那些被囚禁或在荒野受傷的大象扮演了 ___(1)___ 的角色。自從 1980 年開始，庇護所從一間地區中心發展成國際 ___(3)___ 的組織。來自世界各地的訪客到這邊學習關於象群的事或自願協助搜救計畫。 ___(4)___ 除了捐款和當志工，請停止購買象牙產品；如果對這些產品的需求降低，盜獵造成的大象死亡將會減少。

1. (A) 不可缺少的   (B) 可避免的

   (C) 可獲利的   (D) 可測量的

2. (A) 搜救   (B) 搜救   (C) 搜救員   (D) 從…救出來

3. (A) 名聲   (B) 以...出名   (C) 有名的   (D) 匿名

4. (A) 大象是聰明的動物。

⭐(B) 庇護所和幾個國際旅行社合作。

   (C) 庇護所也照顧流浪狗和流浪貓。

   (D) 你有幾個方式能幫助保育這些偉大的動物。

答案：1. A   2. B   3. C   4. D

獵豹 • ● ●

1.

- 看到整句目光直接鎖定在 played an... part。 應該選形容詞修飾名詞 part。根據主詞 Sanctuary 是庇護所、保護機構的意思，應選意義正面的形容詞(A) indispensable。

2.

- 看到整句目光直接鎖定在 of... elephants。因為 of 是介係詞，後面必須接名詞或動名詞，所以選(B) rescuing。

3.

- 看到整句目光直接鎖定在 organization。organization 是名詞，前面要以形容詞修飾，所以選(C) renowned。

4.

- 看到整句目光直接鎖定在 to help with rescue projects... please stop buying...。只有(D)提及 help preserve，故選(D)。

貓頭鷹 ● ● ●

1.

- 除了先考慮緊鄰空格前後的線索字，主詞的意義也常是線索。此題考字義 play a... part 或 play a... role，扮演…的角色。

2.

- 雖然 rescue 是名詞及動詞，但名詞 rescue 之後不能馬上接名詞，要先補上 of，即 the rescue of elephants。動詞 rescue 是及物動詞，能馬上接受詞 elephants。

3.

- 選項中只有(C) renowned 是形容詞。(B) famous for 的 famous 雖然是形容詞，但 famous for 是以......知名，與 organization 的字義無法連貫。空格前的副詞 internationally 也能協助判斷正確選項的詞性，副詞能修飾形容詞，另一個副詞，或動詞。

4.

- 此題上一句描述當志工協助搜救計劃，下一句描述停止購買象牙產品，暗示藉此協助保育大象。根據上下文，正確選項必須提及協助保育，才能維持這三句的連貫性。(D) There are several ways ...數個方式指的是 making donations and volunteering, ...stop buying ivory products。

浣熊 ● ● ●

改寫

1. The Elephant Sanctuary located in Chiang Mai, Northern Thailand, is well-known for its Preservation Movement. The Preservation Movement has <u>rescuers</u> to help injured elephants to recover and captivated ones to be freed. 此時要選 (C)。

2. The sanctuary has eventually earned its <u>fame</u> through a series of development, from a local center to an international organization. 此時要選(A)。

中譯

1. 位於泰國清邁的大象庇護所以保育運動知名。保育運動有急救人員幫助受傷的大象復原，及協助被囚禁的大象被釋放。

2. 庇護所透過一系列的發展贏得名聲，從一間地區中心發展成一個國際組織。

解析

1.

- 此空格前後都有解題線索。空格前是這句的主要動詞 has，has 之後一定要接受詞，而名詞，動名詞或名詞子句能當作受詞，掃描選項，沒有子句，所以正確選項的可能性是(B) rescuing，(C) rescuers。又考慮空格之後搭配不定詞 to help，協助，所以(C) rescuers，急救人員或搜救人員，比(B) rescuing 更適合搭配「協助」之意。

- 另外的解題技巧是考慮(B) rescuing 有可能是動名詞或現在分詞（因為動名詞或現在分詞的拼法都是 Ving），但現在分詞不能當作受詞，所以刪除(B)，也能用同樣技巧刪除(D) rescuing from，而且介系詞 from 之後接不定詞 to help 文法是錯誤的。

2.

- 空格前的所有格 its 是第一線索。所有格之後只能接名詞或動名詞，因此刪除(B) famous for 及(C) renowned，因為 famous 和 renowned 都是形容詞。(A) fame 及(D) anonymity 都是名詞，但是(D) anonymity 意為「匿名的人或事物」，整個篇章主題毫無關聯，因為主題是介紹大象庇護所。

- 而且 anonymity 前面搭配主要動詞 has earned，贏得，句意不合理。搭配主要動詞 has earned 最通順的是(A) fame，名聲。注意 fame 有幾個類似字: renown，celebrity，reputation。

Unit 8
Gym Announcement
市政府公告：健身中心公告

Question 1-4 refer to the following passage

The city government is proud to announce that the __(1)__ Fitness Center will be opened on Oct. 2. Located at the intersection of Maple Street and 1st Boulevard, the center is easily __(2)__ by public transportation, whether you come from the downtown area or suburbs. __(3)__, such as treadmills, elliptical trainers, stair steppers, rowing machines and stationary bikes. __(4)__, users can sign up for group classes that range from moderate to strenuous activities, such as yoga, aerobics, pilates, spinning, zumba, and boxing.

1. (A) Marsupial　　　　(B) Mercantile
   (C) Private　　　　　(D) Municipal
2. (A) arrive　(B) reached　(C) achieve　(D) obtained
3. (A) The monthly membership fee is very reasonable
   (B) You can sign up for one-on-one coaching classes
   (C) There are a variety of exercise machines you can use
   (D) The exercise machines are imported
4. (A) Moreover　　　　(B) Yet
   (C) Nevertheless　　(D) In conclusion

市政府很榮幸宣佈 ___(1)___ 健身中心將在十月二日開幕。中心位於楓樹路和第一大道交叉口，容易透過大眾運輸 ___(2)___ ，不管你來自市中心或郊區。 ___(3)___ ，例如跑步機、橢圓機、踏步機、划船機和腳踏車。 ___(4)___ ，使用者能報名輕度到重度運動的團體課程，例如瑜伽、有氧運動、皮拉提斯、飛輪、zumba 和拳擊。

1. (A) 有袋動物的   (B) 和商業有關的
   (C) 私人的   (D) 市立的

2. (A) 抵達   (B) 抵達或被抵達
   (C) 成就，達成   (D) 獲得

3. (A) 月費非常合理
   (B) 你能報名一對一教練課程
   (C) 你能使用各種運動器材
   (D) 運動器材是進口的

4. (A) 此外   (B) 然而   (C) 然而   (D) 總言之

答案：1.D   2.B   3.C   4.A

獵豹 • • •

1.

- 看到整句目光直接鎖定在 Fitness Center，判斷選形容詞修飾名詞。由主詞 The city government，市政府，推測正確選項應該和「市政的」有關，符合此字義的只有(D) Municipal。

2.

- 看到整句目光直接鎖定在 is... by public transportation。根據 transportation 的字義是運輸，正確選項應表達「到達」，符合此字義的只有(B) reached。

3.

- 看到整句目光直接鎖定在 such as treadmills, elliptical trainers...。只須快速掃描 such as 之後一兩個名詞，瞭解是運動器材的名稱，就能確定正確選項是(C)。There are a variety of exercise machines you can use.

4.

- 看到整句目光直接鎖定在 users can sign up for classes...。上文列舉運動器材，下文描述運動課程，是方向一致的細節，因此正確轉折詞選(A) Moreover。

貓頭鷹

1.

- 因為所有選項都是形容詞，所以此題主要考字義，正確選項必須合理地形容名詞 Fitness Center。其餘選項均與健身中心無關。

2.

- 由空格後的副詞片語 by public transportation，「藉由大眾運輸」的意思，得知應該選表達「抵達或到達」的動詞。大雖然(A) arrive 有到達之意，但必須搭配介系詞 in 或 at。(C) achieve 的字義不符合到達之意。因主詞是 the center，此句的主要動詞須使用被動語態。被動語態的格式是 be 動詞+過去分詞，常搭配介系詞 by。符合過去分詞拼法的選項有(B) reached 及(D) obtained，但只有 reached 有「到達，抵達」之意。obtain 是「獲得」之意。

3.

- such as 是導引例子的常用片語。such as 之前的句意必須與例子有密切關係。雖然(C)和(D)都提及 exercise machines，但(D)的形容詞 imported，進口的，與主題無關。主題是介紹此中心的服務。

4.

- 轉折詞的詞性是副詞，副詞在句首後面要逗號，因此逗號也是詞性的線索。

浣熊 ● ● ●

改寫

1. The center is located at the intersection of Maple Street and 1st Boulevard, and you can <u>arrive</u> at the center by public transportation. 此時要選(A)。

2. <u>You can sign up for one-on-one coaching classes</u> if you have a busy working schedule and seek more flexibility in your training. 此時選(B)。

中譯

1. 此中心位於楓樹路和第一大道交叉口，你能透過大眾運輸抵達中心。

2. 你能報名一對一教練課程，如果你有繁忙的工作行程，而且尋求更有彈性的訓練。

解析

1.

- 首先，注意主詞是 you，暗示主要動詞的語態是主動語態，而且空格前有助動詞 can，助動詞後要接原型動詞，因此刪除(B) reached 及(D) obtained，因為這兩個選項可能是動詞過去式或過去分詞。

● 考慮第一個子句描述健身中心的大致位置，及此句句尾的副詞片語的意思: by public transportation，藉由大眾運輸，綜合以上兩個線索，可推測正確選項的字義是「到達」。到達或抵達的動詞是 arrive，故選(A) arrive。注意 arrive 是不及物動詞，也就是不能馬上接受詞，必須先接介系詞 in 或 at，再接受詞。此句的 arrive at the center 可將動詞片語 arrive at 替換成 reach the center，因為 reach 也有抵達之意，但 reach 是及物動詞，所以後面不需要介系詞。

2.

● 此題型須要選擇一個完整子句套入空格，形成與前後文連貫且意義合理的句子。因為此句的前一句是描述健身中心的位置，但空格後有從屬連接詞 if 連接正確選項子句和另一子句，且 if 導引的從屬子句意思是: 如果你有繁忙的工作行程，且尋求更有彈性的訓練，與前一句中心位置的大意已經無關，所以此情況只要考慮哪個選項與 if 子句最連貫，並呼應 if 子句的大意。

● 首先刪除(A)，因為月費合理與 if 子句的大意毫無關係。而(C)，(D)的大意都是關於運動器材，和尋求更有彈性的訓練也沒有絕對的關係。而(B)你能報名一對一教練課程，與想要上更彈性的訓練課程關係最密切，所以正確選項是(B)。

Unit 1
Best Aquarium
倍斯特水族館：新聞發佈文

First of all, e-mails swarmed into our office like crazy. On behalf of the PR Department of Best Aquarium, I'm here to make an announcement. Best Aquarium is currently under construction and will reopen on Oct. 18, 2018. There are going to be more animals and recreational facilities. We are truly sorry for the inconvenience caused.

Second, unfortunately whales will no longer be in our Aquarium. They do cause problems for our staff to maintain the overall **stability** of our operation. In addition, the glass wall can't seem to endure their pouncing. Also, giving them an individual building won't solve the problem, either. Adult whales are too aggressive. It's pressuring young whales, which cause sickness among young whales.

Third, after doing some serious thinking, our company has decided to release them back to the ocean. For those who are fans of whales, we do have 10 videos containing different aspects of whale life, but you probably have to see them in other places.

1. What is the main purpose of the passage?

(A) to explain why whales are dangerous

(B) to inform new changes of the aquarium

(C) to ask for more funding for the aquarium

(D) to inform fans of whales how they can borrow the videos on whales

2. Which of the followings is NOT the reason that the aquarium decided to release the whales?

(A) it is difficult for the staff to maintain the operation.

(B) The glass wall is too fragile.

(C) Adult whales and young whales cannot get along well.

(D) Taking care of the whales is too expensive.

6 填空式閱讀

7 單篇閱讀

7 雙篇、三篇閱讀

模擬試題

單元 1 ▶ 倍斯特水族館

首先，e-mail 瘋狂似地湧進我們的辦公室。僅代表倍斯特水族館公關部，我在此作宣布。倍斯特水族館現在正在重建且將於 2018 年 10 月 18 日重新開張。水族館將會有更多動物和娛樂設施。我們對於所引起的不便誠摯地感到抱歉。

第二，很不幸地是水族館將不再有鯨魚。鯨魚的確對我們員工在維持運作的整體穩定性上造成困擾。此外，玻璃牆也幾乎無法承受鯨魚的撞擊。而且，給予鯨魚個別的容納處也無法解決此問題。成年鯨魚太具侵略性。它壓迫到年輕鯨魚，引起年輕鯨魚們生病。

第三，再經過謹慎的思慮後，我們公司已經決定將牠們釋放回大海中。對於那些是鯨魚迷的參觀者，我們會有十個影音檔包含鯨魚生活的不同面向，但你可能要去其他地方才能看到牠們的身影了。

1. 這篇文章的主旨是？

   (A) 解釋鯨魚是危險的。

   (B) 告知水族館的新的改變。

   (C) 替水族館要求更多資金。

   (D) 告知鯨魚迷們他們如何借閱有關鯨魚的影音檔。

2. 下列哪個原因不是水族館決定將鯨魚釋放回大海的原因？

   (A) 對員工維持公司營運造成困難。

   (B) 玻璃牆太脆弱。

   (C) 成年鯨魚和年輕鯨魚無法相處。

   (D) 照護鯨魚過於昂貴。

6 填空式閱讀

7 單篇閱讀

7 雙篇、三篇閱讀

模擬試題

答案：1. B　2. D

獵豹

1.

- 看到整句目光直接鎖定在 I'm here to make an announcement。馬上刪去(A) to explain why whales are dangerous。因為動物習性，例如鯨魚是危險的，和做出宣布無關。接續的段落敘述都是在表達新的改變，故選 B。

2.

- 看到整句目光直接鎖定在第三段第一句 ...release them back to the ocean。原因在第二個段落，定位後得知答案為 D。

貓頭鷹

1.

- 讀題時先判斷題目類型，main purpose 是問主題或主旨，通常段落第一段第一～三句或每段第一～三句會敘述主題。

2.

- 此題是細節題型。細節題型先定位相關細節段落。細節題型的選項描述會以類似詞或不同句型將文章敘述重述。(A) it is difficult for the staff to maintain the operation.意思近似 They do cause problems for our staff to maintain the overall stability of our operation。(B) The glass wall is too fragile 重述 the glass wall can't seem to endure their pouncing。(C) Adult whales and young whales cannot get along 重述 Adult whales are too aggressive. It's pressuring young whales...。

浣熊 • • •

NEW

1. In the second paragraph, the word "stability" in paragraph 2, line 3 is closest in meaning to
   (A) vulnerability
   (B) steadiness
   (C) efficiency
   (D) effectiveness

2. What will still be offered to customers after Oct. 18, 2018?

6 填空式閱讀

7 單篇閱讀

7 雙篇、三篇閱讀

模擬試題

(A) Adult whales

(B) swimming pools

(C) sick whales

(D) aggressive whales

中譯

1. 在第二段中,第二段第三行 stability 這個字的意思,最接近哪個字?

(A) 易受傷。

(B) 穩定。

(C) 效率。

(D) 效果。

2. 在 2018 年 10 月 18 日後,何者仍會提供給顧客?

(A) 成年鯨魚。

(B) 游泳池。

(C) 生病的鯨魚。

(D) 具侵略性的鯨魚。

解析

1. 題目詢問「在第二段中,第二段第三行 stability 這個字的意思,最接近哪個字?」先分別從四個選項來看。

• A 選項為 vulnerability 意思是易受傷、弱點,同義詞有 susceptibility 和 defenselessness 等,反義詞有 immunity

和 resistance。可以先排除選項 A。B 選項為 steadiness，與題目的 stability 為同義字，其他同義字有 fixedness, solidity, firmness, secureness 和 solidness 等等，故答案為選項 B。C 選項為 efficiency 同義字有 organization, order, orderliness 和 planning，反義字有 inefficiency 和 incompetence，此選項也與題目的字意思不同，故也可以先排除這個選項。選項 D 為 effectiveness 是有效和有效性的意思也與題目的字意思不同，故也可以先排除這個選項。

2. 題目詢問「在 2018 年 10 月 18 日後，何者仍會提供給顧客？」可以一併來看。

- 文章中提到鯨魚和設施，且會在重新開張後提供更多動物和娛樂設施，先看跟鯨魚有關的部分，選項可能是由出題者修改後造成的混淆。可以很清楚的是，在第二段首句清楚表明了 Second, unfortunately whales will no longer be in our Aquarium.，故可以同時排除選項 ACD。文中雖有提到成年鯨魚、成年鯨魚具侵略性和成年鯨魚的壓迫造成年輕鯨魚生病，但題目是問某時間點後仍會提供的項目，所以 ACD 均不符合。最後是選項 B 游泳池，從更多遊樂設施的敘述中可以推斷，儘管文章中沒有更多關於娛樂設施的敘述，但可能增加的部分會是游泳池，故答案是選項 B。

Unit 2
Best Hotel
倍斯特旅館：結束營業公告

Best Hotel was established in 2008 and was deemed the landmark of southern Europe. Due to economic recession, we have decided to close the hotel next month. Since visitors are mostly visiting western Europe, the number of visitors has dropped from 120 people per day to 120 per month.

This week, with Father's Day coming up, we are offering a 50% off for anyone purchasing our double rooms, and a 30% off for single rooms. __(1)__. For people who are staying over 3 days, we are offering luxurious breakfast for free. __(2)__. Also, we are giving parents with kids a special discount if they want to have a massage in our Spa, which is located on our 10th floor. __(3)__.

Luxurious Cafeteria will also have a special discount for people who want to celebrate Father's Day. __(4)__.

Note: There is no time limit for luxurious breakfast. Luxurious breakfast will always be free as long as you are staying for more than three days.

1. What is the main reason that caused the hotel to go out of business?

   (A) the economic downturn and dramatic reduction of customers

   (B) the decision to move the hotel to western Europe

   (C) the failure of marketing strategy

   (D) the lack of discounts

2. Which of the blanks marked (1), (2), (3), and (4) does the following sentence belong to?

   "Fathers will not be charged for using our facilities from Aug 1st to Aug 8th 2018"

   (A) (1)

   (B) (2)

   (C) (3)

   (D) (4)

單元 2 ▶ 倍斯特旅館

倍斯特旅館創立於 2008 年，被視為是南歐的地標。由於經濟不景氣，我們已經決定於下個月結束旅館營業。既然觀光客都大多參觀西歐，觀光客的數量已從每個日 120 個人下降到每個月 120 個人。

這週，隨著父親節到來，我們將提供任何訂購我們雙人房的訂購者 5 折優惠，單人房七折優惠。對於待超過三天者，我們將提供免費的豪華早餐。而且我們會提供有小孩的父母特別優惠，如果他們想要享受我們的 Spa 按摩服務，位於我們飯店的十樓。

對於想要慶祝父親節者，我們的豪華自助餐也將有特別的折扣。

註：豪華早餐沒有時間限制。只要你待超過三日，豪華早餐都是免費的。

1. 什麼是導致旅館結束營業的主要原因？

(A) 經濟不景氣和顧客急遽地減少。

(B) 決定將旅館移至西歐。

(C) 行銷策略的失敗。

(D) 缺少折扣。

2. 下列句子屬於段落空格 (1), (2), (3), and (4)所標示的哪個欄位中？

「於 2018 年 8 月 1 日至 2018 年 8 月 8 日期間，父親們可以免費使用我們的設施。」

(A) (1)。

(B) (2)。

(C) (3)。

(D) (4)。

答案：1. A　2. D

解析

獵豹 ● ● ●

1.

- 看到整句目光直接鎖定在 Due to economic recession。
  掃描選項裡 economic recession 的類似字，選項 (A) the economic downturn and dramatic reduction of customers，是旅館結束營業的主因，故答案為選項 A。

2.

- 看到整句目光直接鎖定在 Fathers。
  掃描四個空格的上下文，只有標示(4)的空格前提及 Father's Day，故答案為選項 D。

貓頭鷹 • • •

1.

- 此題考 reason，屬於細節題型。due to + N.，因為。to 是介系詞，後面接名詞。表「因為」的片語是此類細節題型的主要線索。除了 due to，同義詞有 because of、owing to、thanks to。再以 recession 的類似字 downturn 決定正確選項。

2.

- 完整句插入正確空格的題型主要測試正確選項與空格前後句意的連貫性。連貫性除了以轉折詞加強，另一個加強連貫性的技巧是重複上一句的關鍵字，例如此題的關鍵字是 fathers。

6 填空式閱讀

7 單篇閱讀

7 雙篇、三篇閱讀

模擬試題

浣熊 ● ● ●

還有可能怎麼問

1. If a visitor plans to stay at Best hotel for four days for his trip to southern Europe with four friends in the fourth week of August, which of the following items will he be getting?

   (A) a 50% off for double rooms

   (B) a discount for a single room

   (C) luxurious breakfast for five people

   (D) a Spa service at the 10th floor

2. Why was the article written?

   (A) to inform the excellent service provided.

   (B) to inform the closure of the business.

   (C) to highlight the importance of Father's Day.

   (D) to celebrate a new opening.

中譯

1. 如果觀光者計劃了四天的南歐，與四位朋友要在八月的第四個禮拜，待在倍斯特旅館四天，下列哪個項目是他能享有的？

   (A) 雙人房五折優惠。

   (B) 單人房的折扣。

   (C) 五人豪華早餐。

   (D) 十樓的 SPA 服務。

2. 寫這篇文章的目的是？

   (A) 告知所提供的優良服務。

   (B) 告知結束營業。

   (C) 強調父親節的重要性。

   (D) 慶祝新開幕。

解析

1. 題目詢問「如果觀光者計劃了四天的南歐之旅，與四位朋友要在八月的第四個禮拜，待在倍斯特旅館四天，下列哪個項目是他能享有的？」先分別從四個選項來看。

- 題目中列出了許多條件，先定位回文章第二段找尋相關的折扣跟優惠，也要注意時間點。文章中無清楚的優惠日期，但可從第二段首句看到 This week, with Father's Day coming up, we are offering a 50% off for anyone purchasing our double rooms, and a 30% off for single rooms.，從這裡可以判定，此三項服務都是在父親節即將到來的那週所提供的，也就是這週才有這些折扣跟優惠，但題目敘述的時間點是八月的第四個禮拜，待在倍斯特旅館四天，所以觀光客無法享有上述優惠，所以可以排除選項 A 的 a 50% off for double rooms，選項 B 的 a discount for a single room。

- 目前就剩下選項 C 和選項 D。選項 D 的部分定位回該段，a Spa service at the 10th floor 也是於父親節該週所享有的部分，所以可以排除選項 D。

- 關於 D 選項，要特別注意雖然在第二段有表明 For people who are staying over 3 days, we are offering luxurious breakfast for free.，表示這是父親節所能享有的部分，但是在註的部分卻又提到待超過三天豪華早餐總是免費所以可以得知答案為選項 C。

2. 題目詢問「寫這篇文章的目的是？」先分別從四個選項來看。

- 選項 A 為 to inform the excellent service provided，文章中提到服務的部分在第二個段落，但是主要的論述是關於所提供的折扣的部分，所以可以先排除選項 A。選項 B 為 to inform the closure of the business，可以從文章首段提到的 Due to economic recession, we have decided to close the hotel next month 和後續表示的原因等得知文章主要是在說 the closure of the business，故答案為選項 B。選項 C 為 to highlight the importance of Father's Day.，文章中雖有父親節活動跟折扣等，但這只是部分文章所提到的服務，文章的主要在講述的部分不是這個，故也可以排除選項 C。選項 D 為 to celebrate a new opening.，文章中要提到慶祝，但是並沒有提到新開幕的內容，而是說明將結束營業，故也可以排除選項 D。

Unit 3
Best Zoo
倍斯特動物園：招聘

Recruitment

Best Zoo is currently looking for health specialists and veterinarians for koalas, brown bears, pandas, and polar bears. Candidates must have a degree in zoology and at least 6 years of training in big agencies, such as ABC Animal Training Center or International Animal Research Center. Familiarity with above-mentioned animals' behavior is a must. We do love people who are enthusiastic about jobs and enjoy spending time with animals. Attributes, such as honesty and reliability, are high on our list. Candidates must enclose their CVs and at least three videos with animals, and e-mail them to us before 8 p.m., Nov 9th, 2018.

We're going to offer a competitive salary. Doctors will have three months of paid vacation during summer, whereas health specialists will have 30 days of paid leave starting their first year. In addition, we do offer meals for lunch and dinner. Our meals are like a godsend, which will give you more incentive to work. Also, this year we are collaborating with other large recreational centers, so we are offering you free tickets. You can go there and enjoy the vacation with your family.

1. Where might readers see this want ad?
   (A) a fashion magazine
   (B) a veterinary journal
   (C) a TV guide
   (D) a zoo guide

2. Which of the followings is TRUE?
   (A) The candidates for this position should hold a degree in veterinary medicine.
   (B) The candidates for this position should have 6 years of working experience with bears
   (C) The benefits include meals, paid leave, and free vacations.
   (D) The candidates do not need to have computer skills.

單元 3 ▶ 倍斯特動物園

人才招募

倍斯特動物園正在尋找無尾熊、棕熊、熊貓和北極熊的保健專家和獸醫。候選人必須要有動物學學歷以及至少六年於大型代理機構的訓練，像是 ABC 動物訓練中心或國際動物研究中心。熟悉上述動物行為是必須的。我們喜愛對工作保有熱忱的人以及喜愛花時間與動物相處的人。我們很重視像是誠實和信賴的特質。候選人必須於 2018 年 11 月 9 日下午 8 點前附上他們的 CV 和至少三個與動物有關的影頻以電子郵件寄給我們。

我們提供與市場行情相近（或高於市場行情）的薪水。在夏季，從開始工作的第一年開始，醫生將有三個月的有薪休假，而保健專家將有三十天的有薪假。此外，我們提供午餐和晚餐。我們的餐點像是天賜般，能給予你更多的工作動機。而且，今年我們將與其他大型的娛樂中心合作，所以我們也會提供免費的門票。你可以去那邊且享受與家人的假期。

1. 讀者可能可以於那裡看到人才招募廣告？

(A) 時尚雜誌。

(B) 獸醫期刊。

(C) 電視節目指南。

(D) 動物園指南。

2. 下列敘述何者為真？

(A) 候選人應徵此職務應該要持有獸醫學歷。

(B) 候選人應徵此職務要有六年照顧熊的工作經驗。

(C) 福利包含餐飲、有薪休假和免費假期。

(D) 候選人不需要電腦技能。

答案：1. B　2. C

獵豹 ● ● ●

1.

- 看到整句目光直接鎖定在 Best Zoo is currently looking for health specialists and veterinarians...。

- 根據 zoo，馬上刪去(A) a fashion magazine 及(C) a TV guide。又根據 health specialists and veterinarians，決定(B) a veterinary journal 比(D) a zoo guide 適合。

2.

- 看到整句目光直接鎖定在 a degree in zoology。必須能判斷出此題屬於細節題，掃描(A)的關鍵字 a degree，定位在第二句 a degree in zoology，與(A) a degree in veterinary medicine 不同，刪去(A)。掃描(B)的關鍵字 6 years，第二句 6 years of training in big agencies 與(B) 6 years of working experience with bears 不同，刪去(B)。

- (C) The benefits include meals, paid leave, and free vacations 將以下這些線索字以更精簡的方式重述：paid vacation... we do offer meals... offering you free tickets. You can go there and enjoy the vacation with your family。所以正確選項是(C) The benefits include meals, paid leave, and free vacations。

貓頭鷹 ● ● ●

1.

● 此題屬於情境題，題目大意詢問文章在哪種媒體或管道出現。

● 因為(D) a zoo guide，動物園指南的讀者群是一般大眾，而(B) a veterinary journal，獸醫期刊的讀者比較偏向獸醫等專業人員。journal 有專業期刊或學術期刊之意。

2.

● 細節題的選項描述會以類似詞或不同句型將文章敘述重述。

● 「下列何者為真或錯」的細節題須先定位每個選項描述裡的關鍵字，同時掃描文章裡是否有相同關鍵字或關鍵字的類似字。關鍵字常是表達條件的名詞，例如(A)的 a degree 及數字，例如(B) 6 years。定位出文章裡的關鍵字或其類似字後再根據那句的大意對照選項描述是否正確。此題(D)是錯誤的，因為全文未提及應徵者是否需要電腦技能。

浣熊 ● ● ●

還有可能怎麼問

1. Which of the following items is Not the requirement of this job?

   (A) solid trainings at International Animal Research Center

   (B) familiarity with the operation of big agencies

   (C) eagerness for this job

   (D) a thorough understanding to bear's behavior

2. What is not mentioned as incentives for potential hires at Best Zoo?

   (A) incredible meals

   (B) free tickets for employees only

   (C) excellent chances of working with other firms

   (D) enjoyment of August vacation

中譯

3. 下列哪個項目不是這份工作的條件？

   (A) 在國際動物研究中心紮實的訓練。

(B) 熟悉大型機構的運作。

(C) 對此工作的熱忱。

(D) 對熊的行為有透徹的了解。

4. 對潛在受僱者下列哪項不是聘僱到倍斯特動物園的潛在誘因？

(A) 驚人的食物。

(B) 只有員工專屬的免費門票。

(C) 與其他公司工作的絕佳機會。

(D) 享有八月假期。

解析

1. 題目詢問「下列哪個項目不是這份工作的條件？」先分別從四個選項來看。

- 選項 A 為 solid trainings at International Animal Research Center 定位回文章中 Candidates must have a degree in zoology and at least 6 years of training in big agencies, such as ABC Animal Training Center or International Animal Research Center.，可以得知至少六年的訓練等同於 solid trainings，故這是工作的條件之一。

- 選項 B 為 familiarity with the operation of big agencies 定位回文章中 Familiarity with above-mentioned animals' behavior is a must.文章中提到的是對上述動物行為的熟悉是必要的，且該段落沒有訊息提到 familiarity with the operation of big agencies，故答案為選項 B。

- 選項 C 為 eagerness for this job，eagerness 為 enthusiasm 的同義字，且 We do love people who are enthusiastic about jobs and enjoy spending time with animals.為此選項的同義表達，故可以排除選項 C。選項 D 為 a thorough understanding to bear's behavior 與段落開頭敘述和 Familiarity with above-mentioned animals' behavior is a must.為同義表達，故也可以排除選項 D。

2. 題目詢問「對潛在受僱者下列哪項不是聘僱到倍斯特動物園的潛在誘因？」先分別從四個選項來看。

- 選項 A 是 Incredible meals，定位到第二段找到 In addition, we do offer meals for lunch and dinner. Our meals are like a godsend, which will give you more incentive to work.與選項 A 為同義表達，故可以排除選項 A。

- 選項 B 為 Free tickets for employees only，同樣定位到第二段，文章中雖然提及 we are offering you free tickets 但沒有清楚說明門票只屬於員工專屬，只提供給員工，故選項 B 為錯誤表達，答案為選項 B。

- 選項 C，同樣定位回文章 Also, this year we are collaborating with other large recreational centers，可以得知此為 excellent chances of working with other firms 的同義表達，故可以排除選項 C。

- 選項 D 為 enjoyment of August vacation，定位回文章中 We're going to offer a competitive salary. Doctors will have three months of paid vacation during summer, whereas health specialists will have 30 days of paid leave starting their first year.可以得知享有假期是在暑假，August vacation 包含在假期裡，員工可以自己選擇故此為其中一個誘因，也可以排除此選項。

113

Unit 4
Skywriting
空中文字：演講稿

Skywriting

It's probably unheard of for some. __1__ . That's why some people are with a confused look when the term skywriting pops into their mind. It's a chance of a lifetime experience. You're going to love it. It can be used as a romantic proposal. I once saw the skywriting with words, like "Mary James. Will you marry me?". The bride immediately said "yes" right on the spot. Soon after there were tears and hugs. People all congratulated them. I'm not going to lie __2__ . The event was so **contagious**. Besides, it can also be used as a warning in places where __3__ , but I don't recommend that since skywriting is not cheap __4__ . Although we are not offering discounts for those who would like to use our service, we do offer two opportunities to use skywriting free of charge to people who actually want to propose to their loved ones, but are sort of on a tight budget. So, any volunteers?

1. What does "The event was so contagious" imply in this context?
   (A) People are easily touched by the romantic event.
   (B) Skywriting can be used to warn people about contagion.
   (C) Skywriting can be used to spread an important message.
   (D) An epidemic might be more contagious if people kiss and hug.

2. Which of the blanks marked (1), (2), (3), and (4) does the following sentence belong to?
   "something might go wrong"
   (A) (1)
   (B) (2)
   (C) (3)
   (D) (4)

單元 4 ▶ 空中文字

對一些人來說可能沒聽過。這也是為何當空中文字這個詞浮現到我們腦海時，有些人有著困惑的神情。這是千載難逢的體驗。你將會喜愛它。它可以用於浪漫的求婚。我曾目睹空中文字寫著文字像是「瑪莉·詹姆士，嫁給我好嗎？」。在當場新娘立刻回答「我願意」。之後就是眼淚跟擁抱。大家都恭喜他們。真的不騙你。這是會感染的。此外，在事情有可能出錯誤的地方會將其用於示警，但是我不推薦就是了，因為空中文字並不便宜。儘管我們沒有提供折扣給那些想要使用我們服務的人，我們提供兩個免費使用空中文字的機會給實際上想要向自己的摯愛求婚，但預算卻有點吃緊的人。所以有人自願嗎？

1. 在上下文中，「這事件深具感染力」意謂著什麼？

   (A) 人們易受浪漫的事件感動。

   (B) 空中文字可以用於警告人們感染。

   (C) 空中文字可以用於傳遞重要訊息。

   (D) 流行病可能更具感染力如果人們親吻和擁抱。

2. 下列句子屬於段落空格 (1), (2), (3), and (4)所標示的哪個欄位中？

   「事情有可能出錯」

   (A) (1)

   (B) (2)

   (C) (3)

   (D) (4)

6 填空式閱讀

7 單篇閱讀

7 雙篇、三篇閱讀

模擬試題

答案：1. A　2. C

獵豹 • • •

1.

- 看到整句目光直接鎖定在 the event。

- 先推測 the event 指的事件，是指這句之前描述的求婚事件，因此推測 contagious 是具感染力的意思。而(A) People are easily touched by the romantic event，人們容易被感動呼應被周遭氣氛感染。

2.

- 看到整句目光直接鎖定在 go wrong。

- 「可能有事情出錯」插入在 ___3___ 與空格前 it can also be used as a warning in places where... 的意思最合理，warning 一字暗示空中文字被用來示警有錯誤或異常事件。

貓頭鷹　● ● ●

1.

- 此題目要求考生選出與句子意思最類似的選項描述。考生須讀出句子的深層意義。

- contagious 的意思有「傳染病方面的」及「氣氛或情緒具感染力的」。而 the event 指的求婚事件也呼應(A) ...the romantic event。

2.

- 單句插入最適合位置的題型除了考慮文意的通順以外，空格在文章裡的位置也是解題主要線索。

- 從空格位置判斷，先刪去(A)，因為「可能有事情出錯」的意思不適合放在文章開頭，刪去(B)，因為(B)的前後文都屬於求婚事件的描述。另外，考生也須有句型結構的知識，例如，刪去(D)，因為(D)上文是副詞子句 ...since skywriting is not cheap，空格前缺乏對等連接詞可連接這個副詞子句和 something might go wrong 這個子句。

浣熊 ● ● ●

1. What is Not mentioned as the function of Skywriting?
   (A) a warning signal
   (B) celebration for a wedding
   (C) other means of message delivery
   (D) reconciliation for romantic rivalry

2. In the paragraph, the word "contagious" in line 9 is closest in meaning to
   (A) contaminated
   (B) remarkable
   (C) cheerful
   (D) infectious

1. 關於空中文字，下列哪個敘述並未提及？
   (A) 警告訊息。
   (B) 慶祝婚禮。

(C) 其他方式的訊息傳遞。

(D) 跟浪漫情敵和解。

2. 在段落中，第九行 contagious 這個字的意思，最接近哪個字？

(A) 污染的。

(B) 著名的。

(C) 愉快的。

(D) 感染的。

解析

1. 題目詢問「關於空中文字，下列哪個敘述並未提及？」先分別從四個選項來看。

- 選項 A 為 a warning signal，定位回 Besides, it can also be used as a warning in places where something might go wrong，雖然沒有清楚表明是警告什麼的細節但是卻表明了這是 warning 的功用，故可以得知選項 A 在文中有提及，可以排除選項 A。

- 選項 B 為 celebration for a wedding，可以定位到 You're going to love it. It can be used as a romantic proposal. I once saw the skywriting with words, like "Mary James. Will you marry me?". The bride immediately said "yes" right on the spot.可以得知與選項 B 表達的訊息相符，故也可以排除選項 B。

- 選項 C 為 other means of message delivery，文中雖沒有在定義 skywriting 這個詞的時候表明是 other means of message delivery 的功用，但是從婚禮敘述跟警告的訊息等可以推斷空中文字其實是另一個形式的訊息傳遞，只是是在空中將訊息表達出來，故可以排除選項 C。

- 選項 D 為 reconciliation for romantic rivalry，以關鍵字 reconciliation 或 romantic rivalry 定位回文章中，均沒有相關的表達，故選項 D 並未於文章中提到，答案為選項 D。

2. 題目詢問「在段落中，第九行 contagious 這個字的意思，最接近哪個字？」先分別從四個選項來看。

- 選項 A 為 contaminated 受汙染的，同義字有 polluted，如果是動詞 contaminate 的話，同義字有 pollute, corrupt, defile, infect. ，與題目的意思並不相符，故可以排除選項 A。

- 選項 B 為 remarkable 意思為值得注意的、卓越的、非凡的，同義字有 unusual, noteworthy, extraordinary, exceptional，與題目的意思並不相符，故可以排除選項 B。

- 選項 C 為 cheerful 意思是興高采烈的、情緒好的，同義詞有 cheery, gay, sunny, blithe，反義詞是 gloomy, cheerless, dismal, melancholy，與題目的意思並不相符，故可以排除選項 C。

- 選項 D 為 infectious 意思為傳染性的、有感染力的，同義詞為 contagious, communicable, transmittable, transmissible. 其意思與題目字相符故答案為選項 D。

Unit 5
Hawaii International Balloon Festival
夏威夷國際氣球節：網路廣告

Best Airline branch office is hosting an International Balloon Festival this summer. For people who love to overlook the gorgeous scenery of the ocean, valleys, and so on, you certainly can't miss it.

Five Major Types of Balloons

	Time	Price	Descriptions
Regular/Type A	5-10 minutes	US 30	assigned balloon
Regular/Type B	60 minutes	US 500	assigned balloon
Luxurious/ Type C	10 minutes	US 300	Choose a favorite
Luxurious/ Type D	120 minutes	US 1000	Choose a favorite
Luxurious/ Type E	24 hours	US 2000	Specifically tailored

Note 1: If there is a rainbow while you are on a balloon, you are getting a 50% off for the ride.

Note 2: If it's your birthday, you're getting a coupon of US 30 dollars or a coupon of US 2000 dollars. You need to draw the lot, so it depends on how lucky you are.

1. How much does it cost if some visitors sign up for a Type A Balloon and two Type C Balloons?
   (A) US 330
   (B) US 600
   (C) US 630
   (D) US 660

2. What does "specifically tailored" mean?
   (A) A tailor can receive more discount for the balloon ride.
   (B) The balloon ride is individually designed.
   (C) People can choose how long they want to stay on the balloon.
   (D) The price for the balloon ride can be negotiated.

單元 5 ▶ 夏威夷國際氣球節

倍斯特國際航空分公司於這個夏天將舉辦國際氣球節。如果你是喜愛俯視海洋、山谷等等美景的人,那你就不能錯過!

五個主要類型的氣球

	時間	價格	描述
普通/類型 A	5-10 分鐘	30 美元	指定氣球
普通/類型 B	60 分鐘	500 美元	指定氣球
豪華/類型 C	10 分鐘	300 美元	可選擇喜愛的氣球
豪華/類型 D	120 分鐘	1000 美元	可選擇喜愛的氣球
豪華/類型 E	24 小時	2000 美元	特別訂做

註 1:當你在氣球上時,如果有彩虹出現,你能享有該趟五折優惠的價格。

註 2:如果是你生日,你能獲得 30 美元的優惠卷或 2000 美元的優惠卷。你需要抽籤,所以要看你有多幸運囉!

1. 如果有些觀光客報名登記 A 類型一次和 C 類型的氣球兩次，花費
   會是多少？
   (A) 330 美元。
   (B) 600 美元。
   (C) 630 美元。
   (D) 660 美元。

2. 「量身訂做」指的是？
   (A) 裁縫師能在氣球乘坐時得到更多折扣。
   (B) 氣球乘坐是個別設計的。
   (C) 人們可以選擇他們想要在氣球上待多久。
   (D) 氣球乘坐的價格是能夠協商的。

答案：1. C　2. B

獵豹 ● ● ●

1.

• 看到整句目光直接鎖定在 Type A Balloon and Type C Balloon。

• 題目是問登記 A 類型氣球一次和 C 類型氣球兩次，A 類型氣球一次是 30 美元，C 類型氣球一次是 300 美元，兩次是 600 美元，所以選（C)US 630。

2.

• 看到整句目光直接鎖定在 specifically tailored。

• 由 tailor 字尾的 ed 可知 tailor 在此篇的情境是當動詞。動詞 tailor 有「量身訂做」之意，選項描述最類似的是(B) The balloon ride is individually designed，尤其是 individually designed。

1.

- 此題是與數字有關的細節題，需要考生做基本的算術。

- 考生只須細心定位題目裡的關鍵字，如此題是氣球的類型，有時此類型題目可能會牽涉單位，如此篇的單位是時間長短。

2.

- 此題測試換句話說的技巧。考生也須認識 tailor 是名詞，也是動詞。

- 大部分情況下，只有動詞能加 ed（Adj. + N-ed 的複合形容詞例外，如 kind-hearted，搭配在形容詞之後的名詞才能加 ed），從 ed 能判斷 tailor 是動詞。

浣熊 ● ● ●

1. Which of the following statement is Not true?

   (A) A bad luck in drawing the lot can end up in getting a coupon of US 30 dollars.

   (B) visitors who get a coupon of US 2000 dollars by drawing the lot can exchange for a luxurious 24-hour journey.

   (C) visitors drawing the lot have a chance to get a coupon of US 2000 dollars, equivalent to the value of a specifically tailored balloon.

   (D) visitors drawing the lot could all get a coupon of US 2000 dollars.

2. For visitors who have such tight lingering time of an hour and a budget of 1000 dollars, and want a balloon of their choices, they should take

   (A) Type A

   (B) Type B

(C) Type C

(D) Type D

 中譯

1. 下列哪個敘述是不正確的？

(A) 如果抽籤時沒那麼幸運則可能得到 30 元美金的優惠卷。

(B) 觀光客如果透過抽籤得到兩千元美金，可以換豪華的 24 小時 旅程。

(C) 觀光客抽籤可以得到兩千元美金的優惠卷，等同於一個量身訂 做的氣球價值。

(D) 觀光客抽籤都能得到兩千美元的優惠卷。

2. 觀光客如果有著有限的停留時間 1 小時整、預算 1000 元而且想 要有自己喜好的氣球，他們應該要搭乘？

(A) 類型 A。

(B) 類型 B。

(C) 類型 C。

(D) 類型 D。

解析

1. 題目詢問「下列哪個敘述是不正確的？」先分別從四個選項來 看。

   • A 選項為 A bad luck in drawing the lot can end up in

getting a coupon of US 30 dollars，可定位回註 2，得知「如果是你生日，你能獲得 30 美元的優惠卷或 2000 美元的優惠卷。你需要抽籤，所以要看你有多幸運囉！」，所以生日能參加抽籤，而抽籤結果是 30 美元的優惠卷或 2000 美元的優惠卷，相對來説 2000 美元的優惠卷是最高獎項，亦等同於很幸運，抽到 30 美元者則會很嘔，符合 A 選項所表達的意思，此敘述正確，故可以排除 A 選項。

- B 選項為 visitors who get a coupon of US 2000 dollars by drawing the lot can exchange for a luxurious 24-hour journey.，可以定位回註 2 和表格，並掌握價格和時間，兩千美元即等同於能購買 24 小時豪華之旅，符合 B 選項所表達的意思，此敘述正確，故可以排除 B 選項。

- C 選項為 visitors drawing the lot have a chance to get a coupon of US 2000 dollars, equivalent to the value of a specifically tailored balloon.，可以定位回註 2 和表格，價格和描述的部分 a coupon of US 2000 dollars 等同於 a specifically tailored balloon.，符合 C 選項所表達的意思，此敘述正確，故可以排除 C 選項。

- D 選項為 visitors drawing the lot could all get a coupon of US 2000 dollars，要特別注意文章敘述中的 all 等字，過於絕對性的字眼，在此 all get a coupon of US 2000 dollars 與註 2 的敘述不合，註 2 所表達的是兩者中其中一個結果，故答案

為選項 D。

2. 題目詢問「觀光客如果有著有限的停留時間 1 小時整、預算 1000 元而且想要有自己喜好的氣球，他們應該要搭乘？」先分別從四個選項來看。

- 選項列出了 A 到 D 類型的氣球，先看題目所敘述的條件，逐一刪除不合的條件，從第一個條件 visitors who have such tight lingering time of an hour 則可以先刪除搭乘時間會超過一小時的選項，故旅客不可能搭乘 D 類型的氣球，先排除選項 D。

- 接著是 a budget of 1000 dollars，得知 A,B,C 類型的價格都在預算內。緊接著看次一個條件 want a balloon of their choices，得知只有 C 類型的氣球符合，A 和 B 的氣球均是 assigned，故可以推斷答案為選項 C。

Unit 6
Best Catering
倍斯特酒席承辦：網路廣告

The Internet and many other social-networking sites have brought some changes to our lives. To counter those changes, Best Catering is now adopting some marketing strategies, and most important of all, we are going to expand our service. In addition to wedding and all forms of ceremonies, we are going to do some events, from as small as a birthday party to as big as a grand promotion party.

For the birthday party, you can see the table below.

Items	Price/Number of people	Descriptions
Bouncing House	US 150/10	• For the luxurious decorations, the price is double.
Monkey	US 300/1	• A monkey only performs two hours. If the performing time exceeds two hours, the price varies.
clown	US 450/1	• A clown performs 8 hours • More than 8 hours: price double
Goodie bags	US 600/10	• More than 50 people: 50% off

Insects collections	US 300/10	• For special animals, such as tarantulas and scorpions, additional 300 dollars are required. • Can only be demonstrated for 2 hours
reptiles	US 600/10	• For special animals, such as poison dart frogs, it's gonna cost another 1200 dollars. • Can only be demonstrated for 2 hours
Children's book	US 30/1	• 20 people: 50% off
Illustration/ portrait	US 150/1	• 20 people: 50% off

Note: even if tarantulas and scorpions are not insects, we categorize them in our list as insects.

1. Who are more likely to hire the catering service?
   (A) graduate school students working on their theses
   (B) parents preparing for their children's birthday parties
   (C) zookeepers
   (D) people who keep insects as pets

2. How much does it cost if a customer order goodie bags for 20 people?
   (A) US 600
   (B) US 800
   (C) US 1200
   (D) US 1800

單元 6 ▶ 倍斯特飲食承辦

　　網路和許多社交網站已經替我們生活上帶來一些改變。為了應對那些改變，倍斯特飲食承辦正採用一些行銷策略，最重要的是，我們將擴大我們的服務。除了婚禮和所有形式的典禮之外，我們還會做一些項目，從小至生日宴會到大至盛大的升遷慶祝派對。

慶生派對的部分，可以看下列表格。

項目	價格/人數	描述
跳房子	每 10 人 150 美元	• 豪華裝飾的部分，價格是兩倍。
猴子	每人 300 美元	• 猴子只表演兩小時。如果時間超過兩小時價格也會有所不同。
小丑	每人 450 美元	• 小丑表演 8 小時。 • 超過八小時：價格是兩倍。
禮物袋	每 10 人 600 美元	• 超過 50 人：五折。
昆蟲收集	每 10 人 300 美元	• 特別的動物像是狼蛛和毒蠍，需要額外 300 美元。 • 只展示兩小時。
爬蟲類	每 10 人 600 美元	• 特別的動物像是箭毒蛙，需要花費 1200 美元。 • 只展示兩小時。
兒童書	每人 30 美元	• 20 人：五折。
插圖/個人畫像	每人 150 美元	• 20 人：五折。

註：即使狼蛛和毒蠍並非昆蟲，我們將它們歸類在昆蟲清單裡。

1. 誰較有可能雇用飲食承辦服務？

(A) 研究所正在撰寫論文的學生。

(B) 父母準備替他們的小孩辦生日派對。

(C) 動物園管理員。

(D) 以昆蟲為寵物的人。

2. 如果一個顧客訂購 20 人份的禮物袋要花費多少錢呢？

(A) 600 美元。

(B) 800 美元。

(C) 1200 美元。

(D) 1800 美元。

答案：1. B　2. C

 獵豹 ● ● ●

1.

- 看到題目目光直接鎖定在 Who... hire。

- 以 party 一字定位解題線索在第一段最後一句,最後一句提及 birthday party,確定正確選項是(B)。

2.

- 看到題目目光直接鎖定在 goodie bags for 20 people。

- 在 Price/ Number of people 欄位下定位 US 600/10,得知 goodie bags 的價格算法是以 10 人為單位。題目問 20 人,US 600*2= 1200,所以選 (C) 1200 美元。

貓頭鷹

1.

- 由題目的 Wh-疑問詞可知此題是細節題，但此題也測試推測能力，選項敘述新的情境，考生須推測或聯想文章的細節在哪個情境會發生。

- 顧客類型和派對內容有密切關係，所以用 party 一字定位解題線索。

2.

- 此題是與數字有關的細節題，需要考生做基本的算術。

- 考生只須細心定位題目裡的關鍵字，如此題是 goodie bags，並注意是否牽涉單位，goodie bags 的價格算法是以 10 人為一個單位。

浣熊 ● ● ●

1. Which of the following statement is Not true?

   (A) If a customer demands to have a special insect, he or she has to pay extra cash.

   (B) poison dart frogs are three times costlier than tarantulas.

   (C) there are three items that offer a 50% discount if the number of people exceeds a certain amount. .

   (D) The price is double for monkeys performing more than two hours.

2. A birthday celebration needs a clown performing more than 8 hours, scorpions for ten, reptiles for ten, children's books for 20 people, poision dart frogs for ten, how much does it cost?

   (A) 3150 dollars

   (B) 3000 dollars

   (C) 3600 dollars

   (D) 4200 dollars

中譯

1. 下列哪個陳述是錯誤的？

   (A) 如果顧客要求要有特別的昆蟲，他或她必須額外付費。

   (B) 箭毒蛙比狼珠貴三倍。

   (C) 有三個項目提供五折折扣，如果人數超過某個量。

   (D) 猴子表演超過兩小時要花費兩倍金額。

2. 有個生日慶生需要小丑表演超過 8 小時、十人份量的毒蠍、十人份量的爬蟲類、20 人的童書和十人份量的箭毒娃，需要花費多少錢？

   (A) 3150 元。

   (B) 3000 元。

   (C) 3600 元。

   (D) 4200 元。

解析

1. 題目詢問「下列哪個陳述是錯誤的？」先分別從四個選項來看。

   • 選項 A 為 If a customer demands to have a special insect, he or she has to pay extra cash.定為回 insect collections 欄得知 For special animals, such as tarantulas and scorpions, additional 300 dollars are required.得知是需要額外付 300 元的，此為同義表達，故可以排除選項 A。

- 選項 B 為 poison dart frogs are three times costlier than tarantulas.分別定位回兩個欄位，得知箭毒蛙跟狼珠的價格分別為 600 元和 1800 元，故可以得知箭毒娃比狼珠貴三倍，故可以排除選項 B。

- 選項 C 為 there are three items that offer a 50% discount if the number of people exceeds a certain amount.對應回表格中可以察覺有三個項目的敘述欄均有五折折扣，故此為同義表達，可以排除選項 C。

- 選項 D 為 The price is double for monkeys performing more than two hours.對應到表格 If the performing time exceeds two hours, the price varies.，僅能得知 the price varies 並不能推斷出是雙倍價格，文中並未表明，故答案為選項 D。

2. 題目詢問「有個生日慶生需要小丑表演超過 8 小時、十人份量的毒蠍、十人份量的爬蟲類、20 人的童書和十人份量的箭毒娃，需要花費多少錢？」先分別從四個選項來看。

- 四個選項均是金額。題目中有提到條件，所以依據所提到的條件將相對應的金額相加。首先是小丑表演超過 8 小時，定位回表格敘述中 More than 8 hours: price double，從此可以得知小丑超過八小時價格雙倍，小丑花費的金額是 900 元。

- 接著是毒蠍，定位回表格 For special animals, such as tarantulas and scorpions, additional 300 dollars are required.，所以毒蠍每 10 人的金額是 300 元加上額外收費 300 元，故是 600 元整。爬蟲類定位回表格描述中 US 600/10，所以是 600 元。

- 接著是 children's books for 20 people，表格中寫道每人 30 美元，20 人等於 20*30=600 元，但是在描述欄中有 20 people: 50% off，表示 20 人的話會有五折優惠，所以童書價格等於 600*50%=300 元。

- 箭毒蛙的部分定位回表格 For special animals, such as poison dart frogs, it's gonna cost another 1200 dollars.所以是 1200 元。最後是將金額相加，故是 900+600+600+300+1200=3600 元，故答案是選項 C。

Unit 7
Best Auditorium
倍斯特禮堂：海報

This year, we are inviting several super stars to perform at Best Auditorium from Dec 22 to 24. Winners of last year's singers and dancers at Best TV will also show up to **invigorate** the show. We are also welcoming members from school dance clubs and music clubs who volunteer to perform.

Show times	
Dec 22	5 P.M. to 10 P.M.
Dec 23	6 P.M. to 10 P.M.
Dec 24	7 P.M. to 10 P.M.

Tickets are available at Books.com and Amazon.com

Note: for people booking tickets from Amazon.com, we only accept money through wire transfer, whereas people buying tickets directly from Best Auditorium, we accept both credit card payments and cash.

1. Which payment method is NOT mentioned?

   (A) credit card

   (B) cash

   (C) debit card

   (D) wire transfer

2. Which might be the theme for the performance at Best Auditorium?

   (A) The Easter Party

   (B) The Spirit of Thanksgiving

   (C) High School Club Performance

   (D) Christmas Celebration

單元 7 ▶ 倍斯特禮堂

今年度從 12 月 22 日到 24 日，我們將邀請幾位超級巨星來倍斯特禮堂表演。去年在倍斯特電視得獎的歌手和舞者也將出席，讓這個場更有活力。我們也將歡迎學校跳舞社和音樂社的成員中自願來參與表演者。

表演時間	
12 月 22 日	下午 5 點到晚上 10 點
12 月 23 日	下午 6 點到晚上 10 點
12 月 24 日	下午 7 點到晚上 10 點

門票能於博客來網站和亞馬遜網站上購買

註：對於欲從亞馬遜網站上購票者，我們只接受電匯的付費方式，而欲從倍斯特禮堂直接購票者，我們接受信用卡付費和現金。

1. 下列哪種付費方式未提及呢？

   (A) 信用卡。

   (B) 現金。

   (C) 借方卡。

   (D) 電匯。

2. 哪個可能是倍斯特禮堂的表演主題呢？

   (A) 復活節派對。

   (B) 感恩節的精神。

   (C) 高中社團表演。

   (D) 聖誕節慶祝。

6 填空式閱讀

7 單篇閱讀

7 雙篇、三篇閱讀

模擬試題

答案：1. C　2. D

解析

獵豹 ● ● ●

1.

- 看到題目目光直接鎖定在 payment method。

- 通常付款方式的描述會接近文章結尾。因此掃描最後一段，付款方式的字有 wire transfer... credit card payments and cash。沒提到(C) debit card。

2.

- 看到題目目光直接鎖定在 theme。

- 根據 from Dec. 22nd to 24th，是接近聖誕節的日期，所以選 (D) Christmas Celebration。

貓頭鷹 ● ● ●

1.

- 此題是細節題型。細節題型先定位相關細節段落。

- 可從文章主題判斷此種細節大致會出現的位置。例如廣告文或此篇主題是介紹並促銷某場活動，付款方式的細節通常在文章後半部，甚至結尾。

2.

- 此題屬於推測題，可先刪去(C) High School Club Performance，因為全文未提及 high school。

- 考生如果對美國文化有基本的背景知識，能加快此題答題速度。例如各選項提到的 Easter，Thanksgiving，Christmas 都是美國的重要節慶。

浣熊 ● ● ●

還有可能怎麼問

1. In the first paragraph, the word "invigorate" in line 3 is closest in meaning to?
   (A) outperform.
   (B) downplay.
   (C) outlive.
   (D) animate.

2. What is included in this article?
   (A) payment method.
   (B) discounts for the tickets.
   (C) prizes for performers.
   (D) exact time frame for each performer.

中譯

1. 在首段中，第三行 invigorate 這個字的意思，最接近哪個字？
   (A) 勝過。
   (B) 將...輕描淡寫。
   (C) 比...活得更長。
   (D) 使有生命。

2. 文章中提到了什麼？
   (A) 付款方式。
   (B) 門票的折扣。
   (C) 表演者的獎項。
   (D) 每個表演者的確切時間。

解析

1. 題目詢問「在首段中，第三行 invigorate 這個字的意思，最接近哪個字？先分別從四個選項來看。

   • 選項 A 為 outperform 意思是在性能或操作上勝過，這個意思與題目 invigorate 的意思不相符，故可以排除選項 A。

   • 選項 B 為 downplay 意思為將...輕描淡寫、貶低，這個意思與題目 invigorate 的意思不相符，故可以排除選項 B。

   • 選項 C 為 outlive 意思是比…活得長、度過危機、風暴。這個意思與題目 invigorate 的意思不相符，故可以排除選項 C。

- 選項 D 為 animate 意思是賦予生命、使有活力，同義詞為 create, vivify, vitalize，反義詞為 depress, enervate, stagnate，invigorate 的意思是賦予精神、活力，使振奮人心，故最貼近此意思的是選項 D，答案為選項 D。

2. 題目詢問「文章中提到了什麼？」先分別從四個選項來看。

- 選項 A 為 payment method 付款方式，可以定位回 Tickets are available at Books.com and Amazon.com. 和「註」的部分 Note: for people booking tickets from Amazon.com, we only accept money through wire transfer, whereas people buying tickets directly from Best Auditorium, we accept both credit card payments and cash.內容都是在講付款的方式，包含在網站上訂購、電匯、直接購買、信用卡付款和現金，故答案為選項 A。

- 選項 B 為 discounts for the tickets，可以定為回文章中，通常折扣的部分都在段落尾或註的部分或提到付款方式的地方，文章中只提到付款方式，但並未提到會提供任何折扣，故可以排除選項 B。

- 選項 C 為 prizes for performers，這部分可以定位到首段文章開頭，文章中未提到表演者的獎項，然後也要特別注意文章只提到 Winners of last year's singers and dancers at Best TV will also show up to invigorate the show.但並未提到 winners 會拿到什麼，故可以排除選項 C。

- 選項 D 為 exact time frame for each performer.定位回表演時間，文中簡單列出了表演時間，但並未以表格等呈現出每個表演時間和對應的表演者，故可以排除選項 D。

Unit 8
Best Medical Center
倍斯特醫療中心：廣告

Best Medical Center has been known as the leading one in the 21th century. We're now making a **remarkable** move towards collaborating with both male and female models. __(1)__ . Models are not getting free services, but are getting the exposure chance through the show and our website. __(2)__ . For school hotties, we are offering free services, such as wrinkle removal, double chin service, teeth whitening, and nose jobs, __(3)__ , but candidates have to be our spokesperson for three months or to be in our shows at least ten times. __(4)__ .

Contact information
www.bestmedicalcenter.com.tw
Dial 999-7891-9010

1. Which section of the classified ads might you see this ad?

   (A) housing

   (B) men seeking women

   (C) used goods

   (D) recruitment

2. Which of the blanks marked (1), (2), (3), and (4) does the following sentence belong to?

   "Another attempt is to work with school handsome guys and hot chicks"

   (A) (1)

   (B) (2)

   (C) (3)

   (D) (4)

單元 8 ▶ 倍斯特醫療中心

在 21 世紀，倍斯特醫療中心一直具有主導地位。我們正使用更驚人的對策朝向與男性和女性模特兒合作。模特兒不具有免費的服務，但是能透過表演和我們網站做曝光。另一個嘗試是與學校英俊的男生和辣妹合作。對於學校的帥哥正妹，我們提供免費的服務，像是除皺、雙下巴服務、牙齒美白和隆鼻，但是候選人必須是我們的代言人三個月或是於我們的表演中至少亮相 10 次。

聯絡資訊

www.bestmedicalcenter.com.tw

撥打 999-7891-9010

1. 在哪個區塊的分類廣告中你可能會看到這則廣告呢？

(A) 家庭。

(B) 男性徵求女性友人。

(C) 二手物品。

(D) 招聘。

2. 下列句子屬於段落空格 (1), (2), (3), and (4)所標示的哪個欄位中？

「另一個嘗試是與學校英俊的男生和辣妹合作。」

(A) (1)。

(B) (2)。

(C) (3)。

(D) (4)。

答案：1. D　2. B

獵豹 ● ● ●

1.

• 看到整句目光直接鎖定在 We're now making a remarkable move towards collaborating with both male and female models.

根據第二句 collaborating with both male and female models，雖然 collaborate with 是「合作」的動詞片語，但能推測是此醫療中心徵求模特兒，所以選(D) recruitment。

2.

• 看到整句目光直接鎖定在 school handsome guys and hot chicks。

• 掃描哪個欄位前後有以上片語的類似詞，定位在 ___(2)___ 之後的 school hotties。所以正確選項是(B) (2)。

貓頭鷹 ● ● ●

1.

- 此題屬於推測題型。也須熟悉招募廣告的常用字彙，如 collaborate with，recruit, recruitment，candidate 等。

- 也能從最後一句 but candidates have to be our spokesperson for three months or to be in our shows at least ten times 的大意推測出答案。因為此句大意是可能的人選必須做出的條件，可推測模特兒與醫療中心是僱傭關係。

2.

- 形容詞常是解題線索，整句插入的題型如果插入句有形容詞，可搭配掃描技巧先找出內文是否有意思相關詞。

- 如此句的 handsome guys and hot chicks，在美式英文厘語的類似字是 hotties。

浣熊

還有可能怎麼問

1. In this article, the word "remarkable" in line 2 is closest in meaning to?

(A) successful

(B) marvelous

(C) ordinary

(D) sophisticated

2. What are most likely to be selected as spokesperson with free services?

(A) experienced models

(B) candidates who want to have wrinkle removal

(C) eloquent spokespersons

(D) a spotted, attractive quarterback studying at a University

中譯

1. 在此文章中，第二行 remarkable 這個字的意思，最接近哪個字？

(A) 成功的。

(B) 驚奇的。

(C) 普通的。

(D) 複雜的。

2. 什麼最可能被選為享有免費服務的代言人呢？

(A) 有經驗的模特兒。

(B) 想要除皺服務的候選人。

(C) 雄辯的代言人。

(D) 被發掘、吸引人的四分衛大學學生。

解析

1. 題目詢問「在此文章中，第二行 remarkable 這個字的意思，最接近哪個字？」。

- 題目中的 remarkable 意思為值得注意的、卓越的、非凡的，同義字有 unusual, noteworthy, extraordinary, exceptional，然後從四個選項來看哪個意思最接近這個字。選項 A 為 successful 意思是成功的、結果圓滿的和勝利的，同義詞是 prosperous, fortunate, thriving, victorious，反義詞為 unsuccessful 不成功的，此意思與題目的字意思不相符，故可以排除選項 A。

- 選項 B 為 marvelous 意思為令人驚歎的、非凡的、不可思議的，同義詞為 wonderful, extraordinary, miraculous, astounding，此意思與題目意思最接近，故答案為選項 B。

- 選項 C 為 ordinary 意思是通常的、平常的，同義詞有 usual, common, normal, aveage，反義詞有 exceptional, unusual, extraordinary, special. 此意思與題目的字意思不相符，故可以排除選項 C。

- 選項 D 為 sophisticated 意思是世故的、複雜的、精通的，同義詞有 wordly, worldly-wise, experienced, enlightened 反義詞有 unsophisticated, naïve, simple，此意思與題目的字意思不相符，故可以排除選項 D。

2. 題目詢問「什麼最可能被選為享有免費服務的代言人呢？」先分別從四個選項來看。

- 選項 A 為 experienced models，出題者在 models 前面多加了 experienced 的形容詞，雖然文章中未提及 experienced 但可以從段落中推測其實 models 就是相對於新招募對象，具經驗的模特兒，此外在 For school hotties, we are offering free services, such as wrinkle removal, double chin service, teeth whitening, and nose jobs 可以得知 school hotties 才是享有免費服務的對象，可以排除選項 A。

- 選項 B 為 candidates who want to have wrinkle removal，要注意段落是敘述成為代言人能享有某些服務並列舉項目，但

題目是候選人想要有該項目者，所以想要 wrinkle removal 的候選人不是 school hotties，此為出題者做出的混淆，故可以排除選項 B。

- 選項 C 為 eloquent spokespersons，我們正常都會理解講者或代言人要會講話或 e l o q u e n t，但文章中並未敘述 spokespersons 要具備那些條件，故可以排除選項 C。

- 選項 D 為 a spotted, attractive quarterback studying at a University，此敘述可以定位回 school hotties，得知其為同義表達，出題者將 school hotties 以另一個形式表達，並使用子句改寫，將本來的 school hotties 換成學校風雲人物或受歡迎的 quarterback 加上 studying at a University，最後在 quarterback 前面加上了形容詞 spotted, attractive，形成 a spotted, attractive quarterback studying at a University 故答案為選項 D，要注意很多時候正確答案都是經過改寫。

Unit 9
ABC Resort & Spa
ABC渡假村和SPA：招募

We are recruiting!

If your dream is to travel around the world and **accumulate** abundant wealth, don't miss the once-in-a-lifetime opportunity. __(1)__ . As an international resort franchise, ABC Resort & Spa is looking for aspiring and talented candidates to compete for our general manager position overseeing our operation in the Southeastern Asia region. __(2)__ . The candidates must have at least 5 years of managerial experience in the hospitality industry as well as excellent negotiation and marketing capabilities. Advanced English proficiency is necessary, and multilingual background is a plus. __(3)__ . Besides frequent business trips in Southeastern Asia, the G.M. will also attend our unique summit conference held in Las Vegas every three years, where our managers from around the world meet up and share their expertise. __(4)__ . Competitive salary and substantial benefits. Interested candidates, please e-mail your C.V. to HR@ABCresort.com

1. Which of the following qualifications is NOT required by the position?
   (A) multilingual background
   (B) advanced English proficiency
   (C) managerial experience
   (D) negotiation ability

2. Which of the blanks marked (1), (2), (3), and (4) does the following sentence belong to?
   "A master's degree relevant to hospitality or business administration is preferred"
   (A) (1)
   (B) (2)
   (C) (3)
   (D) (4)

單元 9 ▶ ABC渡假村和SPA：招募

我們正在招募

如果你的夢想是環遊世界且累積豐沛的財富，別錯過這千載難逢的機會。作為一個國際旅遊勝地的特許店，ABC 旅遊勝地和 Spa 正尋找有抱負和才能的候選人，來角逐總經理職缺，監督東南亞地區的營運。候選人必須至少有五年在旅館業的管理經驗以及卓越的協商和行銷能力。進階的英語能力是必須的，有多語背景是更加分的。偏好具備有觀光服務或商業行政相關的碩士學歷者。除了會頻繁地於東南亞出差之外，總經理將會出席我們每三年於拉斯維加斯的獨特頂峰會議，我們的經理們會從世界各地來此相會並分享專長。具競爭力的薪資和實質的福利。有興趣者請將 CV e-mail 到 HR@ABCresort.com。

1. 該職務不包括下列哪些條件呢？

(A) 多語背景。

(B) 高階英語能力。

(C) 管理經驗。

(D) 協商能力。

2. 下列句子屬於段落空格 (1), (2), (3), and (4)所標示的哪個欄位中？

「偏好具備有觀光服務或商業行政相關的碩士學歷者。」

(A) (1)

(B) (2)

(C) (3)

(D) (4)

答案：1. A　2. C

6 填空式閱讀

7 單篇閱讀

7 雙篇、三篇閱讀

模擬試題

獵豹 • • •

1.

- 看到題目目光直接鎖定在 qualifications is NOT required。

- 根據 The candidates must have... 敘述應徵資格這句，將列舉的必備資格刪去。先刪(C) managerial experience、(D) negotiation ability。再根據下一句 Advanced English proficiency is necessary，刪去 (B) advanced English proficiency。所以答案是(A) multilingual background。

2.

- 看到題目目光鎖定在插入句的 A master's degree，碩士學位。

- 學歷屬於應徵資格方面，所以插入的欄位前後句子應該也敘述應徵資格或條件。所以正確選項是(C) (3)。

貓頭鷹 ● ● ●

1.

● 此題屬於細節題。要選出非必要的應徵資格或條件。required 是過去分詞，表達「被須要」或「被要求」。在徵募廣告的情境可理解成「必要的」。再從文章搜索「必要的」類似字。助動詞 must 意思是「必須」，雖然詞性和 required 不同，意義是類似。根據 must have 之後的受詞 managerial experience 和 negotiation，將(C)，(D)刪除。另一類似字是 necessary，形容詞，必須的。necessary 形容 advanced English proficiency，所以刪去(B)。注意 multilingual background 雖然有提及，但只是 a plus，加分條件，也就是符合題目要求的非必要條件，所以正確選項是(A) multilingual background。

2.

● 先從插入句的主詞 A master's degree 定位敘述應徵資格的句子。這類型句子從 The candidates must have...至 ...multilingual background is a plus。最接近這些句子的欄位有 __(2)__ 和 __(3)__，因此不考慮 __(1)__ 和 __(4)__。又因為應徵資格的句子先描述必要條件（must have... necessary）完，才接著描述會加分的條件（a plus），考慮插入句句尾的形容詞 preferred，被偏好的，在招募廣告中，偏好條件與加分條件是類似詞，所以選擇 __(3)__ 會比 __(2)__ 更通順。也就是連續兩句都有類似詞，這兩句的連貫性會比較強。

還有可能怎麼問

1. In this article, the word "accumulate" in line 2 is closest in meaning to?

   (A) diminish

   (B) diffuse

   (C) dissipate

   (D) amass

2. What is included in this article?

   (A) accumulating immense wealth is increasingly important.

   (B) annual meetings will be held in Las Vagas

   (C) ABC Resort & Spa used to be a domestic company

   (D) there will be recurrent business trips

中譯

1. 在此文章中，第一行 accumulate 這個字的意思，最接近哪個字？
   (A) 減少。
   (B) 擴散。
   (C) 消除。
   (D) 積聚。

2. 在新生介紹中，下列哪項服務公司並未提供？
   (A) 累積巨額財富越來越重要。
   (B) 年度會議將於拉斯維加斯舉行。
   (C) ABC 渡假村和 SPA 過去曾是國產公司。
   (D) 會有頻繁的商業旅行。

解析

1. 題目詢問「在此文章中，第二行 accumulate 這個字的意思，最接近哪個字？」。

   • 題目中的 accumulate 的意思是積聚、累積，同義詞是 gather, amass,compile, increase，反義詞是 dissipate, waste。了解題目字彙意思後再別從四個選項來看。選項 A 是 diminish 減少、減小、縮減，同義詞是 decrease, reduce, lessen, curtail，反義詞是 increase, raise，選項 A 與題目字彙的意思並不相符，故可以排除選項 A。

- 選項 B 為 diffuse 意思為使...擴散、使..滲出和傳播，同義詞為 spread out, scatter, disperse，選項 B 與題目字彙的意思並不相符，故可以排除選想 B。

- 選項 C 為 dissipate 驅散…霧等、使消散、使消失，同義詞有 scatter, spread, dispel, disperse，反義詞是 accumulate，可以得知此選項為選項 C 的反義詞，與題目字彙的意思並不相符，故可以排除選項 C。

- 最後是選項 D，選項 D 是 amass 積聚財富、累積，同義詞有 accumulate, assemble, compile, gather 此為選項 A 的同義詞，故可以得知答案為選項 D。有時候可以依據自己的字彙量和所得知的同反義字直接作答，但仍有少數時候會要根據上下文去推斷真正的意思是什麼，這部分就要多注意，理解在文章中字彙所代表的意思再作答。

2. 題目詢問「在新生介紹中，下列哪項服務公司並未提供？」先分別從四個選項來看。

- 選項 A 為 accumulating immense wealth is increasingly important.，可以定位回文章首句話 If your dream is to travel around the world and accumulate abundant wealth, don't miss the once-in-a-lifetime opportunity.，文章中是表示這是個累積財富的機會，是在說這個職務所能獲得的部分跟吸引點但並未論述看法說 accumulating immense wealth is increasingly important.故可以排除選項 A。

● 選項 B 是 annual meetings will be held in Las Vagas，定位回 Besides frequent business trips in Southeastern Asia, the G.M. will also attend our unique summit conference held in Las Vegas every three years，提到的 frequent trips 和關鍵字 summit conference held in Las Vegas every three years，所以可以得知是每三年開一次的會議，而非題幹說的 annual 每年召開，故可以排除選項 B。

● 選項 C 為 ABC Resort & Spa used to be a domestic company，可以定位回文章中 As an international resort franchise, ABC Resort & Spa is looking for aspiring and talented candidates to compete for our general manager position overseeing our operation in the Southeastern Asia region.，文章中有表明公司是 an international resort franchise 等論述，代表是國際性的，但是文章中並未提到過去是 domestic company，故可以排除選項 C。

● 選項 D 為 there will recurrent business trips 可以定位回 Besides frequent business trips in Southeastern Asia, the G.M. will also attend our unique summit conference held in Las Vegas every three years 得知 recurrent business trips 其實是 frequent trips 的同意轉換，故可以得知答案是選項 D。

Unit 10
Evergreen Assisted Living Community
常綠安養社區：公告

Open House Day, Evergreen Assisted Living Community

We are excited to announce that our annual open house day will be held on June 1st. The event will begin at 9 a.m. and end at 5 p.m. __(1)__. The orientation of the main areas, including medical, residential, and recreational areas, will begin at 10 a.m.

__(2)__. Established in 1960, we have been serving our residents with great enthusiasm and **multifaceted** facilities for over half a century. On the open house day, our staff will be more than glad to answer your questions and guide you through the services we offer. __(3)__.

For more details, call toll free 800-800999. __(4)__.

1. Who might be interested in this Open House Day?

   (A) university students

   (B) medical staff

   (C) entertainers

   (D) retired people

2. Which of the blanks marked (1), (2), (3), and (4) does the following sentence belong to?

   "Evergreen Assisted Living Community, located in the outskirts of Philadelphia, is one of the most reputable assisted living communities in Pennsylvania"

   (A) (1)

   (B) (2)

   (C) (3)

   (D) (4)

單元 10 ▶ 常綠安養社區

開放大眾參觀日，常綠安養社區

我們興奮的宣布我們年度開放大眾參觀日將於六月一日舉行。此事件將於早上九點開始，於下午五點結束。訪客導覽的主要區域包含醫療、住宅和娛樂區，會於早上十點開始。

常綠安養社區位於費城郊區，是賓州最具名望的安養社區。創始於 1960 年代，我們秉持著熱忱和多樣化的設施已經服務了我們居民超過半個世紀。在開幕當天，我們的員工將非常樂意回應您的提問以及引導您認識我們所提供的服務。

更多資訊，致電免費專線 800-800999。

1. 誰可能對此開放大眾參觀日感到有興趣？

   (A) 大學學生。

   (B) 醫療員工。

   (C) 娛樂從業人員。

   (D) 退休人員。

2. 下列句子屬於段落空格 (1), (2), (3), and (4)所標示的哪個欄位中？

   「常綠安養社區位於費城郊區，是賓州最具名望的安養社區。」

   (A) (1)。

   (B) (2)。

   (C) (3)。

   (D) (4)。

答案：1. D   2. B

 獵豹 ● ● ●

1.

- 根據標題 Assisted Living Community 馬上知道此社區不是一般社區，assisted 暗示居民可能日常生活須要協助。

- 既然居民的生活型態可能須要協助，刪去(A)，(B)，(C)。

2.

- 先看懂插入句的大意，是關於此安養社區的背景的介紹句。馬上刪去(A) (1)和(D) (4)。

- 既然是介紹句，不會放在段落結尾，刪去(C) (3)，所以正確選項是(B) (2)。

貓頭鷹 ● ● ●

1.

- 此題屬於推測題，須由文章主題推測對這個社區可能感到有興趣的族群。標題即揭示主題。比較選項的四種族群，最需要協助的應該是(D) retired people。

- 此題也牽涉不同文化慣用語的差異。在美國文化，養老院或安養中心除了被稱為 nursing home，也常稱為 assisted living community，retirement home 或 senior citizen home。另一值得注意的慣用語是 open house day，意思是開放大眾參觀日。

2.

- (A) (1)不能選因為 ___(1)___ 所在段落的句子全都是描述開放大眾參觀日的細節，沒有任何介紹安養社區背景的句子。若插入句放在 ___(1)___，與其它句子毫無連貫性。從文章結構判斷，介紹背景的句子不可能放在段落或文章結尾，所以 ___(3)___，___(4)___ 都不是恰當的插入欄位。

- ___(2)___ 之後的 Established in 1960... 也是描述安養社區背景，所以插入句選擇此欄位和下文的連貫性最強。

浣熊 ● ● ●

1. In the second paragraph, the word "multifaceted" in line 2 is closest in meaning to?

(A) diversified

(B) advanced

(C) wonderful

(D) striking

2. What is NOT a service offered by the company during the orientation?

(A) respond to questions

(B) greet residents with eagerness

(C) offer a variety of facilities

(D) an individual guidance after the service

3. 在第二段中，第二行 multifaceted 這個字的意思，最接近哪個字？

(A) 多樣化的。

(B) 進階的。

(C) 多采多姿的。

(D) 顯著的。

4. 在新生介紹中，下列哪項服務公司並未提供？

(A) 回應問題。

(B) 帶著熱忱問候居民。

(C) 提供各式的設施。

(D) 服務後的個別指導。

解析

1. 題目詢問「在第二段中，第二行 multifaceted 這個字的意思，最接近哪個字？」

- 題目中的字彙 multifaceted 其意思是多方面的、多才多藝的，同義詞近似於 versatile 和 diversified。接下來分別從四個選項來看，選項 A 為 diversified 為多樣化的，其意思與題目意思相近，故可以得知答案為選項 A。

- 選項 B 為 advanced 其意思為在前面的、先進的、高級的，其同義字有 forward, improved, bettered, developed，其意思與題目的意思不相同，故可以排除選項 B。

- 選項 C 為 wonderful 其意思為極好的、精采的、驚人的、奇妙的，其同義詞有 marvelous, remarkable, striking, astonishing，其意思與題目的意思不相同，故可以排除選項 C。

- 選項 D 為 striking 其意思為引人注目的、顯著的、突出的，其同義詞為 attractive, noticeable, obvious, conspicuous，其意思與題目的意思不相同，故可以排除選項 D。

2. 題目詢問「在新生介紹中，下列哪項服務公司並未提供？」先分別從四個選項來看。

- 選項 A 為 respond to questions，可以定位回文章 our staff will be more than glad to answer your questions and guide you through the services we offer.表示很樂意回應提問，此敘述為同義表達，故可以排除選項 A。

- 選項 B 為 greet residents with eagerness 可以定位回 Established in 1960, we have been serving our residents with great enthusiasm and multifaceted facilities for over half a century.，eagerness 即 enthusiasm 的同義表達，serving our residents with great enthusiasm 即是 greet residents with eagerness，故可以排除選項 B。

- 選項 C 為 offer a variety of facilities 可以定位回 Established in 1960, we have been serving our residents with great enthusiasm and multifaceted facilities for over half a century.，a variety of facilities 即是 multifaceted facilities，故可以排除選項 C。

- 選項 D 為 an individual guidance after the service，可以以關鍵字 an individual guidance 和 after the service 定位回文章第二段，文章並未提到任何有關 individual guidance 和 after the service，故答案為選項 D，選項 D 的內容在文章中並未提及。

Unit 11
Best Android TV Box Warranty
倍斯特安卓電視盒保固書：使用說明書

Free One-year Warranty

All of the Best TV boxes are bench-tested with the highest standard prior to sale to **exclude** the possibility of defect. However, if any hardware related issue arises within one year of your purchase, we offer repair or replacement at no cost. Please note that the warranty is only valid after the registration of your TV box on our official website. Within 2 weeks of purchase, defective units can be exchanged or returned for repair in-store. Consumers are responsible for the shipping fee if the units are mailed to our company for repair or replacement.

The warranty does NOT cover:

- any software related issue

- any streaming issue

- user misuse

- physical damage

1. What does the warranty cover?

   (A) streaming issue

   (B) physical damage

   (C) software problems

   (D) hardware issue

2. What should a consumer do for the warranty to take effect?

   (A) register the TV box in-store

   (B) register the TV box online

   (C) mail the registration card to the manufacturer

   (D) fill in the registration card in-store

單元 11 ▶ 倍斯特安卓電視盒保固書

一年免費保固

所有的倍斯特電視盒在銷售前都已最高標準進行測試，以排除產品出現瑕疵的可能性。然而，如果有任何硬體有關的問題在您購買的一年內發生，我們提供無償修護和更換。請注意保固書僅於我們官方網站上註冊您的電視盒後有效。在購買的兩周內，瑕疵的組件可以更換或退回維護店。如果組件是寄至我們公司要求維修或替換，消費者有負擔運送費用的責任。

保固書不包含

- 任何軟體相關問題

- 任何串流問題

- 使用者誤用

- 實體的損壞

1. 保固書包含了什麼呢？

(A) 串流問題。

(B) 實體損害。

(C) 軟體問題。

(D) 硬體問題。

2. 消費者應該要如何做才能使得保固書生效？

(A) 於店內註冊電視盒。

(B) 於線上註冊電視盒。

(C) 寄送註冊卡給製造商。

(D) 於店內填寫註冊卡。

答案：1. D　2. B

獵豹 ● ● ●

1.

- 從轉折副詞 However 引導的第二句 if any hardware related issue arises..., 得到第一個線索字 hardware。

- 又從第二句的第二個子句 we offer repair or replacement at no cost 得知 hardware 免費維修，因此確定保固書涵蓋範圍是 hardware。

2.

- 看到題目目光直接鎖定在 take effect，take effect 是「生效」的意思。

- 掃描 take effect 的類似詞，定位在第三句的 the warranty is only valid after the registration of your TV box on our official website，所以選(B) register the TV box online。

貓頭鷹 ● ● ●

1.

- 閱讀時先找出轉折詞是重要的閱讀技巧，因為轉折詞後常有解題線索，例如表達「然而」的轉折字：however、nevertheless、nonetheless、yet。

- 此題是細節題。除了第二句句尾 at no cost 表達免費維修是線索之外，也能從整篇篇末列出四點保固書不涵蓋的範圍解題。

2.

- 此題是細節題。需要先理解動詞片語 take effect 的意思，再搜尋其類似詞。第三句的 valid 是「有效力的」意思。第三句句中的 after 之後則敘述消費者要讓保固書生效需要做的動作。

- 正確選項(B)的 register 是動詞，文章第三句的 registration 是名詞。

浣熊 ● ● ●

還有可能怎麼問

1. In the first paragraph, the word "exclude" in line 2 is closest in meaning to?

(A) activate

(B) differentiate

(C) prohibit

(D) include

2. What is indicated about Best Android TV Box Warranty?

(A) It offers a refund

(B) It provide free shipping service

(C) It doesn't include a discount

(D) It covers spiritual loss

中譯

1. 在第一段中，第二行 exclude 這個字的意思，最接近哪個字？

(A) 啟動、激活。

(B) 區隔化。

(C) 禁止。

(D) 包括。

2. 關於倍斯特安卓電視盒保證書，何者正確？

(A) 它提供退款。

(B) 它提供免運費服務。

(C) 它不包括折扣。

(D) 它負擔精神損失。

解析

1. 題目詢問「在第一段中，第二行 exclude 這個字的意思，最接近哪個字？」

- 題目中的字彙 exclude 其意思是拒絕接納、把…排除在外、不包括，其同義字有 bar, outlaw, reject, forbid，反義詞有 include。接下來看其他四個選項的意思，選項 A 為 activate 意思為使活動起來、使活潑，若為啟動或觸發其同義詞有 operate, switch on, turn on, start，與題目中的意思所表達的不同，故可以排除選項 A。

- 選項 B 為 differentiate 意思為使有差異、構成…間的差別，其同義詞有 distinguish, discriminate, tell apart, separate，其意思與題目中的意思所表達的不同，故可以排除選項 B。

6 填空式閱讀

7 單篇閱讀

7 雙篇、三篇閱讀

模擬試題

- 選項 C 為 prohibit 其意思有禁止、妨礙和阻止，其同義詞有 forbid, bar, ban, disallow，反義詞有 allow, permit, admit，意思與題目中字彙的表達意思相近，故答案為選項 C。

- 選項 D 為 include 意思是包含，其同義詞有 contain, comprise, cover, enclose，反義詞為 exclude，其意思與題目相反，故也可以排除選項 D。

2. 題目詢問「關於倍斯特安卓電視盒保證書，何者正確？」先分別從四個選項來看。

- 選項 A 為 It offers a refund，可以定位回文章中 However, if any hardware related issue arises within one year of your purchase, we offer repair or replacement at no cost.，寫道在購買的一年內無償提供維修和更換，但未提到會提供退款的部分，在文章其他地方的敘述也未提到關於退款的部分，所以可以排除選項 A。

- 選項 B 為 It provide free shipping service 可以定位回文章中的 Consumers are responsible for the shipping fee if the units are mailed to our company for repair or replacement.，故可以知道如果是將組件寄送到公司的維修的話，是要自己負擔運費的，與選項 B 論述相左，故也可以排除選項 B。

- 選項 C 為 It doesn't include a discount，可以定位回文章中，文章中並未提到有關於折扣的部分，故可以得知答案為選項 C。

- 選項 D 為 It covers spiritual loss，可以定位回 The warranty does NOT cover:和以下的敘述，可以得知不包含的部分，其中有不包含實體損害，綜觀全文文中也沒有提到關於精神損失的部分，故也可以排除選項 D。

Unit 12
Best Caribbean Cruise
倍斯特加勒比海郵輪：廣告

Come have a blast and **pampered** experience on Best Caribbean Cruise! Best Caribbean Cruise sets the bar high in the cruise industry for we never cease to provide innovations and enhance our diverse services. The cruise caters to every clientele, be it honeymooners, family, or retired citizens. Some of our most popular facilities include swimming pools, a miniature golf course, casinos, and spa parlors.　(1)　.

We also take pride in the dining options.　(2)　. There are 8 restaurants with distinctive styles, from formal and casual dining to buffet and steakhouse.　(3)　. To make your dining experience more memorable, cabaret, comedy, and magic shows are held every evening in selected restaurants. 　(4)　.

1. Which of the blanks marked (1), (2), (3), and (4) does the following sentence belong to?

"This year we are proud to unveil a rock-climbing wall and a miniature water park"

(A) (1)

(B) (2)

(C) (3)

(D) (4)

2. Where might you see this passage?

(A) an itinerary

(B) a package tour guide

(C) a restaurant guide

(D) a tabloid magazine

單元 12 ▶ 倍斯特加勒比海郵輪

　　來加勒比海郵輪，玩的盡興且放縱自己的體驗！倍斯特加勒比海郵輪在郵輪業中設定高規格，因為我們未曾停止提供創新和提高我們多樣化的服務。郵輪迎合了每個客戶，包含度蜜月者、家庭或退休居民。有些我們最受歡迎的設施包括游泳池、微型高爾夫課程、賭博場和 spa 美容室。今年我們很引以為傲地揭幕攀岩牆和微型的水上樂園。

　　我們也以用餐選項引以為傲。有八間各有獨特風格的餐廳，有正式風格、休閒風格、自助餐和牛排館。為了使您的用餐體驗更值得回憶，夜總會、喜劇和魔術表演也於每個傍晚在特定幾間餐廳舉行。

1. 下列句子屬於段落空格 (1), (2), (3), and (4)所標示的哪個欄位中？

「今年我們很引以為傲的公布攀岩牆和微型的水公園。」

(A) (1)

(B) (2)

(C) (3)

(D) (4)

2. 你可能在哪裡可以看到這個段落？

(A) 旅行行程表。

(B) 套裝觀光行程導覽。

(C) 餐廳導覽。

(D) 雜誌小報。

答案：1. A　2. B

6 填空式閱讀

7 單篇閱讀

7 雙篇、三篇閱讀

模擬試題

獵豹 ● ● ●

1.

- 看到插入句目光直接鎖定在 __(1)__ 之前的 facilities。

- facilities 的意思是「設施」，插入句提及的 a rock-climbing wall and a miniature water park 是娛樂設施，因此插入句銜接在 facilities 之後，選擇(A) (1)。

2.

- 因為主題是郵輪公司介紹郵輪上的設施，馬上刪去(C) a restaurant guide、(D) a tabloid magazine。

- 因為(A) an itinerary 是「旅行行程表」的意思，也可刪除，所以正確選項是(B) a package tour guide。

貓頭鷹 ● ● ●

1.

- 完整句插入正確空格的題型主要測試正確選項與空格前後句意的連貫性。

- ___(1)___ 欄位上一句一連串的名詞：swimming pools, a miniature golf course, casinos, and spa parlors 都是休閒娛樂設施，與 a rock-climbing wall and a miniature water park 都是同一類型的設施。所以選擇(A) (1)最通順。

2.

- 此題屬於推測題。文章主題是介紹郵輪設施，屬於觀光旅遊方面，與這方面較有關連的選項是(A) an itinerary 及(B) a package tour guide。

- 除了考慮哪個選項與主題關係最密切，或運用刪去法快速找出答案以外，另一個解題方式是考慮不同文類的呈現方式，例如(A) an itinerary「旅行行程表」通常以表格或條列式呈現，因此(B) a package tour guide 更適合作為正確選項。

浣熊 ● ● ●

還有可能怎麼問

1. In the first paragraph, the word "pampered" in line 1 is closest in meaning to?

(A) Superb

(B) indulged

(C) elevated

(D) incredible

2. What is indicated about Best Caribbean Cruise?

(A) It stops providing innovative experience

(B) It uses second-hand facilities to create popular experience

(C) It is not suited to newlyweds

(D) It has unforgettable magic shows

中譯

1. 在第一段中，第一行 pampered 這個字的意思，最接近哪個字？

(A) 一流的。

(B) 縱容的。

(C) 提升的。

(D) 驚人的。

2. 關於倍斯特加勒比海巡航，何者正確？

(A) 它停止提供創新體驗。

(B) 它使用二手設施已創造流行體驗。

(C) 它不適用於新婚夫妻。

(D) 它有難忘的魔術表演。

解析

1. 題目詢問「在第一段中，第一行 pampered 這個字的意思，最接近哪個字？」。

• 先看題目 pamper 的意思，其意思為縱容、姑息、嬌養，同義詞為 humor, favor, indulge, coddle，反義詞為 chasten。緊接著看四個選項分別的意思。選項 A 為 superb 意思是極好的、一流的，同義詞有 excellent, superlative, first-rate, first class，反義詞有 poor, inferior, poor, inferior，意思與題目中表達的意思不同，故可以排除選項 A。

6 填空式閱讀

7 單篇閱讀

7 雙篇、三篇閱讀

模擬試題

- 選項 B 為 indulge 意思是沉迷於、滿足…慾望等，同義詞有 humor, favor, oblige, please，意思與題目相符，故可以得知答案是選項 B。

- 選項 C 為 elevated 意思是升高的、提高的，同義詞有 raised, lifted, upraised, noble，意思與題目中表達的意思不同，故可以排除選項 C。

- 選項 D 為 incredible 其意思為不能相信的、不可信的、驚人的，其同義詞有 inbelievable, doubtful, questionable, staggering，反義詞為 credible，意思與題目中表達的意思不同，故可以排除選項 D。

2. 題目詢問「關於倍斯特加勒比海巡航，何者正確？」先分別從四個選項來看。

- 選項 A 為 It stops providing innovative experience，定位回文章 Best Caribbean Cruise sets the bar high in the cruise industry for we never cease to provide innovations and enhance our diverse services.可以得知與題目敘述相左，選項 A 的敘述是錯誤的，故可以排除選項 A。

- 選項 B 為 It uses second-hand facilities to create popular experience 可以定位回 Some of our most popular facilities include swimming pools, a miniature golf course, casinos, and spa parlors.，文章中指出有提供最流行的設施，但選項 B 卻是 It uses second-hand facilities to create popular experience，為兩個不相干的訊息組織成此論述，且與文章內容不相符，故可以排除選項 B。

- 選項 C 為 It is not suited to newlyweds 可以定位回文章 The cruise caters to every clientele, be it honeymooners, family, or retired citizens.，可以從 newlyweds 即是 honeymooners 的同義轉換，但是要注意題目敘述多出了 not，若選項 C 沒有 not 則選項 C 為正確答案，故也可以選項 C。

- 選項 D 為 It has unforgettable magic shows 可以定位回文章中 To make your dining experience more memorable, cabaret, comedy, and magic shows are held every evening in selected restaurants.得知 magic shows 也是創造難忘體驗的項目，故答案為選項 D。

Unit 1

兼職男友與兼職女友

The following are the line messages among two branch office managers (A and B) and the head of headquarters.

Head: it's pretty urgent... we certainly need some new ideas.

A: ideas?

B: about things other than the ads on our social networking sites?

Head: yep... that's it.

Head: This time... BE BOLDER!!! With successive holidays coming, people are in desperate need of finding a mate.

A: What about PTGF and PTBF?

Head: What do they stand for?

B: Part-time girlfriend and part-time boyfriend.

A: You know how stressful it is for singles to be at major holidays. This can be a way out.

B: With a part-time boyfriend and a part-time girlfriend, they don't have to worry about opinionated friends and family members.

Head: Done!!!

A+B: WHAT?

Head: A, I want you to write an official letter and e-mail to all members of the marketing staff. B, you'll have to schedule a meeting discussing further details about this idea on Dec. 8th, 2018, a week from today, and send me a table of major services we're going to provide.

Letter: table of our major services

To: Mary James Maryjames@dateallyouwant.com
From: Amber Lin Amberlin@dateallyouwant.com
Date: Dec 9
Attachment: Table of our major services

Dear Miss James,

The following is the table of major services that we discussed.

Service	Time	Price	Discount
kissing	2 minutes	$ 30	Valentine's Day: 50% off
shopping	2 hours	$ 35	
Outdoor sports	3 hours	$ 60	Summer time: 40% off
Holding hands	No time limit	$ 10	
Meeting with parents	5 hours	$ 350	New Year's Eve: 20% off

Sincerely,
Amber Lin
Marketing Manager of ABC Dating

6 填空式閱讀

7 單篇閱讀

7 雙篇、三篇閱讀

模擬試題

1. What is the purpose of the Line discussion?
   (A) to post ads on social networks
   (B) to devise new services
   (C) to solve the headquarters' problem
   (D) to find a girlfriend

2. What does the head want the branch office managers to do?
   (A) to think of bold ideas for the holiday season
   (B) to hire people to work as PTGF and PTBF
   (C) to post the table of the major services on Facebook
   (D) to come up with fun holiday activities

3. Which service does not have any restriction on time?
   (A) shopping
   (B) holding hands
   (C) outdoor sports
   (D) meeting with parents

4. How much does it cost for the service of 2-hour shopping and 3-hour outdoor sport?
   (A) $90

(B) $85

(C) $95

(D) $ 65

5. How much does it cost for meeting with parents on New Year's Eve?

(A) $280

(B) $350

(C) $200

(D) $300

中譯

單元 1 ▶ 兼職男友與兼職女友

以下是兩個分公司經理（A 和 B）和總部上司的 line 訊息。

上司： 這相當緊急...我們的確需要一些新想法。

A： 想法？

B： 關於除了我們社交網站上的廣告外的事情。

上司： 是的...就是這個。

上司： 這時候...大膽點！！！隨著接續的假期到來，大家都渴望想要找伴侶。

A： 關於 PTGH 和 PTBF 嗎？

上司： 他們分別代表什麼呢？

B： 兼職女友和兼職男友。

A： 你知道在主要假期時，對單身者來說壓力有多大嗎？這可以是個解決辦法。

B： 有了兼職男友和兼職女友，他們不用擔心說三道四的朋友和家庭成員。

上司： 就這個。

A +B： 什麼？

上司： A，我想要你寫正式信件和 e-mail 給所有行銷職員的成員。B 你必須在 2018 年 12 月 8 日，也就是從今天算起一週後，安排一個會議討論關於這個想法的進一步的訊息，然後寄給我們所要提供的主要服務的表格。

信件：主要服務項目表

致：瑪莉・詹姆士 Maryjames@dateallyouwant.com
從：安柏・林 Amberlin@dateallyouwant.com
日期：12 月 9 日
附件：我們主要服務的表格

親愛的詹姆士小姐，

下列是我們討論過後的主要服務列表。

服務	時間	價格	折扣
親吻	2 分鐘	30 美元	情人節：五折
購物	2 小時	35 美元	
戶外運動	3 小時	60 美元	夏季：六折
牽手	沒時間限制	10 美元	
與父母會面	5 小時	350 美元	除夕夜：八折

Sincerely,

安柏 · 林
ABC 約會行銷經理

1. Line 討論的目的是什麼呢？

(A) 在社交網站上發布廣告。

(B) 設計新的服務。

(C) 解決總部的問題。

(D) 找女友。

2. 上司想要分公司的經理做什麼？

(A) 在假期季節想出大膽想法。

(B) 雇用人來做兼職女友和兼職男友。

(C) 發布臉書上主要服務的表格。

(D) 想出有趣的假期活動。

3. 哪項服務沒有時間限制？

(A) 購物。

(B) 牽手。

(C) 戶外運動。

(D) 與父母會面。

4. 兩小時購物和三小時戶外運動服務要花費多少錢呢？

(A) 90 美元。

(B) 85 美元。

(C) 95 美元。

(D) 65 美元。

5. 除夕夜與父母會面要花費多少錢呢？

(A) 280 美元。

(B) 350 美元。

(C) 200 美元。

(D) 300 美元。

答案：1. B   2. A   3. B   4. C   5. A

獵豹 ● ● ●

1.

● 看到題目目光馬上鎖定在 purpose。

● 根據第一篇 Line 的討論第一句 we certainly need some new ideas 的大意，上司要求員工提出新點子。對照選項找出與這句大意類似的敘述。先刪去(C) to solve the headquarters' problem，(D) to find a girlfriend，又根據第三句 B: about things other than the ads on our social networking sites，刪除(A) to post ads on social networks，所以正確選項是(B) to devise new services。

2.

● 看到題目目光馬上鎖定在 Head: This time... BE BOLDER!!!

● 因為這句是延續 new ideas 的討論，推測 bolder 也是形容 ideas，所以選(A) to think of bold ideas for the holiday season。

3.

● 看到題目目光馬上鎖定在 does not have any restriction on time。

● 在第二篇 Time 的欄位掃描不限制時間的服務。定位在 No

211

time limit，服務是 Holding hands。因此選(B) holding hands。

4.

- 看到題目目光馬上鎖定在 2-hour shopping and 3-hour outdoor sport。

- 在第二篇 Service 欄位找到 shopping 和 outdoor sport。再檢查 Time 欄位。shopping 一次服務以 2 hours 為單位，outdoor sport 一次服務以 3 hours 為單位，所以 $35+$60=$95。

5.

- 看到題目目光馬上鎖定在 meeting with parents on New Year's Eve。

- 在第二篇 Service 欄位找到 meeting with parents，價格是 $350，因為 New Year's Eve 有 20%折扣，即打八折，所以是 $280。

貓頭鷹

1.

- 此題屬於主題題型。此類型題目可能會用 purpose，main idea，main topic 等字詢問主題。主題題型須精讀篇章開頭

212

二～三句。

- 第一個線索是 new ideas，這是 Head，主管，的要求，符合題目問的 purpose。

- 第二個線索是 other than the ads on our social networking sites。other than 是「除了」的意思，所以(A) to post ads on social networks 不能選。

2.

- 此題是推測題。須要綜合 Line 討論的細節推測，也能同時運用刪去法。

- 雖然 PTGF and PTBF 在 Line 討論有提及，但根據第一篇結尾上司的交代事項: A, I want you to write an official letter and e-mail to all members of the marketing staff. B, you'll have to schedule a meeting discussing further details... 並無提及雇用，hire。所以刪除(B) to hire people to work as PTGF and PTBF。

- 刪除(C) to post the table of the major services on Facebook，因為 post，Facebook 整篇都未提及。

- (D) to come up with fun holiday activities 不能選，因為雖然上司的要求與 holiday 有關，但並無明確提到 fun 一字。(A)比(D)更適合當正確選項，因為(A)的形容詞 bold 是上司明確使

用的。

3.

- 此題屬於細節題型。也需以題目的 does not have restriction on time，沒有時間限制，的類似詞定位答案。

- limit 是 restriction 的類似字，所以 No time limit 意思和 ... does not have restriction on time 是近似的。

4.

- 此題是與數字有關的細節題，需要考生做基本的算術。

- 題目是問兩項服務總共的價格。考生只須細心定位題目裡的關鍵字，如此題是 shopping 和 outdoor sport，並注意每項服務的時間單位都不同。

5.

- 此題是與數字有關的細節題，需要考生做基本的算術。

- 須注意特殊細節，此題的特殊細節是 New Year's Eve。

浣熊 ● ● ●

還有可能怎麼問

1. What is NOT the function of these services?

(A) to regain the status as a major marketer.

(B) to find a mate.

(C) to encounter a major holiday.

(D) to prevent from being gossiped from opinionated friends.

2. What is NOT indicated in the article?

(A) there are two items that do not have discounts.

(B) "meeting with parents" is 70 dollars per hour.

(C) There are no time limit for "holding hands".

(D) manager B will write an official letter.

中譯

1. 文中沒有提到哪些服務功用？

(A) 重拾主要行銷者的地位。

(B) 尋找伴侶。

(C) 面對主要假日。

(D) 免於受到愛指指點點的朋友八卦。

2. 文中沒有指出下列哪個項目？

(A) 有兩個項目不包含折扣。

(B) 「與父母見面」每小時花費 70 元。

(C) 「握手」沒有時間限制。

(D) B 經理將寫封正式信件。

解析

1. 題目詢問「文中沒有提到哪些服務功用？」先分別從四個選項來看。

- 文章中未提到重拾主要行銷者的地位，所以 A 選項並未於文章中提到，故答案為 A 選項。再看看其他選項，從上司有提到隨著接續的假期到來，大家都渴望想要找伴侶等等，得知公司推出的服務跟 to find a mate 有關，故 B 選項有提及。

- 另外，A 經理也提到「在主要假期時，對單身者來說壓力有多大嗎？這可以是個解決辦法。」，B 經理也提到「有了兼職男友和兼職女友，他們不用擔心說三道四的朋友和家庭成員。」可以推測出推出兼職男友和兼職女友是要 encounter a major holiday 和 to prevent from being gossiped from opinionated friends，故 C 和 D 選項在文章中均有提到，to prevent from being gossiped from opinionated friends 是 line 訊息中 they don't have to worry about opinionated friends and family members 的同義轉換。

2. 題目詢問「文中沒有指出下列哪個項目？」先分別從四個選項來看。

- A 選項的 there are two items that do not have discounts.，可以回安柏・林寄給瑪莉・詹姆士的提供的主要

服務表格中查看，服務中的五個項目中有其中兩個項目並未提供折扣，故與 A 選項所說的「有兩個項目不包含折扣。」可以先排出 A 選項。

- B 選項的"meeting with parents" is 70 dollars per hour.表達「與父母見面」每小時花費 70 元。立即定位回該表格查看"meeting with parents"每五小時花費 350 美金得知每小時花費 70 元，與題目表達一致，故可以排除 B 選項。

- C 選項 There are no time limit for "holding hands".同樣定位回表格得知"holding hands"沒有時間限制，故也可以排除 C 選項。

- 最後看 D 選項的敘述 manager B will write an official letter.定位回 line 訊息尾上司有請 A 經理寫正式信件和 e-mail 給所有行銷職員的成員，是 A 經理而非選項中所提到的 B 經理，故答案為選項 D。

答案：1. A　2. D

Unit 2

舞台劇表演

Three mothers are discussing their kids' stage performance at a Facebook chatroom.

Linda: Are we still short of costumes?

Cindy: No, we aren't. Some manufacturers are sending us costumes imported from Italy, remember?

Linda: how generous?

Cindy: stop it... stop using that sarcastic tone.

Sally: Do we need to prepare some food and beverages after the show?

Cindy: yep.

Sally: why don't we provide popsicles, like paw-like popsicles from the movie Zootopia?

Linda: kids will like that...

Cindy: Linda, we do want you to contact suppliers who can make paw-like popsicles and make a list of the flavors we are going to provide.

Sally: what about me? What's my job? I already finished sewing a heavy bear costume.

Cindy: why don't you contact the faculty members and set up the stage, and prepare materials and call the ice cream man so that parents can make paw-like popsicles and film the wonderful family time.

Linda: wonderful. I can actually make popsicles with my kids.

Letter ❶: lists of flavors and prices

To: Cindy Cindywang@elitekids.com
From: Linda Lindachen@elitekids.com
Date: Sep 16
Attachment: Lists of flavors and prices

Dear Cindy,

The following is a list of flavors and prices for your reference

Flavor	Size	Price	discount
chocolate	small	$2	
	medium	$3.5	
	large	$5	
watermelon	small	$3	
	medium	$4	
	large	$6	
mango	small	$4	Buy one get one free
	medium	$5.5	Buy two get two free
	large	$7	Buy two get two free
vanilla	small	$1.5	
	medium	$3	
	large	$4	
strawberry	small	$2.5	
	medium	$3.5	
	large	$4.5	

Sincerely,
Linda Chen

Letter ❷: other information

To: Cindy Cindywang@elitekids.com
From: Sally Sallycheng@elitekids.com
Date: Sep 17
Attachment: other information

Dear Cindy,

I've talked with ice cream men. Materials won't be a problem. By the way, I have the exact same thought with them. Five flavors are for selling, and we can add another 10 flavors for family time. Kids can make other ten flavors of their choices with parents. What do you think? Faculty members are also very thrilled about this idea.

Another thing is that, Ken, one of the ice cream men, has an idea that we can make some giant paw-like popsicles. It's gonna be huge. Everyone can take a photo with a giant popsicle, and it will be like the giant vending machine that created a great sensation the other day. Looking forward to your response.

Sincerely,
Sally Cheng

1. Why does Linda ask, "how generous"?

   (A) She has doubts about the costumes imported from Italy.

   (B) She is excited about the costumes imported from

Italy.

(C) She is impressed that the costume manufacturers are generous.

(D) She thinks that it's important to teach children to be generous.

2. Why does Cindy say, "stop it"?

(A) She wants to stop buying costumes.

(B) She wants Linda to stop using a negative tone.

(C) She wants to stop talking about costumes.

(D) She wants to stop the conversation as soon as possible.

3. Which of the following is the closest to the word sarcastic?

(A) sedentary

(B) thrilling

(C) boring

(D) ironic

4. How much does it cost to buy 5 large chocolate popsicles and 5 large mango popsicles?
   (A) $25
   (B) $60
   (C) $46
   (D) $50

5. Why does Sally mention the giant vending machine?
   (A) She thinks it's a good idea to rent a giant vending machine.
   (B) Parents and children can buy many beverages from a giant vending machine.
   (C) She thinks a giant popsicle might create a similar sensation as the giant vending machine.
   (D) A giant vending machine might attract more people to the stage performance.

中譯

單元 2 ▶ 舞台劇表演

三個母親在臉書聊天室討論他們小孩的舞台表演

琳達：我們仍短少服飾嗎？

辛蒂：沒有，我們沒缺了。有些製造商寄了義大利進口的服飾給我們，想起來了嗎？

琳達：真是慷慨阿？

辛蒂：就此打住...停止使用那諷刺語調。

莎莉：表演結束後，我們需要準備一些食物和飲料嗎？

辛蒂：是的。

莎莉：為什麼我們不提供冰棒，像是「動物方城市」裡掌狀形的冰棒？

琳達：小孩子喜歡那樣。

辛蒂：琳達，我們想請你聯繫能製造掌狀形冰棒的供應商，列出我們能提供的口味的清單。

莎莉：那我呢？我的工作是什麼呢？我已經完成了笨重熊的服飾。

辛蒂：那就請你聯繫系上教職員且布置好舞台，然後準備好材料、打電話給冰淇淋男，所以父母可以製造掌狀形的冰棒且拍攝美好的家庭時光。

琳達：好極了。我可以實際跟小孩一起製作冰棒。

信件 ❶：冰品價格和口味表單

給：辛蒂 Cindywang@elitekids.com

從：琳達 Lindachen@elitekids.com

日期：9 月 16 日

附件：口味和價格表

親愛的辛蒂，

下列是口味和價格表的清單提供給妳參考

口味	大小	價格	折扣
巧克力	小	2 美元	
	中	3.5 美元	
	大	5 美元	
西瓜	小	3 美元	
	中	4 美元	
	大	6 美元	
芒果	小	4 美元	買一送一
	中	5.5 美元	買二送二
	大	7 美元	買二送二
香草	小	1.5 美元	
	中	3 美元	
	大	4 美元	
草莓	小	2.5 美元	
	中	3.5 美元	
	大	4.5 美元	

Sincerely,
琳達‧陳

信件 ❷：其他資訊

給：辛蒂 Cindywang@elitekids.com
從：莎莉 Sallycheng@elitekids.com
日期：9 月 17 日
附件：其他資訊

親愛的辛蒂，

我已與冰淇淋男談過了。材料不會是個問題。順便提起，我與他們有相同的想法。五個口味用於銷售，然後我們可以增加額外十個口味用於家庭時光。小還可以依據喜好跟父母製作其他十種冰棒。你覺得呢？系上教職員也會對此感到很興奮的。
另一件事是我們的冰淇淋男，肯，有個想法是，我們可以製作超大的掌狀形冰棒。這會很棒。每個人可以跟巨大冰棒合照，而且就像是其他天有個巨型販賣機那樣可以製造很多轟動。期待您的回應。

Sincerely,
莎莉・鄭

1. 為什麼琳達要說「真是慷慨啊！」？

(A) 她對義大利進口的服飾抱持疑惑。

(B) 她對義大利進口的服飾感到興奮。

(C) 她對於服飾製造商的慷慨感到印象深刻。

(D) 她認為教導小孩要慷慨很重要。

2. 為什麼辛蒂要說「就此打住！」？

(A) 她想要停止購買服飾。

(B) 她想要琳達停止使用負面語調。

(C) 她想要停止談論服飾。

(D) 她想要盡早停止這個話題。

3. 下列哪個字最接近諷刺的這個字？

(A) 靜止的。

(B) 令人感到興奮的。

(C) 無聊的。

(D) 諷刺的。

4. 如果購買 5 個大巧克力冰棒和 5 個大芒果冰棒要花費多少錢呢？

(A) 25 美元。

(B) 60 美元。

(C) 46 美元。

(D) 50 美元。

5. 為什麼莎莉提及大型販賣機呢？

(A) 她認為租一個大型販賣機是好想法。

(B) 父母和小孩能從巨型販賣機購買飲料。

(C) 她認為巨型冰棒可能會創造與巨型販賣機相同的轟動感。

(D) 巨型販賣機可能會吸引更多人到舞台表演。

答案：1. A 2. B 3. D 4. C 5. C

獵豹 • • •

1.
- 看到題目目光馬上鎖定在 How generous?的上一句：Some manufacturers are sending us costumes imported from Italy, remember? 得知 How generous?多慷慨？是指製造商對於提供戲服方面有多慷慨。

- 接著鎖定 How generous?的下一句 stop using that sarcastic tone。因為 sarcastic 的意思是諷刺的，可推測 Linda 並不是單純想知道戲服製造商有多慷慨，而是帶有一點負面情緒的語調，選項中唯一偏向負面情緒的描述是(A) She has doubts about the costumes imported from Italy。

2.
- 看到題目目光馬上鎖定在 it。

- 接著決定代名詞 it 代替的是哪個字，根據 stop it 同一行 stop using that sarcastic tone，得知 it 指的是「使用諷刺語調」這個行為。掃描每個選項 stop 之後的受詞，只有(B)的 using a negative tone 與諷刺語調有關連，因此選(B)。

3.
- 看到題目目光馬上鎖定在 sarcastic 之前的搭配詞 stop it... stop using...。

- 既然 Cindy 要求 Linda 停止，可推測 sarcastic 這個形容詞意義是偏向負面的。sarcastic 的意思是「諷刺的、嘲諷的」，類似字是(D) ironic。

4.

- 看到題目目光馬上鎖定在 flavor 欄位，往下找出 chocolate 和 mango。對照出一支 large 的價格並檢查是否有折扣。

- mango 的折扣是買二送二，3*$7=$21。chocolate 沒有折扣，五支巧克力口味冰棒是 5*$5=$25。$21+$25=$46。所以選(C)。

5.

- 看到題目目光馬上鎖定在 giant vending machine 的上文：Everyone can take a photo with a giant popsicle, and it will be like...，先確定 it 指的是 a giant popsicle。

- 根據 it will be like...，「就像…」的意思，將超大型冰棒比喻成大型販賣機，由(C)的 a similar sensation，得知最接近此意思的選項是(C)。

貓頭鷹 ● ● ●

1.

- 此題屬於推測題型，要考生推測出 Linda 對戲服製造商的態度。而她的態度是根據她的朋友對她的反應來推測的。因此這種推測態度的題型同時也測試考生的單字量和讀出言外之意的能力。

- 因為 Cindy 對 Linda 的反應是：stop it... stop using that sarcastic tone，sarcastic 是下文的關鍵字。Cindy 希望 Linda 停止使用諷刺語調，可推測或許 Linda 過去跟製造商有不愉快的經驗，才會以諷刺語調問「多大方？」，所以正確選項的敘述應偏向負面態度。

- 先刪去(B)及(C)，因為 excited 及 impressed 都是偏向正面的情緒形容詞，(D)的大意是「教小孩大方是重要的」，完全與戲服無關，刪去(D)。因此(A) She has doubts about the costumes imported from Italy，她對進口自義大利的戲服有懷疑，是最恰當的答案。

2.

- 此題屬於推測題型，大部分使用 Why 疑問詞的題目是屬於此題型。理由不一定會直接明確地在上下文交代，須以上下文關鍵字的意義去推測。

229

- 題目有代名詞 it，必須先找出代名詞的先行詞，即代名詞指涉的名詞。從下文 using that sarcastic tone，得知 it 指的是「使用諷刺語調」這個行為。Cindy 一定是覺得 Linda 的發言不適當，才會要求 Linda 停止這麼說。所以對 Cindy 而言，「使用諷刺語調」這個行為是負面的，呼應(A)描述的 a negative tone。

3.
- 此題主要考 sarcastic 的類似字，類似字題型也需要從前後搭配詞去推測哪個類似字替換掉原字，仍然能維持句意通順。

- 如果不確定單字精準的意義時，考生可以從情境推測原字是偏向負面意義或正面意義，再逐一比較每個選項單字的意義是偏向正面或負面。另一找出正確選項的技巧是比較哪個類似字的意義和主題關係最密切。

- 因為 sarcastic 之前的搭配詞是 stop，可推測在這情境 sarcastic 偏向負面意義。(A) sedentary，靜止的或久坐的，(B) thrilling，令人感到興奮的或驚悚的，(A)，(B)不一定是負面形容詞，所以刪去。(C) boring，無聊的，和主題無關，也刪去。因此最合適的選項是(D) ironic，諷刺的。

4.
- 此題是與數字有關的細節題，需要考生做基本的算術。

- 除了先在 flavor，口味欄位下找出 chocolate 和 mango，對照 large 的價格外，也要小心是否有 discount。large mango popsicles 的折扣是買二送二，buy two get two free 是買二送二的意思。題目要求買五支 mango popsicles，芒果口味冰棒，事實上只要付三支芒果口味冰棒的價錢，3*$7=$21。巧克力口味沒有折扣，因此五支巧克力口味冰棒是 5*$5=$25。$21+$25=$46。所以選(C)。

5.

- 此題屬於推測題型，要依照上下文推測出 Sally 提及大型販賣機背後的動機為何。

- 動機的線索可由下文這句推測：it will be like the giant vending machine that created a great sensation the other day。考生需知道 sensation 是「轟動」的意思。

- like 是介係詞，「像」的意思。it will be like... 的 it 指的是 a giant popsicle，即 Sally 認為 a giant popsicle 和 the giant vending machine 會產生類似的效果。「類似的」形容詞是 similar。所以選(C) She thinks a giant popsicle might create a similar sensation as the giant vending machine。

浣熊 ● ● ●

還有可能怎麼問

1. Which of the followings is not mentioned as preparation of this event?

(A) to contact a supplier.

(B) to contact ice cream men.

(C) to contact faculty members.

(D) to contact Italian manufacturers for a heavy bear costume.

2. What is NOT indicated in the article?

(A) Linda will be the one to contact suppliers.

(B) there are 15 flavors of popsicles in total.

(C) mango flavors won't be that costly since you get buy two get two free.

(D) If you are a diabetic, you probably can't enjoy popsicles we sell that day.

中譯

1. 對於準備這項活動，下列哪個敘述並未提及？

(A) 聯絡供應商。

(B) 聯絡冰淇淋男。

(C) 聯絡教職人員。

(D) 聯絡義大利製造商以取得厚重的熊服飾。

2. 文中沒有指出下列哪個項目？

(A) 琳達會是與供應商聯繫的人。

(B) 總共會有 15 總冰棒口味。

(C) 芒果口味不會那樣貴，因為能享有買二送二。

(D) 如果你是糖尿病患者，你可能無法享用我們那天所販賣的冰棒。

解析

1. 題目詢問「對於準備這項活動，下列哪個敘述並未提及？」先分別從四個選項來看。

- 四個選項都以 to contact 開頭，故要分別回 line 對話中釐清文章中的人物分別聯繫過哪些人。先看 A 選項的 to contact a supplier 以 supplier 為關鍵字定位回文章中找，Cindy 對 Linda 講到，Linda, we do want you to contact suppliers who can make paw-like popsicles 得知準備這項活動需要聯繫供應商，故 A 選項於文章提及，與題目敘述不符可以先排出

此選項。

- 然後看 B 選項「聯絡冰淇淋男」，於第三封信莎莉寄給辛蒂的信 I've talked with ice cream men. Materials won't be a problem. 可以得知莎莉與冰淇淋男聯繫過，故 B 選項也可以排除。

- 再看 C 選項的 to contact faculty members 以 faculty members 為關鍵字定位回 line 訊息中得知辛蒂說 why don't you contact faculty members and set up the stage 可以得知莎莉會與教職人員聯繫，故可以排除 C 選項。

- 最後是 D 選項，to contact Italian manufacturers for a heavy bear costume. 得知有兩個關鍵訊息 Italian manufacturers 和 a heavy bear costume 定位回文章中得知前者為開頭時辛蒂說「沒有，我們沒缺了。有些製造商寄了義大利進口的服飾給我們」。而後者是莎莉於後面訊息中表達「那我呢？我的工作是什麼呢？我已經完成了笨重熊的服飾。」兩者並無關聯性，故答案是 D 選項。

2. 題目詢問「文中沒有指出下列哪個項目？」先分別從四個選項來看。

- A 選項 Linda will be the one to contact suppliers，定位回文章中得知琳達會聯繫供應商，故 A 選項有於文章中提及，可

以排除 A 選項。

● B 選項的 there are 15 flavors of popsicles in total. 定位回第三封信件，信件中提到 By the way, I have the exact same thought with them. Five flavors are for selling, and we can add another 10 flavors for family time.，從此得知五個口味會用於販賣，另外 10 種口味會用於家庭時光，故總共有 15 總口味與選項敘述為同義表達，可以排除 B 選項。

● C 選項 mango flavors won't be that costly since you get buy two get two free.，可以定位回表格中，可以看到芒果口味價格較其他口味貴，但是有買二送二，故與選項敘述為同義表達，也可以排除 C 選項。

● 最後是 D 選項 If you are a diabetic, you probably can't enjoy popsicles we sell that day.，綜觀全文並沒有提到糖尿病患者，文章中也未提到後面敘述的訊息，故答案是 D 選項。

答案：1. D　2. D

Unit 3
書籍推薦：森林秘境 The Forest Unseen

Dear faculty members,

It's near the end of the semester. I know you are probably wondering why I am writing this. Summer vacation is near, and you have yet to decide the suggested readings and textbooks for the next semester. For the next semester, we will put a special emphasis on a six-credit course called **Integrated** Biology. It's about plants, insects, and flowers. It's going to be taught consecutively by five professors. I do recommend students of our department to read *The Forest Unseen* by David George Haskell. His writing is beyond anything, quite worth reading. Every square meter of forest is covered in it. Students can read several pieces while doing a field study during summer vacation. That's all.

Sincerely,
Mark Chen
Dean of Best University, Biology

Bulletin board of Best University: Biology Major

Course of next semester

Course Name/ professors	Integrated Biology	Suggested reading: *The Forest Unseen*
Ken	Wild flowers	April 2nd/flowers
Jack	insects	April 14th/Moth July 13th/Fireflies
Sally	Natural phenomena	March 25th/Spring Ephemerals June 10th/Ferns
James	birds	April 16th/Sunrise birds
Jimmy	plants	Jan 30th/Winter plants Feb 16th/Moss

Note: make sure you read those articles

A letter from a student

To: Mark Markchen@bestuniversity.biology.com
From: Mary Marywang@ bestuniversity.biology.com
Date: June 16
Attachment: none

Dear Dean,

I saw the information on the bulletin board that you are suggesting students to read *The Forest Unseen*. Although I'm not a freshman any more, I do want to thank you for doing that. Last year, I was applying for a summer internship program at a top technology firm, and they were asking me some tough questions that I couldn't answer. I was so embarrassed that I looked totally unprepared for a job interview. I really wish someone had told me about that. After that, I was acting like crazy. I actually read some books relevant to biology, attended several forums, and did some serious thinking about my future to make myself look better prepared. I do think *The Forest Unseen* is a good start.

Sincerely,
Mary Wang

1. What is the purpose of the Facebook announcement?

   (A) to inform the faculty members of summer vacation activities

   (B) to ask the faculty members to read a biology book

   (C) to announce a course and recommend a book for it

   (D) to announce some changes to an old biology course

2. Why is The Forest Unseen recommended?

   (A) The dean thinks very highly of this book.

   (B) It covers the information of a forest near the school.

   (C) It is written by the dean.

   (D) It is the best-selling biology textbook.

3. What articles should the students read for the section of natural phenomena in Integrated Biology?
   (A) Moth and Fireflies
   (B) Spring Ephemerals and Fireflies
   (C) Spring Ephemerals and Ferns
   (D) Winter plants and Moss

4. Why does Mary Wang write the email?
   (A) to show her appreciation to the dean for his suggestion
   (B) to ask the dean for some suggestions on her interview
   (C) to thank the dean for teaching her
   (D) to apologize for not taking the biology course

5. What does the word integrated imply?
   (A) comprehensive
   (B) separate
   (C) challenging
   (D) biological

單元 3 ▶ 書籍推薦：森林秘境
The Forest Unseen

臉書公告：生物學院院長臉書公告文

親愛的教職成員們

已經接近學期結尾了。我知道你們可能都在想為什麼我會撰寫這篇文章。暑假近在咫尺，你們也都尚未決定下學期的建議閱讀書籍和教科書。下學期，我們會將重點放在一門，六學分課叫做整合生物學。它是關於植物、昆蟲和花朵。它會由五位教授們接續授課。我建議我們系上的學生閱讀由大衛·喬治·哈思克撰寫的森林秘境。他的寫作超越任何事，相當值得閱讀。每個平方公尺的森林都覆蓋到了。暑假時，學生能夠閱讀幾篇文章，然後一邊做田野調查。就這樣。

Sincerely,
馬克·陳
倍斯特大學生物學院院長

倍斯特大學布告欄：生物主修

下學期課程

課程名稱/教授	整合生物學	建議閱讀：森林秘境
肯	野生花朵	4 月 2 日/花朵
傑克	昆蟲	4 月 14 日/蛾 July 13th/螢火蟲
莎莉	自然現象	3 月 25 日/春天短命春花 6 月 10 日/蕨類
詹姆士	鳥類	4 月 16 日/日出鳥類
吉米	植物	1 月 30 日/冬天植物 2 月 16 日/蘚苔

註：確認你讀了這些文章。

來自學生的信件

致：馬克 Markchen@bestuniversity.biology.com
從：瑪莉 Marywang@ bestuniversity.biology.com
日期：6 月 16 日
附件：無

親愛的院長

我看到了布告欄上，你建議學生閱讀森林秘境。儘管我不是大一新鮮人了，我還是想要感謝你這麼做。去年，我申請了頂尖科技公司暑期工讀計劃，他們詢問了我幾個艱難的問題，而我卻答不出來。我感到尷尬萬分，我像是個全然沒替面試作準備的人。我真的希望當初有人能跟我講。在那之後，我像瘋狂似地，我實際上開始閱讀關於生物學的書籍、參加幾個論

壇和認真思考我的未來，讓自己看起來更充分準備。我真的相信森林秘境
會是個好開始。

Sincerely,
瑪莉・王

1. 此臉書公告的目的是什麼？

(A) 告知教職人員暑期活動。

(B) 要求教職人員閱讀生物學書籍。

(C) 公布課程和推薦書。

(D) 公布舊生物學課程的一些改變。

2. 為什麼森林秘境這本書被推薦呢？

(A) 院長對這本書很推崇。

(B) 它包含學校附近的森林資訊。

(C) 由院長所撰寫的。

(D) 暢銷書生物學教科書。

3. 學生閱讀整合生物學的自然現象那節時，應該會讀到什麼文章
呢？

(A) 蛾和螢火蟲。

(B) 春天短命春花和螢火蟲。

(C) 春天短命春花和蕨類。

(D) 冬天植物和蘚苔。

4. 為什麼瑪莉・王要寫這封信呢？

(A) 表示她對於院長建議的感謝。

(B) 詢問院長一些關於面試的建議。

(C) 感謝院長教導她。

(D) 道歉未選修生物學課。

5. 整合的這個字指的是什麼？

(A) 統整的。

(B) 分開的。

(C) 具挑戰性的。

(D) 生物學的。

答案：1. C　2. A　3. C　4. A　5. A

1.

- 看到題目馬上判斷題型，由 purpose 一字得知屬於主題題型。

- 由第四句 ...we have a special emphasis on a six-credit course called Integrated Biology 得知此篇主題，大意類似 (C)選項敘述的 to announce a course，又根據 I do recommend students of our department to read The Forest Unseen，大意類似(C)選項敘述的 recommend a book for it，所以選(C)。

2.

- 根據 I do recommend... ，馬上推測院長一定認為這本書非常好，才會推薦。

- 又根據 His writing is beyond anything, quite worth reading 的大意，他的寫作值得閱讀，更確定正確選項是(A) The dean thinks very highly of this book。

3.

- 看到題目目光馬上鎖定在 Natural Phenomena。位於第二篇 Bulletin board of Best University。

- 對照 Suggested reading 欄位列出的內容是 Ephemerals 和

Ferns，所以選(C)。

4.

- 由第三篇的第二句 …I do want to thank you for doing that，知道 Mary 寫這封 e-mail 的目的是感謝院長，並同時檢查代名詞 that 代替的名詞，that 是指第一句「建議學生讀 The Forest Unseen」這件事。

- 掃描選項敘述，搜尋感謝的類似詞。有(A)的 appreciation 和 (C)的 thank，但是(C)感謝的理由是 for teaching her，是錯誤的，(A)的理由 for his suggestion 是正確的，因此選(A)。

5.

- 先定位 integrated 第一次出現是在第一篇 Facebook Announcement 第四句。

- 根據第一篇第六句 It's going to be taught consecutively by five professors 的大意:由五位教授接續授課，並掃描第二篇 Bulletin board of Best University，這堂課程由五個主題組合而成，由此可推測 integrated 有綜合的意思，因此選(A) comprehensive。

1.

- 大部分篇章的主題，可由整篇的第一到第四句找到線索。

- 另一解題技巧是先搜索是否有特殊意義的形容詞，如 special，unique，particular 等。這類形容詞可當作定位字，答案常在接近這類形容詞的下文出現。我們讀到第四句 ...we have a special emphasis on...，special 一字就暗示讀者此句是重要的。

- 關於主題的敘述就銜接在介系詞 on 之後。同理，因為 emphasis 的意思是「重心」，emphasis 也是協助我們快速找到答案的定位字。

2.

- 此題屬於推測題型。在 Facebook Announcement 中，主要線索句是 I do recommend students of our department to read The Forest Unseen...，助動詞 do 在此的功能是表達肯定的加強語氣，語氣類似 I highly recommend...。

- 另一線索句是 His writing is beyond anything, quite worth reading。介系詞 beyond 有超越的意思，be beyond anything，超越一切，而 quite worth reading 意思是值得閱

讀的，言外之意是院長對 The Forest Unseen 這本書作者的寫作風格或內容有高度評價。

3.

- 此題屬於細節題型。按照題目給予的細節 Natural phenomena，對照 Suggested reading 欄位下的主題，即可找出正確選項。

- 題目的疑問詞 What articles should the students read...，學生應該閱讀哪些文章，呼應 suggested reading，這個片語意思是規定學生要念的文章。

4.

- 此題的考點較複雜，測試同義字轉換、句意理解及判別代名詞及所代替的先行詞之間的關聯性。

- 這句的 thank 是解題第一線索：Although I'm not a freshman any more, I do want to thank you for doing that，thank 是感謝的動詞，同義字是 appreciate，appreciation 是感謝的名詞，選項中唯一和感謝有關的是(A) to show her appreciation to the dean for his suggestion 和(C) to thank the dean for teaching her。

- 此外，特別注意線索句的最後一個字：代名詞 that。代名詞通常也是解題線索，所以往上一句找 that 所代替的先行詞，先行詞是「建議學生讀 The Forest Unseen」這件事。因此可確定正確選項是(A)。

5.

- 此題測試考生能否依照上下文，推測 integrated 的字義，事實上此題也是測驗同義字轉換，考生其實要思考哪個選項的字義和 integrated 最接近。

- 根據 Integrated 所在句子的下文（第一篇第六句）的敘述：It's going to be taught consecutively by five professors，由五位教授接續授課。

- 又根據第二篇 Bulletin board of Best University，得知這堂課程由五個主題組合而成，由此可推測 integrated 有綜合的意思，因此選(A) comprehensive。其它選項都與課程敘述無關。

浣熊 ● ● ●

還有可能怎麼問

1. Who is Mary Wang?

(A) a freshman.

(B) dean's assistant.

(C) a student majoring in Biology.

(D) professor.

2. What is indicated in the article?

(A) Mark Chen thinks the writing of The Forest Unseen is not superb.

(B) Mary Wang went insane after getting turned down by interviewers, so she turns to the doctor for help.

(C) School dean will be the key person to teach Integrated Biology.

(D) Mary Wang thinks being better prepared is important.

1. 誰是瑪莉・王？

(A) 大學新鮮人。

(B) 院長的助理。

(C) 主修生物學的學生。

(D) 教授。

2. 文中沒有指出下列哪個項目？

(A) 馬克・陳認為森林秘境書籍的寫作不是一流的。

(B) 瑪莉・王在受到面試者拒絕後，發瘋了，所以她向醫生求助。

(C) 學校院長是教授整合生物學的關鍵人。

(D) 瑪莉・王認為更充分的準備是重要的。

解析

1. 題目詢問「誰是瑪莉・王？」先分別從四個選項來看。

- A 選項的 a freshman 可以回到學生瑪莉寫給馬克的信，在信件第二行可以看到敘述 Although I'm not a freshman any more, I do want to thank you for doing that.，從這句話可以知道瑪莉已經不是大學新鮮人了，故 A 選項可以先排除。

- B 選項是 dean's assistant，綜觀全文三篇文章都未提到院長助理，且瑪莉也不是院長助理，故可以排除 B 選項。

- C 選項是關於主修生物學的學生，這個選項與 A 選項類似，只是又加以改寫，以名詞加形容詞子句的方式表達人物，而非名詞，從信件敘述等可以得知瑪莉不是大一新鮮人了但在生物相關的事情上做出許多努力的學生，故可以推測瑪莉是主修生物學的學生，答案為 C 選項。

- D 選項則是教授。可以定位回第二篇文章中的表格中尋找，得知教授名稱中沒有瑪莉，且根據第三篇信件中的敘述推測出瑪莉不是教授，故 D 選項不符合。

2. 題目詢問「文中沒有指出下列哪個項目？」先分別從四個選項來看。

- A 選項寫到 Mark Chen thinks the writing of The Forest Unseen is not superb.，可以定位回第一篇文章敘述，院長寫道 His writing is beyond anything, quite worth reading. Every square meter of forest is covered in it.可以得知 beyond anything 表示 superb 得知院長覺得寫作是一流的，這句只是出題者進行文意的改寫，故可以先排除 A 選項。

- B 選項提到 Mary Wang went insane after getting turned down by interviewers, so she turns to the doctor for help.可以定位回第三封信件，文章中有提到瑪莉受拒絕等，但文中指的是她講這些轉化為更努力學習的動力，此外並未提到她向醫生求助的訊息，故可以排除 B 選項。

- C 選項提到 School dean will be the key person to teach Integrated Biology.可以綜合第一封信和第二個表格內容的訊息，院長未提到自己將教授整合生物學，且表格中沒有提到授課教授有院長名字，故可以排除 C 選項。

- D 選項提到 Mary Wang thinks being better prepared is important. 可以定位回第三封信件，得知瑪莉寫道 did some serious thinking about my future to make myself look better prepared.，故可以得知此敘述與 D 選項相符，答案為 D 選項。

答案：1. C　2. D

Unit 4

生日禮物挑選

The following are the line messages from several friends discussing birthday presents.

Ken: Still struggling to decide which present is the best for my daughter's tenth birthday.

Jenny: Why does that seem like a big burden on you?

Lisa: Buy her a Barbie doll. Problem solved!

Ken: Seriously? A doll? I just didn't see that coming.

Jenny: Not a bad idea. Last year, I sent an expensive doll to a kid of my relative, and she loves it.

Lisa: How much is it? Just out of curiosity.

Jenny: I guess around US 700 dollars

Ken: That much... you are kidding, right.

Jenny: I don't do kidding.

Lisa: Little girls really need an idol to look up to.

Jenny: Gonna grab a late bite with my husband... talk to you guys later.

Ken: Jenny... wait... where did you get that doll?

Letter: Catalogue of Barbie Dolls

Catalogue of Barbie Dolls/BEST Doll Agency

Type	Origin	Descriptions	Price
A	China	Versatile, a great dancer, eyeing for really big things	US$ 850
B	Europe	Living in a castle, a good communicator, incredible blue eyes	US$ 950
C	Taiwan	Diligent, a great chef, inheriting a huge fortune, a rough childhood	US$ 600
D	Japan	Getting married with King of small country, learning martial arts from top Kong Fu artists	US$ 600
E	New York	Rich, beautiful, speak 10 languages	US$ 1000
F	Middle East	Poor, persistent to goals, eventually fulfilling her dreams, has a bunch of stories to share	US$ 750

Note:

1. The table only lists the major type of the dolls. We can customize the ideal doll for you. For more information, please come to our shop.
2. For the doll renting, we do offer 25% off for Type E and 50% off for other Types.
3. For persons buying three dolls, we do offer two coupons, US$ 350 deduction for Type A and us $450 deduction for Type B.

Line messages: follow-up for the birthday present

Ken: I eventually bought three dolls from BEST Doll Agency

Lisa: You are crazy.

Ken: Crazy about dolls... and my daughter loves it.

Jenny: But three dolls? Which one did you buy, anyway?

Ken: The other two dolls are for my client's daughter and my boss' son.

Lisa: So sneaky... you.

Ken: That leaves me with two coupons I don't need.

Lisa: In that case, give me Type A coupon.

Jenny: US$ 450 coupon on Type B. I certainly need one.

1. What does Ken mean by "I just didn't see that coming"?

   (A) He does not like dolls.

   (B) He does not know how to hold a birthday party for his daughter.

   (C) He cannot afford an expensive doll.

   (D) Buying a doll is out of his expectation.

2. What does the description "eyeing for really big things" imply?

   (A) having very high goals

   (B) having big eyes

(C) living in a big house

(D) buying expensive products

3. If a person wants to buy a Barbie doll with European origin and one with Taiwanese origin, how much does he need to spend?

(A) $ 1500

(B) $ 1550

(C) $ 950

(D) $ 1600

4. Why does Ken have two coupons?

(A) He is a long-time customer.

(B) He purchased 3 dolls.

(C) He purchased 2 dolls.

(D) He has a loyalty card.

5. How much does Jenny need to pay if she purchases a Type B doll with a coupon?

(A) $ 850

(B) $ 400

(C) $ 950

(D) $ 500

單元 4 ▶ 生日禮物挑選

下列是幾個朋友間的 line 訊息，討論生日禮物。

肯： 仍在掙扎著該選哪個會是我女兒10歲生日最棒的禮物。

珍妮： 為什麼這對你來說似乎是個大的負擔？

麗莎： 替她買個芭比娃娃。問題解決了。

肯： 當真？一個娃娃？我真的沒想到這個。

珍妮： 還不賴的想法。去年我送了一個昂貴的娃娃給我親戚的小孩，她愛極了。

麗莎： 要花多少年呢？只是出於好奇。

珍妮： 我猜大約 700 美元。

肯： 那麼多錢...你在開玩笑，對吧！

珍妮： 我不開玩笑的。

麗莎： 小女生真的需要一個偶像來仿效。

珍妮： 要跟我丈夫去吃個宵夜...稍後與你們聊喔！

肯： 珍妮...等等你從哪獲得那娃娃的？

信件：芭比娃娃目錄表格

芭比娃娃目錄/倍斯特娃娃代理商

類型	起源	描述	價格
A	中國	多才多藝、良好的舞者、目光放在遠大的事情上	850 美元
B	歐洲	生活於城堡中、是良好溝通者、驚人的藍眼睛	950 美元

C	台灣	勤奮、是個棒廚師、繼承一大筆財產、有艱苦的童年	600 美元
D	日本	與小國家的國王結婚、跟頂尖功夫家學習武術	600 美元
E	紐約	富有、美麗、能講十國語言	1000 美元
F	中東	貧窮、對目標有所堅持、最終達成理想、有很多故事能分享	750 美元

註：
1. 這個表格僅列出主要的娃娃類型。我們能夠替您量身訂做理想類型的娃娃。
2. 關於娃娃出租，我們提供 E 類型 75 折優惠和其他類型的 5 折優惠價格。
3. 關於購買三個娃娃，我們提供兩張優惠卷，A 類型折扣 350 美元和 B 類型折扣 450 美元。

Line 訊息：生日禮物後續

肯： 我最終從倍斯特娃娃代理機構購買了三個娃娃。

麗莎： 你瘋了。

肯： 對娃娃瘋狂...而且我女兒喜愛它。

珍妮： 但三個娃娃？你到底買了哪個？

肯： 另外兩個娃娃是給我的客戶女兒和我老闆的兒子。

麗莎： 真狡猾唉...你。

肯： 這樣讓我多了兩張我不需要的優惠卷。

麗莎： 如果是這樣的話，給我 A 類型的優惠卷。

珍妮： 450 美元優惠卷就能購得 B 類型的娃娃。我確實需要優惠卷。

1. 「我真的沒想到這個」指的是？

    (A) 他不喜歡娃娃。

    (B) 他不知道如何替自己的女兒舉辦生日派對。

    (C) 他負擔不起昂貴的娃娃。

    (D) 購買娃娃在他的意料之外。

2. 「將目光放在真正遠大的事上」的敘述暗指？

    (A) 有非常高遠的目標。

    (B) 有很大的眼睛。

    (C) 住在很大的房子裡。

    (D) 購買昂貴的產品。

3. 如果一個人想要購買具歐裔血統的芭比娃娃和台灣裔血統的娃娃，他需要花費多少錢呢？

    (A) 1500 美元。

    (B) 1550 美元。

    (C) 950 美元。

    (D) 1600 美元。

4. 為什麼肯有兩張優惠卷呢？

    (A) 他是長期顧客。

    (B) 他購買三個娃娃。

(C) 他購買兩個娃娃。

(D) 他有忠誠卡。

5. 如果珍妮以優惠卷購買類型 B 的娃娃，她需要花費多少錢？

(A) 850 美元

(B) 400 美元

(C) 950 美元

(D) 500 美元

答案：1. D　2. A　3. B　4. B　5. D

 獵豹 ● ● ●

1.

• 看到題目目光馬上鎖定在代名詞 that。往 I just don't see that coming 的上一句找出 that 指涉的名詞或事件。上一句有祈使句 Buy her a Barbie doll。得知 that 指的是買芭比娃娃這件事，而動詞 see 有「理解」的意思，前面搭配否定助動詞 don't，因此推測 I just don't see that coming 是「我沒想到這件事」的意思。

• (D)敘述的 out of his expectation，「在他的意料之外」與原句意思類似，所以選(D)。

2.

- 因為 eyeing for really big things 的上文 versatile，a great dancer 都是關於 Type A 娃娃的特色的正面描述，因此推測此片語的含義是正面的。考慮 eye 有加 ing，可得知 eye 在此片語是當動詞使用，由動詞詞性更進一步推測 eye for 有「將目光放在……」的意思，因為(B)，(C)，(D)的大意都與「將目光放在……」無關，所以選(A) having very high goals。

3.

- 看到題目目光馬上鎖定在 Catalogue 的 Europe 和 Taiwan。對照 Price 欄位，源自 Europe 的娃娃價格是$950，源自 Taiwan 的娃娃價格是$600，$950+$600=$1550，所以選(B)。

4.

- 看到題目目光馬上鎖定在 coupons。根據 catalogue 底部 Note 的第三點描述，買三個娃娃可得到兩張優惠卷，因此選(B)。

5.

- 看到題目目光馬上鎖定在 Type B。catalogue 底部 Note 的第三點描述：$450 deduction for Type B，Type B 娃娃可以用優惠卷折抵$450，原價是$950。$950-$450=$500，因此選(D)。

貓頭鷹 ● ● ●

1.

- 此題屬於推測題型，牽涉到慣用語及代名詞。代名詞 that 的先行詞通常在上一句，可能是代替上一句的某個名詞或上一句整句表達的某件事。先行詞指的是代名詞代替的名詞或名詞片語。根據上一句 Buy her a Barbie doll 的句意，得知 that 指的是買芭比娃娃這件事，而動詞 see 有「理解」的意思，前面搭配否定助動詞 don't，可推測 I just don't see that coming 是「我沒想到這件事」的意思。(D)敘述的 out of his expectation，「在他的意料之外」與「我沒想到這件事」意思類似，I don't see that coming 及 Sth. is out of Sb's expectation 都是常用慣用語。所以選(D)。

2.

- 此題測試考生是否知道 eye for 這個動詞片語，或是否能從字尾 ing 推測 eye 在此情境當動詞使用。

- 除了以 eye 的詞性變化推測答案，也能利用 eyeing for really big things 前面的 versatile, a great dancer 當解題線索。正確選項必須在意義上能呼應 versatile，多才多藝的，及 a great dancer，很棒的舞者。因此可刪去(B) having big eyes。(C) living in a big house 及(D) buying expensive products，因為這些選項的意思與多才多藝的，很棒的舞者都

沒有絕對的關係。而正確選項(A) having very high goals，有非常高的目標，能呼應很棒的舞者，因為這兩個特質都屬於抱負或志向。

3.

- 此題是與數字有關的細節題，需要考生做基本的算術。題目常將篇章裡的關鍵字做詞性轉換。如此題，表格的 origin 欄位，是以各個地區，國家及城市的名詞區分娃娃的來源。題目將名詞改成形容詞：Europe (n.)à European (adj.)。Taiwan (n.) à Taiwanese (adj.)

4.

- 此題的線索字是 coupons，題目是問為何肯有兩張優惠卷呢？因此用掃描技巧找出 coupons 一字。Coupons 第一次出現是在表格底部 Note（注意事項）的第三點。根據第三點敘述的大意，得知購買三個娃娃，可得到兩張優惠卷，故選(B) He purchased 3 dolls。

5.

- 此題先找出 Type B 娃娃的原價。以掃描技巧找到 coupon 一字，coupon 位於 Note 的第三點描述，再檢查針對 Type B 娃娃的折扣，$450 deduction for Type B。deduction 是扣除的名詞。Type B 娃娃可以用優惠卷折抵$450，原價是$950。$950-$450=$500。表格類型常在表格底部以 Note 或 N.B.列出特殊事項，或提醒讀者注意重要資訊，是解題線索常出現的地方。N.B.是拉丁文 Nota bene 的縮寫，意思是"note well"。

浣熊 ● ● ●

還有可能怎麼問

1. Which is NOT mentioned about BEST Doll Agency?

(A) It offers coupons.

(B) The doll can be specifically tailored.

(C) It offers discounts in doll renting.

(D) The choice of dolls is quite limiting.

2. What is NOT indicated in the article?

(A) Ken has a hard time for selecting a birthday present for his daughter.

(B) Ken can purchase a doll of European origin at only 500 dollars, if he keeps two coupons for himself.

(C) There are only six types of dolls at BEST Doll Agency

(D) Money spent on renting a type E doll and buying a type F doll is the same.

1. 文中沒有提到有關倍斯特娃娃代理機構的什麼？

(A) 它提供優惠卷。

(B) 娃娃能量身訂做的。

(C) 它提供折扣給娃娃租借。

(D) 娃娃的選擇相當受限。

2. 文中沒有指出下列哪個項目？

(A) 肯對於選擇他女兒的生日禮物有困難。

(B) 肯能只花費 500 元就購得歐裔血統娃娃，如果他將兩張優惠卷都留給自己。

(C) 倍斯特娃娃代理機構只有六個類型的娃娃。

(D) 花費在租一個 E 類型的娃娃的錢和購買一個 F 類型的娃娃相同。

解析

1. 題目詢問「文中沒有提到有關倍斯特娃娃代理機構的什麼？」先分別從四個選項來看。

- A 選項提到 It offers coupons，在第二篇文章 catalogue 表格下方的註 3，可以看到 For the person buying three dolls, we do offer two coupons, US\$ 350 for Type A and 450 for Type B.可以得知有提供 coupons 優惠卷，故可以先排除 A 選項。B 選項提到 The doll can be specifically tailored.，在第二篇文章 catalogue 表格下方的註 1 第二句話，可以看到 We can customize the ideal doll for you.，customize 即 specifically tailored 的同義轉換故可以排除 B 選項。C 選項提

到 It offers discounts in doll renting. 在第二篇文章 catalogue 表格下方的註 2 提到 For the doll renting, we do ....，從這句話可以得知有提供娃娃租借服務，故可以排除 C 選項。D 選項提到 The choice of dolls is quite limiting.，在第二篇文章 catalogue 表格下方的註 1，可以看到 We can customize the ideal doll for you. ...可以得知表格只列出主要的類型公司其實提供不只這些類別的娃娃，甚至可以量身訂做，故可以得知 D 選項敘述並不符合，**答案為 D 選項**。

2. 題目詢問「文中沒有指出下列哪個項目？」先分別從四個選項來看。

• A 選項可以定位回 line 訊息中肯表達 Still struggling to decide which present...為 A 選項的同義表達，故可以排除 A 選項。B 選項 Ken can purchase a doll of European origin at only 500 dollars....，可以定位回目錄表格下方的註得知優惠卷可折抵價格，還有從歐裔血統娃娃得知是類型 B 的娃娃，950 扣掉優惠卷金額 450 元則是 500 元，故此表達與題目相符，句子只是經過改寫，故可以排除 B 選項。C 選項同第一題 D 選項故可以得知不只有六種類型的娃娃，**故答案為 C 選項**。D 選項可以從表格下方註的文字敘述推斷 E 類型的娃娃若是租借的話有 75 折折扣故價格為 750 元與 F 類型娃娃購買的價格相同，故也可以排除 D 選項。

答案：1. D　2. C

Unit 5

電視收視率

TV Ratings Table

Conducted by Best Marketing Team, Oct 11th, 2018

Name of the Program	Ratings 10/1	Ratings 9/1	Ratings 8/1
Finding a Star	10.2	8.6	9.7
Desperate Husbands	21.7	17.9	16.7
Knowing Plants	2.1	1.96	2.8
How to Shop	9.6	15.2	7.8
Asia's Next Top Model	15.2	11.2	13.9
Enjoying Yourself	1.9	2.2	3.0
Top Athletes	10.2	7.8	17.5

Facebook chatroom at TOP TV

Kim: I had this awful feeling this morning while having a drink at Starbucks.

Jack: I can't believe this is happening.

Jessica: Have you guys seen the ratings this morning?

Mary: We got beaten by Knowing Plants.

Jack: I prefer to call it a one-time victory.

Kim: Stop joking around.

Jack:　　　I'm just as serious as you guys. (uploading the file of the Ratings)

Mary:　　Thanks!!!

Jessica:　I just don't think it's that good.

Kim:　　That good? What do you mean? A rating of 2.1 and that's good?

Mary:　　yep, what about the other programs?

Jack:　　　I guess that means we won't have a bonus and international trips this year.

Jessica:　perhaps next year...

Jack:　　　ha ha...

Assistant: (knock knock) Sorry guys... Tim calls a lunch meeting with you

Conference room chat

Tim:　　Kim, you're the producer, what do you think about the ratings?

Kim:　　　I'm sorry.

Tim:　　　I don't want to hear that.

Tim:　　Do you know I got an-email from the headquarters? if things keep going like this, they are going to cut the entire Marketing in half. I'm serious. I might as well need to find a new job in two months.

Tim:　　I'm going to cut the show. The entire Marketing team should come up with something new today.

Assistant: Sorry to interrupt... it's the call from the headquarters.

Tim:　　I'm going to take this call. All of you, grab something from the cafeteria and meet here in ten minutes.

1. Which program received the highest rating on Oct. 1st?

   (A) Asia's Next Top Model

   (B) How to Shop

   (C) Finding a Star

   (D) Desperate Husbands

2. Which program receives the lowest rating on Sept. 1st?

   (A) Enjoying Yourself

   (B) Knowing Plants

   (C) Desperate Husbands

   (D) How to Shop

3. Which of the followings best describes Kim's attitude in the conference room?

   (A) apologetic

   (B) excited

   (C) bored

   (D) angry

4. Which of the followings might be implied by Jack's statement, "I prefer to call it a one-time victory"?
(A) He thinks the victory is short-lived
(B) He thinks the victory is exciting.
(C) He feels one-time victory is enough.
(D) He is satisfied that their program received the highest rating.

5. Which of the followings might be the purpose of the e-mail from the headquarters?
(A) to give the marketing team a suggestion regarding how to improve the rating
(B) to warn the marketing team about the consequence of the low rating
(C) to inform the marketing team that the show will be canceled
(D) to inform the employees of the marketing team that they will be laid off

單元 5 ▶ 電視收視率

電視收視率表格

由倍斯特行銷團隊統計, 2018 年 10 月 11 日

節目名稱	收視率 10/1	收視率 9/1	收視率 8/1
找尋巨星	10.2	8.6	9.7
絕望主夫	21.7	17.9	16.7
認識植物	2.1	1.96	2.8
如何購物	9.6	15.2	7.8
全亞超模	15.2	11.2	13.9
享受自我	1.9	2.2	3.0
頂級運動員	10.2	7.8	17.5

臉書聊天室，在頂尖電視台

金： 我一早在星巴克喝咖啡時就有不好的預感。

傑克： 我不敢相信這真的發生了！

潔西卡： 你們有看今早的收視率嗎？

瑪莉： 我們被「認識植物」擊敗。/收視率輸

傑克： 我傾向將這稱為一次性的勝利。

金： 別再開玩笑了！

傑克： 我跟你們一樣認真好嗎？（上傳收視率的檔案）

瑪莉： 謝謝！！！

潔西卡： 我不認為那節目有這麼好？

金： 那麼好？你指的是什麼？收視率 2.1，這算好。

瑪莉： 是阿，其他節目呢？

傑克： 我猜想這意味著我們今年沒有獎金和國際旅遊了。

潔西卡：可能明年...

傑克： 哈哈...

助理： （敲門聲）抱歉各位...提姆要與各位開午餐會議。

會議室談話

提姆： 金，你是製作人，你覺得收視率怎樣？

金： 我感到抱歉。

提姆： 我不想聽到這個。

提姆： 你知道我收到總部的 e-mail 嗎？如果事情持續這樣的話，他們將會裁一半的行銷部門。我很認真的說。我可能也要在兩個月內找新工作了。

提姆： 我決定要裁掉這個秀。整個行銷團隊今天要想新的東西出來。

助理： 不好意思打斷...是總部打來的電話。

提姆： 我要去接這電話。你們全部去自助餐那拿好吃的，十分鐘後這裡集合。

1. 哪個節目在十月一日獲得最高的收視率呢？

(A) 全亞超模。

(B) 如何購物。

(C) 找尋巨星。

(D) 絕望主夫。

2. 哪個節目在九月一日獲得最低的收視率呢？

(A) 享受自我。

(B) 認識植物。

(C) 絕望主夫。

(D) 如何購物。

3. 下列哪個描述能表示出金在會議室的心情呢？

(A) 感到抱歉的。

(B) 興奮的。

(C) 無聊的。

(D) 生氣的。

4. 下列哪個能推測出傑克的陳述「我傾向將這稱為一次性的勝利」？

(A) 他認為勝利是短暫的。

(B) 他認為勝利令人感到興奮。

(C) 他認為一次性勝利就足夠了。

(D) 他對於他們的節目獲得最高收視率感到滿意。

5. 下列哪個可能是總部寄 e-mail 的目的呢？

(A) 給予行銷團隊關於如何改進收視率的建議。

(B) 警告行銷團隊低收視率的後果。

(C) 告知行銷團隊節目將被取消。

(D) 告知行銷團隊他們將被解雇。

答案：1. D 2. B 3. A 4. A 5. B

獵豹 ● ● ●

1.

- 看到題目目光馬上鎖定在 the highest，在第一個表格 TV Ratings Table 找到 10/1。

- 10/1 欄位下數字最高的是 21.7，節目名稱是 Desperate Husbands，所以選(D)。

2.

- 看到題目目光馬上鎖定在 the lowest，在第一個表格 TV Ratings Table 找到 9/1。

- 9/1 欄位下數字最低的是 1.96，節目名稱是 Knowing Plants，所以選(B)。

3.

- 看到題目目光馬上鎖定在 conference room，跟 Kim 的態度有關係的句子是她說的 I'm sorry。

- 從 I'm sorry 的上下文推測 Kim 的態度，Tim 對 Kim 說的：Kim, you're the producer, what do you think about the ratings?及 I don't want to hear that。

- you're the producer 這句暗示 Tim 期待 Kim 以製作人的身份

發表對收視率的看法，有對 Kim 究責的意思，I don't want to hear that 也像是上司對下屬訓話的語氣，因此可推測 Tim 是 Kim 的主管。由於收視率差，因此 Kim 是對主管表達抱歉。「感覺抱歉的」形容詞是 apologetic。所以選(A) apologetic。

4.

- 看到題目目光馬上鎖定在 one-time victory。

- 以換句話說的技巧判斷正確選項，與 one-time 意思最接近的是 short-lived，所以選(A)。

5.

- 看到題目目光馬上鎖定在 e-mail from the headquarters，定位在第三篇，conference room。

- e-mail from the headquarters 的下一句有解題線索。根據 they are going to cut ...和 I might as well need to...，這兩個子句的大意均暗示如果情況持續沒有改善，將發生的後果，後果的名詞是 consequence，所以選(B)。

貓頭鷹

1.

- 題目裡如果有形容詞最高級及日期，一定是線索字，如此題的

the highest 和 Oct. 1st。

- 定位回文章，找到十月一日收視率最高的數字，再搭配題目疑問詞 Which program，在 the Name of the Program 欄位下對照收視率最高的數字，即可得出節目名稱(D) Desperate Husbands。

2.

- 題目裡如果有形容詞最高級及日期，一定是線索字，如此題的 the lowest 和 Sept. 1st。
- 定位回文章，找到九月一日收視率最高的數字，再搭配題目疑問詞 Which program，在 the Name of the Program 欄位下對照收視率最高的數字，即可得出節目名稱(B) Knowing Plants。

3.

- 此題主要測試考生是否能依照前後文的情境，推測出 Kim 的態度。讀題須細心檢查題目是限定哪一個篇章，此題限定在 conference room。

- 考生須注意 I'm sorry 這句會因情境不同，而有不同的意思。有時表達「我感覺遺憾」，或「我（替某人）感到惋惜」，或「我感到抱歉，對不起」。

- 此題能從談話雙方的關係為何，彼此應答的方式來決定 I'm sorry 的意思。在 conference room 的情境中，Tim 對 Kim 是以上司對下屬的語氣，針對收視率不佳究責。所以能推測 Kim 說 I'm sorry 是「對不起」的意思。

4.

- 此題屬於推測題型，要按照題目所給的句子再搭配原文的情境推測出這句的深層意義。此句的情境是兩個節目互相比較收視率之後，Jack 的個人評語。

- 考生要小心避免思考過程中過度詮釋的陷阱。例如(C) He feels one-time victory is enough 雖然有重複 one-time 這個關鍵字，但在 Jack 的評語的前後文中，他毫無提到一次勝利就足夠。因此不能選(C)。

5.

- 此題屬於推測題型，要推測出來自總部的 e-mail 目的為何。

- e-mail from the headquarters 定位在第三篇的第二個疑問句，此疑問句之後以假設語氣句型給出答案。If things keep gping like this, ... 主詞 things 指的是第二篇 Facebook chatroom 討論的收視率問題，即低收視率，呼應正確選項(B)提及的 low rating。

- 假設語氣句型的 if-子句主要表達條件，主要子句（即 if-子句以外的子句）表達條件如果成立後，可能或將產生的後果。因此此題除了以大意推測，也能從假設語氣句型的功能判斷正確選項應該會提及後果方面的單字。

還有可能怎麼問

1. Which is the program Kim produces?

   (A) Asia's Next Top Model

   (B) Finding a Star

   (C) Desperate Husbands

   (D) Enjoying Yourself

2. What is NOT indicated in the article?

   (A) A low TV rating would result in not having international trips

   (B) The rating of Kim's show was relatively successful than that of Knowing Plants until Oct 1.

   (C) None of the program listed has made a successive progress.

   (D) If the situation does not improve, Tim could lose the job.

1. 金製作的節目是什麼？

    (A) 亞洲超模。

    (B) 尋找巨星。

    (C) 慾望丈夫。

    (D) 享受自己。

2. 文中沒有指出下列哪個項目？

    (A) 低收視率會導致沒有國際性的旅遊。

    (B) 金的節目在 10 月 1 日前比尋找植物相對性的成功。

    (C) 沒有任何節目獲得持續性的進步。

    (D) 如果情況沒有改善，提姆可能會失去工作。

解析

1. 題目詢問「金製作的節目是什麼？」先分別從四個選項來看。

   • **ABCD** 分別代表四個節目亞洲超模、尋找巨星、絕望主夫和享受自己。在第二篇臉書聊天室和會議室文章中均未明顯提及金製作的節目是什麼？但可以定位回收視率表格和臉書聊天室中的訊息，綜合潔西卡和瑪莉的對話「潔西卡：你們有看今早的收視率嗎？瑪莉：我們被「認識植物」擊敗。」定位回表格中認識植物的收視率並找出收視率在 **10/1** 日比認識植物低的節目，從這些訊息可以得知享受自我在 **10/1** 日的收視率低於認識植物，故可以推測出金製作的節目是享受自己，故答案為 **D** 選項。

2. 題目詢問「文中沒有指出下列哪個項目？」先分別從四個選項來看。

- **A 選項**提到 A low TV rating would result in not having international trips，可以由 international trips 定位回聊天內容中 Jack 提到的 I guess that means we won't have a bonus and international trips this year.，故可以得知此為同義表達，故可以排除 A 選項。**B 選項**為 The rating of Kim's show was relatively successful than that of Knowing Plants until Oct 1.，此選項必須先推測出金的節目為何，才能作答，得知後可以定位回表格得知在 10 月 1 日前的兩次收視統計收視率均較認識植物高，故可以得知此敘述也同樣為同義表達，可以排除 B 炫項。

- **C 選項**為 None of the program listed has made a successive progress.，可以定位回表格並將每個節目各三次收視率做比較看數據變化，其中的慾望主夫的收視率是逐步遞升的，故此敘述為非，答案為 C 選項，此為文章中沒提到的部分。**D 選項**提到 If the situation does not improve, Tim could lose the job.可以定位回會議室對話，提姆提到 if things keep going like this, they are going to cut the entire Marketing in half. I'm serious. I might as well need to find a new job in two months.可以推測出如果情況沒有改善，提姆可能會失去工作。

答案：1. D　2. C

Unit 6

萬聖節派對

Line dialogue ❶：discussions of the Halloween dress-up

Katie: Have you seen the list of the Halloween dress-up? It's so limited.

Neal: I'm feeling grateful that our company is having the costume thing. I love Judy Hopps from Zootopia.

Katie: Can't they just make us feel more excited about this festival?

Jimmy: Come on, that's last year's list. Michelle Obama and many other things. Definitely last year, ha ha.

Jimmy: Plus, it's more fun if we get to make the costumes ourselves.

Neal: So, where's this year's list, looking forward to seeing that.

Katie: I'm feeling better now, knowing we're going to have a new list.

Katie: Really looking forward to seeing that, too.

Jimmy: With the festival coming up, I do think HR personnel is going to send us the list before noon.

Neal: Actually, I'm gonna go with something from last year's list. I don't want to cause a scene, since I'm new here. Better be safe than bold.

Jimmy: Ha ha.

Company Bulletin Board: new costumes for the Halloween announced by HR

Bulletin Board of Best Smartphone
New Costumes for the Halloween/ by HR

1. Trump	9. Nick/Sly Fox
2. Sponge BOB	10. Harry Potter
3. Mona	11. Trump junior
4. The Duff/Binaca	12. Arnold
5. Superman	13. Simpson
6. Diana Prince	14. Leonardo da Vinci
7. Judy Hopps/rabbit	15. wonder woman
8. Chief Bogo	16. Spiderman

Note: special for this year, there is going to be a competition. Anyone winning the dress-up award is going to get a bonus of US 500 dollars.

Line dialogue ❷：Halloween follow-up

Katie: So lucky, we did it. We all get that damn bonus.

Neal: How? I just don't know what's good to celebrate? The title of The Oddest Look Award.

Jimmy: I just don't think it's that bad.

Neal: It's going to stay with me... throughout my career... unless I'm making a transfer to the branch office.

Katie: It's not that bad. You're getting a bonus after all.

Jimmy: I don't think making a transfer will change anything. Lucy is going to tell them anyway. She knows everyone.

Katie: yep...

Neal: Why didn't anyone tell me to just wear something from this year's list?

Jimmy: Like Chief Bogo? Why didn't anyone pick him? He looks awesome.

Katie: You beat me on this one, Mr. Decent.

Jimmy: What?

Katie: The Most Decent Look Award.

1. What kind of party might this company hold?

(A) a black-tie party

(B) a masquerade

(C) a luncheon

(D) a banquet

2. What does Neal mean by "Better be safe than bold"?

(A) He does not want to take any risk.

(B) He thinks safety is the most important in a party.

(C) He hopes the co-workers should pay attention to safety.

(D) He thinks courage is crucial.

3. What does Neal mean by "It's going to stay with me"?

(A) People will associate him with the title he won.

(B) He can keep the costume.

(C) He can keep the bonus.

(D) He is thrilled to have won the title.

4. What can be inferred about Lucy?

(A) She is good at making costumes.

(B) She won the Oddest Look Award.

(C) She likes to gossip about other co-workers.

(D) She won the Most Decent Look Award.

5. What does Katie imply by "You beat me on this one"?

(A) Katie does not like Jimmy because he used to beat her.

(B) She thinks that Chief Bogo can beat villains.

(C) She does not like to be beaten.

(D) She does not understand why no one chose the Chief Bogo costume.

單元 6 ▶ 萬聖節派對

Line 對話 ❶：萬聖節裝扮討論

凱蒂：你們看過萬聖節打扮的清單了嗎？選擇好侷限。

尼爾：我覺得感恩，我們公司有服飾這東西。我喜愛動物方城市裡的茱蒂・哈普斯。

凱蒂：他們就不能讓我們對這節慶感到更興奮些嗎？

吉米：拜託，那是去年的清單。歐巴馬夫人和許多東西。絕對是去年的，哈哈。

吉米：再說，如果我們可以自己做服飾的話會更好玩。

尼爾：所以今年的清單在哪呢？期待看到。

凱蒂：我感到好些了，知道我們有新的清單。

凱蒂：我也是，真的期待看到。

吉米：隨著節慶將至，我認為人事部人員將在中午前把清單送給我們。

尼爾：實際上，我想要用去年的清單的有些選擇。我不想要太出眾，因為我是新來的。寧願選擇安全也不要太冒險。

吉米：哈哈。

公司公告欄：人事部公告新的萬聖節服飾

倍斯特手機的布告欄
萬聖節的新服飾/人事部

1. 川普	9. 尼克/狡猾狐狸
2. 海綿寶寶	10. 哈利波特
3. 夢娜	11. 川普小兒子

4. 恐龍尤物/碧昂卡	12. 阿諾
5. 超人	13. 新普森
6. 黛安娜王妃	14. 李奧納多·達文西
7. 茱蒂·哈普斯/兔子	15. 神力女超人
8. Bogo 警長	16. 蜘蛛人

註：今年特別的是將會有競賽。任何贏得盛裝打扮獎的會得到 500 美元的獎金。

Line 對話 ❷：萬聖節後續

凱蒂：好幸運喔！我們做到了。我們都得到該死的獎金了。

尼爾：怎麼會？我都不知道有什麼好慶祝的？最奇怪樣貌獎的頭銜。

吉米：我不覺得有那麼糟。

尼爾：這會跟著我...整個職涯...除非我換到分公司。

凱蒂：沒有那麼糟。你畢竟拿到獎金了。

吉米：我不認為換到分公司就會改變任何事。露西會跟他們說的。她認識每個人。

凱蒂：是阿...。

尼爾：怎麼沒有人告訴我打扮時用今年的清單呢？

吉米：像是 Bogo 警長嗎？為什麼沒人選擇他？他看起來棒極了。

凱蒂：你考倒我了，打扮合宜先生。

吉米：什麼？

凱蒂：最合宜裝扮獎。

---

1. 這公司可能舉辦什麼樣的派對呢？

   (A) 黑領帶派對。

   (B) 化裝舞會。

6 填空式閱讀

7 單篇閱讀

7 雙篇、三篇閱讀

模擬試題

(C) 午餐會。

(D) 宴會。

2. 尼爾所指的「寧願打安全牌也比冒險好」意味著什麼？

(A) 他不想冒任何險。

(B) 他認為派對中最重要的是安全。

(C) 他希望同事應該要注意安全。

(D) 他認為勇氣很重要。

3. 尼爾所指的「這會跟著我了」意味著什麼？

(A) 大家會把他聯想到他所贏的頭銜。

(B) 他能留著服飾。

(C) 他能留著獎金。

(D) 他很興奮贏了頭銜。

4. 能從文章中推測露西是？

(A) 她擅長製作服飾。

(B) 她贏得最奇怪裝扮獎。

(C) 她喜歡八卦其他同事。

(D) 她贏得最合宜裝扮獎。

5. Katie 說的「你考倒我了」意味著什麼？

(A) 凱蒂不喜歡吉米因為他過去打她。

(B) 她認為 Bogo 警長能打敗壞蛋。

(C) 她不喜歡被打敗。

(D) 她不懂為何沒有人挑選 Bogo 警長的戲服。

答案：1.B　2.A　3.A　4.C　5.D

獵豹 ● ● ●

1.

• 根據第二篇 Bulletin Board 的小標題 New Costumes for the Halloween，Costume 的字義是「戲服」，以 costume 當線索字。 對照選項找出與戲服有關的派對類型，masquerade 是「化妝舞會」，所以選(B)。

2.

• 看到題目目光馬上鎖定在 "Better be safe than bold"。因為 bold 是大膽的意思，此句有比較級的 better，有「寧可安全，不要大膽」之意，與(A) He does not want to take any risk，他不想冒險，意思最接近，所以選(A)。

3.

• 看到題目目光馬上鎖定在 "It's going to stay with me" 的主詞

it，因 it 是代名詞，馬上往上一句搜尋 it 的先行詞。

- 因上一句仍使用 it，再往前一句找先行詞，即 the title of The Oddest Look Award。刪去(B)，(C)，因這兩個選項敘述都與 title 無關。雖然(D)有提及 title，但 thrilled 是「興奮的」之意，與題目要求的句子無關，也刪除(D)。故選(A)。

4.

- 看到題目目光馬上搜尋 Lucy，位於第三個篇章: Line messages II/Halloween。根據 Jimmy 說的: Lucy is going to tell them anyway. She knows everyone，Lucy 會告訴每個人關於 Neal 贏得的頭銜，換言之 Lucy 愛說八卦，說八卦的動詞及名詞都是 gossip，所以選(C)。

5.

- 首先判斷 You beat me on this one 是針對上文的疑問句"Like Chief Bogo? Why didn't anyone pick him?"所作出的回答。此句和上文的大意都和 Katie 的喜好無關，因此刪去(A)，(C)。刪除(B)，因 villain，壞蛋，及 Bogo 警長的行為與第三篇章的主題無關。唯一合理的選項是(D) She does not understand why no one chose the Chief Bogo costume。

1.

- 此題須以單字字義為主要線索推測答案。 第一個篇章: Line messages/Halloween，第一及第二句的 dress-up，裝扮，costume，戲服，是線索字。第二個篇章 Bulletin Board 的小標題 New Costumes for the Halloween 也是線索詞，而且列出 16 種名人及電影角色的戲服。由此推測是化妝舞會。化妝舞會是 masquerade。

2.

- 此題屬於推測題型，須以換句話說的技巧推測出答案。也須具備形容詞比較級的基本文法觀念。此句的比較級是 better。bold 有「大膽，厚顏的」意思。Better be safe than bold 是「寧可打安全牌」之意，即「不要冒險」。(A)選項描述將此片語換句話說。也可用刪去法解題。將與篇章主題無關的先刪除。此句在第一個篇章: Line messages/Halloween，主題是討論派對服裝。(B)，(C)雖然提及 safety，安全的名詞，但大意與主題和 bold 毫無關聯。(D)的大意也與主題及 safe，bold 這些關鍵字無關。

3.

- 此題屬於推測題型，也測試考生是否能讀出字面後的深層意義。"It's going to stay with me"也是慣用語（idiom）。因上

一句 Jimmy 說的 I just don't think it's that bad，think 之後的名詞子句的主詞仍是 it，所以再往前一句找 it 的先行詞，確認 it 指的是 the title of The Oddest Look Award。可推測這句的深層意義是 Neal 認為這個頭銜會一直跟著他了。更進一步參考下文 ...throughout my career... unless I'm making a transfer to the branch office。下文的大意暗示他很在意這個頭銜在職場上對他的影響，這點也呼應(A)選項描述 People will associate him with the title he won. 「人們會將他和這頭銜聯想在一起」。

4.

- 此題要考生推測 Lucy 是怎樣的人。因為 Lucy 不是對話角色之一，只能從對話角色對她的評價推測。唯一關於 Lucy 的評價是 Jimmy 說的：I don't think making a transfer will change anything. Lucy is going to tell them anyway. She knows everyone。也是 Jimmy 發表對 Neal 的「除非我換到分公司」的看法。gossip，碎嘴，說三道四。

5.

- 此題須注意 beat 這個動詞在不同情境會有不同字義。主要線索在這句的上文：Like Chief Bogo? Why didn't anyone pick him?。You beat me on this one 也是美式英文常用的慣用語（idiom）。因 You beat me on this one 是 Katie 對以上問題的回應，由此判斷 beat 在此情境不是「打敗」之意，而是「你考倒我了」。換言之，符合(D)的大意：她不懂為何沒有人選 Bogo 警長的戲服。上文的疑問句中，選擇的動詞是 pick，類似動詞是 choose，choose 的過去式是 chose。

還有可能怎麼問

1. Which is most likely to be the costume Neal dresses up at the party?
   (A) Spiderman
   (B) Nick/Sly Fox
   (C) Item 7 from the Bulletin Board of Best Smartphone
   (D) Michelle Obama

2. What is NOT indicated in the article?
   (A) Michelle Obama was on last year's list.
   (B) HR Department will be in charge of making the costume.
   (C) Neal regrets for not using this year's list.
   (D) Jimmy feels surprised that no one at the party dresses up as Chief Bogo.

1. 哪個服飾可能是尼爾於派對中的裝扮呢？
   (A) 蜘蛛人。
   (B) 尼克/狡猾狐狸。

(C) 倍斯特智慧型手機公司布告欄上的項目 7

(D) 歐巴馬夫人。

2. 文中沒有指出下列哪個項目？

　(A) 歐巴馬夫人在去年的清單上。

　(B) 人事部門會負責製作服飾。

　(C) 尼爾後悔沒有使用今年的清單。

　(D) 吉米對於派對中沒有人裝扮成 Bogo 警長感到驚訝。

解析

1. 題目詢問「哪個服飾可能是尼爾於派對中的裝扮呢？」先分別從四個選項來看。

• 此題需要將訊息做出整合，不能僅僅定位回表格中推斷尼爾會打扮成什麼裝飾。首先先看 A 選項和 B 選項，均出現於第二篇文章中所公告的表格內的裝扮項目。

• C 選項則沒有直接使用人物或物品名稱，而是透過改寫，要小心此陷阱，有時候考生會直接猜 C 因為表達不同，推測可能是答案，由 C 選項倍斯特智慧型手機公司布告欄上的項目 7 得知指的是表格中的茱蒂·哈普斯/兔子，但是還無法就此就做出推斷，從一開頭尼爾的對談得知尼爾喜歡茱蒂·哈普斯/兔子，但不能代表尼爾選此裝扮。

• 最後是 D 選項提到歐巴馬夫人，可以由此關鍵字定位回文章

中，得知「吉米：拜託，那是去年的清單。歐巴馬夫人和許多東西。絕對是去年的，哈哈。」從此得知只有歐馬夫人的裝扮是去年的，其他三種裝扮均是今年的，另外還有結尾的對話中尼爾提到「實際上，我想要用去年的清單的有些選擇。我不想要太出眾，因為我是新來的。寧願選擇安全也不要太冒險。」，綜合這些資訊可以得知尼爾最可能選擇去年的人物，故答案是選項 D。

2. 題目詢問「文中沒有指出下列哪個項目？」先分別從四個選項來看。

- A 選項為 Michelle Obama was on last year's list.，可以從吉米的對話中得知此選項文章中有提到，故可以排除 A 選項。

- B 選項為 HR Department will be in charge of making the costume.文章中吉米有提到若能自己製作更好玩等等，另外公佈欄中人事部公告跟其他段落都沒有表明人事部製作萬聖節的服飾，故答案為 B 選項。C 選項為 Neal regrets for not using this year's list.，可以定位回 「尼爾：怎麼沒有人告訴我打扮時用今年的清單呢？」得知在獲獎後尼爾其實後悔沒人跟他說，故為同義轉換，故也可以排除 C 選項。最後是 D 選項，D 選項為 Jimmy feels surprised that no one at the party dresses up as Chief Bogo.可以定位回 吉米在第三篇句尾說的「像是 Bogo 警長嗎？為什麼沒人選擇他？他看起來棒極了。」得知此為同義轉換，故也可以排除 D 選項。

答案：1. D　2. B

Unit 7

報考空服員

Letter ❶: the third round of ABC airline interview

Dear Cindy Lin,

We are writing this letter to inform you that we'd like you to participate in the third round of our interview, a week from today, which is Sep. 10th, 2018. Please find the enclosed files and print out all these forms. Do fill out all columns on each page before coming to the interview. If you have any questions, please let us know.

Sincerely yours,
Linda, HR personnel of ABC Airline

Line messages: discussions with friends

Cindy: Still can't believe that I'm going to the third interview. Third!!!

Rebecca: Congratulations!

Mary: It's not even close to getting hired.

Rebecca: Why can't you just feel happy for Cindy? The waiting process is so arduous.

Mary: In life, you just have to prepare for the worse. That's all.

Cindy: It's Ok. Perhaps Mary is right. You can't just be that lucky, right.

Rebecca: I know it's really is the place where you belong. Stay positive.

Cindy: I'm feeling grateful I'm making this far. Really.

Rebecca: I have faith in you.

Mary: I have faith in you, too... just not as strong as Rebecca's.

(ten minutes later)

Rebecca: Cindy? Are you still here?

Mary: I do hope it's not something I just said.

Cindy: My phone rang... it's a call from Best Airline.

Mary: What?

Cindy: Also the third round.

Rebecca: Some sour grapes perhaps, Mary?

Rebecca: Looking forward to hearing good news from you, Cindy.

Letter ❷: seeking pieces of advice from a professor

Dear Professor Lin,

I'm writing this letter to tell you that I got accepted by two major Airlines, Best Airline and ABC Airline. What a day! I'm beyond flattered. So, what should I do now? Best Airline is offering a competitive salary and bonuses after a six-month training. In addition, it's an international Airline. But it's like I'll never be home. ABC Airline is a domestic one close to home, and I can be around with my family more often. Plus, I heard from a colleague that working at ABC Airline is what you could ever hope for.

Looking at a contract FedExed by Best Airline makes me too thrilled to make a decision right now. Looking forward to the feedback from you.

Best regards,
Cindy Chen

1. What is the purpose of the e-mail from ABC Airline?
   (A) to ask Cindy to give them more personal information
   (B) to invite Cindy for an interview and request her to fill out some documents
   (C) to invite Cindy for an interview and give them more personal information
   (D) to inform Cindy about the process of the interview

2. Which of the followings best describes Mary's attitude toward Cindy's news?
   (A) She has a lot of confidence in Cindy.
   (B) She has doubts about whether Cindy will be hired.
   (C) She is not sure if working in the airline industry is the best for Cindy.
   (D) She does not think Cindy is well-prepared for the

interview.

3. Why does Rebecca say, "Some sour grapes perhaps, Mary"?

(A) She is being sarcastic about Mary's doubtful attitude toward Cindy

(B) She likes to eat sour grapes.

(C) She wants to know if Mary likes grapes.

(D) She is encouraging Mary to have more faith in Cindy.

4. Why did Cindy write the letter to Professor Lin?

(A) She wanted to inform the professor about some airline discounts.

(B) She wanted the professor to know the pros and cons of the two airlines.

(C) She wanted to receive some feedbacks regarding which airline to work for.

(D) She wanted the professor to celebrate with her for being accepted by the two airlines.

5. Why did Cindy write "What a day"?

(A) She went through a terrible day.

(B) She went through a lot that day and it's a unique day.

(C) Working all day long is too much for her.

(D) She did not do much that day.

中譯

單元 7 ▶ 報考空服員

信件 ❶：ABC 航空公司第三回合面試通知

親愛的辛蒂林—

我們寫這封信是想要告知您，我們想要您參加我們第三輪的面試，一星期後也就是 2018 年 9 月 10 日。請見附檔和列印出這些表格。在面試前，請填寫每頁所有欄位。如果你有任何問題請讓我們知道。

Sincerely yours,
琳達，ABC 航空人事部專員

Line 訊息：與友人的討論

辛蒂： 仍然不敢置信我要參加第三回合面試。第三！！！
麗蓓嘉： 恭喜！
瑪莉： 這根本還算不上錄取！
麗蓓嘉： 為什麼你就不能替辛蒂感到高興呢？等待過程很煎熬。

瑪莉：　人生中，你就是要做最壞的打算。就這樣。

辛蒂：　沒關係啦！可能瑪莉是對的。你就是不能那樣幸運，對吧！

麗蓓嘉：我知道這真的是你所屬的地方。保持正向。

辛蒂：　我覺得感恩我走了這麼遠了。真的。

麗蓓嘉：我對你有信念。

瑪莉：　我也對你有信念...只是沒有麗蓓嘉那麼多。

（十分鐘後...）

麗蓓嘉：辛蒂？你還在嗎？

瑪莉：　我希望不是因為我説的話。

辛蒂：　我的手機響了...是來自倍斯特航空公司。

瑪莉：　什麼？

辛蒂：　也是第三回合的面試。

麗蓓嘉：要來些酸葡萄嗎，瑪莉？

麗蓓嘉：期待你的好消息，辛蒂。

信件 ❷：向師長尋求意見

親愛的林教授，

我寫這封信是想告訴您，我錄取兩間主要航空公司了，倍斯特航空和 ABC 航空。真是個漫長的一天！我受寵若驚。所以我該怎麼做呢？倍斯特航空提供了受訓六個月後與市場行情相近（或高於市場行情的）薪資和獎金。此外，這是國際航空。但是這像是好像都不會回家一般。ABC 航空是國內航空，離家近而且我可以有更多與家人相處的時間。另外是我聽説一個在 ABC 航空工作的同事説在那裡工作是你所夢寐以求的。看著倍斯特航空用 FedExed 寄來的合約使我興奮到無法現在就做決定。期待您的回應。

Best regards,
辛蒂・陳

1. ABC 航空公司這封 e-mail 的目的是什麼呢？

   (A) 要求辛蒂給予他們更多個人資訊。

   (B) 邀請辛蒂參加面試且要求她要填一些文件。

   (C) 邀請辛蒂參加面試且給予更多個人資訊。

   (D) 告知辛蒂面試的流程。

2. 下列哪項最能描述瑪莉對辛蒂的消息的態度？

   (A) 她對於辛蒂有很多信心。

   (B) 她對於辛蒂是否能錄取抱持懷疑的態度。

   (C) 她不確定航空產業對於辛蒂是否是最好的。

   (D) 她不認為辛蒂對於面試有充分準備。

3. 為什麼麗蓓嘉說道「要來些酸葡萄嗎，瑪莉」？

   (A) 她是在諷刺瑪莉對辛蒂質疑的態度。

   (B) 她想要吃酸葡萄。

   (C) 她想要知道瑪莉是否喜歡葡萄。

   (D) 她鼓勵瑪莉要對辛蒂有更多信念。

4. 為什麼辛蒂要寫信給林教授呢？

   (A) 她想要告知教授關於航空公司的折扣。

   (B) 她想要教授知道兩間航空公司的優缺點。

   (C) 她想要收到更多關於在哪間航空公司的回應。

   (D) 她想要教授替她慶祝錄取兩間航空公司。

5. 為什麼辛蒂寫道「這真是漫長的一天」？

(A) 她經歷的可怕的一天。

(B) 她在那天經歷了很多，這是很特別的一天。

(C) 整天工作超過她的負荷了。

(D) 她那天沒做什麼。

答案：1.B　2.B　3.A　4.C　5.B

獵豹 ● ● ●

1.

- 由 e-mail 第一句 ...to participate in the third round of our interview，此句大意是通知 Cindy 參與第三輪的面試，換言之是邀請 Cindy 來面試。根據(B)，(C)，to invite 邀請，先鎖定可能的正確選項(B)，(C)。再掃描第二和第三句的大意 Please find the enclosed files and print out all these forms. Do fill out all columns...。大意類似(B)選項敘述的 request her to fill out some documents，所以選(B)。

2.

- 看到題目目光馬上搜尋 Mary，定位在第二篇 Line messages。

- 根據 Mary: It's not even close to getting hired，根本還沒

接近被雇用，能推測 Mary 對 Cindy 的消息的態度。Mary 對這個消息是懷疑的，懷疑的名詞及動詞是 doubt，因此選(B) She has doubts about whether Cindy will be hired。

3.

- 因為第二篇 Line messages 的主題與食物無關，可判斷"Some sour grapes perhaps, Mary?"的 grapes 不是指真的葡萄，所以先刪去(B) She likes to eat sour grapes，(C) She wants to know if Mary likes grapes。考慮上文 Mary 曾説 It's not even close to getting hired，暗示 Mary 對 Cindy 的消息是懷疑的，「感覺懷疑的」形容詞是 doubtful，所以選(A) She is being sarcastic about Mary's doubtful attitude toward Cindy。

4.

- 由信件第一句得知 Cindy 被兩間航空公司錄取，從第三句 So, what should I do now 可知道寫這封信的理由是關於她該選擇哪間公司，想詢問教授的意見。由信件最後一句 Looking forward to the feedback from you，更確定這封信是徵詢意見，因此選(C) She wanted to receive some feedbacks regarding which airline to work for。

5.

- 根據 What a day!的上文，即信件第一句，得知 Cindy 被兩間航空公司錄取。下文：I'm beyond flattered 是「受寵若驚」之意，因此 What a day!應該也是表達正向意義的感嘆語，才能維持這三句的連貫性。比較選項，(A)，(C)，(D)的大意都偏向負面，只有(B) She went through a lot that day and it's a unique day 的大意偏向正面，因此選(B)。

貓頭鷹 ● ● ●

1.
- 看到題目馬上判斷題型，由 purpose 一字得知屬於主題題型。

- 主題題型通常可由篇章開頭一～三句的大意解題。雖然(C)，(D)都有提及 interview，但(C)後半部的描述 give them more personal information 是錯誤的，考生要小心犯下過度詮釋的思考盲點，第二，三句只要求填表格，並沒有明說要 Cindy 給個人資料。而 e-mail 毫無提及面試過程，因此(D) to inform Cindy about the process of the interview 不能選。

2.
- 此題屬於推測題型，要從 Mary 對 Cindy 的消息的反應，推測出她的態度。第一個線索是 It's not even close to getting hired，甚至還談不上被雇用，可知道 Mary 有所質疑。Rebecca 對 Mary 的回應: Why can't you just feel happy for Cindy?也暗示 Mary 對 Cindy 的消息不是很高興。在下一句: In life, you just have to prepare for the worse，Mary 更強調她對此消息是悲觀的。不能選(C) She is not sure if working in the airline industry is the best for Cindy，因為(C)的描述沒有針對面試。不能選(D) She does not think

Cindy is well-prepared for the interview，因為 Mary 並未對 Cindy 是否準備好發表看法。

3.

- 此題屬於推測題型，也牽涉到 sour grapes 這個慣用語。要先確認 Mary 對 Cindy 的消息的態度，再推測出為何 Rebecca 對 Mary 說: Some sour grapes perhaps, Mary?。正確選項必須呼應主題，既然主題不是食物，grapes 就不是指真的葡萄，sour grapes 是隱喻「酸葡萄心理」。即見不得別人好的心理。Rebecca 使用疑問語氣也暗示她在諷刺 Mary 先前懷疑的態度。「諷刺的」形容詞是 sarcastic。

4.

- 題目使用 Why 疑問詞，事實上也是要考生推測 Cindy 寫這封信的目的。因此等同主題題型。通常第一段第一～四句會有主題線索。第四句 So, what should I do now?是線索，明示這封信的目的是徵詢教授看法。雖然第五句起對兩間航空公司的優缺點做出陳述，但不能選(B) She wanted the professor to know the pros and cons of the two airlines，因為這些優缺點只是提供給教授一些背景知識，暗示教授參考這些優缺點對 Cindy 該選哪間公司提出看法。由信件最後一句 Looking forward to the feedback from you，更確定這封信是徵詢意見，所以(C) She wanted to receive some feedbacks regarding which airline to work for 是最恰當的選項。

5.

- What 在句首除了導引疑問句，也能導引感嘆句。句尾是驚嘆號也是提醒考生這是感嘆句。這題牽涉兩個慣用語: What a day 及 I'm beyond flattered。What a day!的意思會因不同情境變化，不一定是正面或負面含義。有時 What a day 的含義可能是「真是糟糕的一天」，有時可能是「好棒的一天」。因此一定要從上下文推測含義。此篇的 What a day!的上文是 Cindy 被兩間航空公司錄取的好消息，下文：I'm beyond flattered 意為「受寵若驚」，表達正面情緒，所以這情境的 What a day 也是正面含義，有「真特別的一天」或「了不起的一天」之意。

浣熊 • • •

還有可能怎麼問

1. Which is stated about Cindy Chen?

(A) she works at an international Airline.

(B) she is making a transition about her job.

(C) She feels tentative about the third interviews at ABC Airline

(D) She's got two offers.

2. What is NOT the advantage of working at Best Airline?

(A) It is an international Airline.

(B) It offers a competitive salary.

(C) It offers a corner office.

(D) It gives candidates moments of thrill

1. 文中指出 Cindy Chen 的什麼事？

(A) 她在國際航空公司工作。

(B) 她在轉換工作跑道。

(C) 她對於 ABC 航空公司的第三輪面試感到躊躇不前。

(D) 她獲得兩個錄取通知。

2. 下列哪個項目並非在倍斯特航空公司工作的優點？

(A) 它是國際航空公司。

(B) 它提供與市場行情相近（或高於市場行情的）薪資。

(C) 它提供高級辦公室。

(D) 它給予候選人興奮的時刻。

解析

1. 題目詢問「文中指出 Cindy Chen 的什麼事？」先分別從四個選項來看。

- 選項 A 為 she works at an international Airline.，但綜觀全文可以得知 Cindy 是求職者正在參與航空公司面試，故此敘述為非，可以排除 A 選項。B 為 she is making a transition about her job.，但文章中未提及 Cindy 是否是在轉換跑道所以投遞航空公司的面試並參與面試，僅能從文章中得知她正參

與航空面試。故可以排除 B 選項。C 選項 She feels tentative about the third interviews at ABC Airline，可以定位回第一封信，Cindy 有收到 ABC Airline 寄的第三輪面試通知，但並未提到她對於 ABC 航空公司的第三輪面試感到躊躇不前。故可以排除 C 選項。D 選項為 She's got two offers，從文章中可以得知 Cindy 參加兩間航空公司的面試 ABC 和 BEST，第一封信中僅說 ABC Airline 寄的第三輪面試通知，第二篇的 line 訊息中可以得知錄取了 BEST 航空，最後一篇文章的信件中可以得知 Cindy 錄取了兩間公司的聘書，所以可以得知答案為 D 選項，她兩間都錄取了。

2. 題目詢問「下列哪個項目並非在倍斯特航空公司工作的優點？」先分別從四個選項來看。

- A 選項為 It is an international Airline.可以定位回最後一封信件，得知倍斯特航空為國際性航空公司，所以可以先排除 A 選項。B 選項為 It offers a competitive salary.同樣定位回最後一封信件可以得知它提供與市場行情相近（或高於市場行情的）薪資，故可以排除 B 選項。C 選項為 It offers a corner office.定位回最後一封信可以得知並未提到 corner office 故可以得知答案為 C 選項。D 選項為 It gives candidates moments of thrill 可以定位回最後一封信件，Cindy 說道 too thrilled to make a decision right now.可以得知 Cindy 收到合約後很興奮，此為同義轉換，此敘述在文章中提到為在倍斯特航空公司工作的優點故可以排除此選項。

答案：1. D　2. C

Unit 8

訂購書籍

Letter ❶: order

Dear Rick,

Thanks for your enquiry no. CX966200001, ISBN 978-xxx-9xxxx-y-z dated 10th of Oct 2018 regarding our bestselling book, Interpretation 101. Due to its high demand from several suppliers and dealers, we have already contacted our printing plant for further information to see if they can actually deliver printed books to us before 16th of Oct 2018. Since it's an international order, there is going to be another 14 days, including packaging and shipping. So the earliest day for you to actually get the Interpretation 101 is perhaps around 31th of Oct. Thanks again for placing such a high order. If you still have any questions, please let us know.

Best regards,
Ann Lin, assistant sales rep of ABC Publishing

Letter ❷: reply from the customer

Dear Ann,

Thanks for such a quick response. I was wondering whether it is possible for you to give us a discount since it's the order of such a large number. Plus, we do like other books of yours. After discussing with our managers, I believe it is highly likely that we are going to purchase other books from you. Looking forward to hearing from you.

Best regards,
Rick Wang

Letter ❸: reply from the company

Dear Rick,

I've asked our boss about the discount. With a bulk order of around 500 books, we normally would give suppliers 35% off. Since it's with you, we would love to give you more discounts. In this case, we are going to offer you 40% off. In addition, if the order exceeds 750 books and 1000 books, it is going to be 45% off and 50% off respectively. Really feeling excited about further purchase.

Best regards,
Ann Lin

1. Why does Rick Wang write, "… it is highly likely that we are going to purchase other books from you"?

   (A) He wants to know what other books they can buy.

   (B) He wants to know what other books will be published.

   (C) He hopes the publisher will ship more books as soon as possible.

   (D) He hopes to receive more discounts with more purchases.

2. Why did ABC Publishing contact the printing plant?

   (A) to know whether the printing plant could ship the books before a certain date

   (B) to know the day the printing plant will finish the printing process

   (C) to ask the printing plant to send the books on Oct. 31th

   (D) to ask the printing plant to contact Rick directly

3. Which of the following is the closest to the phrase "a bulk order"?

(A) an order that is shipped in a large package

(B) an order of a few products

(C) an order of many products

(D) an order that is shipped internationally

4. What does the sentence, "Since it's with you, we would love to give you more discounts" indicate?

(A) The publisher would like to give Rick an extra favor.

(B) Ann enjoys hanging out with Rick.

(C) If Rick comes to visit the publisher, he might receive more discounts.

(D) The publisher is pleased with doing business with Rick in the past.

5. What might Rick Wang do next?

(A) requesting a catalogue from the publisher

(B) placing another order for other books

(C) asking for more discounts

(D) asking when he will receive the books

6 填空式閱讀

7 單篇閱讀

7 雙篇、三篇閱讀

模擬試題

單元 8 ▶ 訂購書籍

信件 ❶：訂單

親愛的瑞克，

謝謝您詢問編號 CX966200001, ISBN 978-xxx-9xxxx-y-z，於 2018 年 10 月 10 日開始販售的暢銷書，口譯 101。由於幾個供應商和經銷商的高度需求，我們已經聯繫了印刷廠詢問進一步資訊，看是否他們能在 2018 年 10 月 16 日將印好的書籍交給我們。既然這是國際訂單，將會需要額外 14 個工作天，包含包裝和運送。所以你實際上能最快拿到口譯 101 書籍可能是 10 月 31 日。再次感謝您下了這樣高額量的訂單。如果你還有任何問題，請讓我們知道。

致上最高的問候，
安・林，ABC出版公司銷售助理

信件 ❷：客戶信件回覆

親愛的安，

謝謝您這麼快的回覆。我在想既然是這麼大量的訂單，您是否有可能給予我們更多折扣。外加，我們的確喜歡你的其他書籍。在與我們經理討論後，我相信我們極有可能再向您訂購其他書。期待聽到您的消息。

致上最高的問候，
瑞克・王

信件 ❸：公司信件回覆

親愛的瑞克，

我已經詢問我們老闆關於折扣的事。訂購近 500 本這樣的大量訂單，我們通常會給予供應商 65 折。但既然是您的話，我們會想給您更多的折扣。在這樣的情況下，我們將給您 6 折的折扣。此外，如果訂購量超過 750 本和 1000 本的話，將會享有分別是 55 折和 5 折的折扣。對於您進一步的訂購感到興奮。

致上最高的問候，
安・林

1. 為什麼瑞克・王寫到「我相信我們極有可能再向您訂購其他書。」呢？

    (A) 他想要知道他們還能買其他哪些書。

    (B) 他想要知道其他書會於何時出版。

    (C) 他希望出版商能盡快運送更多書籍。

    (D) 他希望更多購買量能收到更多折扣。

2. 為什麼 ABC 出版商聯繫印刷廠？

    (A) 在特定日期前，知道印刷廠可能運送書籍。

    (B) 知道印刷廠在哪天會完成印刷流程。

    (C) 要求印刷廠在 10 月 31 日寄送書籍。

    (D) 要求印刷廠直接向瑞克聯繫。

3. 下列哪個與「大量的訂單」的片語意思最相近呢？

   (A) 以大包裹運送的訂單。

   (B) 幾個產品的訂單。

   (C) 許多產品的訂單。

   (D) 由國際運送的訂單。

4. 這句「既然是您的話，我們會想給您更多的折扣。」指的是什麼？

   (A) 出版商想要給瑞克額外的優惠。

   (B) 安喜歡跟瑞克混在一起。

   (C) 如果瑞克拜訪出版商，他可能會收到更多的折扣。

   (D) 過去出版商對和瑞克做生意感到滿意。

5. 瑞克·王可能接下來會做什麼呢？

   (A) 向出版商要求目錄。

   (B) 下另一筆訂單訂別的書。

   (C) 詢問更多折扣。

   (D) 詢問何時他會收到書。

答案：1.D　2.A　3.C　4.A　5.B

獵豹 ● ● ●

1.

- 根據第二篇信件，第二句，I was wondering whether it is possible for you to give us a discount since it's the order of such a large number 得知此信件的主題或目的。

- 從主題句能推測 Rick 寫這句的動機，他提出很可能會買其它書，是希望對方能給折扣，所以選(D)。

2.

- 看到題目目光馬上搜尋 printing plant。定位在第一篇信件第二句。

- 因為 see 有「瞭解」之意，to see 之後很可能接著描述聯絡印刷廠的原因。...to see if they can actually deliver printed books to us before 16th of Oct 2018，大意是出版社想瞭解是否能在十月十六日之前寄送書。所以選(A)。

3.

- 看到題目目光馬上搜尋 bulk order，定位在第三篇第二句 With a bulk order of around 500 books。

- 除了 500 暗示 a bulk order 是一筆數量很多的訂單，也考慮第三篇是回覆第二篇的信件。對照第二篇第二句，...since it's the order of such a large number，更確定正確選項是(C) an order of many products。

4.

- 看到題目目光馬上鎖定 more discounts 及指定句子的前後兩句。

- Since it's with you，既然是您的話，暗示對 Rick 有特殊優待。「給優待」或「給好處」的片語是 give... a favor，因此選 (A)。

5.

- 首先綜合第二篇及第三篇的主題的共同點，是關於大筆訂單是否能獲得折扣。

- 由第二篇 ...it is highly likely that we are going to purchase other books from you，我們極有可能再向您訂購其他書。 推測出 Rick 下一個動作是再下一筆訂單，故選(B)。

貓頭鷹 ● ● ●

1.

- 此題屬於推測題型，因為正確選項必須呼應主題，答案可由主題句推測。解題過程要避免過度詮釋選項的敘述。例如(A) He wants to know what other books they can buy.和(B) He wants to know what other books will be published. 不能選，因為 Rick 的信件毫無詢問其它書籍或未來將出版的書。

- (C) 選項的 ship more books 與信件的主題無關，也無提及運送書籍方面的細節，因此要馬上刪除。

2.

- 此題屬於細節題型，只須定位出 contact 及 printing plant，再搭配換句話說的技巧，很快能找出答案。

- 正確選項(A) 用類似字將 to see if they can actually deliver printed books to us before... 重述。考生除了要知道 see 有「瞭解，想知道」之意，也須知道連接詞 if 在此是「是否」。表達「是否」的連接詞還有 whether。而在信件，「寄送」的動詞是 deliver，(A)選項將 deliver 改成類似字 ship。before 16th of Oct 2018 改寫成 before a certain date。

3.

- 此題測試哪個選項的意思最接近 a bulk order 這個名詞片語。

- 因為雙篇章或三篇章間互相呼應。線索除了在最接近 a bulk order 的下文，即 around 500 books，也能將第二篇的主題句當作線索，第三篇是針對第二篇的主題句做出回應。

- a large number 是「很多的數量」。注意不能選(A) an order that is shipped in a large package。雖然(A)也使用 large，但修飾 package，(A)選項意思是「一筆用大型包裹或包裝運送

6 填空式閱讀

7 單篇閱讀

7 雙篇、三篇閱讀

模擬試題

的訂單」。

4.

- 題目指定的句子的前一句指出 500 本書有 35%折扣，下一句描述願意給 Rick 40%折扣，由此可見給他特別優待。

- 選項(A) The publisher would like to give Rick an extra favor 將 more discounts 改寫成 extra favor。extra favor 有「額外優待」，「額外好處」之意。

- 雖然(C)的第二個子句 he might receive more discounts 提及更多折扣，注意不能選(C)，因為(C)的第一個子句 If Rick comes to visit the publisher，假如 Rick 拜訪出版社，在全文均無提及。

5.

- 此題須綜合至少兩個篇章的主題，再推測 Rick 讀完 Ann 的回信後，合理的下一個動作是什麼。

- (A)不能選，因為三封信都沒提到目錄（catalogue），刪除(C) asking for more discounts，因為 Rick 已經在第二封信要求更多折扣。刪除(D) asking when he will receive the books，因為在第一封信，Ann 已經交代 Rick 能收到書的日期。

還有可能怎麼問

1. Which is NOT stated about Interpretation 101?

(A) Its demand is high among suppliers and dealers.

(B) It's a bestselling book.

(C) Rick will get the discount.

(D) Rick will get the reprinted version sooner than Oct 31

2. What is offered by ABC Publishing?

(A) It provides shipping service.

(B) It prints books for major suppliers and dealers.

(C) It teaches interpreters skills necessary for their job-hunting.

(D) It offers a significant discount for a bulk order.

 中譯

1. 文中沒有指出口譯 101 的什麼事？

(A) 它在供應商和經銷商中需求量高。

(B) 它是暢銷書。

(C) 瑞奇會得到折扣。

(D) 瑞奇會於比 10 月 31 日前更早收到再版的印刷版書。

2. ABC 出版社提供什麼服務？

(A) 它提供運送服務。

(B) 它替主要供應商和經銷商印製書籍。

(C) 它教導口譯員找工作所需的技能。

(D) 它提供相當的折扣給大量訂單。

解析

1. 題目詢問「文中沒有指出口譯 101 的什麼事？」先分別從四個選項來看。

- A 選項為 Its demand is high among suppliers and dealers. 可以定位回第一封信件 Due to its high demand from several suppliers and dealers, we have already contacted our printing plant for further information to see if they can actually deliver printed books to us before 16th of Oct 2018.得知此為同義轉換，故可以排除 A 選項。選項 B 為 It's a bestselling book.同樣定位回第一封信件可以得知此為同義轉換，故可以排除此選項。

- C 選項為 Rick will get the discount.可以定位回最後一封信 Ann 寫道 Since it's with you, we would love to give you more discounts.得知 Rick 有得到折扣，故可以排除此選項。

D 選項為 Rick will get the reprinted version sooner than Oct 31.定位回第一封信件可以得知不可能於 10 月 31 日前就拿到再版書，故答案為 D 選項。

2. 題目詢問「ABC出版社提供什麼服務？」先分別從四個選項來看。

- **A 選項**為 It provides shipping service.可以定位回第一封信，可以得知公司有請印刷廠送書但並未說公司有運送服務，故可以排除 A 選項。**B 選項**為 It prints books for major suppliers and dealers.同樣定位回第一封信得知並未提到公司有印刷書籍且替主要供應商和經銷商印製書籍，僅提到公司口譯書籍在供應商和經銷商中需求量高故可以排除 B 選項。

- **C 選項**為 It teaches interpreters skills necessary for their job-hunting.同樣定位回第一封信件，可以得知公司有口譯書籍且為暢銷書，但並未提到公司有在教導口譯員找工作所需的技能，故可以排除此選項。**D 選項**為 It offers a significant discount for a bulk order.可以定位回最後一封信，安寫道 With a bulk order of around 500 books, we normally would give suppliers 35% off. Since it's with you, we would love to give you more discounts.，從這部分可以得知大量訂書有折扣，故答案為 D 選項。

Unit 9

內部升遷名單

Meeting

Boss: There is going to be an adjustment since Judy is going to be **transferred** to our branch office. The promotion will come into effect on 9th of July 2018, which means I'm in desperate need of finding a person who can do her job. I do need Sales Department to provide me with a list of candidates. Each with the evaluation sheets from HR managers. <u>meeting adjourned</u>

Line messages

Jack: <u>I don't have time for this.</u>

Mary: What?

Kim: The list? Just randomly give him the list, we'll just be fine.

Mary: I just don't think it's gonna be that easy.

Jack: Can anyone just write long evaluation sheets and hand them to him before tomorrow morning?

Mary: There is no way that I have time to do that. I received a letter from our end users that the shipment was delayed.

Kim: Why did Judy make that move, transferring to the branch office?

Jack:	Perhaps it's because our boss is too demanding.
Kim:	Oh! Lord.
Jack, Mary:	What?
Kim:	The other shipment is delayed, too. We are getting a penalty for the losses caused. Apparently, there is going to be a typhoon, which will hamper our product release in Tokyo on Wednesday morning.
Jack:	Kim your phone just rang.
Kim:	(I'm not busy enough?) Hey... this is she.
Kim:	Thank God. HR Department has all the papers and evaluation sheets ready.
Mary:	What a relief.
Jack:	we owe them Big!
Kim:	That's not all... we are all on the list.
Mary, Jack:	What?

Internal Bulletin Board

Candidates being considered for filling in Judy's position

Name	Descriptions	Time/experience
Kim	Sales Rep	4 years
Mary	Sales Rep	3 years
Jack	Sales Rep	3 years
Sally	Assistant Sales Rep	1 year

Note: The person getting promoted to the position will receive a 20% increase in salary

1. Which of the followings is the closest to "meeting adjourned"?

    (A) Do you enjoy the meeting?

    (B) I don't like the meeting.

    (C) Let's call it a day for the meeting.

    (D) The meeting went well.

2. "Jack: I don't have time for this." What does "this" refer to?

    (A) working on a list

    (B) working on evaluation sheets

    (C) doing Judy's job

    (D) writing a letter

3. Which can be inferred about Judy's motive for transferring to the branch office?

    (A) She did not maintain a good relationship with her boss.

    (B) Her previous boss expected too much from her

working performance

(C) She did not get along with her co-workers.

(D) The branch office is closer to her house.

4. Why does Kim say, "Oh! Lord"?

(A) She tries to pray.

(B) She's a Christian.

(C) She's shocked about the delayed shipment.

(D) She's relieved that the problem is finally solved.

5. "Jack: we owe them Big!"—What does Jack imply?

(A) The HR department owes his department some evaluation sheets.

(B) He owes some money to the employees in the HR department.

(C) The tables of the evaluation sheets are too big.

(D) His department owes the HR department a big favor.

6 填空式閱讀

7 單篇閱讀

7 雙篇、三篇閱讀

模擬試題

中譯

1. 下列哪個項目最接近「會議結束」？

   (A) 你喜歡會議嗎？

   (B) 我不喜歡會議。

   (C) 今天會議就到此為止。

   (D) 會議進行的順利。

2. 「傑克：我沒時間耗在這上面。」，「這」指的是什麼呢？

   (A) 正在處理清單事宜。

   (B) 正在處理評估表單。

   (C) 做茱蒂的工作。

   (D) 寫信。

3. 哪項可以推測出關於茱蒂調往分公司的動機是什麼呢？

   (A) 她與老闆並未維持良好的關係。

   (B) 她前老闆對於她工作表現要求過多。

   (C) 她與同事相處不來。

   (D) 分公司離她家較近。

4. 為什麼金說，「喔！我的天啊」？

   (A) 她嘗試禱告。

   (B) 她是基督徒。

   (C) 她對於送貨延遲感到吃驚。

   (D) 她對於問題最終解決了感到如釋重負。

5.「傑克：我們欠他們一個大人情」—傑克指的是什麼呢？

(A) 人事部門欠他們部門一些評估表單。

(B) 他欠人事部門的員工們一些錢。

(C) 評估表單的表格太大。

(D) 他的部門欠人事部門一個大人情。

答案：1. C　2.A　3.B　4.C　5. D

單元 9 ▶ 內部升遷名單

會議

老闆： 自從茉蒂調到我們分公司後，將會做出調整。這個升遷會於 2018 年 7 月 9 日生效，意味著我迫切找到能替補她工作的人選。我需要銷售部門提供給我候選人列表。每份均附上人事經理的評估單。會議結束。

Line 訊息

傑克： 我沒時間管這個。

瑪莉： 什麼？

金： 那份單子嗎？只要隨便給他個表，我們就沒事了。

瑪莉： 我不覺得會這麼簡單。

傑克： 有任何人可以只寫下長的評估表單，明早前把它們交給老闆嗎？

瑪莉： 我不可能有時間去做這個。我收到我們使用者對於貨物運送延遲的信件。

金： 為什麼茉蒂要有此舉，調到分公司呢？

傑克： 或許是因為老闆要求太多了。

金： 嘔！天啊。

傑克、瑪莉： 什麼？

金： 其他的運送也延遲了。我們將因此而要受到對對方引起損失的懲罰。顯然有個颱風，將危害到我們在星期三早上東京產品發佈。

傑克： 金，你的電話剛響。

金： （我還不夠忙嗎？）嘿...我就是金。

金： 謝天謝地。人事部門把所有文件和評估表都準備好了。

瑪莉：	真是鬆了一口氣。
傑克：	我們欠他們一個大人情！
金：	還不只這樣...我們都在表上。
瑪莉、傑克：	什麼？

內部公告欄

被考慮替補茱蒂職位的候選人

名字	描述	時間/經驗
金	銷售業務	4 年
瑪莉	銷售業務	3 年
傑克	銷售業務	3 年
莎莉	銷售業務助理	1 年

註：因此職缺而升遷者，薪資會增加 20%。

獵豹 ● ● ●

1.

- 首先注意 meeting adjourned 這個片語位於第一個篇章 Meeting 結尾。此片語的上一句是老闆交代事情，沒有牽涉個人情緒，因此(A)，(B)均刪除，因為這些選項描述有 enjoy，don't like 等情緒方面的動詞。(D) The meeting went well

是老闆對會議的正面評價，與 meeting adjourned 的上一句不連貫，也刪除(D)。故選(C)。

2.

- 看到題目目光馬上鎖定在"I don't have time for this"的代名詞 this，因這句是第二篇章的第一句，馬上往第一篇章搜尋 this 的先行詞。最接近 this 且意思能搭配 have time 的單數先行詞是此句 list：I do need Sales Department to provide me with a list of candidates。又參考這句的下文，Kim 的回應：The list?，更確定答案選(A) working on a list。

3.

- 看到題目目光馬上搜尋 Judy 和 transfer。雖然第一篇章第一句有提及 Judy 和 transfer，但未提及她轉任的原因，所以往第二篇章搜尋其它線索。

- 第二篇章的線索為 Kim: Why did Judy make that move, transferring to the branch office?及對此疑問句的回應：Perhaps it's because our boss is too demanding，對照選項找尋與此回應大意類似的描述，因此選(B)。

4.

- 搜尋"Oh! Lord"的上下文是否有為何 Kim 這麼説的原因。

- 在下文 Kim 解釋: The other shipment is delayed, too，對照選項找尋與此句大意類似的描述，所以選(C)。

5.

- 看到題目目光馬上鎖定在 we owe them Big!的代名詞 them。

- We 指的是 Jack 自己的部門同事。再往上文搜尋 them 代替的先行詞。由 Kim: Thank God. HR Department has all the papers and evaluation sheets ready 得知 them 指的是 HR Department 的同事。

- 對照代名詞指涉的先行詞，就能判斷正確選項是(D) His department owes the HR department a big favor。

 貓頭鷹 ● ● ●

1.

- 此題要選出 meeting adjourned 的類似詞。meeting adjourned 是宣佈會議結束的慣用語。即使不熟悉慣用語，也能以片語所在的位置（整篇結尾）及上文大意，推測出答案。正確選項 (C) Let's call it a day for the meeting。Let's call it a day 也是慣用語，「到此為止」之意。

2.

- 如果題目指定的句子包含代名詞，代名詞一定是解題線索。且多重篇章的題目要注意代名詞指涉的對象可能在上一個篇章。例如"I don't have time for this"的 this，呼應第一篇章裡，老闆交代的做表格這件事。另外，由於第二篇是同事間的 Line 對話，藉由同事間的回應，也能找出解題線索。在 I don't have time for this 下兩句，Kim 就對 Jack 回應：The list?。

3.

- 題目指定的句子包含專有名詞，例如人名，地名，公司名稱等，一定是要先搜尋的線索字，此題的線索字是 Judy。疑問句也常是解題線索，正確選項常將該疑問句的回答換句話說，在第二篇章 Kim 問了為何 Judy 要轉任到分公司之後，Jack 回答她: Perhaps it's because our boss is too demanding，demanding 是「苛求的」，換言之老闆要求太多，和 (B) ...expected too much... 意思是接近的。

4.

- 此題屬於推測題型，要從 Kim 說出 Oh! Lord 的情境找出她這麼說的原因。Oh! Lord 是比較偏口語化的感嘆詞，類似 My God 或 My Gosh。藉由下文 The other shipment is delayed, too 得知原因是貨運延遲。雖然 Lord 有「上帝」之意，但第二篇章的主題與宗教無關，因此不能選(A) She tries to pray，她嘗試祈禱，和 (B) She's a Christian，她是基督徒。

5.

- 此題牽涉慣用語:We owe them big，owe 是「虧欠」之意。因為此句上下文都沒牽涉到金錢，此句不是欠款，而是「我們欠他們一個大人情」。正確選項 (D) His department owes the HR department a big favor 將此慣用語改寫成「他的部門欠人資部門一個大恩惠」。另外，搭配刪去法解題。只須掃描(B)，(C) 的主詞:He，the tables 就馬上刪去，因為不符合代名詞 we 和 them 指涉的先行詞，we 和 them 分別指 Jack 自己部門的同事和 HR Department 的同事。

浣熊 ● ● ●

還有可能怎麼問

1. In the meeting section, the word "transferred" in line 2 is closest in meaning to?
   (A) fulfilled.
   (B) moved.
   (C) succeeded.
   (D) transfused.

2. What is NOT indicated in the article?
   (A) Km is swamped with work.
   (B) the product release will be impeded.
   (C) there is going to be a replacement for Judy.
   (D) Sally has the slightest chance of getting promoted because she is just an assistant.

中譯

1. 在會議的部分，在第二行「轉移」這個字最貼近於？

6 填空式閱讀

7 單篇閱讀

7 雙篇、三篇閱讀

模擬試題

(A) 履行。

(B) 移至。

(C) 成功。

(D) 傳遞。

2. 文中沒有指出下列哪個項目？

(A) 金對於工作應接不暇。

(B) 產品發佈會受到阻礙。

(C) 將會有茱蒂的替補人選。

(D) 莎莉因為僅是個助理所以獲得升遷的機會很渺茫。

解析

1. 題目詢問「在會議的部分，在第一行「轉移」這個字最貼近於？」先分別從四個選項來看。

- A 選項為 fulfilled，有履行諾言、執行、服從等意思，同義字有 perform, do, execute, finish.。，與題目字彙意思不相符，故可以排除 A 選項。B 選項為 move，有移動和移至…的意思，同義字有 relocate, shift, transfer 等等，此意思與題目的字彙 transferred 同，故答案為選項 B。

- C 選項為 succeeded，有成功、接連發生、繼任和接連發生等意思，同義字有 achieve, prosper, thrive, flourish 等等，與題目字彙意思不相符，故可以排除 C 選項。D 選項為 transfused，有輸血和注射的意思，與題目字彙意思不相符，

故可以排除 D 選項。

2. 題目詢問「文中沒有指出下列哪個項目」先分別從四個選項來看。

- A 選項為 Km is swamped with work.可以得知「金對於工作應接不暇。」。從與金有關對話話進行尋找，可以得知她很忙碌故與選項表達的敘述相符，故可以排除 A 選項。

- B 選項為 the product release will be impeded.對應到後來金說的話，此敘述為同義轉換，表示在週三早上東京的產品發佈會受阻，故可以排除此選項。

- C 選項為 there is going to be a replacement for Judy.，定位回一開頭 Boss 說的那段話可以推測出會尋找人替補 Judy 的職缺，此為同義轉換，故也可以排除 C 選項。

- D 選項為 Sally has the slightest chance of getting promoted because she is just an assistant.定位回最後一篇的布告欄，從中可以看到公告內容跟被考慮為替補 Judy 職缺的名單，可以看到 Sally 的名字跟年資，但無法從表格中推斷出莎莉因為僅是個助理所以獲得升遷的機會很渺茫，故答案為 D 選項，因為 D 選項在文章中未提及。

答案：1. B　2. D

Unit 10

運送動物

Letter ❶：rhinos' condition during shipping

Dear Mr. Smith

I'm writing this letter to inform you that there are some problems in the delivery. The truck was 2 hours late, which made the delivery a lot worse than we thought. When our staff arrived at the scene, the truck was not what we asked for. It was way too small for two rhinos even though they were sedated. We couldn't risk it. In addition, we had to wait there for another two hours for the giant truck to arrive. What's worse, there was terrible traffic on the highway, which took us another 2 hours. By the time we reached the destination, Best Zoo, the door was closed with a notice stating "Open tomorrow at 2 p.m.". We gave the delivery man US 200 as a compensation. We shipped the rhinos back to Best Conservation Center for a temporary stay. I'll contact the staff there tomorrow morning for further details. Really sorry for everything.

Best regards,
Jenny Chen

Letter ❷：letter from Animal Conservation Center

Dear Jenny,

This is Mark Wang from Best Conservation Center. I'm writing this letter to let you know that we won't be able to ship the rhinos tomorrow morning for you. We're currently running out of anesthetics. I've been told that the rhinos were in the worst condition. Their teeth were bleeding badly, and there was some vomiting involved. Their blood pressure was quite low. They need constant care. Under this circumstance, we might as well ship them a week from now, which is July 20, to Best Zoo. I do need you to give me Mr. Smith's contact information. I do think perhaps by having a little talk to our doctors here, he will understand this is totally under extenuating circumstances.

Best regards,
Mark Wang

1. Which of the followings is NOT one of the problems during the delivery?

(A) The truck was too small.

(B) It took extra hours for the right truck to arrive.

(C) The delivery was stuck in a traffic jam.

(D) The truck driver took the wrong route.

2. Why does Mark Wang write, "...we won't be able to

ship the rhinos..."?

(A) Because Best Conservation Center does not have enough anesthetics

(B) Because the rhinos feel anxious

(C) Because they don't have the right truck

(D) Because the zoo won't be opened tomorrow

3. What happened to the rhinos?

(A) They felt restless.

(B) They were in terrible physical condition.

(C) They hated long travel.

(D) They were trapped in a small truck.

4. Which of the followings is the closest to "extenuating circumstances"?

(A) an exciting situation

(B) a situation in which there is no solution

(C) a situation that provides an excuse for an action

(D) a condition that hurts wild animals

5. Why does Mark Wang want to know Mr. Smith's contact information?

(A) He wants to tell Mr. Smith about what happened during the delivery.

(B) He wants to arrange a talk between Mr. Smith and the vets at the center.

(C) He wants Mr. Smith to take back the rhinos.

(D) He wants to talk to Mr. Smith directly about the rhinos' condition.

中譯

單元 10 ▶ 運送動物

信件 ❶：犀牛運送狀況

親愛的史密斯先生您好

我寫這封信是想要告知您在運送過程中出現了幾個問題。卡車晚了兩小時，使得運送過程比想像中遭很多。當我們的員工抵達現場時，卡車並非我們要求的。對於乘載兩隻犀牛來説，太小了，即便他們都處於鎮靜劑狀態。我們無法冒這個險。更糟的是，在高速公路上交通很擁擠，這也使得我們多花了額外兩小時的時間。當我們抵達目的地，倍斯特動物園時，門上寫著「於明天下午兩點開門」。於是我們給了運送元 200 美元作為補償。我們將犀牛運送回倍斯特保護中心，讓犀牛作短暫停留。我明早會聯繫那裡的員工詢問進一步資訊。對所有事情感到抱歉。

致上最高的問候
珍妮・陳

6
填空式閱讀

7
單篇閱讀

7
雙篇、三篇閱讀

模擬試題

信件 **②**：動物保護中心來信

親愛的珍妮

我是倍斯特保育中心的馬克・王。我寫這封信是想要您知道我們明早無法替您運送犀牛。我們目前用完鎮定劑了。我已被告知犀牛在最糟的情況。牠們的牙齒流血流得很嚴重，還包含有些嘔吐情況。牠們的血壓也相當低。牠們需要悉心照護。在這種情況下，我們可能要從現在起算一周後，也就是 7 月 20 日，才能送至倍斯特動物園。我需要你給我史密斯先生的連絡資訊。我想可能藉由和我們的醫生有些談話，他會了解到這是在情有可原的情況下。

致上最高的問候
馬克・王

1. 下列哪個敘述不是運送期間的問題之一呢？

   (A) 卡車太小。

   (B) 花費了額外小時的時間型號符合的卡車才抵達。

   (C) 運送時受困於擁擠的交通。

   (D) 卡車司機行駛錯誤路線。

2. 為什麼馬克・王寫道「...我們無法運送犀牛...」？

   (A) 因為倍斯特保護中心沒有足夠的鎮定劑。

   (B) 因為犀牛感到焦慮。

   (C) 因為他們沒有合適的卡車。

   (D) 因為動物園明天沒有營業。

3. 犀牛發生了什麼事？

(A) 牠們感到煩躁。

(B) 牠們處於糟的身體狀況。

(C) 牠們討厭長途旅程。

(D) 牠們困於小卡車中。

4. 下列哪個敘述最接近「情有可原的請況」？

(A) 令人興奮的情況。

(B) 無解的情況。

(C) 對於行為能提供藉口的情況。

(D) 可能傷害到野生動物的情況。

5. 為什麼馬克・王想要知道史密斯先生的連絡資訊呢？

(A) 他想要告訴史密斯先生在運送期間發生了什麼事。

(B) 他想要替史密斯先生和保護中心的獸醫安排談話。

(C) 他想要史密斯先生帶回犀牛。

(D) 他想要直接與史密斯先生談論犀牛的情況。

答案：1. D　2.A　3.B　4.C　5.B

獵豹

1.

- 先在第一篇章掃描(A)的形容詞 small，定位在第四句 It was way too small...。

- 根據 It was way too small... 下兩句句首都有轉折詞 In addition 和 What's worse，可知下兩句是延伸第四句的細節，分別提到 another two hours 和 terrible traffic，呼應 (B) It took extra hours for the right truck to arrive.及(C) The delivery was stuck in a traffic jam，因此選(D)。

2.

- 看到題目目光馬上搜尋 we won't be able to ship the rhinos...，定位在第二篇章第二句。

- 往第三句搜尋是否有表達不能運送犀牛的原因。第三句 We're currently running out of anesthetics 大意是「我們現在用完了麻醉劑」。(A)選項 ...does not have enough anesthetics 大意類似，因此選(A)。

3.

- 關於犀牛的狀況，第一個線索句是第二篇的第四句 the rhinos were in the worst condition，犀牛處於最糟的狀況。

- 第五和六句提供更多細節: Their teeth were bleeding badly, and there was some vomiting involved. Their blood pressure was quite low，都是關於犀牛生理上的問題，因此刪去(A)，(C)，因為(A)，(C)都是描述情緒問題。「生理的」形容詞是 physical，故選(B) They were in terrible physical condition。

4.

- 因為第二篇的主文解釋犀牛處於最糟的生理狀況，circumstances 也是狀況之意，可推測 Mark Wang 想讓 Mr. Smith 瞭解犀牛的狀況。extenuating circumstances

- 先刪去(A) an exciting situation，再刪去(B) a situation in which there is no solution，因為第二篇有明示一星期之後可以運送犀牛，與(B)的大意抵觸。也刪去(D) a condition that hurts wild animals，因為 wild animals 泛指所有野生動物，不符合主題。因此正確選項是(C) a situation that provides an excuse for an action。

5.

- 看到題目目光馬上鎖定在 contact information。

- 定位 contact information 在第二篇倒數第二句，下一句馬上描述 Mark Wang 想知道 Mr. Smith 的聯絡資訊的原因: by having a little talk to our doctors here...，他想聯絡 Mr. Smith，讓他跟倍斯特保育中心的獸醫談話。而獸醫是 vet，因此選 (B) He wants to arrange a talk between Mr. Smith and the vets at the center。

 貓頭鷹 ● ● ●

1.

- 題目問哪一個選項不是運送期間的問題，屬於細節題型。須逐一將有提到的細節刪去。先確定運送方面的問題比較可能在哪一個篇章描述，根據第一篇章的第一句: I'm writing this letter to inform you that there are some problems in the delivery，確定相關細節都在第一篇。

- 定位出其中一個有描述的細節後，如此題先定位 small，再掃描是否有轉折詞，轉折詞後常有答案的線索。In addition，此外，及 What's worse，更糟的是，這些轉折詞 都暗示考生它們引導的句子也是敘述運送方面的問題。

2.

- 此題正確選項只須在下文找出理由句，再運用換句話說的技巧，很快能確定答案。

- run out of... 是「用完」之意。用刪去法也能解題。注意 (B) 選項的 anxious 是「焦慮的」，在第二篇毫無提及，故刪除 (B)，刪除 (C) Because they don't have the right truck，因為卡車不適合，在第一篇已經提出。刪除(D) Because the zoo won't be opened tomorrow，動物園明天不會開，第二篇也毫無提及，事實上，第一篇倒數第四句有明示"Open tomorrow at 2 p.m."，明天下午兩點營業，因此(D)選項的敘述是錯誤的。

3.

- 正確選項(B) They were in terrible physical condition 總結了第二篇第四～六句的大意。

- (A) 的 restless 是「坐立不安的」，(C) They hated long travel，他們討厭長程旅行，這兩個選項都牽涉犀牛的心理層次，在第二篇完全沒描述。(D) They were trapped in a small truck 不能選，因為雖然第一篇有提到卡車太小，並沒有提及犀牛被困住。

4.

- 正確選項(C) a situation that provides an excuse for an action 中，an excuse 指的是犀牛身體狀況很糟的情況，an action 指的是一星期之後才能運送犀牛這個動作。

- 動詞 extenuate 有 to offer excuses for...，提供理由或藉口之意，或「辯解」。在 under extenuating circumstances 這個片語中，extenuating 是現在分詞轉成形容詞使用，under extenuating circumstances 形成慣用語，是「情有可原的狀況」。

5.

- 此題是詢問理由的細節題。也須知道獸醫的單字是

veterinarian，可縮寫為 vet。

• 運用換句話說的技巧，很快能確定答案。by having a little talk to our doctors here... 換言之是 Mark Wang 想安排 Mr. Smith 跟保育中心的獸醫談話，由獸醫解釋延遲運送犀牛這件事，是情有可原的。he will understand this is totally under extenuating circumstances 這句的代名詞 this 指的就是上文提出的一星期之後才能運送犀牛這件事。

還有可能怎麼問

1. Why was the first e-mail written?

   (A) to demonstrate her enthusiasm for the job.

   (B) to offer a shoulder to cry on.

   (C) to tell her colleague that she was in a dilemma during the delivery

   (D) to notify delivery problems first hand

2. When will likely to be the date for rhinos to safely arrive at Best Zoo?

(A) July 14 2 p.m. after Best Zoo opens

(B) July 14

(C) July 15

(D) July 20

中譯

1. 為什麼寫第一封信件？

(A) 顯示她對於工作的熱忱。

(B) 提供患難時的慰藉。

(C) 告訴她同事在運送期間她陷入兩難。

(D) 第一步告知運送問題。

2. 何時可能是犀牛能安全抵達倍斯特動物園的日期呢？

(A) 7 月 14 日下午 2 點在倍斯特動物園開幕後。

(B) 7 月 14 日。

(C) 7 月 15 日。

(D) 7 月 20 日。

解析

1. 題目詢問「為什麼寫第一封信件？」先分別從四個選項來看。

• A 選項 to demonstrate her enthusiasm for the job.與寫這封信的目的不相符，Jenny 身為這個職務負責這項工作，本就有責任在第一時間告知為何犀牛無法準時運送至倍斯特動物

園，若要選擇 A 選項則在信件中需表達出向上司等表達對工作的熱愛跟積極度，讓人覺得她對工作很有熱忱，故可以排除 A 選項。

- B 選項為 to offer a shoulder to cry on.，此與信件中敘述不符，Jenny 是遇到問題者並非同事等向她抱怨問題，而她提供患難時的慰藉，故可以排除 B 選項。

- C 選項則是 to tell her colleague that she was in a dilemma during the delivery，信件中並未提到這是她與同事間的對話，或她向同事表明運送中出現了問題，讓她深陷兩難，故可以排除 C 選項。

- D 選項是 to notify delivery problems first hand，在運送期間出了這麼多問題，Jenny 寫這封信最有可能就是在第一時間告知對方犀牛為何無法準時送至倍斯特動物園，故答案為 D 選項。

2. 題目詢問「何時可能是犀牛能安全抵達倍斯特動物園的日期呢？」先分別從四個選項來看。

- A 選項是 July 14 2 p.m. after Best Zoo opens，可以從第二封信中 Mark 回 Jenny 的信作出日期的推測，They need constant care. Under this circumstance, we might as well ship them a week from now, which is July 20, to Best

Zoo.，故可以推測運送日期是 7 月 20 日，回推運送當天是 7 月 14 日，而且第一封信件中有說明了 By the time we reached the destination, Best Zoo, the door was closed with a notice stating "Open tomorrow at 2 p.m."，且第二封信件中有說道 I'm writing this letter to let you know that we won't be able to ship the rhinos tomorrow morning for you.，故可以得知即使隔天下午兩天動物園開始營業也無法運送，故可以排除 ABC 三個選項，此題答案為選項 D。

Unit 11

倍斯特商業會議中心

Letter ❶: table of the business convention

Dear Jimmy,

I'm writing this letter to let you know that we have finalized the activities of Best Business Conventions, including activities for the plus ones. I totally understand they have nothing to do but wait for their partners outside the lecture room. In addition to giving them the SPA time as usual, this year, the employees of our department have come up with some interesting activities, such as having a personal portrait and film watching. Below are the things that we are going to do for the following three days.

Table of activities

SPA Time	Racing with animals
Film watching	Surfing under water
Shopping Center	Learning photography
Best Resort	Making pottery
Fashion Week	Treasure Hunt
Making a doll	Book Fair
Cooking (learning from a master)	Art Gallery

Best regards,
Cindy Wang

Letter ❷: alteration of the table

Dear Jimmy,

Sorry for sending you the wrong table. Please find the new one below and each with points. We removed two items in a meeting on July 3, since it's beyond our budgets, and for those plus ones who get the most points in three days by attending the most activities and completing the challenges, they will receive the ultimate prize.

Table of activities

SPA Time	5 points	Racing with animals	25 points
Film watching	5 points	Surfing under water	15 points
Shopping Center	5 points	Learning photography	10 points
Best Resort	10 points	Making pottery	15 points
Making a doll	35 points	Treasure Hunt	10 points
Cooking (learning from a master)	20 points	Book Fair	10 points

Note 1: The activity "Making a doll" requires participants to be away from the Business Convention Center for a day, so its points are 35.

Note 2: there will be lecturers giving speeches at Book Fair. This year we're lucky enough to invite Taylor Swift to speak at Book Fair.

Best regards,
Cindy Wang

1. What does the phrase "the plus ones" refer to?

   (A) the partners of convention attendees

   (B) the attendees who receive more points

   (C) the partners of the employees of the convention center

   (D) the partners of convention attendees who receive the most points

2. Which of the following activities is removed from the first table?

   (A) Book Fair

   (B) Fashion Week

   (C) Racing with animals

   (D) Best resort

3. Why did Cindy Wang send the second letter?

   (A) to explain how to gain more points

   (B) to inform the number of plus ones

   (C) to correct a mistake she made earlier

   (D) to give the route to the convention center

4. If a person participates in SPA time, film watching, and making a doll, how many points will he/she receive?
   (A) 40 points
   (B) 45 points
   (C) 35 points
   (D) 25 points

5. Why does making a doll give the highest points?
   (A) Making a doll is very difficult.
   (B) The activity requires many skills.
   (C) The activity costs the highest price.
   (D) It takes much more time to complete the activity.

單元 11 ▶ 倍斯特商業會議中心

信件 ❶：會議中心活動表單

親愛的吉米，

我寫這封信是要讓您知道，我們已經決定好倍斯特商業會議的活動，包括配偶或伴侶的活動。我全然了解他們沒事做，只是在演講廳外等候他們另一半。除了給予他們如同往常的 SPA 時光外，今年，我們部門的員工已經想一些有趣的活動，像是個人畫像或電影觀賞。下列是我們接下來三天要進行的活動。

活動的表格

SPA 時光	與動物競賽
電影觀賞	在水下浮潛
購物中心	學習攝影
倍斯特渡假勝地	製作陶瓷
時尚周	寶藏獵捕
製作娃娃	書展
烹飪（從大師身上學習）	藝廊

致上最高的問候，
辛蒂・王

信件 ❷：更正後活動表單

親愛的吉米，

很抱歉寄給你錯誤的表格。請查收下列的新表格，每項均有對應的分數。我們於 7 月 3 日的會議後移除了兩個項目，因為超過了我們的預算，對於在三天行程中，參與最多行程、完成挑戰和獲得最多的分數者將會得到最終獎。

活動表格

SPA 時光	5 分	與動物競賽	25 分
電影欣賞	5 分	在水下潛水	15 分
購物中心	5 分	學習攝影	10 分
倍斯特渡假勝地	10 分	製作陶瓷	15 分
製作娃娃	35 分	寶藏獵捕	10 分
烹飪 （從大師身上學習）	20 分	書展	10 分

註 1：「製作娃娃」活動需要參與者離開倍斯特商業會議中心一天，所以分數是 35 分。

註 2：書展時會有演講者發表演説。今年我們很幸運能邀請到泰勒?史威夫特在書展上致詞。

致上最高的問候，
辛蒂・王

1. 「配偶或伴侶」指的是什麼呢？

　(A) 會議參加者的另一半。

　(B) 獲得更多分數的參加者。

　(C) 會議中心員工的另一半。

(D) 得到最多分數的會議參與者的另一半。

2. 下列哪項活動從第一個表格從移除了呢？

(A) 書展。

(B) 時尚週。

(C) 與動物競賽。

(D) 倍斯特渡假勝地。

3. 為什麼辛蒂‧王寄送第二封信呢？

(A) 解釋如何獲得更多分數。

(B) 告知配偶或伴侶人數。

(C) 更正她先前犯的錯誤。

(D) 給予會議中心的路線。

4. 如果一個人參加了 SPA 時光、電影欣賞和製作娃娃，那他/她將得到幾分？

(A) 40 分

(B) 45 分

(C) 35 分

(D) 25 分

5. 為什麼製作娃娃給予最高的分數呢？

(A) 製作娃娃非常困難。

(B) 此活動需要許多技能。

(C) 此活動花費最高額的費用。

(D) 要花費更多時間來完成這個活動。

答案：1. A　2. B　3. C　4. B　5.D

獵豹　● ● ●

1.

• 因為 plus ones 在第一篇章的第一句，馬上往第二句搜尋線索。由第二句: I totally understand they have nothing to do but wait for their partners outside the lecture room，得知其中的代名詞 they 指 plus ones，又根據 wait for their partners，推測 plus ones 指的是在演講室外等待配偶或伴侶的人，因此他們也是配偶或伴侶，所以選(A) the partners of convention attendees。

2.

• 看到題目目光馬上鎖定在 removed from the first table。確認題目的關鍵字意思是「從第一個表格被移除」。

• 直接掃描第二個表格的活動，同時對照選項。將選項中與第二個表格的活動符合的刪去，很快就得出唯一沒提到的活動，也

就是被移除的活動是(B) Fashion Week。

3.

- 第二封信的第一句即是為何 Cindy Wang 要再寄一次信的線索句。根據 Sorry for sending you the wrong table，她之前寄錯表格，換言之第二封信是更正錯誤，因此選(C) to correct a mistake she made earlier。

4.

- 看到題目目光馬上鎖定在 SPA time, film watching, and making a doll。對照第二個表格，SPA time 和 film watching 分別是五分，5 points。making a doll 是 35 分。加總是 45 points。因此選(B) 45 points。

5.

- 看到題目目光馬上鎖定在 Making a doll。在第二封信搜尋 Making a doll 這項活動提供最多分數的原因，根據表格下方的 Note: The activity "Making a doll" requires participants to be away from the Business Convention Center for a day, so its points are 35，關鍵字是 to be away... for a day。因此選(D) It takes much more time to complete the activity。

1.

- 此題除了要運用基本代名詞和先行詞的觀念，看懂第一篇章第二句的代名詞 they 指 plus ones，也須以同義詞轉換找出正確選項。此題主要線索是第二句的大意: I totally understand they have nothing to do but wait for their partners outside the lecture room，推測出 plus ones 指的是在演講室外等待配偶或伴侶的人， 當然 plus ones 就是配偶或伴侶。他們的配偶或伴侶換言之就是參加會議者，符合(A)的 convention attendees。

2.

- 此題屬於難度不高的細節題型，即使有些活動的單字不知道字義，考生也能使用掃描技巧找出答案。除了運用刪去法，將選項中第二個表格的活動也有提到的刪除，也可檢查兩個表格的差異，第二個表格少兩項活動，只須一邊掃描，一邊對照兩個表格裡每項活動的的第一 個字，就能找出從第一個表格被移除的是 Fashion Week 和 Art Gallery。

3.

- 此題屬於推測題型，找出表達原因的線索句後，再以換句話說的技巧判斷正確選項。Sorry for sending you the wrong table，她之前寄錯表格，換句話說第二封信是更正錯誤，因此選(C) to correct a mistake she made earlier。考題測驗換句

話説的技巧時，不一定會使用詞性一樣的字，例如此題 wrong，「錯誤的」，是形容詞，正確選項改寫成 a mistake，「錯誤」，是名詞。

4.
- 此題是與數字有關的細節題，需要考生做基本的算術。題目問參加三項活動總共可得到的分數。考生只須細心定位題目裡的關鍵字，如此題是 SPA time，film watching， making a doll，將各項活動的分數加總即可。

5.
- 表格類型常在表格底部以 Note 或 N.B.列出特殊事項，或提醒讀者注意重要資訊，是解題線索常出現的地方。 表格下方 Note 導引的句子裡，關鍵字是 to be away... for a day。這些關鍵字就是暗示 Making a doll 跟其它活動比較下，此活動的特殊點，也就是它提供最高分數的原因。再以換句話説的技巧選擇(D) It takes much more time to complete the activity。

浣熊 ● ● ●

還有可能怎麼問

1. What information is NOT provided in this article?
   (A) the prize.

(B) activities.

(C) the number of participants.

(D) the name of the lecturer.

2. Why is Cindy's company hosting an event of 12 activities for the plus ones?

(A) to inform them that they get the chance to meet a super star.

(B) to make them feel less bored.

(C) to make them feel comfortable outside the Business Convention Center.

(D) to make them get competitive for the ultimate prize.

1. 這篇文章中沒有提供什麼資訊？

(A) 獎項。

(B) 活動。

(C) 參加者的數量。

(D) 講師的名字。

2. 為什麼 Cindy 的公司要替家屬們辦 12 項活動？

(A) 通知他們他們有機會遇到巨星。

(B) 讓他們覺得較不無聊。

(C) 讓他們在倍斯特會議中心外覺得舒適。

(D) 讓他們更具競爭感角逐最終獎。

解析

1. 題目詢問「這篇文章中沒有提供什麼資訊？」先分別從四個選項來看。

- A 選項為 the prize.可以定位回第二封信件，提到 for those plus ones who get the most points in three days by attending the most activities and completing the challenges, they will receive the ultimate prize.可以得知 A 選項在文章中有提到，故可以排除 A 選項。

- B 選項為 activities.從第一封信中寫道的 In addition to giving them the SPA time as usual, this year, the employees of our department have come up with some interesting activities, such as having a personal portrait and film watching.和兩封信的表格中可以很清楚知道，文中有提到這個資訊，故可以排除 B 選項。

- C 選項為 the number of participants.，從兩封信的敘述等，可以知道文中未提到任何有關參加者數量為多少的訊息，可以得知答案為選項 C。

- D 選項為 the name of the lecturer.可以定位回第二封信的註

2 得知會有講者且講者會是巨星 Taylor Swift，故可以排除 D 選項。

2. 題目詢問「為什麼 Cindy 的公司要替家屬們辦 12 項活動？」先分別從四個選項來看。

- A 選項為 to inform them that they get the chance to meet a super star.，從文章中可以得知有提到巨星 Taylor Swift 會在書展中現身，但這並非題目所問的原因，故可以排除選項 A。

- B 選項為 to make them feel less bored.，可以回第一封信件中找到相關敘述 I totally understand they have nothing to do but wait for their partners outside the lecture room...從這段敘述可以得知，其實辦書展的原因是讓家屬們較不無聊，此為同義詞轉換，故答案為選項 B。C 選項為 to make them feel comfortable outside the Business Convention Center.，文章中有敘述到 outside the Business Convention Center 但未提到此與讓家屬更舒適有關，而且這與題目詢問的原因無關，故可以排除選項 C。選項 D 是 to make them get competitive for the ultimate prize.，可以從文章中找到有 ultimate prize 這件事，但未提到要讓家屬們更 competitive，而且這並非當初公司想做出跟往年不同的做法和替家屬辦活動的原因，故可以排除選項 D。

答案：1. C　2. D.

Unit 12

倍斯特體育場

Letter ❶：the table of selling food prices

Dear Teri,

Have you heard about Best City Field? It's really crowded over there. It can accommodate 5,000 people, to my amazement. My son had a blast there last Friday. He enjoyed gourmet there. Then it hit me – why don't we sell some of our foods at Best City Field. This can be another channel for us to sell our foods. More channels mean more profits, right. I've narrowed down the list of foods we are going to sell there, and detailed information as to why we should sell foods there. I'm going to do a PPT presentation in our monthly meeting on Friday. Please see the table below.

Table of foods

Name/Price	Original Price	Price at BCF
Hot dog	US 2.5	US 2
Tomato Garlic Bread	US 3	US 3
Stroopwafel	US 4	US 3
Croque Madame	US 5	US 4
Satay	US 5	US 5
Oden	US 2	US 2
Pineapple Bun with Butter	US 4	US 3
Tanghulu	US 2	US 2

Best regards,
Cindy Wang

Letter ❷：reply

Dear Cindy,

I've seen the food list. It's quite intriguing, but what about drinks? Drinks go with the food we are going to sell there. It will be more feasible, but I don't think we should have more than two drinks, perhaps coke and black tea. What do you think? In addition, what about flavors? Flavors of Tanghulu and Satay. Also, Tanghulu can be so appealing to kids. I'm thinking about adding other flavors. Satay can be a good choice for people who just don't want to be too stuffed while watching sports game at night. I do need a new list before Monday morning 10 a.m., and who do you think is more suitable for handling this? We certainly need someone who has lots of experience in this. Make a list of the possible candidates on your team and from other departments.

Last but not the least, I do think we should give customers coupons. It's just similar to things other shops are trying to do. I saw that from newspapers. There is no harm in that right? I'm thinking about giving customers coupons at our shop, customers who buy foods and at the same time it can be a free advertisement for customers to know we are going to sell foods at BCF.

Best regards,
Teri

1. Who might be Teri in terms of her relationship with Cindy?

   (A) Teri might be Cindy's chef.

   (B) Teri might be Cindy's supervisor.

   (C) Teri might be Cindy's colleague.

   (D) Teri might be Cindy's PR contact.

2. What kind of company might Cindy and Teri work for?

   (A) a fast food diner

   (B) a catering service

   (C) a beverage manufacturer

   (D) a Japanese restaurant

3. Which of the followings is NOT mentioned in Teri's letter?

   (A) flavors

   (B) drinks

   (C) the person who can take charge of the project

   (D) the cook who can prepare all of the foods

4. What does Cindy mean by "Then it hit me"?

   (A) She was hit in an accident in Best City Field.

(B) She suddenly thought of a new idea.

(C) She was hit by her son.

(D) She suddenly decided to go to Best City Field.

5. What does Cindy mean by "My son had a blast there"?

(A) Her son had a superb time there.

(B) Her son was caught in an accident there.

(C) Her son did not like Best City Field.

(D) Her son ate too much in Best City Field.

單元 12 ▶ 倍斯特體育場

信件 ❶：販售食物價格表

親愛的泰瑞，

你曾聽過倍斯特體育場嗎？這裡真的相當擁擠。令我感到驚訝的是，這裡能容納 5000 人。我的兒子上周五在這玩得很高興。他喜愛那裡的美食。然後靈光閃現 — 為什麼我們不在倍斯特體育場販賣一些我們的食物呢？這可以是我們另一個銷售食物的管道。更多的管道意味著更多的利潤，對吧！我已經縮限我們在那裡要販賣的食物清單以及詳細的資訊包含為什麼我們要銷售這些食物。在我們周五的月會上我將會做簡報。請看下列表格。

食物表格

名稱/價格	原始價格	在 BCF 的價格
熱狗	2.5 美元	2 美元
番茄大蒜麵包	3 美元	3 美元
焦糖煎餅	4 美元	3 美元
焗烤火腿乳酪吐司	5 美元	4 美元
沙嗲	5 美元	5 美元
關東煮	2 美元	2 美元
冰火菠蘿油包	4 美元	3 美元
糖葫蘆	2 美元	2 美元

致上最高的問候，
辛蒂‧王

信件❷：回覆

親愛的辛蒂，

我已經看過食物清單了。令人感到相當有興趣，但飲料的部分呢？飲料搭我們要銷售的食物。將會更可行，但我不認為我們應該要銷售超過兩樣飲品，可能可樂和紅茶。你覺得呢？此外，口味的部分呢？糖葫蘆和沙嗲的口味。而且糖葫蘆可以很吸引小孩子。我有在思考關於增加其他口味。沙嗲對於不想吃太飽的人來說是個好選擇，一邊於晚上觀看體育節目。星期一早上十點我會需要新的清單。你覺得誰更適合處理這部分呢？我確定需要一些在這部分有許多經驗的人。列出你們團隊和其他部門可能的候選人。

最後要説的是，我認為我們應該要給顧客優惠卷。這類似其他店家正在做的部分。我從報紙上看到的。試試也無訪對吧？我正考慮要在我們店裡提供優惠卷給顧客，有在店裡賣食物的顧客，同時這可以是免費的廣告，讓顧客知道我們將在倍斯特體育場販賣食物。

致上最高的問候，
泰瑞

1. 辛蒂和泰瑞的關係可能是什麼呢？

(A) 她可能是辛蒂的廚師。

(B) 她可能是辛蒂的管理者。

(C) 她可能是辛蒂的同事。

(D) 她可能是辛蒂的公關聯絡人。

2. 辛蒂和泰瑞可能是替哪種類型的公司工作？

(A) 速食餐館。

6 填空式閱讀

7 單篇閱讀

7 雙篇、三篇閱讀

模擬試題

(B) 外燴服務。

(C) 飲料製造商。

(D) 日式餐廳。

3. 下列哪些在泰瑞的信件中未提及呢？

(A) 口味。

(B) 飲料。

(C) 負責這個計畫的人員。

(D) 能準備所有食物的廚師。

4. 辛蒂說的「然後我就突然想到」意味著什麼呢？

(A) 她在體育館發生意外被打到。

(B) 她突然想到一個新想法。

(C) 她被她兒子毆打。

(D) 她突然決定要去倍斯特體育館。

5. 辛蒂說的「我的兒子玩得很盡興」指的是什麼呢？

(A) 她兒子在那裡有美好的時光。

(B) 她的兒子在那裏發生的意外。

(C) 她的兒子不喜歡倍斯特體育館。

(D) 她的兒子在倍斯特體育館吃太多。

答案：1. B　2. B　3. D　4. B　5.A

獵豹 ● ● ●

1.

- 看到題目目光馬上鎖定在 in terms of her relationship with Cindy。確認題目的意思是要求推測對 Cindy 而言，Teri 的身份是什麼。運用掃描技巧，首先刪除 (A) 與 (D)，因為 chef 及 PR 兩字及相關細節都未提及。接著掃描 Teri 寫的信，即第二封信的開頭及結尾兩句。由最後一句的句型得到線索：Make a list of the possible candidates on your team and from other departments，是祈使句，祈使句的語氣是上對下，因此確定選擇(B) Teri might be Cindy's supervisor。Teri 可能是 Cindy 的主管。

2.

- 由第一封信第六句得知 Cindy 提議公司能在 Best City Field 販賣食物。先將不會在戶外販賣食物的公司刪除，因此刪除(A) a fast food diner 及(D) a Japanese restaurant。接著刪除(C) a beverage manufacturer，因為 manufacturer 是製造商，通常不會在戶外直接販賣產品，且第一封信毫無提及 beverage，飲料。因此選(B) a catering service，外燴服務公司。

3.

- 由第一句 what about drinks?刪去(B) drinks。根據 what about flavors?及 who do you think is more suitable for

371

handling this? 刪除(A) flavors 及(C) the person who can take charge of the project。所以正確選項是(D) the cook who can prepare all of the foods。

4.

- 先刪去(A) She was hit in an accident in Best City Field 和(D) She suddenly decided to go to Best City Field。這兩句的大意與第一封信的主題毫無關聯。刪去(C) She was hit by her son，這句大意也與主題毫無關。所以正確選項是(B) She suddenly thought of a new idea。

5.

- 由下文 He enjoyed gourmet there 推測 Cindy 的兒子在體育場的經驗非常好，因此 My son had a blast there 應該也是正面意涵。將有負面意涵的選項描述刪除，先刪除 (B) Her son was caught in an accident there 及(C) Her son did not like Best City Field。(D) Her son ate too much in Best City Field 的大意也偏向負面，所以正確選項是(A) Her son had a superb time there。

貓頭鷹 ● ● ●

1.

- 此題屬於推測題型。要推測對 Cindy 而言，Teri 的身份是什麼。首先判斷應該從 Teri 對 Cindy 的回應方式或態度能得到線

索，所以鎖定在第二封信。第二封信最後三句的語氣都非常強烈，暗示 Teri 的身份是可以對 Cindy 下指令的，因此合理推測 Teri 是主管。

- 在此句: I do need a new list before Monday morning 10 a.m., and who do you think is more suitable for handling this?，表達強烈語氣的線索字是助動詞 do。而在 We certainly need someone who has lots of experience in this 中，表達強烈語氣的線索字是副詞 certainly。第二封信最後一句是祈使句。祈使句是原型動詞放在句首的句型。表達要求或命令。通常是表達權力高者對權力低者的語氣，因此可從祈使句判斷 Teri 可能是 Cindy 的主管。

2.

- 此題屬於推測題型。要綜合地點及商品類型，推測哪種公司最有可能是 Cindy 和 Teri 的公司。

- 有固定營業場所的公司先刪去，刪除 (A) a fast food diner 及 (D) a Japanese restaurant，diner 是小餐館。因為表格列出的商品全是食物，沒有飲料，所以刪除 (C) a beverage manufacturer，飲料製造商。(B) a catering service，外燴服務公司，考慮地點在體育場，而外燴服務公司提供食物的地點比較有彈性，因此此選項較合理。

3.

- 此題屬於細節題型。要選出第二封信沒提到的細節。先搜尋 轉折詞及疑問句，因為轉折詞及疑問句之後常有線索。將有提及

的細節逐一刪除。主文中的轉折詞 In addition，此外，導引 what about flavors?因此刪除 (A) flavors，疑問句 who do you think is more suitable for handling this? 換句話說是 Terri 想知道誰適合處理這件事，意思近似 (C) the person who can take charge of the project，能負責這個案子的人。所以刪去 (C)。

4.

- 此題屬於推測題型，牽涉到慣用語 it hit me 及代名詞 it。慣用語常有深層意義，與字面意思不同。在此 hit 不是「打擊」的意思，it hit me 是「我突然想到一個點子」。將此慣用語換句話說，就是正確選項(B) She suddenly thought of a new idea，她突然想到一個新想法。先從 "Then it hit me"的上文搜尋線索。上兩句描述 Cindy 的兒子在體育場度過好時光，他享受那裏的美食—這提供給 Cindy 提議在體育場販賣食物的靈感。注意大部份代名詞的先行詞位於代名詞的上文，但 it hit me 因為是慣用語，比較特殊，it 的先行詞位於下文，下文才解釋突然想到的內容: why don't we sell some of our foods at Best City Field。

5.

- 此題牽涉慣用語: have a blast 的深層意義。考生若不確定慣用語的深層意義，可考慮連貫性原則，將選項敘述套入慣用語在篇章中的位置，將與上下文不連貫的選項刪除。因為下文 He enjoyed gourmet there 暗示 Cindy 的兒子在體育場的經驗非常好，因此 My son had a blast there 應該也是正面意涵。(A) Her son had a superb time there。由於 superb 意思是

「很棒的」，是正面意涵的形容詞。(A)表達「她兒子在那裡有美好的時光」。

還有可能怎麼問

1. What is mentioned about Cindy's company?

(A) It seeks for a foreign investor.

(B) It is trying to find other channels.

(C) It owns a branch office.

(D) It needs good suppliers.

2. How can customers get coupons?

(A) customers who can memorize the slogan of the company.

(B) customers who buy a newspaper.

(C) customers who shop at the store.

(D) customers who watch ads on TV.

1. 文中提到有關 Cindy 公司的什麼？

(A) 它尋找國外投資者。

(B) 它試著找其他管道。

(C) 它擁有分公司辦公室。

(D) 它需要好的供應商。

2. 顧客要如何拿到優惠卷呢？

　　(A) 能記住公司口號的顧客。

　　(B) 買報紙的顧客。

　　(C) 在店裡購物的顧客。

　　(D) 在電視上觀看到廣告的顧客。

解析

1. 題目詢問「文中提到有關 Cindy 公司的什麼？」先分別從四個選項來看。

　• 選項 A 為 It seeks for a foreign investor. 可以定位回第一封信件，故可以得知文章中未提及找尋國外投資者，可以排除選項 A。選項 B 為 It is trying to find other channels. 可以定位回第一封信件，Cindy 提到 This can be another channel for us to sell our foods. More channels mean more profits, right. ，故可以得知此可以替公司找尋更多管道，故答案為選項 B。選項 C 為 It owns a branch office. 可以定位回兩封信件尋找，故可以得知文章中未提及擁有分公司辦公室的敘述，故可以排除選項 C。選項 D 為 It needs good suppliers. 可以定位回兩封信件尋找，故可以得知文章中未提及它需要好的供應商

的相關敘述，故可以排除選項 D。

2. 題目詢問「顧客要如何拿到優惠卷呢？」先分別從四個選項來看。

- 四個選項均為 customers 開頭後面接形容詞子句的設計，重點在形容詞子句對 customers 的描述，故可以看哪項敘述在文中有提到。選項 A 為 customers who can memorize the slogan of the company.，此部分在文章中未提及，沒有任何訊息跟 memorize 和 slogan 有關，故可以排除此選項，此為杜撰的內容。選項 B 為 customers who buy a newspaper.定位到第二封信最後幾句話文中有提及 Teri 在報上看到的，但這與題目問的顧客要如何拿到優惠卷呢？無關，故可以排除此選項。C 選項為 customers who shop at the store.可以從第二封信最後幾句話可以得知答案為選項 C。D 選項為 customers who watch ads on TV.，文章中有提到 a free advertisement 但是這並非顧客能拿到優惠卷的原因，故可以排除 D 選項。

答案：1. B　2. C

Unit 13

韓國自助行

Line messages ❶：about the final boarding call

James: oh lord! That's the final boarding call.
Jack:　I knew it...
Neal:　such an awful feeling.

(5 minutes later)
James: swear to god that we would never do this again.
Jack:　we made it.
Neal:　such a close call.
James: we're now heading to HK, and our destination is Seoul.
　　　　We will make a transfer at HK.
Jack:　let me see our itinerary. We're going to take XX676 at
　　　　20:05 from HK to Seoul, will be arriving at 00:45.
Neal:　three hours and 45 minutes.
James: that's quick.

Line messages ❷：about the final boarding call

James: can't believe we have to be back now.
Jack:　totally hating the morning flight.
Neal:　quick quick quick
Jack:　the plane will depart at 6:35 a.m.
Neal:　Taxi...
James: we will be taking XX6499. We'll be arriving at HK 9:30 a.m.

Neal: we still haven't had our breakfast yet.

Jack: you can eat that once we get on the plane.

Board

Flight Number	Flight Information
CX7899	Cancelled
CV7458	Cancelled
XX6499	Cancelled
XX9878	Cancelled
CV9878	Cancelled
CX5439	Delayed
XX9988	Delayed
XX5698	Delayed

Note/broadcasting: due to a typhoon, all flights taking a transfer through HK are cancelled. Due to some mechanical problems, three flights will be delayed. We're still trying to figure out why. Please contact our ground crew for further information, and we are reimbursing you by giving coupons.

1. What does Neal mean by "such a close call"?

(A) He wanted to call his friend.

(B) He heard the final call for boarding.

(C) They barely made it to the boarding gate.

(D) They were very close to the boarding gate.

2. Which of the followings might be the reason that the three people begin their Line messages in the first passage?

(A) to ask for the directions to the boarding gate

(B) to remind one another to hurry up for boarding

(C) to remind one another to bring the itinerary

(D) to ask when to board the flight

3. Which of the followings is the closest to itinerary?

(A) a schedule for a trip

(B) a boarding pass

(C) a coupon

(D) a ticket

4. What might they do after they arrive at the airport for the return flight?

(A) They might check in a hotel.

(B) They might take a nap at the airport.

(C) They might have some Hong Kong gourmets.

(D) They might talk to the ground crew.

5. Which of the followings is the closest to reimbursing?

(A) arranging lodging

(B) enjoying local cuisines

(C) informing the next flight

(D) giving compensation

中譯

單元 13 ▶ 韓國自助行

Line 訊息 ❶：關於最後登機呼叫

詹姆士： 我的天啊！那是最後登機呼叫。
傑克： 我知道...
尼爾： 有個奇怪的感覺。

（5 分鐘過後）

詹姆士： 發誓我們下次別再這樣了。
傑克： 我們成功了。
尼爾： 真的是千鈞一髮。
詹姆士： 我們現在往香港出發，我們的目的地是首爾。我們將於香港轉機。
傑克： 讓我看下我們的旅遊行程。我們現在搭乘晚間 8 點 5 分的 XX676 班機從香港到首爾，會於 12 點 45 分抵達首爾。
尼爾： 三小時又 45 分鐘。
詹姆士： 真快。

Line 訊息 ❷：關於最後登機呼叫

詹姆士： 不敢相信我們要回去了。
傑克： 完全討厭早晨航班。
尼爾： 快快快。
傑克： 飛機將於 6 點 35 分起飛。
尼爾： 計程車...
詹姆士： 我們將搭乘 XX6499 航班。我們會於上午 9 點 30 分抵達香港。
尼爾： 我們都還沒吃早餐。
傑克： 你可以在我們上機後吃。

公告欄

班機號碼	班機資訊
CX7899	取消
CV7458	取消
XX6499	取消
XX9878	取消
CV9878	取消
CX5439	延誤
XX9988	延誤
XX5698	延誤

註/廣播：由於颱風的關係，所有經由香港轉機的航班均取消。由於一些機械問題，三個班次將延遲。我們仍試著了解原因。請聯繫我們地勤人員獲取更進一步資訊，我們會補償您優惠卷。

1. 尼爾說的「真的是千鈞一髮」指的是什麼呢？

   (A) 他想要打電話給他的朋友。

   (B) 他聽到最後登機呼叫的廣播。

   (C) 他們勉強趕至登機門。

   (D) 他們離登機門很近。

2. 下列哪個可能是首段三人開始 **LINE** 訊息的可能原因呢？

   (A) 要求去登機門的指示。

   (B) 提醒彼此要快點登機。

   (C) 提醒彼此要攜帶旅行計畫。

   (D) 詢問何時要登機。

3. 下列哪個與旅遊行程意思最接近呢？

   (A) 旅行的時程表。

   (B) 登機通行證。

   (C) 優惠卷。

   (D) 門票。

4. 在抵達機場搭回程班機後他們可能做什麼呢？

   (A) 他們可能在旅館下塌。

   (B) 他們可能在機場小睡一下。

   (C) 他們可能吃些香港美食。

(D) 他們可能與地勤人員談話。

5. 下列哪個跟補償的意思最接近呢？

(A) 安排住所。

(B) 享用當地佳餚。

(C) 通知下個航班。

(D) 給予補償。

答案：1.C　2.B　3.A　4.D　5.D

獵豹 ● ● ●

1.

- 先掃描第一篇章的第一句，判斷主題。由 That's the final boarding call，boarding call，登機呼叫廣播一詞，得知主題是朋友間趕著登機時候的 Line 對話。先刪除(A) He wanted to call his friend，因為(A)他想打電話給朋友，與主題沒有密切的關聯。根據 such a close call 的上一句: we made it，意思是「我們做到了」，又搭配登機主題，所以是「我們成功登機了」，進一步推測 such a close call 有「好驚險」之意，換句話說是他們勉強趕至登機門，因此選 (C) They barely made it to the boarding gate。

2.

- 題目詢問在第一篇章，這些人開始互傳 Line 訊息的原因是什麼，因此掃描第一篇第一～三句。根據第一篇第一～三句對話將(A) to ask for the directions to the boarding gate 及(C) to remind one another to bring the itinerary 都先刪除，因為毫無提及 directions 和 itinerary 這兩個名詞。刪去(D) to ask when to board the flight，問何時登機，因為第一～三句沒提到任何時間點。因此正確選項是(B) to remind one another to hurry up for boarding。

3.

- 看到題目目光馬上搜尋 itinerary，定位在第一篇章接近結尾 Jack: let me see our itinerary。由 Jack 接著下一句: We're going to take XX676 at 20:05 from HK to Seoul, will be arriving at 00:45，得知他在 itinerary 看到的資訊是航班號碼，出發/抵達時間，地點。由此推測 itinerary 的字義一定與旅行有關，所以選(A) a schedule for a trip。

4.

- 看到題目目光馬上鎖定在 for the return flight，以此片語定位解題線索在第二篇章，因為第二篇章第一句: can't believe we have to be back now，不敢相信我們現在必須回去了，就暗示此篇是關於 return flight，回程班機。根據第三篇的表格下方 Note/broadcasting: ...Please contact our ground crew for further information...，得出答案是(D) They might talk to the ground crew。

5.

- 看到題目目光馬上搜尋 reimbursing。定位 reimbursing 在第三篇章表格下方的 Note/broadcasting: ...we are reimbursing you by giving free coupons。此句前後文都無提及 lodging，cuisines，因此刪去(A) arranging lodging，(B) enjoying local cuisines。也沒告知下一個航班，故刪除(C) informing the next flight。正確選項是(D) giving compensation，給予補償。

1.

- 此題屬於推測題型，也牽涉到 a close call 這個慣用語。正確選項必須呼應主題，因此可將與登機主題無關的(A)先刪除。a close call 是「千鈞一髮」的慣用語。正確選項(C) They barely made it to the boarding gate，他們勉強趕至登機門。如果不確定 a close call 的意思，也能以上文 we made it，推測他們事實上有趕上飛機。而(B) He heard the final call for boarding 和(D) They were very close to the boarding gate 不能選，因為(B) 他聽到最後登機呼叫的廣播和(D) 他們離登機門很近，這兩個行為應該是發生在他們登機前，但 Neal 說 such a close call 是登機後說的。

2.

- 此題屬於推測題型， 要綜合第一篇章的主題和開頭的訊息所暗示的語氣，推測出這些人開始這場 Line 對話的原因，也就是問開始互傳訊息的動機。

- 由第一句 James 的訊息: That's the final boarding call，推測 James 打這句話時，他正聽到登機呼叫廣播。這句也暗示第一篇的主題是他們趕著登機。要推測動機或態度的題型，考生可以利用感嘆詞或形容情緒的形容詞當線索。如 James 說的 oh lord! 是帶有一點緊張或驚慌語氣的感嘆詞，第三句 Neal 回應: such an awful feeling 也暗示負面情緒。綜合以上，(B) to remind one another to hurry up for boarding，提醒彼此加快動作以趕上登機，是最合理的答案。

3.

- 此題主要考 itinerary 的字義與哪個選項的單字最接近。除了 itinerary 的下一句大意是線索，另一線索是上一句: we're now heading to HK, and our destination is Seoul. We will make a transfer at HK，也是描述行程規劃，因此 itinerary 的字義與行程 schedule 類似，故選(A) a schedule for a trip。

- 此題另一解題方式是互相比較選項單字的意思，和篇章主題關係越密切，越可能是答案。(C) a coupon，折價券或優待券，及(D) a ticket，入場券，因為與主題無關，一定先刪除。

4.

- 此題屬於推測題型，要推測這些朋友抵達回程航班的機場後，可能的動作。此題的線索分別位於兩個篇章，考生要先從題目的 for the return flight 定位回第二篇章第一句: can't believe we have to be back now。再將第二篇章結尾提到的班機編號 XX6499 和第三篇章的表格對照，確定此班機取消。而表格下方的 Note/broadcasting 提供航空公司因應班機取消，所做的措施/給旅客的指示: Please contact our ground crew for further information...，按照此指示，得出答案是(D) They might talk to the ground crew。

5.

- 此題主要考 reimbursing 的字義與哪個選項的單字最接近。原型動詞是 reimburse。由 reimbursing 之後的搭配詞: by giving coupons，因應班機取消，給予乘客優待券。換言之，以優待券補償乘客。而補償的名詞類似字是 compensation。所以選(D) giving compensation。

浣熊

還有可能怎麼問

1. What is NOT indicated about flight information?

   (A) CV 9878 is cancelled.

(B) there is a typhoon approaching.

(C) Neal will get the coupon.

(D) Ground crews will not be able to show up because the typhoon is too violent.

2. How can passengers get coupons?

(A) passengers who take a direct flight.

(B) passengers whose flight is delayed.

(C) passengers who know the crew members.

(D) passengers who can fix mechanical problems.

（中譯）

1. 關於班機資訊，何者錯誤？

(A) CV9878 班機遭到取消。

(B) 有颱風正在靠近。

(C) 尼爾會得到優惠卷。

(D) 地勤人員無法現身因為颱風太強烈。

2. 顧客要如何拿到優惠卷呢？

(A) 搭乘直航航班的乘客。

(B) 搭乘的班機受到延誤的乘客。

(C) 知道地勤人員的乘客。

(D) 能修理機械問題的乘客。

解析

1. 題目詢問「關於班機資訊，何者錯誤？」先分別從四個選項來看。

- 選項 A，CV 9878 is cancelled.，可以定位回最後的布告欄中找到相對應的資訊，所以可以得知該班機遭到取消了，故可以排除選項 A。選項 B 是 there is a typhoon approaching.可以從布告欄中的公告中得知 due to a typhoon, all flights taking a transfer through HK are cancelled.故可以排除 B 選項。選項 C 是 Neal will get the coupon.，可以從 line 訊息和布告欄中的資訊得知，尼爾所搭乘的航班名稱和他和朋友們正趕往機場，但機場公告他所搭乘的航班取消，雖然文章沒有進一步敘述他後續的舉動，但綜合這些資訊可以得知，因航班取消所以他也會得到優惠卷，故可以排除選項 C。選項 D 是 Ground crews will not be able to show up because the typhoon is too violent，佈告欄的公告有表明說可以聯繫地勤人員，也是唯一出現此訊息的地方，但是並未說明地勤人員會因為颱風太強烈而無法出現，故答案為選項 D。

2. 題目詢問「顧客要如何拿到優惠卷呢？」先分別從四個選項來看。

- 四個選項均為 passengers 開頭後面接形容詞子句的設計，重點在形容詞子句對 passengers 的描述，故可以看哪項敘述在文中有提到。

- A 選項為 passengers who take a direct flight.但文章中並未提到 direct flight，只有提到轉機，故可以排除 A 選項。B 選項為 passengers whose flight is delayed.可以從佈告欄的 Please contact our ground crew for further information, and we are reimbursing you by giving free coupons.得知對於航班取消跟航班延誤者航空公司將給予優惠卷補償，故可以得知答案為選項 B。選項 C 為 passengers who know the crew members.，但文章中並未提到與聯繫地勤人員外，地勤人員的其他描述，故可以得知此敘述為非，可以排除 C 選項。

- 選項 D 為 passengers who can fix mechanical problems.，同樣可以定位回佈告欄下方的公告 Due to some mechanical problems, three flights will be delayed. We're still trying to figure out why.這兩句話只表明出現的機械問題但並未提到能修理機械問題的乘客會得到優惠卷，此為張冠李戴，故可以得知此選項為錯誤的，可以排除選項 D。

答案：1. D　2. B

READING TEST

In the Reading test, you will read a variety of texts and answer several different types of reading comprehension questions. The entire Reading test will last 75 minutes. There are three parts, and directions are given for each part. You are encouraged to answer as many questions as possible within the time allowed.

You must mark your answer on the separate answer sheet. Do not write answers in your test book.

PART 5

Directions: A word or phrase is missing in each of the sentences below. Four answer choices are given below each sentence. Select the best answer to complete the sentence. Then mark the letter (A), (B), (C), or (D) on your answer sheet.

101. People working in an underground tunnel for a long period of time are exposed to harmful chemical substances, which can ultimately lead to _____ illness.
    (A) regular
    (B) unharmful
    (C) chronic
    (D) sustained

102. Health experts are constantly reminding people of not taking foods that contain cholesterol, but totally forgetting the fact that cholesterol does have a _____ effect.

(A) harmful

(B) rough

(C) chronic

(D) beneficial

103. Farmers are beginning to abandon chemical substances that are extremely useful, but _____ toxic.

(A) credulous

(B) incredibly

(C) credible

(D) believable

104. Drinking water in certain areas of Africa is _____ with germs and microorganisms.

(A) contaminated

(B) contamination

(C) contained

(D) pollution

105. Without the electricity _____ by nuclear power plants, local residents are worried that there is going to be a scarcity of power during summer.

(A) generation

(B) generating

(C) generate

(D) generated

106. Complexities of insect life cycle are _____ intriguing to life science students than to students majoring in Chinese.

(A) less

(B) more

(C) as

(D) far

107. Tourists are finding that places with a rich biodiversity _____ more money than a less diversified one.

(A) costs

(B) cost

(C) take

(D) spend

108. _____ viewing on smartphone does cause eyestrain so that there are other devices being developed to alleviate the symptom.

(A) prolong

(B) prolonged

(C) prolonging

(D) a prolong

109. Although transportation facilities, such as road juggernauts and RV, are not _____, they are

considered more modern by today's teenagers.

(A) uncommon

(B) rampant

(C) widespread

(D) wide

110. The CEO of Best Hotel is considering using a _____ glass that is going to withstand gun shots and tornadoes.

(A) rough

(B) tough

(C) toughness

(D) toughened

111. _____ a hit song that has been on the bestseller's list on Amazon.com for 6 months in a row, this super star is getting a three-year contract by Best Studio.

(A) Whose

(B) With

(C) Without

(D) That

112. _____ to renew the contract with an employer, a foreign domestic helper cannot help but return to her home country.

(A) incapable

6 填空式閱讀

7 單篇閱讀

7 雙篇、三篇閱讀

模擬試題

(B) unable

(C) capable

(D) ability

113. Poaching ivory of elephants _____ illegal, but ivory hunters value money over precious life.

(A) are

(B) once

(C) is

(D) were

114. Education experts are devoted to _____ less successful students by lowering the ratio between pupils and teachers.

(A) helping

(B) helped

(C) helps

(D) have helped

115. Best Tech is shifting from putting _____ on manufacturing to overall quality of its goods.

(A) emphasized

(B) stress

(C) emphasis

(D) emphasize

116. Animals _____ are adept at temperature changes and human interference are more likely to survive.
    (A) whose
    (B) who
    (C) which
    (D) of which

117. Dog lovers have a _____ for prioritizing the needs of dogs above everything else.
    (A) prefer
    (B) favorable
    (C) favorite
    (D) penchant

118. The medical device _____ eventually choose to showcase on new product launch is IDM wheelchair.
    (A) us
    (B) we
    (C) that
    (D) our

119. Consumers now favor movies with _____ techniques and dramatic visual and sound effects over moving narratives.
    (A) cinema

(B) cinematic

(C) cinematography

(D) cinematical

120. Since two manufacturing workers are on a maternity leave for three months, employees are now having a _____ working schedule than before.

(A) busy

(B) busily

(C) busied

(D) busier

121. All learning materials are _____ to employees of Best Publishing, including workers from the branch office.

(A) uncommon

(B) rampant

(C) accessible

(D) native

122. Candidates of Best Airline are expected to _____ their loyalty, enthusiasm, and a willingness to learn during the trial period.

(A) showing

(B) show

(C) showed

(D) shown

123. Flowers _____ fragrance attracts the most pollinators, such as bees and butterflies, are bound to prosper during early spring.
    (A) whose
    (B) who
    (C) which
    (D) that

124. Some elevators are _____ tailored for people with chronic illness, such as diabetes and high blood pressure.
    (A) specifically
    (B) specialty
    (C) special
    (D) specific

125. Neither the branch office manager _____ the Chief Marketing Officer received the opportunity of the long-waited promotion.
    (A) or
    (B) both
    (C) nor
    (D) while

126. It is essential _____ all workers follow the instruction carefully since the working condition is rather hazardous.
(A) among
(B) why
(C) that
(D) with

127. Though John is not as strong _____ other competitors or gold medalists, his courage of managing to swim back to the shore wins the heart of viewers.
(A) among
(B) than
(C) as
(D) in

128. To celebrate his tenth _____ , Jack not only hires a violinist to perform music during dinner, but also employs a horse drawn carrier to give them a ride home.
(A) concert
(B) ceremony
(C) activity
(D) anniversary

129. One way to collect Line points is to share an assigned article to your line page, _____ another method is to accomplish things at a certain level of game.

    (A) when

    (B) with

    (C) whereas

    (D) however

130. _____ came up with the practical strategies to impress potential clients will receive a year-end bonus.

    (A) whatever

    (B) whoever

    (C) however

    (D) whenever

Directions: Read the texts that follow. A word, phrase, or sentence is missing in parts of each text. Four answer choices for each question are given below the text Select the best answer to complete the text. Then mark the letter (A), (B), (C), or (D) on your answer sheet.

Questions 131-134 refer to the following letter.

To Whom It May Concern,

I'm honored to announce that the Craft & Hobby Fair will __ (131)__ in the World Trade Center on July 2nd.

The fair gathers designers, craftsmen, retailers, distributors, buyers and suppliers. Attendees will not only familiarize themselves with traditional American crafts, but also interact with the __(132)__ craftsmen from around the globe.
I'm also pleased to inform you of a new sector, the upcycling sector, which is highly informative on __(133)__ lifestyle. The fair has received accolades for the diverse products in the paper and textile sectors. Besides, the jewelry sector has seen unabated boom according to our statistics of visitors and orders.
__(134)__ If you have any questions, please contact us via e-mail or phone.

Sincerely,

Jeff Benson

the Craft & Hobby Fair Organizer

131. (A) command
     (B) commence
     (C) commend
     (D) comment

132. (A) promised
     (B) prominence
     (C) prominent
     (D) compromising

133. (A) sustainable
     (B) sustain
     (C) sustainability
     (D) sustaining

134. (A) Attached is the information of the schedule, exhibition booths, and transportation.
     (B) We have invited craftsmen from Asia.
     (C) It takes only 10 minutes to walk from the MRT station to the World Trade Center.
     (D) The number of transactions is the highest in the

jewelry sector.

Questions 135-138 refer to the following article.

While the connections between home security systems and your smart phones are not uncommon, smart homes will eventually ___(135)___ devices of all areas, and those devices will communicate with one another. ___(136)___

Various smart devices will form an ___(137)___ web. These devices include automatic temperature control, smart fridges that track your food, and sensors in bins that detect the kinds of trash. The more these devices talk to one another, the more they will understand your lifestyle and personal preference ___(138)___ they adjust their operations. A smart home will become a living entity that responds to your lifestyle.

135. (A) comprehend
     (B) add
     (C) compass
     (D) encompass

136. (A) Smart devices are becoming more and more affordable.

(B) IT allows us to control devices remotely.

(C) A smart home is equipped with sensors.

(D) They will help you manage your household, so you can focus on more crucial parts of your life.

137. (A) moderate
  (B) intricate
  (C) modest
  (D) inexpensive

138. (A) through
  (B) by
  (C) whereby
  (D) or

Questions 139-142 refer to the following advertisement.

Bangkok Culinary School: Learn from the master chef of Thai cuisines!

---

* Learn how to cook mouthwatering Thai cuisines with fun

* Hands-on experience: International tourists do not need to fuss over the materials and ingredients. The tuition includes materials, utensils, and containers. Our school __(39)__ __(40)__ the freshest and highest-quality produce and ingredients. Just register online or on site. You will receive a 10% discount for in-advance payment 1 month __(41)__ the class.

Types of Classes: All classes are taught in English.
* Short-term classes:
  2~4 hours in the morning or afternoon, 2 recipes per hour
* Intensive classes:
  6 hours from Monday to Thursday, 48 hours in total, 90 recipes.
* One-on-one classes
* __(42)__

easy transportation
located in downtown Bangkok/ only 5-min. walk from BTS Skytrain station

For more details, please visit our website:
https://www.bangkokcuisineschool.com/

---

139. (A) takes pride for

(B) is proud that

(C) prides itself for

(D) takes pride in

140 (A) utility

(B) utilize

(C) utilizing

(D) utilization

141. (A) beforehand

(B) prior to

(C) in advance

(D) prioritizing

142. (A) Ingredients and cooking equipment will be provided.

(B) Most attendees are tourists from western countries.

(C) Attendees must be able to communicate in Thai.

(D) Attendees will receive certificates varying in formats according to class levels.

Questions 143-146 refer to the following letter.

Dear Customers,

After   (143)   the local community here in Lexington for 20 years, the Gift Store Around the Corner is saddened to inform you that the store will close down on December 20th due to declining revenues. It has been an honor to play a role in the local residents' childhood memories.

We will begin the   (144)   sale on Oct. 1. As the holiday

6 填空式閱讀

7 單篇閱讀

7 雙篇、三篇閱讀

模擬試題

season is around the corner, it is the perfect timing to store up on Thanksgiving and Christmas decorations, and purchase the gifts for your loved ones.   (145)   If you have our loyalty card, you will enjoy an additional 10% discount. Don't miss out on this once in a lifetime opportunity!

We look forward to your   (146) .

Sincerely,
the Gift Store Around the Corner

143. (A) having service
    (B) having served
    (C) has served
    (D) have service

144. (A) liquidate
    (B) liquid
    (C) liquidation
    (D) liquidating

145. (A) There is no other store like ours.
    (B) Most of the products will be 50% off.
    (C) Tourists will love our souvenirs.
    (D) Thanksgiving is a traditional American holiday.

146. (A) patron

    (B) patronizing

    (C) patronize

    (D) patronage

PART 7

Directions: in this part, you will read a selection of texts, such as magazine and newspapers articles, e-mails, and instant messages. Each text or set of texts is followed by several questions. Select the best answer for each question and mark the letter (A), (B), (C), or (D) on your answer sheet.

Questions 147-149 refer to the following advertisement.

Best English Class Schedules

Courses	Fee	Time
Vocabulary Basic	US 300	Mon 1 p.m. to 6 p.m
Vocabulary Basic II	US 600	Wed 2 p.m. to 7 p.m.
Grammar Basic	US 450	Mon 1 p.m. to 6 p.m
Grammar Basic II	US 900	Tue 2 p.m. to 7 p.m.
Refresher/Vocabulary	US 300	Thu 1 p.m. to 6 p.m
Refresher/ Grammar	US 450	Fri 2 p.m. to 7 p.m.

Note:

1. There's been a scheduling conflict between Vocabulary Basic and Grammar Basic. People can choose either Refresher/ Vocabulary or Refresher/ Grammar since the content is the same.

2. A free teaching DVD will be given to students taking four courses from Best English.
3. Textbook fees are not included in the fees listed above.

147. What is the main purpose of the passage?

(A) to inform the change to the class schedule

(B) to inform the class arrangement and tuition

(C) to give away a free DVD

(D) to raise the tuition

148. What is suggested in case of a scheduling conflict?

(A) People can take another course with the same content but under a different title

(B) People can ask for a refund

(C) People can sign up for a private tutoring session

(D) People can watch a teaching DVD to make up for the course they miss

149. How much does it cost if a person decides to sign up for Vocabulary Basic II and Grammar Basic II?

(A) US 600

(B) US 900

(C) US 1500

(D) US 1000

Questions 150-151 refer to the following advertisement.

Best Garage Sale

This year, we are having baby clothes, as you all know how quick a baby can grow. We also have a list of baby strollers for you to choose from. It's 85% new, and will totally save you lots of money. If you'd like to buy baby-related stuffs as a gift to your friend, you will also find it exhilarating to be here. For those who are about to have a baby soon, visiting won't do any harm. We also have interior designers here. They can help you visualize your ideal baby room whether it's going to be a room full of cartoon characters on the wall or a trendy palace style. Anyway, our Garage Sell will open as usual from Dec 12 to Dec 20. For more information, you can see more information on our flyer.

150. How many days will the garage sale last?
    (A) 9 days
    (B) 12 days
    (C) 8 days
    (D) 20 days

151. Which item is recommended by the passage?
    (A) cartoon characters
    (B) baby strollers

(C) wall decoration stickers

(D) interior design blueprints

Questions 152-155 refer to the following advertisement.

Best Antique Shop

Normally, people come here for crystal balls of all sorts, but we're running out of them this year. However, we do have ancient pearls that can be a treasure not only for collectors, but also for newlyweds. It can be seen as a way to symbolize long-lasting love. Ancient pearls are so rare that they can only be found in some places where poisonous sea weeds are rampant. They have to be harvested for at least 10 years. Some are found from the shipwreck down the sea. The value of ancient pearls is invaluable, and it even outweighs diamonds, money, and jade. For people who'd like to buy it as a gift to your loved one during Valentine's Day, you're in luck. We have craftsmen who can make specifically designed pearls for you, and of course with carved names on it. The craftsmen will only come to our shop for three days from Jan 16 to Jan 18.

152. What kind of product did consumers usually buy in the antique store in the past?

(A) crystal pendants

(B) ancient pearls

(C) pearl necklaces

(D) crystal balls

153. What does the writer mean by "rampant"?

 (A) extremely poisonous

(B) very rare and expensive

(C) widespread and uncontrolled

(D) quite precious

154. What does the writer mean by "invaluable"?

 (A) valuable beyond estimation

(B) lacking any value

(C) the value differs according to different buyers

(D) the value is undecided

155. Which one of the following about ancient pearls is FALSE?

(A) It takes a long time to harvest these pearls.

(B) They are not as valuable as diamonds.

(C) They have a symbolic meaning.

(D) They are very rare.

Best Yoga Farm

Best Yoga Farm is dedicated to differentiating itself from the rest of the Yoga-related service. We'll include organic foods in the cafeteria area. People can eat foods of lower calories at our cafeteria. All calories are carefully calculated by our nutritionists, so you don't need to worry about consuming more than you should. In addition, you can experience cultivation of organic foods at the backyard of our farm. You get to purchase seeds of organic foods and can cultivate them right after you finish exercising or stretching out. Also, we are adding another cool thing to our Yoga Farm. With sweltering summer coming up, we do provide free ice creams to people who sign up our courses before June 1 2018. (free ice creams for the first three days of our course)

156. What is the main purpose of the passage?
    (A) to describe the benefits of organic foods
    (B) to list the qualifications of the coaches in this yoga center
    (C) to explain how people can get free ice cream
    (D) the introduce the services that distinguish this yoga center from others

157. Which service is NOT included in this yoga center?

(A) cultivating organic foods

(B) low calorie foods

(C) foods designed by dietician

(D) free trial yoga classes

Questions 158-159 refer to the following advertisement.

Best Restaurant

An enough open space for dining is what most consumers desire. Eating at traditional restaurants is too crowded. That's why Best Restaurant is adding the prairie experience to dining. You get the chance to have a barbecue with your friends on the prairie where you can smell the scene of green grass. We'll have all kinds of meats and meals prepared on the side. You can also taste the milk from our cattle. All the Mongolian-like experience will turn the night into an unforgettable one. Besides, there is a mysterious magic place behind our cabins. Fireflies gather in the woods, forming the incredible scene that all children fancy. If you're the romantic type of the person, you'll love this. For natural-lovers, walking down the trail while viewing groups of fireflies showing up is like a godsend. For more information, please visit www.bestrestaurant.greatview.com.

158. Why did Best Restaurant add the prairie experience?

    (A) Some customers have requested this experience

    (B) The meat barbecued on a prairie tastes more delicious

    (C) An open space experience is more comfortable for customers

    (D) The restaurant owner wanted to keep cattle on the prairie

159. Why did the passage mention "a mysterious magic place"?

    (A) No one has ever been to the area behind the cabins

    (B) A magician will perform magic tricks at the barbecue

    (C) The origin of the fireflies is very mysterious

    (D) People can see the incredible scene of the fireflies in this place

Questions 160-163 refer to the following advertisement.

Best Travel and Tours

If you're looking for an adventurous tour in the US, Best Travel and Tours is the one for you. We've designed a 10 day tour. Our tour package includes RV and Road juggernaut experience. You'll be like giant stars, such as Justin Bieber taking a grand tour by taking Road juggernaut. In addition, __

(1) . We maybe stop by whenever we see something new and exciting. You won't feel bored. You get to photograph a bison or wild animals. We might as well have the tent ready at any camp site, have a barbecue there. Plus, our tour package includes a special chef, who will have all ingredients and foods ready whether we are at a river basin or national park. (2) . Don't worry. (3) . Our price is quite reasonable, always falling under the range that students are able to afford, and there won't be a discount unless you are a vegetarian. (4) .

160. What can you receive if you sign up for the trip and are a vegetarian?
(A) free vegetarian food
(B) grilled vegetables
(C) meal coupons
(D) a discount

161. Which of the blanks marked (1), (2), (3), and (4) does the following sentence belong to?
"we don't have a specific schedule for the whole day"
(A) (1)
(B) (2)
(C) (3)
(D) (4)

162. What kind of activity is NOT mentioned in this passage?

    (A) going to Justin Bieber's concert

    (B) barbecue

    (C) camping

    (D) taking an RV

163. Why does the passage mention "bison"?

    (A) to give an example of an endangered species

    (B) to point out that bisons look very handsome

    (C) to give an example of how the tour will stop for something exciting

    (D) to explain how to take photos of bisons

Questions 164-166 refer to the following letter.

Best F&B

Dear Jack,

   (1) . I have seen the quote for raw materials and several items. It's not slightly adjusted prices. (2) . I've discussed with our boss and several managers during a product launch meeting on March 18 2018. Since you're our main supplier and we've worked with you for at least 10 years, so I was wondering is it possible for you to make some adjustments to the price. Another thing that is on our mind is whether there will be any discount on raw materials if we order for 20 tons of flour, rice, and sugar. We do have an enlarged warehouse since March 3 2018. (3) . Also, we are going to reposition our market place by narrowing down several products we are selling worldwide. (4) . If there won't be any openness to discussion, we might as well have to

find another supplier by cutting down 30% of our recent order from you. Looking forward to your response.

Best regards,
Jenny Wang

164. Which of the blanks marked (1), (2), (3), and (4) does the following sentence belong to?

"For that kind of prices, there is no way that we can make any more profits"

(A) (1)

(B) (2)

(C) (3)

(D) (4)

165. What request is made in this letter?

(A) a reposition of the company's market place

(B) help with building the warehouse

(C) a discount for a large amount of order

(D) more supplies of rice, flour and sugar

166. What can be inferred if the supplier refused to accept the request?

(A) The company might carry out more negotiations with the supplier

(B) The company might do business with another supplier

(C) The supplier might go out of business

(D) The suppliers' orders will not be affected

Questions 167-168 refer to the following advertisement.

Christmas Special Offer

This year, Best Festival is having a new service. We're offering a customized service for decorating neighborhoods, communities, and companies. You don't have to worry about the Christmas stuff like you used to. Like should we put those light bulbs back to our warehouse, it's not trendy enough? Or should we spent time rewashing those things before we decorate? Or why do we have to spend time decorating Christmas trees in the house while kids only want us to take them to participate in community grand Christmas festival where they can get cotton candy while enjoying the festival. Remember worries give you wrinkles. With us, you won't have these worries. We have the latest technology and you can get a customized Christmas decoration at a cheap price.

167. What does "customized service" imply?

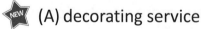 (A) decorating service

(B) service according to cultural customs

(C) much more popular service

(D) tailor-made service

168. Which of the following service is NOT implied in this passage?

(A) light bulb display

(B) cleaning decorations

(C) a Santa Claus character

(D) decorating a Christmas tree

Questions 169-171 refer to the following memo.

Memo

To: Cindy Chen, Assistant Editor
From: Jane Wang, Mangers
Date: July 22
Re: ideas about the Book Fair

I've seen your ideas about the Book Fair. __(1)__. It's quite interesting that you want to add the interaction session. __(2)__. In addition, it's a lovely thought that you think some people attending Book Fair might bring their kids there. I remember we do have some snacks for them, right? I won't be at the company, since I have other errands to do. __(3)__. This my Line ID: XXXXBESTBEST please add me the moment you see this memo. We can discuss other things through Line contact. __(4)__.

Thanks,
Jane Wang

169. Why was the memo sent?

(A) to initiate a discussion on the Book Fair

(B) to encourage more new ideas on the Book Fair

(C) to congratulate Cindy Chen on her achievement

(D) to discuss whether they should buy snacks

170. Which of the blanks marked (1), (2), (3), and (4) does the following sentence belong to?

"I think it's great"

(A) (1)

(B) (2)

(C) (3)

(D) (4)

171. Why did Jane Wang give Cindy Chen her Line ID?

(A) to tell her about the errands

(B) to have more interactions with Cindy

(C) to have a more private relationship with Cindy

(D) to continue further discussion on the same topic in the memo

Questions 172-175 refer to the following announcement.

Best Department Store

   (1)   . A ransacking yesterday at Best Department Store raised a security problem. Police haven't yet had a clue as to why they broke into.   (2)   . This may seem like the worst shoplifting in thirty years, but at least no one got injured. Best Department Store owner announced a statement to us that the store won't be opened unless the police have found enough evidence. The jewelry collections on Oct 13, which is two weeks from now, might also be declined.   (3)   . Sports Club won't give club members any compensation regarding to this incident. We can only hope the police find the evidence sooner than we think.   (4)   . Reporter Lisa Lin at Best Department Store

172. What does "ransacking" mean in this passage?
 (A) running away from a crime scene
    (B) searching a place violently to commit robbery
    (C) demanding a ransom
    (D) pointing a gun at a victim

173. Which of the following is TRUE according to this

passage?

(A) Only gold was stolen

(B) The motive behind the break-in remains unclear

(C) The members of Sports Club will receive compensations

(D) All operations of the department store will remain normal

174. Which of the blanks marked (1), (2), (3), and (4) does the following sentence belong to?

"According to several employees, jewelry and gold were all gone"

(A) (1)

(B) (2)

(C) (3)

(D) (4)

175. What might happen to the jewelry collection exhibition?

(A) It might not be held

(B) It will be held as scheduled

(C) More security measures will be taken

(D) There will be more security guards

Questions 176-180 refer to the following advertisement.

Best Breast Cancer Center

Breast cancer has been known as a terrifying disease for most women. It can happen at a time when you least expect it. Best Breast Cancer Center is having a symposium today to help women learn more about breast cancer, hopefully raising more funds for those who are still battling against this disease.

Name	Descriptions	Time
Dr. John	Introduction	9:00-10:00
Dr. Mary	Treatment	10:00-12:00
Break		
Patient Linda	Sharing ideas	2:00-2:30
Dr. Lin	precaution	2:30-4:30
host	Fund-raising	4:30-5:30

Note:

1. Dr. John will use PPT slides, whereas Dr. Lin will play videos.
2. All speaking sessions will be recorded except for the patient part.

Dear Frank,

I thought you did a great job being a host that day. I was actually a patient combating the breast cancer. I never knew I was going to be one of them. When I found out I got breast cancer, it was stage 2. Miraculously, after meticulous care and a series of treatment by my family members and doctors, I started to feel better and eventually recovered. I want to thank you for doing this. I am grateful for Best Breast Cancer Center, assisting patients through the hard-time of their lives. Now I do want to help by donating US 2,000 for fund-raising. I know it's not a huge amount of money, but it's just a small way for me to say "Thank You".

Best regards,
Cindy Lin

176. What does the term "symposium" refer to?

(A) a conference where people share ideas

(B) a meeting where doctors order medicines

(C) a party especially for medical professionals

(D) a meeting similar to an auction

177. Who is Frank?

(A) a doctor specializing in breast cancer

(B) the host of the symposium

(C) a breast cancer survivor

(D) a breast cancer patient

178. What is the purpose of Cindy's letter?

(A) to show her appreciation to Frank

(B) to ask how much money she should donate

(C) to show her appreciation to Best Breast Cancer Center

(D) to inquire the way to donate some money

179. How long will the symposium last?

(A) 6 hours

(B) 7 hours

(C) 6.5 hours

(D) 5.5 hours

180. What will Dr. Lin talk about?

(A) how to take preventive measures against breast cancer

(B) how to survive breast cancer

(C) the most effective treatment

(D) the best way to raise money for breast cancer research

Questions 181-185 refer to the following letter and statement.

Letter to the school principal

Dear Mr. Jack,

Due to a **negligence** of your school lifeguard, my kid is still in the hospital right now. For a moment, these questions rushed through my mind: why did they call the ambulance so late? What were those lifeguards doing? Are they well-trained lifeguards? According to some parents, some of them were scrolling smartphones, while kids were swimming for fun? I do need an explanation for this. Why didn't they supervise the kids as they should have. You're the school dean. You'd better explain this. I'm bringing the lawyer to school today.

Best regards,
Jane Wang

Statement from the school

Best Elite School won't tolerate this kind of behavior. Any behavior that can endanger a kid's safety is not allowed. We condemn those who challenge school authority and those who are **loose cannons**. All lifeguards who were on duty that day were handcuffed to the police station for statements. We sincerely apologize to those kids who were injured at the swimming pool the other day. Not only are those lifeguards going to face penalties from the court, they will be expelled from Best Elite School, starting from April 15, 2018. The school has decided to close the swimming pool from now on to prevent further injuries and damage that might put the life of any kid at risk.

Best Elite School
April 13, 2018

181. What does the term "negligence" imply about the lifeguard?

    (A) His mistake is negligible

    (B) His lack of attention to the kids

    (C) Negligence is unavoidable sometimes

    (D) His lack of passion for his job

182. What might Jane Wang do when she meets Mr. Jack?

    (A) She might shout at Mr. Jack

    (B) She might discuss legal matters with Mr. Jack

    (C) She might ask for some compensation

    (D) She might ask Mr. Jack about how to treat her kid

183. What does the term "loose cannons" refer to?

    (A) People who know a lot about the trade of cannons

    (B) People who like to wear loose clothes

    (C) People who hurt children on purpose

    (D) People whose behaviors are unexpected and might cause problems

184. Who is Mr. Jack?

    (A) a lifeguard

    (B) the swimming pool director

    (C) the school dean

    (D) a concerned parent

185. According to the statement, what might NOT happen to the lifeguards?

    (A) They will receive penalties.

    (B) They will lose their jobs.

    (C) They will leave some records at the police station.

    (D) They will be forgiven after apologizing to the injured kids' parents.

Questions 186-190 refer to the following line messages and form.

Best Museum

Line messages ❶

Betty:	It seems that we won't be able to see portraits at Best Museum
Linda:	The tickets are officially sold out. Maybe next year.
Cindy:	I know a guy from Best Museum who can get the tickets.
Betty:	Even at this time?
Cindy:	It's probably for employees and their family members. I can ask him if you guys really want to go.
Linda:	ASK HIM! You know I can't resist those artworks.

(ten minutes later)

Cindy:	he says he has three tickets left. His colleagues have to spend the weekend with the family in another city.
Linda:	That means we can still go, right?
Betty:	Can't believe we are that lucky?
Cindy:	yep, but **on one condition**? He wants us to add him as a Facebook friend.
Linda:	**Deal!**
Betty:	I saw him sending the request... alright..for damn tickets.

Line messages ❷

Betty: Amazing! Thank God we went to the museum.
Linda: Some paintings are recently discovered, right?
Cindy: Perhaps... I wasn't paying too much attention.
Cindy: But I do love the coffee there, pretty invigorating
Betty: It's too expensive.
Linda: I'm posting all the photos taken that day.
Betty: Meaning clicking the "Like" button?
Cindy: Of course... **click** click click
Linda: What are the requirements for working at Best Museum?
Linda: It would be a combination of my interest and my major.
Betty: Why not ask Tom?
Linda: He is sending me the scanned form.

Form

Education: should be college or above, and history or arts related majors
English proficiency: advanced
Language: French or German as a second language will be a plus

Note: Normally, we prefer candidates who have taken a summer internship at Best Museum. Candidates working at other museums are welcomed. Candidates who major in architecture or design will also be considered. Recommendations from employees of Best Museum are favored. Candidates should prepare a CV and four video clips about four different museums. (Best Museum: excluded)

186. What does Cindy mean by "on one condition"?

(A) The condition of adding one more person to her Facebook friends is complicated.

(B) After adding the guy to their Line friends, she and her

friends will receive the tickets.

(C) The condition of the exhibition at Best Museum is of very high quality.

(D) She and her friends will receive the tickets only if they agree to do something.

187. What does Linda mean by "deal"?

 (A) She is not sure if they should deal with the guy.

(B) Dealing with the guy is a piece of cake.

(C) She has no problem adding the guy to her Facebook friends.

(D) After sealing the deal, she will pay the guy immediately.

188. What does Cindy mean by "click"?

 (A) She's clicking on the Like button

(B) She's uploading some pictures

(C) She's clicking the mouse

(D) She's sending her CV

189. Which of the following is NOT mentioned in the form?

(A) educational background

(B) language proficiency

(C) job responsibility

(D) internship experience

190. Which of the following candidates might have the best qualifications for the position in Best Museum?

(A) someone who speaks English and French fluently and holds a degree in arts

(B) someone who holds a degree in arts and speaks Chinese fluently

(C) someone who has taken a summer internship in Best Museum and has a high school diploma

(D) someone who is very interested in arts and donates a large sum of money to Best Museum

Questions 191-195 refer to the following advertisement and letter.

Best Conservation Center

Best Conservation Center is dedicated to saving native wildlife. This year we are lucky enough to get a tremendous sum of money from overseas companies. The money will be used to save mammals which are hurt or trapped in the wild. An extra care will be given to those animals which have a serious wound. They will be taken to our conservation center, and of course our veterinarians will be there. For those volunteers who participate in our program and help lighten our staff's workload in certain activities, such as cleaning the beach and preparing meals for animals, they will receive gifts in exchange for their volunteer hours.

The table below is a list of gifts

Gift Name	Time spent	Descriptions
Huge black bear bag	150 hours	For those who have completed the program for more than 600 hours, you will be getting a certificate, and get to apply for a job position at Best Conservation Center worldwide since you have demonstrated your enthusiasm for animals and conservation.
Raccoon hand gloves	150 hours	
Luxurious Best handbag	300 hours	
Luxurious kitchenware	600 hours	
Brown bear jacket	150 hours	

Letter

Dear HR personnel of Best Conservation Center,

I'm a student majoring in zoology. I've volunteered at Best Conservation Center and worked there for two whole summers, 8 hours per day. That's 1920 hours in total. What's more interesting is that those working hours can be valued and exchanged for gifts. Now I've exchanged a whole kitchenware for my mother, three brown bear jackets for me and my sisters, four huge black bear bags for kids at Children Center.

Assisting doctors and spending the day with animals are really meaningful. This is really an ideal job for me. Even though I do not have a fancy degree, I do think those two past summers there have shown my dedication and enthusiasm for wild animals. Enclosed is my CV. Looking forward to hearing from you.

Best regards,
Linda Lee

191. Where does most of the funding this year come from?

(A) volunteers

(B) university students

(C) foreign companies

(D) veterinarians

192. What is the criteria for obtaining the gifts?

(A) reaching a certain number of hours

(B) cleaning the beach

(C) preparing meals for animals

(D) taking an internship at the conservation center

193. How will most of the funding this year be spent?

(A) to invest in gifts

(B) to help the mammals hurt in the wilderness

(C) to save to endangered mammals

(D) to hire more workers

194. If a volunteer wants to exchange for a luxurious Best handbag and a brown bear jacket, how many hours should she accumulate?

(A) 300 hours

(B) 450 hours

(C) 150 hours

(D) 600 hours

195. Which of the following is NOT mentioned in the letter?

    (A) various gifts

    (B) volunteer hours

    (C) the applicant's major

    (D) an internship program

Questions 196-200 refer to the following letters and line messages.

Letter ❶

Dear Jason,

I bought a house through one of your sales reps at Best House Rental. I was pleased with your service until yesterday, and lately I found several problems about the house that just don't seem right. The wall of the backyard is rusty. It's ruined to a point that a new paint can't cover that. We have contacted a handyman to our house. He finds out other problems in plumbing and kitchen pipes. We can't cook meals, and there are some leaking problems, so water pours on the front yard whenever we use water in the toilet or kitchen. It's totally your sales rep's negligence for not letting us know all the conditions of the house.

Best regards,
Ann Chen

Line messages

Jason: this is Best House Rental, I'm Jason by the way.

Ann: I just can't stand this anymore, so I think what the heck talking on a phone is quicker.

Ann's husband: Tell him if it's not fixed we're going to sue.

Ann: have you received the letter? How are you going to deal with this?

Ann: there're termites!!! Things I recently discover.

Jason: I'm sorry. I didn't know all about this. Perhaps I come to your house with our sales reps to see what we can do.

Ann: when?

Jason: this afternoon 2 p.m. is that ok?

Ann: ok see you then.

Letter ❷

Dear Ann,

After visiting your house the other day, we try to come up with several solutions to this particular and unusual condition. We obviously have no clue about the conditions of the house. It's covered with luxurious decoration and paint. Perhaps arranging you to live in a house of the same size is the way to go. I'm contacting the construction workers. They're going to renovate the house we'd like to arrange for you. We also book a hotel near your house, so that you can have a sound sleep after two weeks of horrible nights. There won't be any insects or weird things in your new house I guarantee, except for some earthworms on the backyard.

Best regards,
Jason
Nov 19 2018

196. Which of the following problems about the house is NOT

mentioned in the letter?

(A) leaking

(B) a plumbing problem

(C) an insect problem

(D) a rusty wall

197. What problem did Ann later find out?

(A) a pipe problem

(B) a pest problem

(C) rusty pipes

(D) earthworms

198. What solution did Best House Rental offer?

(A) buying an apartment for Ann and her family

(B) arranging for Ann and her family to live in another house

(C) paying the hotel fees for Ann and her family until they buy a new house

(D) arranging for Ann and her family to move to a new apartment

199. Why did Jason write "We obviously have no clue about the conditions of the house" in his letter?

(A) Because the sales representative did not tell Jason the truth

(B) Because Jason did not see the rusty wall

(C) Because the house is covered with luxurious decoration and paint

(D) Because clues about the condition of the house were difficult to identify

200. What will the construction workers do?

(A) They will tear down Ann's house.

(B) They will refurbish the new house for Ann.

(C) They will conduct some pest control.

(D) They will repaint Ann's house.

新多益模擬試題解析

Part 5

101. 長期於地下隧道工作的人暴露在有害化學物質之下，最終會導致慢性病。

 解析

　　第 101 題考的是字彙，chronic 是形容詞：慢性的，特別指疾病或壞事長期持續或不斷重演，例如 She suffers from chronic pain in her arms.（她忍受手臂的慢性疼痛。）/ The hospital is facing a chronic shortage of nursing staff.（這間醫院正面對長期缺乏護理人員。）定位回題目，長時間暴露於有害物質下的工作，最終將導致慢性疾病的發生：故此題答案為 C。

(A) regular，定期的 adj.：Corporate emails require regular attention from employees.

(B) unharmful，無害的 adj.：The design of the working environment should be unharmful to employees.

(D) sustained，持續的 adj.：The fans reacted to the performance with sustained applause.

102. 保健專家們不斷地提醒人們不要攝取含膽固醇的食物，但卻全然忘記了膽固醇是有益處的。

第 102 題考的是字彙，beneficial 是形容詞：有益的，例如：Running, like any other form of exercise, is beneficial to your health. （和任何其他形式的運動一樣，慢跑有益於健康。） 定位回題目，保健專家建議人們不要攝取含膽固醇的食物，但其實膽固醇仍有益於人體健康的功效：故此題答案為 D。benefit 可作名詞或動詞使用，有效益和造福的意思：例如：The discovery of oil brought many benefits to the state. (油田的發現為該州帶來了許多好處。) / The new plant will benefit the local community. （新的工廠將造福當地社區。）

(A) harmful，有害的 adj.：Food must be heated to a high temperature to kill harmful bacteria.
(B) rough，粗糙的 adj.：I made a rough table out of some cardboards.
(C) chronic，慢性的 adj.：Chronic illness recently compelled him to retire from the service.

103. 農夫開始棄用極有效卻相當毒的化學物質。

第 103 題考的是文法，定位回題目，toxic 是形容詞：有毒的：所以加在 toxic 前面用以修飾 toxic 的就必須是一個副詞：故此題答案為 B。incredibly，是令人難以置信地，用以修飾 toxic，表示具有非常驚人的毒性。

(A) credulous，輕信的，容易被騙的 adj.：Most people are credulous and impressed by things they don't understand.
(C) credible，可信的 adj.：They haven't produced any credible evidence.
(D) believable，可信的 adj.：Generally, the more details a person

remembers, the more believable and convincing his description is.

---

104. 在特定的非洲地區飲用水受到細菌跟微生物的汙染。

 解析

第 104 題考的是字彙，contaminate 是動詞：汙染，這裡做被動式使用，be contaminated with Sth..，表示被什麼東西所污染；配合題目敘述邏輯，表示飲用水受到了細菌和微生物的汙染；故此題答案為 A。

(B) contamination，汙染 n.：We discovered lead contamination in the toy.
(C) contained，包含 v.：The essay contained a number of grammar mistakes.
(D) pollution，汙染 n.：Greenery is an essential process to improve air quality and reduce pollution.

---

105. 少了由核能電廠產生的電力，當地居民開始擔憂在夏季期間將可能電力短缺。

 解析

第 105 題考的是文法，generate 是動詞：產生的意思，這裡搭配電力，因為電力是「被產生」，修飾電力必須以被動語態。被動語態基本的格式是 be 動詞+過去分詞，beV. generated by Sth.，表示藉由某物所產生的，這裡 generated 是過去分詞。定位回題目，the electricity (which 或 that was) generated by nuclear power plants：此句原本用形容詞子句形容 the electricity，進一步可以省略關係代名詞：which 或 that 及省略 be 動詞 was，保留過去分詞 generated。故此題答案為 D。

106. 比起中文系為主修的學生來說，昆蟲的生活週期的複雜度對於生命科學的學生來說更具吸引力。

 解析

第 106 題考的是形容詞比較級的句型：A + be 動詞 + 比較級 than + B，表示 A 比 B 更…。intriguing 是形容詞：讓人著迷的或奇妙的，這裡用 be intriguing to Sb.，表示對某人來說是令人著迷的：加上比較級的句型，intriguing 的比較級是 more intriguing 或 less intriguing。根據題目大意，生命科學系的學生對昆蟲生態的興趣，應比中文系的學生來得多，所以用 more intriguing 比較合乎邏輯，故此題答案為 B。

107. 觀光客察覺出具物種豐富多樣性的地方比起較不具多樣性的地方花費更高昂。

 解析

第 107 題考的是文法及字義。cost/take/spend 的用法，可以從主詞是人或物，以及受詞是錢或時間來判斷。根據題目，名詞子句 that... 裡的主詞是複數的 places，花費金錢，所以用複數動詞 cost 而不是單數動詞 costs：故此題答案為 B。

a. cost 的本意為「價值」，故僅限用於「主詞」為「物」、受詞為「金錢」。

物 + cost + 人 + $ (+ to v.) → [物] 花了 [人] 多少錢 [做…]

例：This room costs me 500 dollars to rent tonight.

b. take 用於花費「時間」，主詞可能是人、物，或是動作。
物 + take + 人 + 時間 + to v. →[物] 花了 [人] 多少時間 [做…]
人 + take + 時間 + to v. →[人] 花了多少時間 [做…]
動名詞 Ving + take + 人 + 時間 →[做…] 花了 [人] 多少時間
例：Those trees took him ten years to grow.

c. spend 用於花費「時間、金錢」，主詞只能是「人」。
人 + spend + 時間/金錢 + v-ing →[人] 花了 多少時間/金錢 [做…]
人 + spend + 時間/金錢 + on + N. →[人] 花了 多少時間/金錢 在…上
例：I spent three hours reading the novel.

---

108. 冗長的瀏覽智慧型手機的確引起眼睛不適，以致於有其他裝置
是被開發於能減輕此症狀的。

 解析

　　第 108 題考的是文法，主要測試 prolong 的詞性變化。prolong 是動詞：延長、持續，例如：We were having such a good time that we decided to prolong our stay by another week.（我們有一段很好的時光，所以決定多待一個星期。） prolong 的過去分詞 prolonged 常轉化為形容詞使用，例如：These drugs can be continued for a prolonged period.（這些藥物可以長期使用。）定位回題目，因為空格之後是主詞 viewing，因此正確選項是形容詞。這裡用過去分詞 prolonged 當形容詞，形容主詞，也是動名詞 viewing，表示長時間的瀏覽；故此題答案為 B。

---

109. 儘管交通設施，像是道路重型卡車和露營車都不普遍，他們是
現今年輕人覺得很時髦的交通工具。

第 109 題考的是字彙，widespread 是形容詞：普及的、廣泛的；例如：There has been widespread concern about road safety. 根據題目大意，road juggernauts 和 RV 雖然不普遍，但現今的年輕人還是覺得很時髦，故此題答案為 C。其餘選項的均無「普及的」字義。

(A) uncommon，罕見的 adj.：He does have an uncommon intuition.（他的確擁有不尋常的直覺。）
(B) rampant，猖獗的 adj.：Epidemics are rampant in third-world countries.（在第三世界國家傳染病是猖獗的。）
(D) wide，寬廣的 adj.：Someone left the window wide open.

110. 倍斯特旅館將考慮使用能抵抗槍枝射擊和颶風的強化玻璃。

第 110 題考的是字彙，toughen 是動詞：鍛鍊、使…強化；例如 Working in the army certainly toughened him up.（在軍隊工作確實使他更堅強。）定位回題目，這裡 toughened 是過去分詞，過去分詞常當形容詞使用，表示被強化的，指的就是強化玻璃；故此題答案為 D。

(A) rough，粗糙的 adj.：It was a rough mountain road, so very few travelled here.
(B) tough，強硬的 adj.：We need a mayor who is tough enough to declare a war on the mafia.
(C) toughness，韌性 n.：He lacks the inner toughness needed to survive in a foreign country.

111. 有熱銷單曲在亞馬遜暢銷榜蟬聯連續六個月，這位巨星獲得了與倍斯特影音三年的合約。

 解析

第 111 題考的是文法，首先注意到空格後不是完整子句，而是接名詞 a hit song，再以形容詞子句 that has been... 修飾 a hit song。因此正確選項應該是介系詞，因為介系詞之後馬上接名詞。介系詞只有(B)，(C)。又根據題目主要子句的大意，這位巨星獲得了與倍斯特影音三年的合約，所以應該選 (B) With。故此題答案為 B。With 表達「有，附帶，伴隨著」。With... 片語是副詞片語，修飾主要子句。

112. 無法向雇主更新合約，外籍傭人只能返回他們家鄉。

 解析

第 112 題考的是字彙，unable 是形容詞：無法的，後面接不定詞 to V.，主要線索是不定詞，表示無法完成某事：例如：We were unable to contact him at the time. （當時我們無法聯繫他。)根據題目，這裡不能選(A) incapable 及(C) capable，因為這兩個形容詞後面都要接 of Ving，例如 capable/incapable of renewing the contract：故此題答案為 B。

(A) incapable，無能力的 adj.：She was incapable of refusing others' demands.
(C) capable，有能力的 adj.：She's a very capable accountant.
(D) ability，能力 n.：The teacher has the ability to explain things clearly and concisely.

113. 盜獵象牙是非法的，但獵捕象牙者重視金錢大於珍貴的生命。

解析

第 113 題考的是文法，poach 是動詞盜獵的意思，題目用動名詞 poaching ivory (of elephants) 當主詞，表示盜獵象牙這一件事，所以是一個單數主詞，要搭配單數動詞：故此題答案為 C。

114. 教育專家們致力於降低師生比來幫助較不成功的學生

解析

第 114 題考的是文法，主要測試「貢獻於，致力於」的動詞片語。devote 是動詞：貢獻、致力於的意思，動詞片語有 devote oneself/Sth. to Sth./Sb./動名詞 Ving 或 beV. devoted to Sth./動名詞 Ving，要特別注意 to 在此是介係詞。例如：He devoted himself/his life to serving his family and friends.（他致力於為家人和朋友服務）。根據題目，空格前是 are devoted to，因為 to 在此是介係詞，且因為空格後有受詞 students，可推測 help 在此是及物動詞，不是名詞。所以應該將 help 加上 ing，形成動名詞。故此題答案為 A。

115. 倍斯特科技將重心由強調製造上轉向整體的貨物品質上。

解析

第 115 題考的是字彙，emphasis 是名詞：重點、要點：一般用 put/place/add emphasis on Sth.的句型，表示強調某件事物，例如：To achieve the transition, they put a lot of emphasis on innovations.（為了成功轉型，他們大幅強調創新。）：故此題答案為 C。

(A) emphasized，強調 v.（動詞過去式或過去分詞）：It was emphasized that European integration would pose controversies.

(B) stress,壓力 n.：Pilates is a very effective sport for combating stress.

(D) emphasize,強調 v.：He emphasized that all the people participating in the research were volunteers.

---

116. 擅長於適應溫度變化和人類干擾的動物更能存活。

　　第 116 題考的是文法，主要測試形容詞子句的關係代名詞。正確的關係代名詞依賴的是它的先行詞，即關係代名詞代替的名詞。這題的關係代名詞的先行詞剛好是主詞 animals，而且當先行詞是普通名詞，不是名字或世界上獨一無二之人，事，物時，這種先行詞要用限定的形容詞子句形容：限定的形容詞子句在關代前不能有逗號，換言之，關代（空格處）前沒有逗號，就是暗示考生這是限定形容詞子句的線索。在限定形容詞子句中，不管先行詞是人類，動物/事物，關代都能用 that，人類以外的先行詞，關係代名詞也能用 which。由於選項中沒有關代 that，**因此選 (C) which**。此題的限定形容詞子句是 which are adept at temperature changes and human interference。

---

117. 愛狗者都有偏好將狗狗的需求置於所有事情之上。

　　第 117 題考的是字彙及詞性，penchant 是名詞：傾向、偏好、嗜好：通常用單數 a penchant for sth 表示傾向於某事物，例如：He had a penchant for mountain climbing.（他有登山的嗜好。）根據題目，也可以用詞性去判斷，have a... for 中間應填入名詞，可以用 they have a penchant for... 或是直接用 they prefer...：故此題答案為 D。

(A) prefer,較喜歡 v.：She prefers western food, while I prefer Chinese food.

(B) favorable，良好的 adj.：You can enjoy favorable sunlight at the morning here.

(C) favorite，喜愛的 adj.：She'll make my favorite cake when I am back.

---

118. 我們最終選擇在新產品發表會上展示的醫療裝置是 IDM 輪椅。

 解析

　　第 118 題考的是文法：形容詞子句的用法。根據題目，這裡用「我們最終選擇在新產品發表會上展示的」來形容 the medical device，句子的主詞是物，可以用 which 或 that 連接：we choose the device. / the device is IDM wheelchair.，可以合併為 the device (which/that) we choose is IDM wheelchair.。which/that 當做 choose 的受詞，可省略，形容詞子句的主詞 we 不能省略**故此題答案為 B**。

---

119. 消費者現在認定電影中的電影技術和誇張的視覺效果和音效比動人的故事敘述更重要。

 解析

　　第 119 題考的是字彙，cinematic 是形容詞：電影的，例如：The novel has a cinematic quality that you can picture it in your brain.（那小說具有電影特質，可以在腦中顯現畫面。）根據題目，movies with... techniques 中間應放入形容詞，表示影片的拍攝技巧，故此題答案為 B。

(A) cinema，電影 n.：She is famous for her work in the cinema.

(C) cinematography，攝影 n.：The cinematography in this film

makes it different from the others.

(D) cinematical，錯誤用法，正確的「電影的」形容詞應為 cinematic。

---

120. 既然兩個製造工人都請了三個月的產假，員工現在比起以往工作更忙碌了。

 解析

第 120 題考的是文法，形容詞比較級的句型：A + be動詞 + 形容詞比較級 than + B，表示 A 比 B 更…。根據題目裡副詞子句 Since... 的大意：因為兩位製作工人請了三個月的產假，可推測主要子句表達其他員工更忙。主要子句的主要動詞是現在進行式的 are having，空格後的名詞是 working schedule，所以這題用 busy 的比較級 busier 形容 working schedule，表示現在有一個更繁忙的工作時間表，故此題答案為 D。

---

121. 所有學習資料倍斯特出版的員工都可以取用，包含分公司的員工。

 解析

第 121 題考的是字彙，accessible 是形容詞：可接近的、可觸及的、可取得的：例如：The ingredients for the meal are very accessible here.（那道料理的材料在這裡很容易取得。）此外，也常用 be accessible to 表示可通過、可到達，例如：All parts of the library are accessible to wheelchairs.（圖書館的所有區域都是可以使用輪椅的。）因為要形容主詞 learning materials，(C) accessible 的字義比其它選項合理，故此題答案為 C。

(A) uncommon，罕見的 adj.：Porcelain made by traditional ways is uncommon nowadays.

(B) rampant，猖獗的 adj.：Poverty is rampant on the barren land.

(D) native，原生的 adj.：He returned to live and work in his native country.

122. 倍斯特航空公司的候選人們在試用期期間都期許要表現出忠誠、熱忱和學習意願。

 解析

　　第 122 題考的是文法，expect 是動詞：期望、預期，後面接不定詞 to V.：例如：He expected his friends to hold a birthday party for him. （他期望他的朋友為他舉辦生日派對。）題目以被動語態表達員工候選人被期待表現出忠誠、熱忱和學習意願。被動語態 beV. expected to 後面應接上原型動詞 show，表示他們被期望表現出…：故此題答案為 B。

123. 花的香氣吸引最多授粉者，例如蜜蜂和蝴蝶，的花種必定能於早春就盛開。

 解析

　　第 123 題考的是文法，主要測試關係代名詞的用法，whose 是關係代名詞的所有格，代替先行詞的所有格，表示屬於某人或某物的。此題的關係代名詞的先行詞剛好是主詞 Flowers，空格後是 fragrance，香味，可由空格前後的字義推測大意是：花的香氣…，是所有格的大意，**故選 (A) whose**。先行詞是事物時，關係代名詞的所有格也能用 of which，所以此題也能寫成：Flowers of which fragrance...。定位回題目，關係代名詞主要有兩個功能：(1) 導引形容詞子句形容先行詞。(2)合併原本獨立存在的兩個完整句。例如此題原本是兩個完整句：Flowers are bound to prosper during early spring. / Fragrance of flowers attracts the most pollinators, such as bees and butterflies.進一步以關係代名詞的所有格 whose 合併為 Flowers whose fragrance attracts the most pollinators are bound to prosper during early spring. 其它例子如：The boy is my student. / The boy's eyes are blue. ，可合併為 The boy whose eyes are blue is my student.。

124. 有些電梯是特地為患有慢性病像是糖尿病和高血壓患者所量身打造的。

 解析

　　第 124 題考的是文法，主要考詞性。tailor 是名詞：裁縫師，也可作動詞使用，訂製的意思，例如：We tailor the weeding program for your specific needs. （我們為您的特殊需求量身打造這個婚禮企劃。）由空格後 tailor 字尾的 ed，得知 tailor 在此題目是當動詞使用，因為主詞是電梯，所以主要動詞以被動語態表達：電梯是被訂做的。tailored 在此是過去分詞，搭配空格前的 be 動詞 are，形成被動語態：are tailored，被訂做。動詞只能用副詞修飾，所以選 (A) specifically。：故此題答案為 A。

(B) specialty，專長 n.：Her specialty was writing. （她的專長是寫作。）

(C) special，特別的 adj.：She got a special talent for dancing. （她擁有特別的舞蹈天分。）

(D) specific，特定的 adj.：Some of these dresses are specific for particular occasions. （其中某些洋裝是特別配合特定場合的。）

125. 分公司經理或首席行銷長都沒能獲得等待已久的升遷機會。

 解析

　　第 125 題考的是文法，Neither A nor B，（不是 A 也不是 B）兩者皆非的句型，故此題答案為C。neither 是副詞，nor 是對等連接詞，兩者的意思都是「也不」。因為 nor 是對等連接詞，A 和 B 必須是同詞性的單字。例如：

a. 連接名詞

例如：Neither Mia nor Anna made the cookies.

b. 連接動詞

例如：I can neither do the laundry nor clean the house.

c. 連接形容詞

例如：Fast food is neither delicious nor healthy.

126. 既然工作情況是相當的危險，所有員工都仔細地遵守指示是很
重要的。

第 126 題考的是文法，題目第一個字是虛主詞 it，馬上往後面找 it 代
替的真主詞。空格後有主詞 all workers+動詞 follow，符合任何子句的基
本必備結構 (S+V)，由此推測是名詞子句當真主詞，名詞子句常見的結構是
that S+V，此時 that 可省略。此題中，it 代替的真主詞是 that 導引的名詞
子句：that all workers follow the instruction carefully，表示「所有員
工都仔細地遵守指示」這一件事。此題的 that 其實是可以省略的。也可寫
成 That all workers follow the instruction carefully is essential，特別
注意名詞子句當主詞，不使用虛主詞 it 代替名詞子句時，句首的 that 不能
省略。

127. 雖然約翰沒有其他競爭者或金牌選手強壯，他設法游回岸邊的
勇氣替他贏得了觀眾的心。

第 127 題考的是文法的同等比較句型，A + be動詞 + as 原級形容詞/
副詞 as+ B，A 和 B 一樣…。例如：He is as tall as my brother.（他和我
哥哥一樣高）。主要動詞是 be 動詞時搭配原級形容詞/ She can dance as

well as me.（她可以跳舞跳得像我一樣好）。主要動詞是 be 動詞以外的普通動詞時，必須搭配副詞修飾普通動詞。題目用的是 be 動詞的否定句：A + is not so/as 原級形容詞 as+ B，A 不像 B 一樣…。否定的同等比較句型中，not 後面也可以搭配 so。例如：He is not so tall as my brother.

128. 為了慶祝他的第十個結婚周年紀念日，傑克不只在晚餐期間雇用了小提琴手來表演音樂，而且還聘用了馬車來載他們回家。

 解析

第 128 題考的是字彙，anniversary 是名詞：周年紀念的意思：例如：The department store has a big sale for its 20th anniversary.（那間百貨公司為二十周年慶舉辦了特賣。）由空格前的 celebrate，慶祝，和 tenth，第十，可聯想哪個選項的字義和「慶祝」及「第十」關係最密切，anniversary 的字義比其它選項更適合搭配以上兩個線索字，故選 (D) anniversary。

(A) concert，音樂會 n.：I'll go to the concert at the church hall next weekend.（我下週末會去教堂的音樂會。）
(B) ceremony，儀式 n.：The attendees were divided into groups at a special ceremony.（參加者在一個特別的儀式上分組。）
(C) activity，活動 n.：There will be a fun activity for Halloween.（這裡將會有一個有趣的萬聖活動。）

129. 一個收集 line 點數的方式是於你的 line 頁面中分享指定的文章，而另一個方式是於特定等級的遊戲中完成事項。

 解析

第 129 題考的是字彙及文法，因為空格前後都是子句，必須選連接詞。先刪除 (B) with，因為 with 是介係詞。刪除(D) however，however

是副詞。(A) when 雖然是連接詞，但不能選，因為兩個子句的語意和時間觀念無關，如果用 when，當…的時候，連接兩個子句，邏輯是不通順的。(C) whereas 是連接詞，有然而的意思，連接兩個前後語意相反或語意落差極大的子句，等同於 while 的用法：例如：She enjoys cooking, whereas I prefer eating.（她享受烹飪，而我更喜歡品嚐）。題目及以上例句的 whereas 都能換成 while，故此題答案為C。

130. 不論是誰想出實用的策略來打動潛在客戶都將獲得年終獎金。

 解析

　　第 130 題考的是文法，主要測試複合關係代名詞，複合關係代名詞包括 whoever（無論誰）、 whomever（無論誰<只能當受格>）、whosever（無論誰的）、 whatever（無論什麼）、whichever（無論哪一個）。whoever= anyone who，whomever= anyone whom，whosever= anyone whose，whatever= anything which，whichever= anything which。空格後的動詞片語 came up with，想出…是線索，因此知道正確選項是代稱人的主詞，選項中代稱人的只有 (B) whoever。其餘選項的字義均無法搭配動詞片語 came up with the practical strategies，想出實用的策略的詞意。：故此題答案為 B。

Part 6

問題 131-134

　　敬啟者：

　　我很榮幸地宣布，工藝愛好博覽會將於七月二號在世界貿易中心 __(131)__ 。

展覽會聚集設計師、工匠、零售商、經銷商、買家和供應商。參加者不僅將熟悉傳統的美國手工藝，還可以與來自全球 ___(132)___ 工匠互動。

我也很高興告訴你一個新部門，升級改造部門，這是在 ___(133)___ 生活具有高度信息的。因為紙品和紡織部門的多樣化產品，該展覽贏得了讚譽。此外，根據我們對來賓和訂單的統計，珠寶部門一直享有不減的榮景。

___(134)___ 如果您有任何問題，請通過電子郵件或電話與我們聯繫。

誠摯地，
傑夫·本森
工藝愛好博覽會主辦單位

解析

131.
  (A) command.
  (B) commence.
  (C) commend.
  (D) comment.

131.
  (A) 命令。
  (B) 開始。
  (C) 表彰。
  (D) 評論。

---

　　131 題考的是字彙，commence 是一個動詞，有開始的意思，後面可接現在分詞(Ving)，用於表示著手進行某個動作，定位回文章，表示工藝愛好博覽會將於七月二號在世界貿易中心開跑，故此題答案為 B。

(A) command，命令 n.：The command was given to rescue the hostage.

(C) commend，表彰 v.：Her teacher commended her on her honesty.

(D) comment，評論 n.：He made negative comments on my report.

132.
(A) promised.
(B) prominence.
(C) prominent.
(D) compromising.

132.
(A) 許諾。
(B) 卓越。
(C) 傑出的。
(D) 妥協的。

---

132 題考的是字彙，prominent 是形容詞，有傑出、突出的意思：例如: He is a prominent member of the baseball team. 定位回文章，因為空格後是名 craftsmen，名詞必須以形容詞形容，又考慮整句大意是「參加者可與來自全球的傑出工匠互動」，與下承諾或妥協的均無關，所以刪除 (A)及(D)：(B) prominence 是名詞，也刪除，故此題答案為 C。

(A) promised，許諾 v. (過去式或過去分詞)：Her father promised her a new computer if she won the prize.（她的父親許諾她一台新電腦，如果她能獲獎。） promise 也可做名詞使用，例如: make/keep/break a promise。另外，promise 的現在分詞 promising，作為形容詞：有為的、有希望的。

(B) prominence，卓越或顯著之事物 n.

(D) compromising，妥協的 adj.：It is a compromising way to solve the dilemma.（這是可以解決窘境的折衷辦法。）原形的 compromise 可作名詞或動詞使用，有妥協的意思：例如: reach a compromise 和 compromise on sth。

133.
(A) sustainable.
(B) sustain.
(C) sustainability.
(D) sustaining.

133.
(A) 可持續發展的。
(B) 支持。
(C) 可持續性。
(D) 持續的。

133 題考的是文法，定位回文章，可知空格 (133) 是一個形容詞，用形容來 lifestyle，可由 A 選項字尾-able 判斷。sustainable 是一個形容詞，有永續發展的意思，用以形容 lifestyle，可呼應 upcycling sector 的循環再造；故此題答案為 A。

(B) sustain，支持 v.：His family will no longer sustain him for the heavy losses of the company.（他的家人無法再支持他嚴重虧損的公司。）

(C) sustainability，可持續性 n.：The program shows great sustainability of the new technique.（那項計畫顯示了新技術的巨大可持續性。）

(D) sustaining，持續的 adj.：This would be a sustaining electricity for 72 hours.（這將是可以維 72 小時的電力。）

134.
(A) Attached is the information of the schedule, exhibition booths, and transportation.
(B) We have invited craftsmen from Asia.
(C) It takes only 10 minutes to walk from the MRT station to the World Trade Center.
(D) The number of transactions is the highest in the jewelry sector.

134.
(A) 附檔是時間表、展位和交通資訊的相關資料。
(B) 我們邀請了亞洲的工匠們。
(C) 從地鐵站步行到世貿中心只需 10 分鐘。
(D) 珠寶部門的交易數量是最高的。

6 填空式閱讀

7 單篇閱讀

7 雙篇、三篇閱讀

模擬試題

134 題考的是邏輯，可以把選項一一帶入空格 (134)，選出最符合敘述邏輯的選項。定位回文章，可知信件內容即將結束，末段通常用於補述尚未提及的或特別提醒收信人要注意的重要事項：即可先刪除與前段內容重複的 B、D 選項。而 A、C 選項在內容上皆適合填入空格 (134)，就敘述條理而言，C 選項可以接在 A 選項後面，作為補充說明，單獨填入空格稍嫌突兀；所以 A 選項是最適合的答案。

問題 135-138

雖然家庭安全系統和智慧手機之間的聯繫並不罕見，但智能家居終將 ___(135)___ 所有領域的裝置，並且這些裝置將可以相互通信。 ___(136)___

各種智能裝置將形成一個 ___(137)___ 網絡。這些裝置包括自動溫度控制、可以追踪食物的智慧冰箱，以及垃圾箱中可以檢測垃圾種類的感應器。這些裝置彼此的交流越多，它們將越了解您的生活方式和個人偏好， ___(138)___ 調整它們自己的操作。一個智能家居將成為一個響應你的生活方式的活體。

 解析

135.
    (A) comprehend.
    (B) add.
    (C) compass.
    (D) encompass.

135.
    (A) 理解。
    (B) 添加。
    (C) 羅盤。
    (D) 涵蓋。

135 題考的是字彙 encompass 是動詞，有環繞、擁有的意思：例如：The book is to encompass everything from music to literature and cinema.（那本書將涵蓋所有從音樂到文學和電影的一切。）定位回題目，這裡用 encompass 表示涵蓋所有層面的裝置，故此題答案為 D。

(A) comprehend，理解 v.：She couldn't comprehend his reasons for buying the old car.（她無法理解他買下那輛老車的理由。）

(B) add，增加 v.：You can add blue color to the yellow and get green.（你可以把藍色顏料加進黃色，然後得到綠色。）

(C) compass，指南針 n.：Sometimes, people take divination as a moral compass for direction.（有時候，人們用占卜作為心靈的方向指南。）

136.

(A) Smart devices are becoming more and more affordable.

(B) IT allows us to control devices remotely.

(C) A smart home is equipped with sensors.

(D) **They will help you manage your household, so you can focus on more crucial parts of your life.**

136.

(A) 智能裝置變得越來越負擔得起。

(B) 他使我們能遠端遙控裝置。

(C) 智能家居配有感應器。

(D) **他們將幫助您管理家庭，所以您可以專注於生活中更重要的部分。**

---

136 題考的是邏輯和與上一句的連貫性，可以把選項一一帶入空格 (136)，選出最符合敘述邏輯的選項。根據文章，空格 (136) 位於第一段的結尾，敘述這些可以互相通信的裝置，有助於我們管理家庭，並在下一段舉例驗證：而上一句的大意是智能家居終將涵蓋所有領域的裝置，並且這些裝置 (those devices) 將可以相互通信，此句的主詞 They 指的就是上一句的 those devices，代名詞與先行詞之間的關係，也是解題線索。其餘選項的大意和上一句都沒有密切的連貫性，也不像 D 選項的句子有承先啟後（承先：連貫上一句：啟後：下一段舉例驗證各式各樣的智能裝置）的作用。故

D 選項是最適合的答案。

137.
    (A) moderate.
    (B) intricate.
    (C) modest.
    (D) inexpensive.

137.
    (A) 中等的。
    (B) 錯綜複雜的。
    (C) 謙虛的。
    (D) 便宜的。

---

137 題考的是字彙，intricate 是形容詞錯綜複雜的，例如：This sculpture is a masterpiece with intricate details.（這個雕塑是一個有複雜細節的傑作。）定位回文章，用 intricate 形容網路，表示智能裝置將形成一個錯綜複雜的網路，故此題答案為 B。

(A)   moderate，中等的 adj.：A moderate intake of sugar will excite your brain to work.（適量的糖分攝取可以刺激大腦工作。）

(C)   modest，謙虛的 adj.：She is a modest girl who is too shy to accept compliments.（她是一個謙虛的女孩，太害羞而不敢接受稱讚。）

(D)   inexpensive，廉價的 adj.：He made inexpensive perfume that young girls can afford.（他製作年輕女孩買得起的廉價香水。）

138.
    (A) through.
    (B) by.
    (C) whereby.
    (D) or.

138.
    (A) 通過。
    (B) 藉著。
    (C) 藉此。
    (D) 或。

---

138 題考的是文法，whereby 是副詞，等同於 by which 的用法，有憑著、藉此的意思：例如：She signed up for a course whereby she can learn to cook.（她參加了一個課程，藉此學習烹飪。）定位回文章，空格前後文大意是它們將越了解您的生活方式和個人偏好，⋯調整它們自己的操

作。空格填入 by which 或 whereby，大意是最通順的，也就是藉由「越了解您的生活方式和個人偏好」這個過程或方式，智能裝置能自我調整。故此題答案為 C。

問題 139-142

曼谷烹飪學校：向泰國美食的主廚學習！

---

* 學習如何快樂烹飪令人垂涎的泰國美食

* 實作經驗：國際旅客不需要為器材和材料而忙亂。學費已包含材料、器具和容器。我們學校以 __(140)__ 最新鮮，最優質的產品和材料 __(139)__ 。只需在網上或現場註冊，您將因在上課 __(141)__ 1 個月付款，收到 10%的折扣。

課程類型：所有課程皆為英語授課
* 短期班：
  上午或下午的 2~4 小時，每小時 2 份食譜
* 密集班
  星期一到星期四每日 6 小時，總共 48 個小時，共有 90 個食譜
* 一對一教學班
* __(142)__

交通便利
位於曼谷市中心/從 BTS 輕軌站步行只需 5 分鐘。

欲知詳情，請拜訪我們的網站：
https://www.bangkokcuisineschool.com/

解析

139.
(A) takes pride for.
(B) is proud that.
(C) prides itself for.
(D) takes pride in.

139.
(A) 感到自豪。
(B) 很自豪。
(C) 以自己為榮。
(D) 引以為傲。

139 題考的是片語 takes pride in sth/sb 的用法，表示以某人或某事為傲：例如：The coach takes pride in her students.（教練為她的選手們感到驕傲。）也可以用 be proud of sth/sb，例如：The coach is proud of her students.。按造文法規則，只有選項 D 正確，故此題答案為 D。

140
(A) utility.
(B) utilize.
(C) utilizing.
(D) utilization.

140.
(A) 效用。
(B) 利用。
(C) 利用。
(D) 採用。

140 題考的是文法，utilize 是動詞：利用的意思，例如 The government utilized the army to overwhelm rebellion.(政府用軍隊鎮壓叛亂。) 承接上題 takes pride in sth/sb，在介係詞 in 後面應接名詞或動名詞 v-ing，可用 utilizing 或是 the utilization of：故此題答案為 C。

(A) utility，效用 n.：The medicine has been proven to have the utility of relieving pain. （該藥物被證明有舒緩疼痛的效用。）

141.
   (A) beforehand.
   (B) prior to.
   (C) in advance.
   (D) prioritizing.

141.
   (A) 預先。
   (B) 之前。
   (C) 提前。
   (D) 優先。

141 題考的是字彙，定位回文章，in-advance payment 1 month... the class，由 in-advance 這個形容詞的字義「預先的」可推測空格是表達「之前」，才能搭配 the class，表上課一個月之前。prior，形容詞，意思是之前的。prior to= before，故選 (B) prior to。刪除 (A) beforehand 及 (C) in advance，beforehand 和 in advance 都是副詞，副詞後面馬上接名詞 the class 文法是錯誤的。(D) prioritizing 是原型動詞 prioritize，排列優先順序，的動名詞或現在分詞，字義及文法上搭配 the class 都是錯誤的；故此題答案為 B。

142.
   (A) Ingredients and cooking equipment will be provided.
   (B) Most attendees are tourists from western countries.
   (C) Attendees must be able to communicate in Thai.
   (D) Attendees will receive certificates varying in formats according to class levels.

142.
   (A) 將提供材料和烹飪設備。
   (B) 大多數參加者是來自西方國家的遊客。
   (C) 參加者必須能夠用泰語進行交流。
   (D) 根據班級，參加者將收到不同格式的證書。

142 題考的是邏輯，可以把選項一一帶入空格 (142)，選出最符合敘述邏輯的選項。定位回文章，空格 (142) 應與課程類別有關，D 選項承接上面

的課程分級的內容，最合乎敘述邏輯。A 選項在第一段已經敘述過了，故刪除(A)。由「課程類型：所有課程皆為英語授課」，可知 C 選項是錯誤的，也刪除(C)。B 選項無法從文章中論證：故此題答案為 D。

問題 143-146

親愛的顧客：

在列克興敦的當地社區 ___(143)___ 了 20 年之久，街角禮物店很遺憾地通知您，由於收入下降，該商店將於 12 月 20 日關閉。能在當地居民的童年回憶中扮演一個角色，我們深感榮幸。

我們將於 10 月 1 日開始 ___(144)___ 拍賣。隨著假期季節即將到來，這是一個很好的時機，先將感恩節和聖誕節裝飾品囤放起來，並為您的親友購買禮物。 ___(145)___ 如果您有我們的會員卡，您將額外享有 10% 的折扣。千萬別錯過這一生一次的機會！

我們期待您的 ___(146)___ 。

此致
街角禮物店

143.
   (A) having service.
   (B) having served.
   (C) has served.
   (D) have service.

143.
   (A) 有服務。
   (B) 已服務。
   (C) 已服務。
   (D) 有服務。

　　143 題考的是文法，主要測試分詞構句裡，主詞的省略及分詞變化。根據文章，可以把第一句解構成：the Gift Store Around the Corner has served the local community... / the Gift Store Around the Corner is saddened to inform you...：可知這裡用連接詞 after 將兩句合併，更進一步改成分詞構句: 兩句主詞一樣時，其中一句的主詞要省略，並將該句的主要動詞改成現在分詞或過去分詞，如果原句的主要動詞是以主動語態表達，就改成現在分詞；如果原句的主要動詞是以被動語態表達，就改成過去分詞。由以上解構的句子可知 has served 是主動語態，所以改成現在分詞 having served：故此題答案為 B。

144.
   (A) liquidate.
   (B) liquid.
   (C) liquidation.
   (D) liquidating.

144.
   (A) 清算。
   (B) 液體。
   (C) 出清。
   (D) 清算。

　　144 題考的是字彙，由空格後的 sale 得知是拍賣，出清大拍賣的慣用片語是 liquidation sale，是名詞+名詞的搭配。

145.
(A) There is no other store like ours.
(B) **Most of the products will be 50% off.**
(C) Tourists will love our souvenirs.
(D) Thanksgiving is a traditional American holiday.

145.
(A) 沒有其他像我們這樣的商店。
(B) **大部分產品將以半價出售。**
(C) 遊客將會喜歡我們的紀念品。
(D) 感恩節是美國傳統節日。

　　145 題考的是邏輯，可以把選項一一帶入空格 (145)，選出最符合敘述邏輯的選項。根據文章敘述，現在是買禮品的好時機、會員可以打折，可以先刪除與敘述無關的 A、D 選項：從文章敘述：持有會員卡可額外享有 10％的折扣，往前推測，上句應與價錢相關：帶入 B 選項，合乎邏輯、文意通暢：故 B 是最適合的答案。

146.
(A) patron.
(B) patronizing.
(C) patronize.
(D) **patronage.**

146.
(A) 顧客。
(B) 自以為高人一等的、頤指氣使的。
(C) 光顧。
(D) **光臨。**

　　146 題考的是文法，從 We look forward to your (146).判斷，所有格後面接名詞，所以正確選項是名詞，所以這題的答案為 D。patronize 是動詞光顧、寵幸的意思，它的名詞作 patronage：而 patron 則是顧客的意思。We look forward to your patronage.，我們期待您的光臨。要特別注意 (B) patronizing 是一個意義負面的形容詞，意為自以為高人一等的，頤指氣使的。

Part 7

問題 147-149

倍斯特英語課程表

課程	價格	時間
基礎字彙	300 美元	星期一下午 1 點到下午 6 點
基礎字彙 II	600 美元	星期三下午 2 點到下午 7 點
基礎文法	450 美元	星期一下午 1 點到下午 6 點
基礎文法 II	900 美元	星期二下午 2 點到下午 7 點
複習班/字彙	300 美元	星期四下午 1 點到下午 6 點
複習班/文法	450 美元	星期五下午 2 點到下午 7 點

註：

1. 基礎字彙和基礎文法課有排課上的衝突。大家可以選擇複習班/字彙或複習班/文法因為課程內容是相同的。
2. 修倍斯特英語 4 堂課將獲贈免費的教學 DVD。
3. 教科書費用不包含在上列的費用裡。

答案：147. B　148. A　149.C

 解析

147. What is the main purpose of the passage?
   (A) to inform the change to the class schedule.
   (B) to inform the class arrangement and tuition.
   (C) to give away a free DVD.
   (D) to raise the tuition.

147. 這篇文章的主旨是什麼呢？
   (A) 告知課程進度的改變。
   (B) 告知課程安排和學費。
   (C) 贈與免費的 DVD。
   (D) 增加學費。

147 題題目是詢問這篇文章的主旨是什麼呢？可以定位回表格，由表格的名稱和表格的第一行，可得知這是由「課程」、「費用」和「時間」構成的一個英語課程表，也就和選項 B 的課程安排和學費最相符，故答案是 B。主要考的是字彙，class arrangement 和 tuition，文章並未提及課程進度的改變和增加學費，可以先刪除 A、D 選項；而贈與的免費 DVD 只是備註的其中一項，並不是整篇文章的主要述說目標，所以選項 C 也不是本題的答案。

---

148. What is suggested in case of a scheduling conflict?

(A) People can take another course with the same content but under a different title.

(B) People can ask for a refund.

(C) People can sign up for a private tutoring session.

(D) People can watch a teaching DVD to make up for the course they miss.

148. 對於排課衝突此例的建議是什麼呢？

(A) 大家可以修其他課程內容相同的課程只是課程名稱不同。

(B) 大家可以要求退款。

(C) 大家可以報名私人家教課程。

(D) 大家可以藉由觀賞教學 DVD 補償所缺的課。

---

148 題題目是詢問對於排課衝突此例的建議是什麼呢？可以由 scheduling conflict 定位回文章的備註第一項，衝突的基礎字彙課和基礎文法課，與複習班的字彙課和文法課內容相同，可以做為排課衝突的解決方案；也就是選項 A 所指的，不同名稱的相同課程，故此題答案為 A。文章中也沒有提及退費和家教課程，B、C 選項可以先刪去；而從文章，我們也無法得知教學 DVD 的內容，無法保證觀賞教學 DVD 可以補償所缺的課程，所以選項 D 也不是正解。

149. How much does it cost if a person decides to sign up for Vocabulary Basic II and Grammar Basic II?
(A) US 600.
(B) US 900.
(C) US 1500.
(D) US 1000.

149. 如果決定報名基礎字彙 II 和基礎文法 II 要花費多少錢呢？
(A) 600 美元。
(B) 900 美元。
(C) 1500 美元。
(D) 1000 美元。

149 題題目是詢問報名基礎字彙 II 和基礎文法 II 要花費多少錢呢？定位回表格，基礎字彙 II 和基礎文法 II 的課程費用分別是 600 美元和 900 美元，兩堂課程費用相加，即是 1500 美元，故答案是 C 1500 美元。

問題 150-151

倍斯特車庫拍賣會

今年我們有嬰兒服飾，你們都知道嬰兒長得多快。我們還有嬰兒推車的清單能供您選擇。85 成新而且完全省了你許多錢。如果你想要買嬰兒相關的東西當禮物送你的朋友的話，這在你會覺得振奮。對於那些將有小孩者，參觀下也沒有甚麼損失。我們也會有室內設計師在此。他們能幫助你設想出理想的嬰兒房，不論是房間牆上充滿著卡通人物或者是時尚的宮殿風格。不論怎樣，我們的車庫拍賣會於 12 月 12 日到 12 月 20 日如往常般的開幕。更多資訊可以看我們的傳單。

答案：150. A　151. B

150. How many days will the garage sale last?
(A) **9 days.**
(B) 12 days.
(C) 8 days.
(D) 20 days.

150. 車庫拍賣會持續多少天呢？
(A) **9 天。**
(B) 12 天。
(C) 8 天。
(D) 20 天。

150 題題目是詢問車庫拍賣會持續多少天呢？可以定位回文章最後，open from Dec 12 to Dec 20，可得知車庫銷售的營業日期是從 12 月 12 日到 12 月 20 日，總共 9 天，故答案為 A。

151. Which item is recommended by the passage?
(A) cartoon characters.
(B) **baby strollers.**
(C) wall decoration stickers.
(D) interior design blueprints.

151. 哪個項目是段落中推薦的呢？
(A) 卡通人物。
(B) **嬰兒推車。**
(C) 牆上的裝飾貼紙。
(D) 室內設計藍圖。

151 題題目是詢問哪個項目是段落中推薦的呢？定位回文章前段，可以得知車庫銷售的項目包含嬰兒服飾、嬰兒推車和嬰兒相關的產品；其中特別描述嬰兒推車為 85 成新，所以刪除 A、C、D 選項，答案即為 B 嬰兒推車。文章後段提到，現場有室內設計師可以提供意見，但並沒有明確指出現場有販售室內設計藍圖，故 D 是一個干擾選項，要特別小心。

問題 152-155

倍斯特古董店

通常大家來這是因為各類型的水晶球，但是我們今年賣完了。然而，我們有古董珍珠，對於收藏家或新婚夫妻來說，它也能充當寶藏。他也被視為是象徵持久的戀愛的方式。古董珍珠很稀有，它只能於一些有毒海藻蔓延的地方中找到。它們需要至少 10 年的孕育。有些於海中的船骸中找到。古董珍珠的價值是無價的，它甚至勝過鑽石、錢和玉。對於在情人節想要買它當作禮物贈送給愛人的人，你發了。我們有工匠可以替您特別設計珍珠，當然也附雕刻名字在上面。工匠只會於 1 月 16 日到 1 月 18 日到我們店裡。

答案：152.D　153. C　154.A　155.B

解析

---

152. What kind of product did consumers usually buy in the antique store in the past?
(A) crystal pendants.
(B) ancient pearls.
(C) pearl necklaces.
(D) crystal balls.

152. 消費者過去通常在古董店裡購買哪個產品呢？
(A) 水晶掛飾。
(B) 古董珍珠。
(C) 珍珠項鍊。
(D) 水晶球。

---

152 題題目是詢問消費者過去通常在古董店裡購買哪個產品呢？定位回文章第一句，「通常大家來這是因為各類型的水晶球」，可以得知答案即為 D 水晶球。古董珍珠是今年推薦的新產品，並不是大家以往購買的產品，所以 B 不是答案。

153. What does the writer mean by "rampant"?
(A) extremely poisonous.
(B) very rare and expensive.
(C) widespread and uncontrolled.
(D) quite precious.

153. 作者所指的「蔓延的」是什麼呢？
(A) 極有毒性的。
(B) 非常稀有且昂貴的。
(C) 廣布且不受控制的。
(D) 相當珍貴的。

153 題題目是詢問作者所指的「蔓延的」是什麼呢？這題考的是字彙，rampant 是蔓延的意思，可以直接刪除意義不符的選項，得到答案 C 廣布且不受控制的。也可以由 rampant 定位回文章，作者用形容詞子句描述可以找到古董珍珠的地方，我們可以由句意推測，rampant 是一個跟毒海藻的「生長」有關的形容詞，即可先刪除選項 B 和 D；如果套上選項 A，極有毒性的，會變得句意不通順，所以 A 也不是答案。

154. What does the writer mean by "invaluable"?
(A) valuable beyond estimation.
(B) lacking any value.
(C) the value differs according to different buyers.
(D) the value is undecided.

154. 作者所指的「無價的」是什麼呢？
(A) 超過所能估計的價值。
(B) 缺乏任何價值的。
(C) 根據不同買家價值也不同。
(D) 價值是無法決定的。

154 題題目是詢問作者所指的「無價的」是什麼呢？這題考的是字彙，invaluable 是無價的意思，可以直接刪除意義不符的選項，得到答案 A 超過所能估計的價值。也可以由 invaluable 定位回文章，作者用 invaluable 形容古董珍珠，價值超過鑽石、錢和玉，而得知 invaluable 有非常珍貴、價值極高的意思，就可以刪除 B、C 選項；D 選項的 undecided，有尚未決定的意思，並不是作者所指的無價的意思，所以 D 也不是答案：故此題答案為 A。

155. Which one of the following about ancient pearls is FALSE?
   (A) It takes a long time to harvest these pearls.
   (B) **They are not as valuable as diamonds.**
   (C) They have a symbolic meaning.
   (D) They are very rare.

155. 下列哪個關於古董珍珠的敘述是錯誤的呢？
   (A) 這些珍珠要花費相當長的時間孕育。
   (B) **他們不像鑽石那樣珍貴。**
   (C) 他們有象徵意義。
   (D) 他們非常稀有。

　　155 題題目是詢問下列哪個關於古董珍珠的敘述是錯誤的呢？定位回文章，作者形容古董珍珠的價值超過鑽石、錢和玉，可知選項 B「他們不像鑽石那樣珍貴」是錯誤的敘述，故答案為 B。另外，文章提到它們需要至少 10 年的孕育；他們可用來象徵長久的愛情；他們很稀有、很難被找到；證明 A、C、D 選項皆為正確的敘述；故此題答案為 B。

問題 156-157

倍斯特瑜珈農場

　　倍斯特瑜珈農場致力於與其餘的瑜珈相關服務作出區隔化。我們將在自助餐區納入有機食物。大家可以在我們自助餐吃熱量較低的食物。所有卡路里都經過我們營養師精心計算過，所以你不用擔心攝取超過你本該攝取的量。此外，你能在我們農場後院體驗種植有機食物。你能購買有機食物的種子，於你運動完或伸展後耕種它們。而且我們還在我們瑜珈農場另外增加了酷的東西。隨著悶熱的夏季到來，我們再 2018 年 6 月 1 日提供免費的冰淇淋給報名我們課程的報名者。（免費冰淇淋於首三天課程）

答案：156.D　157.D

解析

156. What is the main purpose of the passage?
(A) to describe the benefits of organic foods.
(B) to list the qualifications of the coaches in this yoga center.
(C) to explain how people can get free ice cream.
(D) the introduce the services that distinguish this yoga center from others.

156. 這個段落的主旨是什麼呢？
(A) 描述有機食物的益處。
(B) 列出此瑜珈中心的教練資格清單。
(C) 解釋人們如何獲取免費冰淇淋。
(D) 引進服務包括如何將瑜珈中心與其他區隔化。

　　156 題題目是詢問這個段落的主旨是什麼呢？定位回文章，第一句就闡述「倍斯特瑜珈農場致力於與其他瑜珈的相關服務作出區隔」，接著說明他們提供了營養師設計的低卡有機食物、和有機作物的耕種體驗，可知答案為 D 介紹他們與其他瑜珈中心不同的服務。文末提出了夏季的優惠活動，但並不是整篇的主要敘述目的，所以 C 並不是正解；故此題答案為 D。

157. Which service is NOT included in this yoga center?
(A) cultivating organic foods.
(B) low calorie foods.
(C) foods designed by dietician.
(D) free trial yoga classes.

157. 哪項服務不包含在此瑜珈中心呢？
(A) 耕種有機食物。
(B) 低卡路里食物。
(C) 食物由營養學家設計。
(D) 免費體驗瑜珈課程。

　　157 題題目是詢問哪項服務不包含在此瑜珈中心呢？定位回文章，可知

瑜珈中心的服務項目包含了營養師設計的低卡有機食物、和有機作物的耕種體驗，並沒有免費瑜珈課程，故答案為 D。

問題 158-159

倍斯特餐廳

　　大多數消費者都渴望在足夠空曠的地方用餐。在傳統餐廳用餐太過擁擠。這就是為什麼倍斯特餐廳增加了草原用餐的體驗。你能與朋友在草原烤肉，聞到綠草香味的機會。我們有各式的肉類，肉類都準備在旁。你也能品嚐我們牛的牛奶。所有的類似蒙古的體驗將這晚轉變成難忘的體驗。此外，我們小木屋後有神祕魔力的地方。螢火蟲聚集在林間形成所有小孩都朝思暮想的難以置信的場景。如果你是浪漫類型的人，你會喜愛這個。對於大自然的愛好者，在小徑間行走觀看成群的螢火蟲現身就像是天賜。更多資訊請參訪 www.bestrestaurant.greatview.com。

答案：158.C　159.D

 解析

158. Why did Best Restaurant add the prairie experience?
  (A) Some customers have requested this experience.
  (B) The meat barbecued on a prairie tastes more delicious.

158. 倍斯特餐廳為什麼增加草原體驗呢？
  (A) 有些顧客已經要求這個體驗。
  (B) 在草原烤肉品嚐起來更美味。
  (C) 開放的寬廣空間的體驗對於顧客來說更舒適。

(C) An open space experience is more comfortable for customers.

(D) The restaurant owner wanted to keep cattle on the prairie.

(D) 餐廳雇主想要在草原養小牛。

---

158 題題目是詢問倍斯特餐廳為什麼增加草原體驗呢？定位回文章，首兩句「大多數消費者都渴望在足夠空曠的地方用餐」、「在傳統餐廳用餐太過擁擠」；可知倍斯特餐廳認為，開放的空間對顧客來說更為舒適，故答案為 C。

---

159. Why did the passage mention "a mysterious magic place"?

(A) No one has ever been to the area behind the cabins.

(B) A magician will perform magic tricks at the barbecue.

(C) The origin of the fireflies is very mysterious.

(D) People can see the incredible scene of the fireflies in this place.

159. 為什麼這個篇章提到「神秘魔力的地方」呢？

(A) 沒人曾到過小木屋後的地方。

(B) 魔術師將在烤肉地方表演魔術雜技。

(C) 螢火蟲的起源非常神秘。

(D) 大家可以在這個地方看到驚人的螢火蟲場景。

---

159 題題目是詢問為什麼這個篇章提到「神秘魔力的地方」呢？可以從 a mysterious magic place 定位回文章，得知這個擁有神秘魔力的地方，是因為有螢火蟲聚集的壯觀場景；故答案為 D。文章敘述螢火蟲聚集的場景，是孩子們憧憬的、浪漫的人喜愛的、愛好自然的人視為天賜的，所以充滿了神祕魔力，與螢火蟲的起源無關，所以 C 並不是答案。

6 填空式閱讀

7 單篇閱讀

7 雙篇、三篇閱讀

模擬試題

問題 160-163

倍斯特旅行和遊覽

　　如果你在尋找到美國的冒險旅遊，倍斯特旅行和導覽就是你要的。我們設計了十天的導覽。我們的組合包括 RV 和重型卡車體驗。你會像巨星例如小賈斯汀那樣搭乘重型卡車來場盛大旅遊。此外，我們不需要特定的一天排程。可能每當遇到我們想看一些新鮮和令人興奮的東西就會停留。你不會感到無聊。你可以拍攝北美野牛或野生動物。我們也可能在任何露營地點總有帳篷準備好，在那裏就烤起肉來。外加我們旅遊組合包含了特別的廚師，他會將所有原料和食物都準備好，不論我們在河流盆地或國家公園。別擔心。我們的價格相當合理，總是在學生能負擔的範圍內，然後除非你是素食者，不然就不會有折扣。

答案：160.D　161.A　162. A　163.C

160. What can you receive if you sign up for the trip and are a vegetarian?
　(A) free vegetarian food.
　(B) grilled vegetables.
　(C) meal coupons.
　(D) a discount.

160. 如果你是素食者且報名這個旅遊，你能得到什麼呢？
　(A) 免費素食食物。
　(B) 燻烤蔬菜。
　(C) 肉品優惠卷。
　(D) 折扣。

6
填空式閱讀

7
單篇閱讀

7
雙篇、三篇閱讀

模擬試題

160 題題目是詢問如果你是素食者且報名這個旅遊，你能得到什麼呢？可以由 vegetarian 定位回文章的最後：there won't be a discount unless you are a vegetarian，敘述與費用相關的內容，並說明只有素食者可以得到折扣，故答案為 D。

---

161. Which of the blanks marked (1), (2), (3), and (4) does the following sentence belong to?

"we don't have a specific schedule for the whole day"

(A) (1).

(B) (2).

(C) (3).

(D) (4).

161. 下列句子屬於段落空格 (1), (2), (3), (4)所標示的哪個欄位中？

「我們不需要特定的一天排程」

(A) (1)。

(B) (2)。

(C) (3)。

(D) (4)。

---

161 題題目是詢問下列句子：「我們不需要一整天的特定行程」屬於段落空格 (1), (2), (3), (4)所標示的哪個欄位中？定位回文章，把「我們不需要一整天的特定行程」分別帶入段落空格(1), (2), (3), (4)中，由前後文意判斷敘述是否順暢並合乎邏輯。將句子填入段落空格 (1)，下一句接著「可能每當遇到一些新鮮和令人興奮的事物，我們就會停留」；表示行程的安排是很隨意的、不緊湊的，承接上句「我們不需要一整天的特定行程」，文意通暢，故答案為 A。段落空格 (3), (4) 前後文已脫離與行程相關的內容，填入句子並不通順，可以先刪除 C、D 選項；而段落空格 (2) 的前段，已將隨意的行程項目舉例出來，若再填入「不需要特定行程」，會顯得冗贅多餘，所以 B 並不是最佳解答。

---

162. What kind of activity is NOT mentioned in this passage?

(A) going to Justin Bieber's concert.

(B) barbecue.

162. 下列哪個活動未在這段落中提到呢？

(A) 去小賈斯汀的音樂會。

(B) 烤肉。

(C) 露營。

(C) camping.
(D) taking an RV.

(D) 搭乘 RV。

---

162 題題目是詢問下列哪個活動未在這段落中提到呢？定位回文章，作者形容顧客將會有巨星般的待遇，就像小賈斯汀那樣，可以搭乘重型卡車來場盛大的旅遊；並沒有提到行程中安排要去小賈斯汀的音樂會，所以答案為 A。

---

163. Why does the passage mention "bison"?

(A) to give an example of an endangered species.

(B) to point out that bisons look very handsome.

(C) **to give an example of how the tour will stop for something exciting.**

(D) to explain how to take photos of bisons.

163. 為什麼段落中提及「北美野牛」呢？

(A) 給予一個瀕臨絕種的一個生物的例子。

(B) 指出北美野牛看起來非常俊美。

(C) **給予這個行程停留地方會有些令人興奮的東西的例子。**

(D) 解釋如何拍攝北美野牛的照片。

---

163 題題目是詢問為什麼段落中提及「北美野牛」呢？可以由 bison 定位回文章，作者並沒有對北美野牛多做描述，或是解釋如何拍照，即可以刪除 A、B、D 選項。另外，文章闡述他們會為了一些新鮮和令人興奮的事物而停留，並舉出拍攝北美野牛或野生動物、就地露營烤肉為例，故答案為 C。

問題 164-166

倍斯特飲食

親愛的傑克，

我看了訂單的原物料和幾個項目。這不是些微調整價格。以那樣的價格，我們幾乎不太能獲取更多利潤。在 2018 年 3 月 18 日產品發佈會議時，我已經與我們老闆和幾個經理討論過了。既然您是我們的主要供應商而且也與我們合作了至少 10 年了，所以我想詢問您是否有可能在價格部分作些調整。另一件在我們心頭上的事是在原物料上是否有任何折扣，如果我們訂購 20 噸的麵粉、米和糖。在 2018 年 3 月 3 日後，我們有加大的倉庫。而且我們將重新定位我們的市場定位，縮限幾項我們在世界各地正在銷售的產品。如果沒有任何討論的空間的話，我們可能會尋找其他供應商並且降低 30%近期與您的訂購量。期待您的回應。

致上最高的問候，
珍妮·王

答案：164.B　165.C　166.B

 解析

164. Which of the blanks marked (1), (2), (3), and (4) does the following sentence belong to?
"For that kind of prices, there is no way that we can make any more profits"
(A) (1).
(B) (2).
(C) (3).
(D) (4).

164. 下列句子屬於段落空格 (1), (2), (3), (4)所標示的哪個欄位中？
「以那樣的價格，我們幾乎不太能獲取更多利潤」
(A) (1)。
(B) (2)。
(C) (3)。
(D) (4)。

164 題題目是詢問下列句子：「以那樣的價格，我們幾乎不太能獲取更多利潤」屬於段落空格 (1), (2), (3), (4)所標示的哪個欄位中？定位回文章，可以把「以那樣的價格，我們幾乎不太能獲取更多利潤」分別帶入段落空格(1), (2), (3), (4)中，由前後文意判斷敘述是否順暢並合乎邏輯。段落空格(2)的前兩句，敘述作者看了訂單並且不滿意價格，接著填入以那樣的價格無法獲利，文意通暢，故答案為 B。也可以由「以那樣的價格，我們幾乎不太能獲取更多利潤」這句話來推測，前一句話跟價格有關，即可排除文意不通的段落空格(3), (4)；而段落空格(1)的後句雖然與價格相關，但因果關係顛倒，所以 A、C、D 選項都不正確。

---

165. What request is made in this letter?
   (A) a reposition of the company's market place.
   (B) help with building the warehouse.
   (C) a discount for a large amount of order.
   (D) more supplies of rice, flour and sugar.

165. 這封信的請求是什麼呢？
   (A) 公司重新定位市場。
   (B) 協助建立倉庫。
   (C) 大量訂單的折扣。
   (D) 更多的麵粉、米和糖供應。

---

165 題題目是詢問這封信的請求是什麼呢？定位回文章，可知這是一封與供應商的協商信件，由於原物料價格上漲，公司難以獲利，信件的主要訴求便是希望供應商能調降價格，或是給予大量訂單一些折扣，故答案為 C。作者提到公司將縮限部分產品，但希望藉由大量訂單取得一些折扣，也擴充了倉儲設備，所以並不是因為需要更多原物料的供應，故 D 是一個干擾選項，要特別小心。

---

166. What can be inferred if the supplier refused to accept the request?
   (A) The company might carry out more negotiations with the supplier.

166. 能從文章中推測出，如果供應商拒絕這個請求的話會如何呢？
   (A) 公司可能實行與供應商更多的協商。
   (B) 公司可能尋找與其他供應商合作。

(B) The company might do business with another supplier.

(C) The supplier might go out of business.

(D) The suppliers' orders will not be affected.

(C) 公司可能無法營業。

(D) 供應商的訂單可能不受影響。

---

166 題題目是詢問能從文章中推測出，如果供應商拒絕這個請求的話會如何呢？定位回文章末段，信中敘述如果價格沒有協商空間，他們可能會尋找其他供應商並且降低原本的訂購量，故答案為 B。此外，我們也可以推測雙方的合作機會會減少、供應商的訂單數量會下降，但不至於完全沒有；所以 A、C、D 選項都不正確。

問題 167-168

聖誕特別提供服務

今年倍斯特節慶將有新的服務。我們在裝飾街坊、社區和公司提供客製化的服務。你不需要像過去那樣擔心聖誕節的東西。像是我需要將這些燈泡拿回倉庫嗎？這夠時髦嗎？或者是在裝飾前我們該花時間重新洗那些東西嗎？或者是我們該花時間在家裡裝飾聖誕樹而小孩們卻只想要我們帶他們參加社區的聖誕樹節慶，他們能拿到棉花糖且享受節慶。記住擔憂讓您長皺紋。有我們在，您不用在有這些擔憂。我們有最新的科技，你可以以便宜的價格享有客製化的聖誕樹。

答案：167.D　168.C

167. What does "customized service" imply?
   (A) decorating service.
   (B) service according to cultural customs.
   (C) much more popular service.
   (D) tailor-made service.

167.「客製化服務」指的是什麼呢?
   (A) 裝飾服務。
   (B) 根據不同文化習俗服務。
   (C) 更多的流行服務。
   (D) 量身訂做的服務。

　　167 題題目是詢問「客製化服務」指的是什麼呢?這題考的是字彙,customized service 是客製化服務的意思,可以直接刪除意義不符的選項,得到答案 D 量身訂做的服務。如果不清楚 customized 是什麼意思,也可以從字根上去推測,custom 是習俗的意思、customer 是顧客的意思;我們可以推測 customized 是一個跟顧客和習慣有關的形容詞,並且先排除 A、C 選項。而 tailor 是裁縫師的意思,tailor-made 是一個複合形容詞,形容就像是裁縫師量身訂做的一樣,也最符合客製化的意思;相較之下,選項 B 提到的文化差異與文意較不合,是一個干擾選項,要特別小心;故此題答案為 D。

168. Which of the following service is NOT implied in this passage?
   (A) light bulb display.
   (B) cleaning decorations.
   (C) a Santa Claus character.
   (D) decorating a Christmas tree.

168. 下列哪個服務不在這篇文章中指出呢?
   (A) 電燈泡展示。
   (B) 清理裝飾。
   (C) 聖誕老人角色。
   (D) 裝飾聖誕樹。

　　168 題題目是詢問下列哪個服務不在這篇文章中指出呢?定位回文章前

段，作者敘述他們提供裝飾街坊、社區和公司的客製化服務，並舉例包含了聖誕裝飾的清潔整理和佈置，但並不包含聖誕老人的角色扮演，故答案為 C。

問題 169-171

備忘錄

致：辛蒂・陳，助理編輯
從：簡・王，經理
日期：7 月 22 日
回覆：書展的想法

我已經看過妳關於書展的想法。妳想要增加互動課程的部分相當有趣。我覺得很棒。此外，你想到有些人參加書展可能會攜帶小孩的這個想法是美好的。我記得我們有替他們準備點心，對吧？我不會在公司，因為我有其他差事要做。這是我的 Line ID: XXXXBESTBEST，請於看到這備忘錄時加我。我們可以透過 Line 聯繫討論此事。

謝謝，
簡・王

答案：169.A　170.B　171.D

 解析

169. Why was the memo sent?
   (A) to initiate a discussion on the Book Fair.
   (B) to encourage more new ideas on the Book Fair.

169. 為什麼會寄這封備忘錄呢？
   (A) 發起書展討論。
   (B) 鼓勵在書展更多新想法。
   (C) 恭喜辛蒂・陳她的成就。
   (D) 討論他們是否需要買點心。

(C) to congratulate Cindy Chen on her achievement.

(D) to discuss whether they should buy snacks.

---

169 題題目是詢問為什麼會寄這封備忘錄呢？定位回文章，我們可以從「回覆」的信件主旨和信件的第一句得知，這是簡‧王回覆辛蒂‧陳關於書展想法的信件，並藉由這篇備忘錄希望得到辛蒂‧陳進一步地回應，以討論有關書展的想法，故答案為 A 引起討論。信中提到辛蒂‧陳想要增加互動課程，引起了簡‧王的興趣，因而希望能有進一步的討論；所以「引起討論」的目的，相較於「激起更多新想法」來得更為明顯，故 B 選項不是最佳解答；故此題答案為 A。

---

170. Which of the blanks marked (1), (2), (3), and (4) does the following sentence belong to?

"I think it's great"

(A) (1).

(B) (2).

(C) (3).

(D) (4).

170. 下列句子屬於段落空格 (1), (2), (3), (4)所標示的哪個欄位中？

「我覺得很棒」

(A) (1)。

(B) (2)。

(C) (3)。

(D) (4)。

---

170 題題目是詢問下列句子：「我覺得很棒」屬於段落空格 (1), (2), (3), (4) 所標示的哪個欄位中？定位回文章，可以把「我覺得很棒」分別帶入段落空格 (1), (2), (3), (4) 中，由前後文意判斷敘述是否順暢並合乎邏輯。也可以從「我覺得很棒」推測，前一句應與某個想法或提議有關，即可先刪除文意不通順的段落空格 (3) 跟 (4)。從文意上來看，段落空格 (1) 跟 (2) 都適合填入句子；但就文法而言，從段落空格(1)的前句「I've seen your ideas about the Book Fair.」來看，若作者想表達他覺得很棒，用「I think they're great.」來敘述會比較合文法。所以把 I think it's great 填入段落空格(2)，用來表達對「增加互動課程」的看法最為恰當，故此題

答案為 B。

---

171. Why did Jane Wang give Cindy Chen her Line ID?
   (A) to tell her about the errands.
   (B) to have more interactions with Cindy.
   (C) to have a more private relationship with Cindy.
   (D) to continue further discussion on the same topic in the memo.

171. 為什麼簡‧王給辛蒂‧陳她的 Line ID 呢？
   (A) 告訴她更多的差事。
   (B) 與辛蒂有更多互動。
   (C) 與辛蒂有更多私人關係。
   (D) 持續在備忘錄上相同話題的進一步討論。

---

171 題題目是詢問為什麼簡‧王給辛蒂‧陳她的 Line ID 呢？定位回文章末段，簡‧王表示她不在公司，希望辛蒂‧陳透過 Line 聯繫她並藉此討論。可知主要是因為針對的書展的討論，尚未完成又無法當面進行，才會希望能用 Line 來溝通，所以 D 選項的「進一步討論」會比 B 選項的「增加互動」更適合，故此題答案為 D。

問題 172-175

倍斯特百貨公司

記者/公告

倍斯特百貨公司昨日的搶劫引起安全問題的關注。警方對於他們為什麼闖入尚未有線索。根據幾個員工的描述，珠寶和金飾都不見了。這可能似乎是近 30 年來最糟的搶劫，但至少沒有人受傷。倍斯特百貨公司雇主向我們宣布聲明，在警方未找到足夠證據前，百貨公司不會開張。10 月 13 日的珠寶系列，也就是從現在起的兩週，可

能也要取消。關於此事件，健身俱樂部不會給予俱樂部成員任何補償。我們只能希望警方比我們想像中更快找到證據。記者麗莎‧林在倍斯特百貨公司。

答案：172.B　173.B　174.B　175.A

 解析

172. What does "ransacking" mean in this passage?
(A) running away from a crime scene.
(B) **searching a place violently to commit robbery.**
(C) demanding a ransom.
(D) pointing a gun at a victim.

172. 此段落中的「搶劫」指的是什麼呢？
(A) 逃離犯罪現場。
(B) **瘋狂地尋找犯搶案的地方。**
(C) 要求贖金。
(D) 對受害者指著槍。

　　172 題題目是詢問此段落中的「搶劫」指的是什麼呢？這題考的是字彙，ransack，是搶劫的意思，一般作動詞使用，而在此作者以進行式 ransacking 做名詞使用，等同於 robbery 的用法，表示大肆的搜括掠奪；故此題答案為 B。如果不清楚 ransack 的意思，我們也可以從文章中推測，像是從 broke into、shoplifting 和 no one got injured 等字詞來看，可知有人強行闖入行竊、沒有人受傷，從選項來比較，B 選項也是最適合的答案。

173. Which of the following is TRUE according to this passage?
(A) Only gold was stolen.
(B) **The motive behind the break-in remains unclear.**

173. 根據這個段落，下列哪項敘述為真呢？
(A) 只有金飾被偷了。
(B) **非法侵入的動機仍未明。**
(C) 健身俱樂部的成員將收到補償。

(C) The members of Sports Club will receive compensations.

(D) All operations of the department store will remain normal.

(D) 百貨公司的所有運作將維持正常。

---

173 題題目是詢問根據這個段落，下列哪項敘述為真呢？定位回文章前段，作者明確闡述「警方尚未找出犯案動機的相關線索」，可知此題答案為 B。而文章中也提到，在警方未找足證據前，百貨公司不會開張，也不會給予健身俱樂部成員任何補償；故 C、D 選項皆為錯誤敘述。此外，在未知段落填空缺失的句子內容前，我們無法得知犯人行搶的內容，不能證明選項 A 的敘述正確，所以 A 選項也不是答案。

---

174. Which of the blanks marked (1), (2), (3), and (4) does the following sentence belong to?

"According to several employees, jewelry and gold were all gone"

(A) (1).
(B) (2).
(C) (3).
(D) (4).

174. 下列句子屬於段落空格 (1), (2), (3), (4)所標示的哪個欄位中？
「根據幾個員工的描述，珠寶和金飾都不見了」
(A) (1)。
(B) (2)。
(C) (3)。
(D) (4)。

---

174 題題目是詢問下列句子：「根據幾個員工的描述，珠寶和金飾都不見了」屬於段落空格 (1), (2), (3), (4) 所標示的哪個欄位中？定位回文章，可以把「根據幾個員工的描述，珠寶和金飾都不見了」分別帶入段落空格 (1), (2), (3), (4) 中，由前後文意判斷敘述是否順暢並合乎邏輯。將句子填入段落空格 (2)，下句接著表示「這可能為近 30 年來最糟的搶案」，呼應了金飾珠寶不見的消息，文意通暢；故答案為 B。而段落空格(3)跟(4)的前

後文，跟搶案內容沒有直接關係，所以可先刪除選項 C 和 D。此外，如果將句子填入位於文章首句的段落空格(1)，文章的敘述和因果關係無法合乎邏輯，所以 A 也不是答案。

---

175. What might happen to the jewelry collection exhibition?
    (A) **It might not be held.**
    (B) It will be held as scheduled.
    (C) More security measures will be taken.
    (D) There will be more security guards.

175. 珠寶系列展可能發生何事呢？
    (A) **可能不會舉辦。**
    (B) 可能如期舉行。
    (C) 會採取更多的安全措施。
    (D) 會有更多的保全。

---

175 題題目是詢問珠寶系列展可能發生何事呢？由 jewelry collection exhibition 定位回文章，可知原定於 10 月 13 日開始的珠寶系列展，有可能會取消；故答案為 A。這題考的是字彙 declined，這裡做動詞使用，有下降、拒絕的意思，作者使用被動式 be declined，表示這個珠寶展可能「被推辭」；我們可以由此推測，珠寶展會被延期或取消。此外，如果不清楚 declined 的意思，我們也可以根據前文敘述「在警方未找到足夠證據前，百貨公司不會開張」，推測如果 10 月 13 日百貨公司不會開張，珠寶展也不會舉行。

問題 176-180

倍斯特乳癌中心

對於大多數女性來說，對乳癌的認知一直是可怕的疾病。它可能發生在你最意想不到的時候。乳癌中心在今天有個研討會幫助女性更認識乳癌，希望能獲得更多資金來幫助那些正在與此疾病搏鬥者。

姓名	描述	時間
約翰醫生	介紹	9:00-10:00
瑪莉醫生	治療	10:00-12:00
休息時間		
病人琳達	想法分享	2:00-2:30
林醫生	預防	2:30-4:30
主持人	募款	4:30-5:30

註：

1. 約翰醫生會使用簡報，而林醫生會播放視頻。

2. 除了病人分享的部分，所有演說內容都會錄音。

親愛的法蘭克，

我認為你在當天主持得很好。我過去也是個與乳癌搏鬥的病人。我從不知道我會是當中之一。當我發現我得了乳癌時，已經是第二期。奇蹟似地，在悉心的照護和我家人及醫生一系列的治療後，我開始轉好且最終康復。我想要感謝你所作的。我感激倍斯特乳癌中心在病人最艱苦的時期協助病人。現在我想要藉由募款捐贈兩千美元來幫助。我知道這金額並不多，但是這是我小小的感謝之道以表示「謝謝你」。

致上最高的問候，
辛蒂·林

答案：176.A　　177.B　　178.C　　179.C　　180.A

6 填空式閱讀

7 單篇閱讀

7 雙篇、三篇閱讀

模擬試題

176. What does the term "symposium" refer to?

(A) a conference where people share ideas.

(B) a meeting where doctors order medicines.

(C) a party especially for medical professionals.

(D) a meeting similar to an auction.

176. 詞彙「研討會」指的是什麼呢？

(A) 大家分享想法的會議。

(B) 醫生訂購藥品的會議

(C) 特別是給醫療專業人員的派對

(D) 和拍賣相似的會議。

---

176 題題目是詢問詞彙「研討會」指的是什麼呢？，這題考的是字彙，如果懂這個字的可以很快就知道答案要選 A，如果不知道這個字是什麼意思，可以從每個選項的敘述跟文章內容加以判斷。每個選項都是在定義這個字的意思，加上逐步閱讀文章內容後可以刪除 B 因為文章中未提及 order medicine，也可以刪除 C，因為敘述中包含 especially for medical professionals，因為文章中提到是「幫助女性更認識乳癌，希望能獲得更多資金來幫助那些正在與此疾病搏鬥者。」，不是只開放給醫療專業人員的派對。D 選項也不對，因為他提到拍賣：故此題答案為 A。

---

177. Who is Frank?

(A) a doctor specializing in breast cancer.

(B) the host of the symposium.

(C) a breast cancer survivor.

(D) a breast cancer patient.

177. 誰是法蘭克呢？

(A) 專攻乳癌的醫生。

(B) 研討會主持人。

(C) 乳癌生存者。

(D) 乳癌病患。

---

177 題題目是詢問誰是法蘭克呢？，在新多益中此為常考題旨在考考生對於文章中人物關係的理解程度。有的人物很清楚就能知道可能是指那個職

位的人，有的就需要整篇理解或推測出，較不容易察覺。有的比較簡單的可以從表格中直接找到相對應的人物。在這篇中，可以由兩個地方分別連結到法蘭克是誰。首先先從表格中看到有個人物欄並未指出是誰，僅寫了 host，再由信件中辛蒂‧林寫信開頭跟信件中第一句稱讚主持的部分可以得知法蘭克是當天的主持人，故答案是 B。

---

178. What is the purpose of Cindy's letter?
   (A) to show her appreciation to Frank.
   (B) to ask how much money she should donate.
   (C) to show her appreciation to Best Breast Cancer Center.
   (D) to inquire the way to donate some money.

178. 辛蒂寫這封信的目的是什麼呢？
   (A) 表示對法蘭克的感謝。
   (B) 詢問她該捐贈多少錢。
   (C) 表示它對倍斯特乳癌中心的感謝。
   (D) 詢問捐贈一些錢的方法。

---

178 題題目是詢問辛蒂寫這封信的目的是什麼呢？可以定位回信中找到，她寫道「我想要感謝你所作的。我感激倍斯特乳癌中心在病人最艱苦的時期協助病人。」等等得知她是想要對倍斯特乳癌中心表達感謝，故選 C。A 選項是干擾選項，要特別小心。

---

179. How long will the symposium last?
   (A) 6 hours.
   (B) 7 hours.
   (C) 6.5 hours.
   (D) 5.5 hours.

179. 研討會會持續多久呢？
   (A) 6 小時。
   (B) 7 小時。
   (C) 6.5 小時。
   (D) 5.5 小時。

---

179 題題目是詢問研討會會持續多久呢？，可以定位回表格，表格中有

時間點，將上午跟下午研討會加起來的時間就是研討會進行的時間，故答案
是 C 6.5 小時。

---

180. What will Dr. Lin talk about?
  (A) how to take preventive measures against breast cancer.
  (B) how to survive breast cancer.
  (C) the most effective treatment.
  (D) the best way to raise money for breast cancer research.

180. 林醫生會談論什麼呢？
  (A) 如何採用預防措施對抗乳癌。
  (B) 如何於乳癌中存活。
  (C) 最有效的治療。
  (D) 最佳替乳癌中心研究募款的方式。

---

　　180 題題目是詢問林醫生會談論什麼呢？，可以在定位回表格，找到林醫生跟描述的部分，林醫生的描述欄位是預防，所以可以推測出他可能會談到預防相關的話題，故選 A。

問題 181-185

親愛的傑克先生，

由於你們學校救生員的疏忽，我的小孩現在仍在醫院。有些時刻，這些問題很快地於我腦海中飄過：為什麼他們這麼晚才叫救護車呢？他們是受過良好訓練的救生員嗎？根據有些父母，他們有些人當時在滑手機，而小孩正在游泳玩樂。我需要關於此事的一個解釋。為什麼他們未盡到本該監督小孩的責任呢？你是學校院長。你最好把這解釋清楚。我今天會帶律師到學校。

致上最高的問候，
簡・王

學校的聲明

倍斯特菁英學校不會容忍這個行為。任何會危及小孩安全的事都不被允許的。我們譴責那些挑戰學校權威和那些自行其事的人。所有當時都在值勤救生員都被上銬至警局作聲明。我們誠摯地向那天在游泳池所受傷的那些小孩道歉。不只那些救生員都將面臨法庭的刑罰，他們會被倍斯特菁英學校開除，始於 2018 年 4 月 15 日。學校已經決定從現在起關閉游泳池以免除對任何生命危急的小孩進一步地傷害和損害。

倍斯特菁英學校，
2018 年 4 月 13 日

答案：181.B　182.B　183.D　184.C　185.D

 解析

181. What does the term "negligence" imply about the lifeguard?
    (A) His mistake is negligible.
    (B) His lack of attention to the kids.
    (C) Negligence is unavoidable sometimes.
    (D) His lack of passion for his job.

181.「疏忽」這個詞彙可能暗指救生員什麼呢？
    (A) 他的錯誤是可以忽略的。
    (B) 他對小孩缺乏關注。
    (C) 忽略有時候是無可避免的。
    (D) 他對於工作缺乏熱忱。

　　181 題題目是詢問「疏忽」這個詞彙可能暗指救生員什麼呢？，A 選項有了題目 negligence 的形容詞，但意思完全扭曲了，指稱救生員的錯是可以忽略的，故可以先排除 A 選項，C 選項指忽略有時候是無可避免的，這部分也與文意不合。D 選項是救生員可能導致該行為的原因，但未在文章中討論到，文章中僅提到因滑手機而導致疏失。B 選項中的 lack of attention 其實是 negligence 的同義字轉換，加上文章敘述輔證，故可以推斷答案是

B 選項。

---

182. What might Jane Wang do when she meets Mr. Jack?
    (A) She might shout at Mr. Jack.
    (B) She might discuss legal matters with Mr. Jack.
    (C) She might ask for some compensation.
    (D) She might ask Mr. Jack about how to treat her kid.

182. 當她遇到傑克先生時，簡·王可能做什麼呢？
    (A) 她可能對傑克先生大呼小叫。
    (B) 她可能與傑克先生討論法律事情。
    (C) 她可能會要求一些補償。
    (D) 她可能詢問傑克先生關於如何照顧她的小孩。

---

182 題題目是詢問當她遇到傑克先生時，簡·王可能做什麼呢？，可以定位回文章中她寫道「你是學校院長。你最好把這解釋清楚。我今天會帶律師到學校。」所以最有可能是與傑克先生討論法律事情，故答案選 B。A 選項是家長可能會做出的行為但文章中並未提到，所以可以排除 A 選項。C 選項中的提出補償和 D 選項中的如何照顧她的孩子文章中均未提到，故也可以排除。

---

183. What does the term "loose cannons" refer to?
    (A) People who know a lot about the trade of cannons.
    (B) People who like to wear loose clothes.
    (C) People who hurt children on purpose
    (D) People whose behaviors are unexpected and might cause problems.

183. 術語「自行其事的人」指的是什麼呢？
    (A) 知道許多關於大砲交易的人。
    (B) 喜歡穿寬鬆服飾的人。
    (C) 故意傷害小孩的人。
    (D) 行為我行我素且可能造成問題的人。

183 題題目是詢問術語「自行其事的人」指的是什麼呢？，如果對慣用語熟悉的人可以很輕易答出這題是 D 選項行為我行我素且可能造成問題的人。而 A 選項和 B 選項敘述均是包含該術語的字 cannon 和 loose，但全是跟文章和該慣用語無關的敘述。而 C 選項中的 hurt on purpose 也無文章中提到的內容不相符，故排除。

---

184. Who is Mr. Jack?
    (A) a lifeguard.
    (B) the swimming pool director.
    (C) the school dean.
    (D) a concerned parent.

184. 誰是傑克先生呢？
    (A) 救生員。
    (B) 游泳池指導。
    (C) 學校院長。
    (D) 關心的父母。

---

184 題題目是詢問誰是傑克先生呢？，定位回信件，可以很清楚知道傑克先生是學校院長，故答案選 C。

---

185. According to the statement, what might NOT happen to the lifeguards?
    (A) They will receive penalties.
    (B) They will lose their jobs.
    (C) They will leave some records at the police station.
    (D) They will be forgiven after apologizing to the injured kids' parents.

185. 根據這個聲明，哪個可能不會發生在救生員身上呢？
    (A) 他們會收到處罰。
    (B) 他們會失去工作。
    (C) 他們會在警局留下些紀錄。
    (D) 他們會因為向受傷父母道歉後得到原諒。

---

185 題題目是詢問根據這個聲明，哪個可能不會發生在救生員身上呢？，此題是細節題，可以定位回文章中的聲明，找到救生員會面臨的處罰等，包含 ABC 三個選項。而 D 選項在文章中未提及，且該聲明是由學校發佈，不代表父母的立場等，故答案是 D。

問題 186-190

倍斯特博物館

Line 訊息

貝蒂：似乎我們無法看到倍斯特博物館的人物畫像了。

琳達：票已經售光了。可能要下年。

辛蒂：我知道倍斯特博物館一個男子可以拿到票。

貝蒂：即使是在這時候嗎？

辛蒂：可能是給員工或他們家庭成員的。我可以詢問他如果你們真的想去。

琳達：問他！你知道我無法抗拒藝術品。

（十分鐘之後）

辛蒂：他說他有剩餘三張票。他同事周末要與家人去另一個城市。

琳達：那指的是我們仍可以去，對吧？

貝蒂：真不敢相信我們這麼幸運呢？

辛蒂：是阿，但有個條件？他想要我們加他臉書好友。

琳達：好！

貝蒂：我看到他傳的邀請了...好吧...為了該死的票。

Line 訊息

貝蒂：很棒！還好我們有去博物館。

琳達：有些人物畫像是近期發現的對吧？

辛蒂：可能...我沒注意到。

辛蒂：我喜愛那裏的咖啡，相當令人感到有活力。

貝蒂：太貴了。

琳達：我發佈了那天拍了所有照片。

貝蒂：指的是要點「讚」嗎？

辛蒂：當然...點點點。

琳達：在倍斯特博物館工作的條件是什麼呢？

琳達：這會是能結合我們興趣和主修的工作。

貝蒂：為什麼不問 Tim 呢？

琳達：他寄給我掃描表格了。

表格

教育程度：應至少大學學歷或以上，歷史或藝術相關主修
英語程度：進階
語言：法語或德語為第二外語會是加分

註：通常我們偏好候選人有倍斯特博物館暑期工讀實習經驗。候選人在其他博物館工作過也歡迎。候選人在建築或設計也會考慮。有倍斯特博物館員工的推薦函是有利的。候選人應該要準備 CV 和四個不同博物館的影音檔。（倍斯特博物館除外）。

答案：186.D　187.C　188.A　189.C　190.A

186. What does Cindy mean by "on one condition"?
  (A) The condition of adding one more person to her Facebook friends is complicated.
  (B) After adding the guy to their Line friends, she and her friends will receive the tickets.
  (C) The condition of the exhibition at Best Museum is of very high quality.
  (D) She and her friends will receive the tickets only if they agree to do something.

186.「有個條件」辛蒂所指的是什麼呢？
  (A) 在她臉書朋友中多新增一個人的情況是很複雜的。
  (B) 在加入那個男生到 Line 朋友後，她和她朋友會收到票。
  (C) 倍斯特博物館的展示情況是非常高品質的。
  (D) 她和她朋友會收到票除非他們同意做些事。

186 題題目是詢問「有個條件」辛蒂所指的是什麼呢？，可以定位回 line 對話，得知她們要拿到票的話要同意加男方臉書好友，所以答案是 D She and her friends will receive the tickets only if they agree to do something.，其中 something 指的就是加男方臉書好友。

---

187. What does Linda mean by "deal"?
   (A) She is not sure if they should deal with the guy.
   (B) Dealing with the guy is a piece of cake.
   (C) **She has no problem adding the guy to her Facebook friends.**
   (D) After sealing the deal, she will pay the guy immediately.

187.「一言為定」琳達所指的是什麼呢？
   (A) 她不確定如果他們應該要應付那個男子。
   (B) 應付那個男子是小菜一碟。
   (C) **她對於將男子加入她臉書朋友沒意見。**
   (D) 達成協議後她會立刻付錢給男子。

---

187 題題目是詢問「一言為定」琳達所指的是什麼呢？，ABD 的選項均與琳達她們的對話無關，故選 C。

---

188. What does Cindy mean by "click"?
   (A) **She's clicking on the Like button.**
   (B) She's uploading some pictures.
   (C) She's clicking the mouse.
   (D) She's sending her CV.

188.「點擊」辛蒂所指的是什麼呢？
   (A) **她點了讚。**
   (B) 她上傳一些照片。
   (C) 她點擊了滑鼠。
   (D) 她寄了她的 CV。

---

188 題題目是詢問.「點擊」辛蒂所指的是什麼呢？，其實指的就是點

了讚，B 選項是在文章中有提到的敘述，但與題目無關，而 C 選項和 D 選項均不對。文章中未提及點擊滑鼠且表格中雖有提到候選人要附 CV，但為提及有寄送這個動作，故均可以排除：故此題答案為 A。

---

189. Which of the following is NOT mentioned in the form?
   (A) educational background.
   (B) language proficiency.
   (C) job responsibility.
   (D) internship experience.

189. 下列哪個敘述在表格中未提及？
   (A) 教育背景。
   (B) 語言程度。
   (C) 工作責任。
   (D) 實習經驗。

---

189 題題目是詢問下列哪個敘述在表格中未提及？，可以定位回表格中並找出未提及的部分，A, B ,D 均在敘述中可以找到，唯一沒提到的是工作責任為何，故選 C。

---

190. Which of the following candidates might have the best qualifications for the position in Best Museum?
   (A) someone who speaks English and French fluently and holds a degree in arts.
   (B) someone who holds a degree in arts and speaks Chinese fluently.
   (C) someone who has taken a summer internship in Best Museum and has a high school diploma.
   (D) someone who is very interested in arts and donates a large sum of money to Best Museum.

190. 對倍斯特博物館應徵職缺來說，下列哪個候選人可能有最佳的條件呢？
   (A) 能流利地說英語和法語且有藝術學歷。
   (B) 有藝術學歷且中文流利。
   (C) 有倍斯特博物館暑期工讀實習經驗且有高中學歷。
   (D) 對藝術有興趣且捐贈鉅額給倍斯特博物館。

190 題題目是詢問對倍斯特博物館應徵職缺來說，下列哪個候選人可能有最佳的條件呢？對應到表格中的敘述條件，可以發現 A 選項即是答案。B 選項、C 選項和 D 選項均為列舉兩個項目，但僅有一個是敘述中提及的，而另一個條件文章中未提及，B 選項的中文流利部分文章中未提及。C 選項的高中學歷與敘述不符合。D 選項中的捐贈大筆資金給倍斯特博物館也與文章不符合。

問題 191-195

倍斯特保護中心

倍斯特保護中心致力於拯救原生野外生物。今年我們很幸運能獲得海外公司的鉅額。這些錢會用於拯救在野外受傷或受困的哺乳類動物。那些有重傷的動物也會給予特別照護。他們會被帶至我們的保護中心，當然我們的獸醫也會在那裡。對於自願參予我們計畫的參與者和幫助我們在特定活動中減輕我們員工負擔者，像是淨灘和準備餐點給動物，他們會擁有能更換禮物的自願服務時數。

下列表格是禮物清單

禮物名稱	花費時間	描述
大黑熊包	150 小時	
浣熊手套	150 小時	對於那些已完成此計畫超過 600 小時者，你會獲得證照，且能申請倍斯特世界各地的保護中心工作，因為你已展示出你對動物和保護的熱忱。
豪華倍斯特手提包	300 小時	
豪華廚具	600 小時	
棕熊夾克	150 小時	

信件

親愛的倍斯特保護中心人事部，

我是主修動物學的學生。我已經自願在倍斯特保護中心服務了兩個暑假，每天八小時。總共 **1920** 個小時。更令人覺得有趣的是，那些工作時數能有價值且用於更換禮物。我已經更換了整套的廚具給媽媽、三個棕熊夾克給我自己和妹妹們、四個巨大黑熊包給兒童中心。

協助醫生和花費整天時間陪伴動物真的很有意義。這對我來說真的是很理想的工作。即使我不具有美好的學歷，我認為過去這兩個暑期在這裡已經展現了我對於野生動物的奉獻和熱忱。附件是我的 **CV**。期待收到您的消息。

致上最高的問候，
琳達・李

答案：191.C　192.A　193.B　194.B　195.D

191. Where does most of the funding this year come from?	191. 今年大多數的募款要從哪來呢？
(A) volunteers.	(A) 自願者。
(B) university students.	(B) 大學學生。
(C) foreign companies.	**(C) 外國公司。**
(D) veterinarians.	(D) 獸醫。

　191 題題目是詢問今年大多數的募款要從哪來呢？，可以從首段中 This year we are lucky enough to get a tremendous sum of money from overseas companies.得知會從海外公司中獲得募款故答案要選 C。而 foreign company 是 overseas company 的同義字轉換。

192. What is the criteria for obtaining the gifts?
    (A) reaching a certain number of hours.
    (B) cleaning the beach.
    (C) preparing meals for animals.
    (D) taking an internship at the conservation center.

192. 獲得禮物需要的標準是什麼呢？
    (A) 達到特定的時數。
    (B) 清理海灘。
    (C) 替動物準備餐點。
    (D) 在保護中心參予實習工讀。

192 題題目是詢問獲得禮物需要的標準是什麼呢？，可以由禮物表格清單中得知，特定時數有對應的禮物，所以是達到特定時數後即可換得，故答案是 A。BCD 的選項敘述均為文章中提到但卻不是題目所問的部分故可以排除。

193. How will most of the funding this year be spent?
    (A) to invest in gifts.
    (B) to help the mammals hurt in the wilderness.
    (C) to save to endangered mammals
    (D) to hire more workers.

193. 今年大多數的募款資金會用於哪裡呢？
    (A) 投資在禮物上。
    (B) 幫助野外受傷的哺乳類動物。
    (C) 拯救瀕臨絕種的哺乳類動物。
    (D) 雇用更多工人。

193 題題目是詢問今年大多數的募款資金會用於哪裡呢？，定位回文章首段，提及「這些錢會用於拯救在野外受傷或受困的哺乳類動物。那些有重傷的動物也會給予特別照護。」故答案是 B 幫助野外受傷的哺乳類動物。

194. If a volunteer wants to exchange for a luxurious Best handbag and a brown bear jacket, how many hours should she accumulate?
(A) 300 hours.
(B) 450 hours.
(C) 150 hours.
(D) 600 hours.

194. 如果一個自願者想要交換一個豪華貝斯特包包和棕熊夾克，她應該要累積幾小時呢？
(A) 300 小時。
(B) 450 小時。
(C) 150 小時。
(D) 600 小時。

194 題題目是詢問如果一個自願者想要交換一個豪華倍斯特包包和棕熊夾克，她應該要累積幾小時呢？，可以定位回表格並將敘述的部分對應到相對的時數，相加後就是累積時數，故是 B 選項 450 小時。

195. Which of the following is NOT mentioned in the letter?
(A) various gifts.
(B) volunteer hours.
(C) the applicant's major.
(D) an internship program.

195. 下列哪個項目在信中未提及呢？
(A) 不同的禮物。
(B) 自願的時數。
(C) 申請者的主修。
(D) 實習計畫。

195 題題目是詢問下列哪個項目在信中未提及呢？文章中其實未提到具體的實習計畫故答案為 D。

問題 196-200

親愛的傑森您好，

我透過你們倍斯特房仲銷售代表買了間房子。我很滿意你們的服務直到昨天。最近我發現了關於房子的幾個問題似乎不太對。後院的牆生鏽了。它損壞至一個程度，到了新粉刷的漆無法覆蓋上去。我們已經聯繫了水電工到我們家裡。他發現其他問題包括水管和廚房管線。我們無法煮餐點，而且還有些漏水問題，所以每當我們在廁所或廚房使用水時，水由前院湧出。這全是你們銷售代表的疏忽，沒有讓我們知道房子的所有情況。

致上最高的問候，
安・陳

Line 訊息

傑森： 這裡是倍斯特房仲，附帶説下我是傑森。
安： 我真是無法再忍受了，所以我想用電話講更快。
安的丈夫： 告訴他問題沒解決的話我們要提告了。
安： 你們有收到信嗎？你們將如何處理這問題。
安： 有白蟻出現！！！我的近期新發現。
傑森： 很抱歉。我不知道這些事。或許我跟我們銷售代表一同前往你們家看我們能怎麼處理。
安： 何時？
傑森： 今天下午兩點，可以嗎？
安： 到時見。

信件

親愛的安您好，

前幾天拜訪你們房子時，我們試著想出幾個解決這特別且不尋常的情況的方案。我們顯然對於房子的情況沒有線索。它覆蓋著豪華的裝飾和漆。或許安排你們至相同類型的房子是個解決辦法。我聯繫了建築工人。他們正翻修我們想要安排您入住的房子。我們也會訂離您們最近的旅館，這樣你們在兩周的可怕夜晚後，可

以先有個安穩的覺。在新房子那裡不會有任何昆蟲或奇怪的事，除了一些在後院的蚯蚓。

致上最高的問候，
傑森
2018 年 11 月 19 日

答案：196.C　197.B　198.B　199.C　200.B

196. Which of the following problems about the house is NOT mentioned in the letter? (A) leaking. (B) a plumbing problem. **(C) an insect problem.** (D) a rusty wall.	196. 下列哪個房屋問題在信件中未提及呢？ (A) 漏水問題。 (B) 水管問題。 **(C) 昆蟲問題。** (D) 生鏽牆。

　　第 196 題題目是詢問下列哪個項目在信件中未提及呢？，文章中四個選項均有提到，但是要很注意題目中的敘述，是詢問「在信件中」未提及，信件中的問題包括 (A) 漏水問題 (B) 水管問題 (D) 生鏽牆，所以答案是 (C) 昆蟲問題。另外要注意的是，題目有可能改寫成 in the reading passage or in this article，如果是這樣的話那就包含四個選項的內容。還有一點是 line 對話中提到白蟻問題，題目中也做了同義字轉換，不熟悉這類型轉換跟白蟻這個單字的讀者要多注意這樣的題目變化。

197. What problem did Ann later find out?
   (A) a pipe problem.
   (B) a pest problem.
   (C) rusty pipes.
   (D) earthworms.

197. 安會於之後發現什麼問題呢？
   (A) 管線問題。
   (B) 害蟲問題。
   (C) 生鏽水管。
   (D) 蚯蚓。

第 197 題題目是詢問安會於之後發現什麼問題呢？關於這問題可以回 line 對話段落中找出，安在對話中講到有白蟻出現！！！，從這點可以得知安所發現的問題是白蟻問題，白蟻也就是害蟲所以答案是 (B) 害蟲問題。

198. What solution did Best House Rental offer?
   (A) buying an apartment for Ann and her family.
   (B) arranging for Ann and her family to live in another house.
   (C) paying the hotel fees for Ann and her family until they buy a new house.
   (D) arranging for Ann and her family to move to a new apartment.

198. 倍斯特房仲提出的解決方案是什麼呢？
   (A) 替安和他家人購買一間公寓。
   (B) 安排安和他家人入住另一間房子。
   (C) 直到買新房子，會替安和他家人付旅館費用。
   (D) 安排安和他家人搬到新公寓。

第 198 題題目是詢問倍斯特房仲提出的解決方案是什麼呢？，這點可以定位回傑森回覆安的信件中，傑森寫道「或許安排你們至相同類型的房子是個解決辦法。我聯繫了建築工人。他們正翻修我們想要安排您入住的房子。」A 選項和 D 選項是錯誤的因為文中沒有提到公寓，外加安的房子有前、後院等，可以推測安其實不是住公寓。C 選項也是錯誤的因為文章中只提到在安排入住前會訂購旅館讓安家人有暫時安穩棲身之所，所以也不能

選：故此題答案為 B。

---

199. Why did Jason write "We obviously have no clue about the conditions of the house" in his letter?
   (A) Because the sales representative did not tell Jason the truth.
   (B) Because Jason did not see the rusty wall.
   (C) Because the house is covered with luxurious decoration and paint.
   (D) Because clues about the condition of the house were difficult to identify.

199. 為什麼傑森在信中寫到「我們顯然對房子的情況毫無頭緒」呢？
   (A) 因為銷售代表無法告訴傑森真相。
   (B) 因為傑森無法看到生鏽牆。
   (C) 因為房子覆蓋了豪華的裝飾和漆。
   (D) 因為房子的情況的線索很難辨識出。

　　第 199 題題目是詢問為什麼傑森在信中寫到「我們顯然對房子的情況毫無頭緒」呢？，傑森在信見有寫道「我們顯然對於房子的情況沒有線索。它覆蓋著豪華的裝飾和漆。」這題根據文章閱讀定位很容易就能知道答案是 C 選項。A 選項在文章中並無交代所以無從推測。

200. What will the construction workers do?

(A) They will tear down Ann's house.

(B) They will refurbish the new house for Ann.

(C) They will conduct some pest control.

(D) They will repaint Ann's house.

200. 建築工人會做什麼呢？

(A) 他們會拆除安的房子。

(B) 他們會翻修新房子給安。

(C) 他們會執行一些害蟲防治。

(D) 他們會重新上漆安的房子。

第 200 題題目是詢問建築工人會做什麼呢？，關於這題也能從信件中很快找到答案，答案是 B 選項。只是信件中的翻修 renovate 在問題中換成了另一個同義字 refurbish。只要掌握這兩個字的同義轉換要答這題其實不難。

新多益閱讀模擬試題答案表

PART 5				
101. C	102. D	103. B	104. A	105. D
106. B	107. B	108. B	109. C	110. D
111. B	112. B	113. C	114. A	115. C
116. C	117. D	118. B	119. B	120. D
121. C	122. B	123. A	124. A	125. C
126. C	127. C	128. D	129. C	130. B
PART 6				
131. B	132. C	133. A	134. A	135. D
136. D	137. B	138. C	139. D	140. C
141. B	142. D	143. B	144. C	145. B
146. D	147. B	148. A	149. C	150. A
PART 7				
151. B	152. D	153. C	154. A	155. B
156. D	157. D	158. C	159. D	160. D
161. A	162. A	163. C	164. B	165. C
166. B	167. D	168. C	169. A	170. B
171. D	172. B	173. B	174. B	175. A
176. A	177. B	178. C	179. C	180. A
181. B	182. B	183. D	184. C	185. D
186. D	187. C	188. A	189. C	190. A
191. C	192. A	193. B	194. B	195. D
196. C	197. B	198. B	199. C	200. B

國家圖書館出版品預行編目(CIP)資料

全新制新多益閱讀：金色證書/ 韋爾、莊琬君
著. -- 初版. -- 臺北市：倍斯特, 2018.2　面；
公分. --（考用英語 系列; 7）
ISBN 978-986-95288-8-7（平裝）
1.多益測驗

805.1895　　　　　　　　　　107000463

考用英語系列 007

全新制—新多益閱讀：金色證書

初　　版　　2018年2月
定　　價　　新台幣480元

作　　者　　韋爾、莊琬君
出　　版　　倍斯特出版事業有限公司
發 行 人　　周瑞德
電　　話　　886-2-2351-2007
傳　　真　　886-2-2351-0887
地　　址　　100 台北市中正區福州街1號10樓之2
E - m a i l　　best.books.service@gmail.com
官　　網　　www.bestbookstw.com
執行總監　　齊心瑀
行銷經理　　楊景輝
企劃編輯　　陳韋佑
封面構成　　盧穎作
內頁構成　　菩薩蠻數位文化有限公司
印　　製　　大亞彩色印刷製版股份有限公司

港澳地區總經銷　　泛華發行代理有限公司
地　　址　　香港新界軍澳工業邨駿昌街7號2樓
電　　話　　852-2798-2323
傳　　真　　852-2796-5471